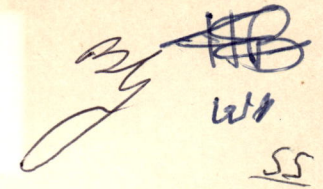

The Price of Fame

Also by Jonathan Havard

Blood and Judgment
The Stockholm Syndrome
Coming of Age

The Price of Fame

JONATHAN HAVARD

HEINEMANN : LONDON

William Heinemann Ltd
Michelin House, 81 Fulham Road, London SW3 6RB
LONDON   MELBOURNE   AUCKLAND

First published
Copyright © Jonathan Havard 1991

A CIP catalogue record for this book
is held by the British Library
ISBN 0 434 31384 X

Phototypeset by Input Typesetting Ltd, London
Printed and bound in Great Britain by
Mackays of Chatham PLC, Chatham, Kent

To my ex-colleagues at the
Princess of Wales Hospital, Bridgend,
to whom, both in sickness and in health,
I have never turned unavailingly for help

Vanity of vanities, saith the Preacher, vanity of vanities; all is vanity.

        Ecclesiastes 1:2.

1

David Royall – Master of Surgery, past Hunterian Professor and Member of the Court of Examiners of the Royal College of Surgeons of England, examiner to the University of London, consultant surgeon to Queen's College Hospital, Fellow of the Royal Society of Medicine, Harley Street specialist – smiled.

He glanced down appreciatively to where his left hand rested on the gear lever. It felt smooth, vibrating gently to the engine's throb. The BMW 635CSi still had the showroom smell about it. Buying his first BMW had been one of the thrills of his life. Now the novelty was wearing off and he had contemplated a change of image. A Porsche perhaps? Or a Ferrari? No. Brash surgical yuppies rarely made the real big time. A Rolls, then? Too soon. Time enough for that. It was all a question of timing. For the present, he would have to make do with a BMW. Or perhaps a Bentley . . . ?

The lunchtime traffic in Tooting High Street ground to a standstill. The BMW, halted amongst the surburban drabness, glinted like a speck of gold in alluvial silt. David Royall stared at the tailboard of the lorry in front, trying to ignore the movement to his left. Life on the pavement: the walkers, the queuers; the other world. He knew only too well what he'd see. Envy, distrust – that's what he'd see. Admiration? Respect? No chance.

Sod 'em. Sod 'em to hell.

Inexorably, as if to reassure himself that he was not afraid of them, his head and eyes turned to face them. He wasn't sure who affected him more, the ones who ignored him or the ones who looked right through him, staring him down. The woman, forty-five to fifty, stocky, strong, her square jaw set, her mouth firm, its corners dragged down as if by the weight of the bags she carried. That could have been his mother, striding up Cory Street, eyes front, saving the bus fare as she had pinched and saved to fuel a son's ability and ambition. Women like that didn't look at him now. Why not? Hadn't he done everything his mother had ever dreamed of? Hadn't he made her proud of him? Why then did she not look at him, smile at him? The man, one shoulder against the lamppost, hands in empty pockets, ankles crossed – David's grandfather must have stood like that in 1926. But then there had been respect for the doctor driving by – the straightened back, the touched cap. Or had they too spat – thick black phlegm – into the gutter between them?

David engaged low gear as the lorry in front edged forward. Cursing gently, he waited as a group of sixth-formers, duffle bags over their shoulders, took their insolent time to cross in front of him. He felt his jaw clamp tight and his left foot ease on the clutch as he inched the car forward, compressing the jostling, irreverent youthfulness. A face turned and two males stared at each other across a generation. A shoulder dropped; a football boot, its studs gleaming sharp, dragged across the car bonnet. There was a taunting blur of grins and tongues and fingers as, darting and shoving, the boys scooted away between two thundering buses.

Grinding his teeth in silent fury, David let in the clutch to drive the fifty yards to where the lorry's tailboard waited for him once more. Impelled by frustration, his left hand picked up the phone. He stabbed out a number.

'Mr David Royall's consulting rooms. Good afternoon. Can I help you?'

Martha. Thank God for Martha. David did just that, almost every day. Martha, who had looked after Sir Geoffrey for thirty years until his stroke. The one-bedroomed flat just off Westbourne Grove, and the Harley Street consulting rooms. The neighbours locked away like battery hens, and the wealthy and the titled, stripped and vulnerable. The secret silence of the intruder-proof bedroom, and the whispered confidences of the examination couch. Martha's two worlds, linked by the 27 bus.

What Martha did not know about private practice in London was not worth knowing. Before Martha, David had suffered from either good typists who had stood tongue-tied in the presence of the aristocracy, or languid Sloane Rangers who had found seventeen different ways of spelling intussusception. How he had managed to get Martha ahead of half Harley Street he would never know.

'Hullo, Martha, how're things? Any problems?'

'Not really, Mr Royall. Where are you?'

'On my way to the Merton. I'm stuck in a traffic jam in Tooting High Street.'

Martha made a querying noise, as if she had no idea where that was. Thirty years with Sir Geoffrey had made her something of a snob.

'What about Mrs Da Costa? How did you get on there?' she asked.

'Benign.'

'Oh, I'm so pleased. She's such a beautiful woman; just like her mother was. But I'm glad you've called. I was going to ring you at the Merton.' Sir Geoffrey had always had a Rolls. BMWs with phones in them were for those greedy young men in the City, the ones with the rolled-up shirt sleeves and sweaty armpits, shouting at each other all day, not for surgeons. 'I'm afraid I've had to squeeze someone in at five o'clock for you.'

'That could be a bit awkward, Martha.' So another couple of patients in his clinic would have to see his registrar – so what? – it happened. 'Why the urgency?'

'It's Lady Alicia.'

'Shit.'

Sir Geoffrey had never sworn. In thirty years, Martha had never heard him raise his voice. David held the phone at arm's length, his face pinched and vicious.

'Are you there?' he heard in the distance.

'Yes, I'm here, Martha,' he answered. The 'What the hell's the matter with the stupid old bat now?' hissing through his mind was censored to 'What's the matter this time?'

'Same thing.' She heard him groan. 'Now, Mr Royall, that's not fair. Lady Alicia is a very frightened woman. All she needs is a bit of reassuring now and then.'

'If you weren't such a lady, Martha, I'd tell you exactly what she needs.'

'Mr Royall – there's no need to be crude.'

3

David grinned. He could see the pursed lips, the sudden lift of the chin.

Lady Alicia had breasts like bean bags. He was tempted at times to shake one to see if it rattled. Under the NHS, one lump would have been removed, just for the record, and she would have been sent on her way, told not to worry. The first two, even the third, of Lady Alicia's private biopsies, he had been able to justify, even to himself. Now, many scars later, and with further operation fees virtually impossible to justify, her tearfully adoring but financially unrewarding consultations were becoming a bit of a drag.

Martha was talking again.

'What's that?' he asked.

'You haven't forgotten you have guests to dinner tonight?'

Martha savoured her links with the rich and successful. It would be pâté on toast for her, securely locked away from the muggers and the rapists, listening to Radio 4 – so much nicer people on Radio 4 than on TV these days. All that sex. Couldn't even watch a nature programme these days.

'So don't be late – you have two other patients after Lady Alicia.'

'Martha, Sir Geoffrey warned me you were a tyrant.' He was going to add 'no wonder he had a stroke' but decided against it. He replaced the phone.

The cause of the hold-up become more obvious as the traffic edged its way towards the flashing blue lamps, the crumpled car, the broken glass and dripping oil, the mangled remains of the bus shelter. David saw a man bending over a stretcher as it was being loaded into an ambulance, his grey suit conspicuous amongst the uniforms. One of the local GPs – had to be. Nobody bleeding to death by the roadside. No point in stopping. Hanging around to give evidence in some magistrates' court, worse still some crown court, was no longer his idea of making money. He had been glad enough of the extra cash as an impoverished registrar. Now it was just a pain in the rear.

The only thing to make him wince was the sight of the black Porsche deformed beyond repair. As he drove past he felt the compassion of a bomber pilot who sees a comrade shot down on a raid over enemy territory.

Just short of the hospital, he pulled to the side to let the ambulance go screeching by, then he followed it through the hospital gates. The parking spaces reserved for visiting consultants were full. It took time to squeeze between two rusting, dented old bangers in the public car park. The vision of some lout denting the side of the BMW deepened his irritation. He ran a finger along the scratch the football studs had caused. BMW owners do not 'touch up' scratches; they respray. It was going to cost a bomb.

He was late starting his clinic. It wasn't his fault. He could not help it if half of Tooting had ground to a halt because of a simple road accident. And why was it that whenever he started late, in a hurry, there were always problems over notes and X-rays?

He snapped at the outpatient sister.

'Come on, Sister. What the hell's going on today?'

Sister Fox snapped back. She had not had lunch either.

'I'm doing my best, Mr Royall, but you haven't got a registrar today. Mr Shah's up with that RTA that just came in.'

No registrar. And Lady Alicia booked for five.

Shit.

'So it's just your houseman on the other side, and I'm doing my best to pick out some he can send for a chest X-ray or something and bring back again next week. It's not easy, Mr Royall.'

A file fell on the floor, disgorging papers, as she struggled to select Royall's first patient.

'But he's not on call today,' he said.

'Who?'

'Shah.'

'Don't bark at me, Mr Royall. I don't arrange the doctors' rotas. I've got enough troubles of my own. They've had to take two or three patients to theatre at the same time.'

'But . . .' He got no further. A file was thrust into his hands and he was pointed in the direction of his first patient. It was not the way he was treated at Queen's. Was it worth it?

He strode from cubicle to cubicle, trailing his secretary behind him, dictating his notes and letters as he went. There was no time for the sympathetic chatter that was part and parcel of his private practice. No handshake, no unhurried preamble; all pleasantries were crushed out of the system by the sheer weight of numbers. Bodies had been bathed, clean underwear laid out, stories rehearsed till they were word-perfect, taxis hired in case the bus was late – all irrelevancies, brushed aside by a man in a white coat with one eye on the clock. 'David, take a tip from me: never let the beggars get their word in first,' an old chief had warned him. 'Otherwise you'll never get the clinic finished. And always have the next question ready; get it in before they've finished answering the previous one.'

Did everyone in south-west London have piles? David consciously stopped his foot from tapping out his impatience as, gloved hand at the ready, he watched Sister Fox heave the fourth successive expanse of buttocks, vast and pale, towards him. Shifting buttocks across couches for the convenience of consultants in a hurry is part of a nurse's duties. Faced with wide expanses of skin in patients too fat or too frightened or too stupid to comply with his every wish, even senior departmental sisters are expected to put their backs in jeopardy for a member of the profession's ruling class. The target set to her lord and master's satisfaction, Sister Fox, panting slightly, stood back. David Royall, Master of Surgery, Hunterian Professor, advanced. When not so rushed, he frequently indulged in a small, silent snigger as all the pomp and nobility of an ancient profession was coned down to the gobbet of lubricant jelly shimmering on the tip of an index finger arrowing its way towards yet another fundament. But, with no registrar to help and Lady Alicia's breasts at five o'clock, there was no time for such frivolity.

He made the standard reassuring noises as he began his examination. There are set words, noises, touchings, that go mindlessly with the fourth identical case in succession – until the probing finger suddenly stops, then goes back to make sure.

Halfway through a sentence, both the sister's and the secretary's heads came up as they detected the change in David's tone the sudden sight or feel of a cancer always produced. They saw the momentary confusion in his face as impulses from a probing fingertip sped upwards and inwards, searching out the core of caring compassion encased beneath layer on layer of vanity. For a few minutes the tempo slowed as, with soothing voice and smiling eyes, he explained to a frightened face, in words that were specific and personal, that admission to hospital was necessary – just for investigation – nothing to worry about at this stage – just a precaution – fuller examination – yes, it was possible, an operation, but not certain at the moment – have a longer chat when he was in hospital – no need to worry – Sister would tell him where to go, what to do.

David turned his back and looked at his watch.

'Right, Sister Fox. Let's get on then.'

He was going to make it after all, though it meant another adrenaline-boosted rush against the evening traffic coming out of London. Why did he do it? Why did he bother with the Merton? Two patients later, he heard the phone ring in the next room and sensed his secretary behind him leave to answer it. When she came back, she looked at him nervously.

'It's for you, Mr Royall.'

'Who is it?'

'Theatre.'

For a moment, David stood quite still, his eyes closed. Ten seconds earlier and he was just going to make it. Now, that one word later, he knew in his heart that something had happened to screw it all up. Sod it, sod it, sod it.

'Tell them I'll ring them back as soon as I've finished here.'

'It's not that sort of call, Mr Royall.'

'Who is it?'

'One of the anaesthetic registrars.'

The next patient lay listening, beginning to wonder whether he wanted to be looked after by such a rushed, angry consultant.

'Sh——' David completed the word under his breath. The name on the other end of the phone meant nothing to him, and nervous pleas for help fell on deaf ears. 'That's quite impossible. I'm virtually alone down here. I can't be in two places at once. Put Shah on the phone.'

'He's scrubbed, sir. He can't leave the table.'

'Ask him . . .'

He heard the phone change hands and a quieter, firmer voice take over.

'Hullo, David, it's Digger here. I'm afraid we need your help, old son, pronto. Your lad's getting out of his depth, I'm afraid. He's done very well so far, but he's not coping now – I was going to call you myself if he hadn't asked us to. Quick as you can, David. This fella's crook.'

The faintest of Australian accents remained.

David made one last desperate effort. 'Where the hell's Brian?'

'In the next theatre resecting a bowel, with a ruptured bladder to follow.'

'And Harry?'

'Harry's on study leave.'

Digger Drew was not the sort of man one cursed at. David shuffled his feet as he suppressed an instinctive reply. 'Always on study leave, that man,' he muttered. He paused before giving a theatrical sigh signalling his resignation to fate. 'All right. What's the problem then, Digger?'

'Ruptured liver – amongst other things. Quick as you can, David. Shah's standing there, can't move – bit like a boy with his finger in a dyke. He needs a hand, David. I rather think he's just about filling his pants.'

David put down the phone, shrugged his shoulders at Sister Fox and his secretary, then turned and walked out. Changed into operating garb, he walked into theatre with the measured tread of the infallible that was designed to instil a confidence not always felt by the surgeon. He looked over the anxious registrar's shoulder.

'What've you got, Shah?'

David had worked with Shah long enough to have developed a considerable respect for his judgment. He had also worked long enough in the heady atmosphere of a teaching hospital for that respect to be grudgingly bestowed. Shah was, after all, an overseas graduate. But he had been in the UK a long time. With a string of registrar's appointments behind him in gritty northern industrial towns and in the surgical fastnesses of the Welsh valleys, his operative experience was considerable, his judgment excellent, his prospects negligible. Even so, it was obvious from the slight tremor in his voice that he was at the frontier of his ability.

'I am glad to be seeing you, sir. We have big trouble here.'

'What have you found so far?'

'He is the driver of a car that is running into a bus queue. He is deeply unconscious when he is coming in and he has a fracture of his tibia.' Shah nodded in the direction of a vague lump under the far end of the drapes. 'But his abdomen also is very rigid, with some bruising over his left ribs. So, when I am getting blood in my syringe, I am diagnosing a ruptured spleen, and that is what he has.'

Shah pointed with his free hand, and the theatre sister held a large steel bowl under David's nose. He saw the jagged tear in the spleen, flopped and slithering amongst the blood clots.

'So – what's the problem now?'

'After taking the spleen out, I am sucking all the blood out and everything is looking very dry, but then I'm feeling his liver for tears, and suddenly there is this rush of blood that I am not controlling very well.'

As if to convince his chief, Shah lifted the hand that was hidden inside the patient's abdomen, and the level of blood around his wrist rose sharply.

'All right,' David said hurriedly. 'Stay just like that. I'll go and wash.'

His scrub was a compromise, just about long enough to ensure sterility. People who are bleeding to death do not worry unduly about becoming infected. On his way to the table he saw Digger Drew putting up a second intravenous line, his orderly hovering nearby, a unit of blood in each hand.

'How is he?' David asked.

'Rough.'

David took no further interest in the top end of the patient. If Digger Drew said the patient was rough, so be it.

At the table, David slid a hand in on top of Shah's, now

quivering under the combined influence of muscle fatigue and fear, and made a quick assessment.

'I'll need some rib shears.' He did not take his eyes off the patient as he spoke, but still saw the sister uncover a separate trolley. 'But give me a knife first. Keep your hand there, Shah. Don't move. I won't cut you, I promise.'

Shah had, quite correctly, made his incision just to the left of the midline, the logical place with a diagnosis of ruptured spleen. From there, however, there was no real chance of controlling bleeding from the back of the liver's right lobe. With one long sweeping movement, David cut obliquely up and to the right, extending the existing wound up on to the right chest. It would be a scar to be proud of, strutting round a crowded swimming pool in Tenerife. The muscle wall was well developed, with surprisingly little fat for someone David judged to be in his early forties. A crunch of the shears, and the rib margin gaped. An incision of the muscles between the ribs, and the chest was open. Snips of the scissors divided the diaphragm. There was no time for the usual looks of mock horror as ribs cracked loudly as a steel retractor was cranked open.

Now there was no Lady Alicia, no BMW, no dinner party, no guilt at wandering emotions, no professional ambitions and jealousies. There was just someone bleeding to death, and David Royall, Master of Surgery, was the end of the line. The patient might die of his head injury or some post-operative complication generally ascribed to God. He might fall out of bed later and break his neck. He might jump through the ward window after hearing his wife had deserted him. Tough luck – but acceptable. But what this patient must *not* do was bleed to death. Patients do *not* bleed to death beneath a consultant surgeon's hand. That's why the consultants were paid so much. Everyone knew that. What everyone did *not* know was that the surgeon was not particularly interested at that moment in what the hell they thought. Already seducing David away from the trivialities of the petty world outside was the strange, addictive bonding that brings the surgeon back to the table time and time again. This was a simple matter between him and the patient now. Everything else was blotted out. If he failed, then it would be a personal failure – not in anyone else's eyes, just his own. Later that evening, come what may, he would be sitting at a dinner table, the perfect host, the imperfect husband, the adoring father, the brilliantly successful surgeon. But what would he be thinking? That was going to be decided within the next ten minutes.

'Let me have some of those long fine half-circle atraumatics, Sister, please – about six or eight of them. Put them there in a row. Shah – you keep your hand where it is while I put the sutures in. If I stick one through your finger, you will tell me, won't you?'

Shah managed a small, polite laugh.

'When we've got the sutures in place, we'll put some omentum where your finger is now and tie the sutures round it as a tampon.'

Five minutes later and a row of sutures were in place, their untied ends anchored with artery forceps. David took a deep breath.

'Right – here we go.'

In the welter of blood that surged up as Shah took his finger away, removing with it the swab he had been pressing on, David pulled up a fold of the fatty tissues that hung from the stomach. Plugging the tear with it, he tied the sutures over it. Tied too loose, they would not stop the bleeding; pulled too tight and they would cheese-wire their way through the friable liver, only increasing the bleeding. Somewhere in his head, behind a mask-like face, a voice screamed over and over again, 'Do it slowly; do it once. Do it slowly; do it once.'

The last suture tied, Michael Drew joined them as they peered anxiously into the wound. He heard David give a grunt of satisfaction. The anaesthetist smiled beneath his mask, jerking his head upwards. 'Someone up there's looking after you, David,' he said quietly.

David grinned. 'More likely the Devil looking after his own, I'm afraid.'

Why was it he always felt a little cleaner, that much more at peace, in Digger Drew's company? He stripped off his gloves.

'He should be all right now, Shah. Can you close him up?

You'll need to put an underwater seal in his chest. You did well to control that.'

'Thank you, sir. But what am I doing if you are not around, sir?'

David was able to smile expansively. Things had gone well.

'Well, you'll know what to do next time, won't you.'

He watched for a moment, appreciating the way a born operator handled his instruments, before he turned to Drew. 'I'm afraid I'll have to dash, Digger. Jackie's got one of her literary dinner parties tonight.'

'Typical. You're all the same, you teaching hospital guys – just stay for the glamour – leave us to cope with the dross.'

They both chuckled.

'Now you've stopped that bleeding, I'll give the orthopods a ring, get them to fix that leg. As for the head inury . . .' Drew's forehead furrowed. 'And then we must not forget the small matter of the law pacing up and down outside. They're after this guy's blood – literally.'

'You mean booze?'

Drew nodded. 'They've been nagging for a specimen ever since he came in.'

'At this time of day?'

The words were hardly out of his mouth before David felt the old awkwardness. Would it always be the same? Drew had been dry for years now. No need to be careful what one said any more – surely?

Drew smiled gently, forgivingly, sensing David's thoughts. 'What's the time of day got to do with it?' A vision of the glass of vodka beside the shaving mirror passed before his eyes.

'Have you given them a specimen?' David asked.

'No.'

'Going to?'

'No.'

Embarrassed, David said nothing. Was it possible Digger Drew still harboured a fellow feeling for a drunk who had mowed down a bus queue? Shame welled up inside him as the anaesthetist explained.

'This fella was unconscious when he came in. They got me to

see him in Cas, and the cut of his suit suggested a business lunch. So I needed to know. I imagine even a bone-headed surgeon can see that a patient already stewed to the gills can make the anaesthetic a bit dodgy.' He smiled at David as if to reassure him he need not worry. A born-again abstainer had done the right thing. 'But I'm not going to risk being sued for assault by giving the police a specimen without his consent.'

'And was he?'

'What?'

'Drunk.'

Digger Drew's smile broadened into a grin. 'No. Not a trace.' He nodded to the orderly who, wordlessly, had held up the label on another unit of blood for him to check. 'Which is strange for a Welshman. I imagine he's got to be a compatriot of yours, with a name like Evans. D'you know any Welshmen called Evans living in Wimbledon?'

'Don't be bloody silly. Only rich Englishmen live in Wimbledon. Everyone knows that. Why d'you think I bother to slum it down here? We poor Celts, ground into the dust as we are under the Saxon heel, we can't afford places like that. I thought you knew that.'

Drew's shoulders shook above a wheezy chest. He might have given up smoking sixty a day, but his chest was never going to get any better.

One last look at how Shah was coping and David thanked the theatre sister before heading for the door. He turned for one final word with Digger Drew.

'All right for Friday?'

'Yes. What time?'

'Usual time – knife to skin eight-thirty?'

'I'll be there. Give my love to Jackie.'

Much to the disgust of his anaesthetist colleagues at Queen's, David gave the bulk of his private anaesthesia to Digger Drew. Drew, like David, had a part-time NHS contract, but there was a difference. Drew would not take on private work outside the sessions set aside. David had tried, but Drew had always gently but firmly refused, knowing that by doing so he risked losing it all. It had not pleased them at Queen's. So – they had said – it was all right for that bastard at the Merton to scoop all the major cases while they at Queen's had to put themselves out, cutting their NHS work, dodging here and there across London at short notice, coping with the untidy, unpredictable, demanding fringes of Royall's practice. So Drew was a bloody good anaesthetist – weren't they all? What the hell – Royall might spread the loot around a bit more. It was hardly playing the game, giving the cream of one of the biggest surgical practices in London to a dried-out lush in a DGH, for God's sake.

David had worked at the Merton and District General Hospital while on the registrars' rotation scheme from Queen's College Hospital. Even amongst the junior staff, Drew's drinking had been an open secret: the whispered conferences amongst his colleagues, his absence for days at a time covered by registrars to whom a wink had to be as good as a nod – registrars who had hopes of consultant status themselves one day and no desire to rock the selection boat. It was the oldest joke in the NHS that the consultants had their registrars by the testimonials. But, as in all such unstable conditions, there was a logical progression to an inevitable conclusion.

David had been on call the day Drew's mentally handicapped son, his only son, had been admitted with third-degree burns, the result of the cigarette end dropped in an alcoholic whiteout. The boy, brutally scarred, had survived, and it had been as if Drew had been given a second chance. David had witnessed the agonising transformation as what many had said was the cause of his drinking had become his reason for living.

David, now the successful surgeon, knew where Drew's private earnings went – the modified minibus designed to take four or five handicapped children, the trips to the coast with Drew at the wheel, the plans for the small specialised centre Drew was building with his own hands from a derelict garage. Putting money Drew's way gave David a warm feeling inside, a vicarious sense of absolution. He saw it as a method of offering a libation to the gods of charity without giving offence to the rather more avaricious deities he had chosen to serve.

*

Lady Alicia's breasts were as lumpy as ever. She had not minded being kept waiting, and the reason for his being late, so modestly let slip, the bleeding, the life saved, only added to her adoration. David looked at the scars, scattered over both breasts, and wondered whether, in her craving for more surgery, she was developing a sort of mammary Münchhausen syndrome. Or was it that she wanted to be ahead of the field at the next Embassy party? There was hardly a breast in Mayfair now, over the age of forty, on which David's hand had not come to rest. It was a competitive arena with an exotic method of scoring and, as he moved amongst them socially, gin and tonic in hand, like some suave ringmaster, he had to make a conscious effort to gaze at their faces rather than at what he knew lay beneath the silk and lace.

High-fliers in busy worlds of their own, at the centres of eccentric social vortices in a teeming city, David and Jackie Royall had few friends, fewer still mutual ones. Dinner parties were either 'his' or 'hers'. David had spent many hours listening with one ear to an American publisher drawling on about some auction he had just won against all the odds while, with the other, he could hear Jackie, the editorial director of Janssen and Paul, gently seducing some odiously ill-mannered bestselling author they did not even publish. In return, Jackie had sat, the perfect hostess, listening to endless hours of medical politics from which even gory clinical 'shop' was a diversion. Reluctantly, she had had to admit that some of her husband's guests had been more interesting recently. His contacts with the Embassies seemed to be bearing fruit. She remembered the challenge of giving her first Muslim dinner party. Now, their flowing robes and gentle manners regularly added a certain something that never failed to impress the other guests.

It was a great help, living 'over the shop'. It was also fortunate that this evening's dinner party was one of Jackie's. David heard the sound of voices in the drawing room as he raced upstairs to change. He would never quite get used to seeing his DJ laid out on the bed. How Jackie managed it all he would never know. Did she never make a mistake, leave herself vulnerable, show some sign of weakness? Minutes later he stood, taking a deep breath, before opening the drawing room door. The strange faces would mean nothing to him; they all looked the same. The one face that would register would be his wife's, that keen, penetrating glance as if her eyes, like retrograde scanning sensors, could see, minute by minute, what he had done all day.

Two days later, David drove into the Merton to do his ward round. His three sessions at the Merton consisted of one out-patients clinic, one ward round and one operating session. He was never on call for emergencies – a sore point with the other two surgeons, particularly Brian Pullman, five years his senior. Harry O'Connor, the other, recently appointed consultant, was sufficiently generous to concede that David's sessions gave them at least a tenuous connection with a teaching hospital, but there was no doubt in Brian Pullman's mind.

'He's here for the private work, pure and bloody simple,' he said. 'What other reason could he possibly have for straying this far from Harley Street and the London Clinic – and Lincoln's Inn Fields?'

Which was correct. David explained his presence by pointing to the dearth of good clinical material to be found in a depopulating city centre. Clustered cheek by jowl around the Royal Colleges and embattled by an outer ring of excellent DGHs, too many teaching hospitals fought for their long and honoured existences by filling their beds with the esoteric specialities of the profession's high-fliers. If a medical student at Queen's, thirsting for knowledge, picked a bed at random, the chances were that the patient he would find therein would not have acute appendicitis or gallstone colic, but some exotic and incurable liver disease or some tropical parasitic infestation upon which an international reputation had been built.

'Some of my best cases I use to teach on at Queen's come from the Merton,' David argued.

Which again was the truth – but not the whole truth.

The truth was that he had seen south-west London as a fertile field that contact with local GPs might help him harvest. All those wealthy Wimbledon homes and the lush pastures of the stockbroker belt. But the sessions were now something of a burden. He was becoming known internationally, what with the papers he had read abroad and his father-in-law's contacts in the Middle East. He had reached the stage where he could pick and choose. He was beginning to wonder whether the Merton was worth it.

On the ward, Shah, his usual polite, self-effacing self, offered David a white coat.

David shook his head. 'I can't stay long this morning, I'm afraid, Shah.' He saw two students lurking hungrily in the background and avoided their eyes. Hell – he'd talked to them for a good half-hour the previous week. 'D'you think you could have a chat with them about something after I've gone? I've got to get away.'

The ward sister and the house surgeon fell in behind them as they made the rounds of David's patients. One bed had the screens drawn round it. He raised one eyebrow at the sister.

'Mr Evans, the ruptured liver. He's on a bedpan.'

David turned to Shah as they moved on.

'How is he?'

'He is fine, sir. No problems.'

'Conscious yet?'

'Oh, yes, sir. Straight afterwards. Dr Drew thinks he is probably regaining consciousness under the anaesthetic, if you know what I mean, sir.'

The ward sister butted in. 'His sister would like to see you before you leave, sir.'

David pulled a face. 'Perhaps you could . . . Tell her I'll see her the next time . . .'

'I think you'd better see her, Mr Royall. I don't think she's that sort of woman, somehow. Flown over from America just to see her brother and looks the sort you'd be wise to see even if she lived next door.'

'Oh, God, one of those. All right, I'll see her before I leave. But tell her – just two minutes.'

David would still have walked out if the ward sister had not reminded him.

'Mr Royall – Mr Evans's sister? In here?'

She opened the door for him.

The woman was tall, made to look even taller by the upturned collar of a long, elegant leather coat. She knew the trick of keeping the light at her back, and David struggled to see her features as he heard her drawl.

'Hullo, David. Remember me? It costs more than a penny to see my knickers now.'

And memories came pouring back.

2

'Give me ewr penny an' my sister'll show ew 'er knickers.'

Maldwyn Evans, aged eight, was already beginning to show his flair as an entrepreneur. He and his sister, Faye, aged nine, stood solemnly side by side, looking for David Royall's reaction to what they obviously considered a reasonable business proposition. For a moment, the only sound was that of Maldwyn's breathing. Mal Evans did ninety per cent of his breathing through parched encrusted lips. The only time he closed his mouth was periodically to suck air noisily through his nose, dragging into the dark recesses the snotty gob that, summer and winter, adorned his nostrils. His voice had all the tonal resonance of sodden driftwood.

'Give it me 'en – or I'll knock ewr bloody block off f'r ew.'

The precious coin firmly clenched, David shook his head, his face expressionless. He looked at their feet, hiding from Mal his fear, from Faye the earliest tremors of guilt. Girls. Faye Evans. Pale, smooth legs. Knickers. Disturbing things he thought about at times – secret thoughts – his – pleasurable in a warm, ill-defined, disturbing sort of way. He'd seen knickers before – quick glimpses of black as slim white legs climbed a gate or swirled in a playground cartwheel – but it would be different, someone slowly, deliberately showing them, just for him.

The problem was he could think of better ways of spending

his money. And it had been a penny this week. Not all Saturdays were penny days. David never asked for his pocket money. Pocket money? – he had never heard the term. He just stood, after breakfast on Saturdays, beneath the mantelpiece on which rested the old tobacco jar with the purse wedged behind it. He always knew, without looking, whether it was a penny or halfpenny that had been pressed into his palm. The smaller coin always brought with it the gentle push propelling him in the direction of the door, with no demand for gratitude, from someone who did not want to witness his disappointment.

For a whole penny meant twice as long to ponder over the row on row of wide-necked jars of sweets – or 'loshins' as they were called in that part of the Rhondda Valley – in 'Llewellyn's the Shop', the Gossip Exchange at the end of Cory Street. With a penny, anything up to ten minutes could be spent in careful selection under the old lady's patient, watchful eye before emerging, one pocket bulging with the paper bag secreted within. But now, a flinty, pain-immune brother and sinuous, predatory sister, shoulder to shoulder, barred his way. There would have been one sweet for his Gran, one for his Mam, but now they would have to wait.

Mal Evans saw the sales resistance in David's face and was prepared to improve his offer.

'Touch 'em 'en. Ew can feel 'em if ew like.'

David shook his head vigorously, his cheeks flushing, and Mal was quick to see the futility of further bargaining. Enough of the soft sell. He closed in, his fists clenching menacingly. His sister stepped forward with him, her pretty, prematurely adult face hard and merciless. Between them, they pinned David into a corner of the Infants' yard where David, having seen them further down the street, had tried to escape. Cory Street Junior School was always referred to as 'The Infants'. No one knew why.

Apart from the obvious matter of gender, the three were similar in many ways. Their differences were more a matter of degree than anything else. Except that one wore a skirt, the other two trousers, their dress was uniform – thick grey shirt and ragged jumper, crumpled socks and heavy black shoes. The difference was that one's clothes were carefully darned, his feet well shod, the others' torn and holed. All three gave off the same stale body smell – not one of them had yet seen the inside of a bathroom. That was not to say there were no bathrooms in Cory Street in 1951; they were beginning to appear, here and there, ugly outcrops of breeze blocks jutting out into the black back gardens. But for David Royall, nurtured on the razor-edge economy of a part-time theatre staff nurse, there was no such luxury. For him it was still the tin bath in front of the fire, to stand, naked and shivering, while his Mam grunted at the steamy weight of the great iron kettles. Maggie Evans's children washed themselves under a cold tap.

The children differed most in their physical appearances. David and Faye might have been of similar height, he with the promise of his parents' physical strength, she with the lean muscular look of the survivor, but where his hair was jet, combed to the shine and grain of a gramophone record, his eyes grey-green, her hair, long, unwashed and unbrushed, hung honey-blonde to her waist. Her eyes, a bright blue that defied the clouds of hurt and mistrust, she kept half closed in constant vigilance. Mal was inches shorter than both, his hair, curly and red, cropped close enough to show the pink scalp. His green eyes darted restlessly in their challenge to anything that moved or talked.

A hard little fist thudded into David's chest before being held threateningly under his nose.

'I'll smash ewr face in f'r ew, if ew don't give me 'at penny. Ew give it bloody 'ere.'

David's jaw set firmer as his pulse began to race. A collier, walking home within a few yards of them, laughed at memories of his own childhood. He might as well have been a million miles away as David's world now contracted to a few square feet, populated only by his two oppressors. The face in front of him became blurred, the sound of voices made indistinct by the thumping in his head. But on one point he was quite clear. Somehow, he must not, would not submit to the vicious green eyes that came ever closer.

'I'll break ewr arm f'r ew.' Mal Evans paused as he struggled for words. 'I'll cut ewr bloody 'ead off.'

The ultimate threat had its calming effect. David knew he had won. That much was clear. What he could not understand was – why? Desperate to hide all sign of his fear, he had not moved. He had seen other children submit to Mal's bullying often enough. Most handed over a prized possession without demur – a new ball, a pencil box, a precious toy. Others put off the moment of capitulation only to exchange a bloody nose or a bruised shin for a few moments of defiance. But David knew the penny was his, that Mal and his sister were not going to get it. And it was going to be without his having to say a word or raise a finger, even in self-defence. It could not just be his size – he had seen Mal take on boys much bigger than he was. Why then?

'Why're ew so stuck up 'en?' Mal inched back and David breathed more easily. 'Wot ew got to be so bloody stuck up about 'en?'

'I'm not stuck up.'

'Ew are. Ew bloody are. And ew're teacher's pet.'

'I'm not.'

'Ew are. Ew're bloody teacher's pet.'

'Teacher's pet. Teacher's pet.' The facial contortions that accompanied Faye's chanted chorus contrasted with her eyes which remained still, holding David's in a level, steady, half-closed gaze.

'Ewr mother's only a bloody nurse. 'Es nothin to get stuck up about in 'at. Nothin special, bloody nurse.'

'She's not just a nurse. She works in the hospital with the doctors. She helps them take things out of people when they're ill.'

'And' I'll take somethin' out of ew too if ew don' watch.' Once more Mal raised a fist beneath a nose, this time his own. He pushed upwards, his nostrils squelching, his upper lip rising to expose yellow, carious teeth, the skin between his eyes corrugating into ridge and furrow. 'Don' ew be so stuck up. Ew watch, tha's all. Ew watch.'

He turned and, in one sweeping movement, picked up a stone

which, hurled in a low, flat arc, sent a passing dog yelping painfully out into Cory Street. He did not look back. Faye did.

Megan Royall paused in her ironing to sigh. It had been a long hot day in theatre and she was tired, but that was not the reason for her sigh. She picked up the shirt she had just finished, holding it at arm's length before hanging it to air over the brass rail bolted beneath the heavy slate mantelpiece. So small and yet so big. She remembered the thick flannel shirts of her father and of Ben – always white shirts. Why did colliers always have to wear white shirts? And stiff, starched collars on Sundays. She remembered the losing battle against the grey with knuckle-bruising washboards and creaking mangles on steaming wet Mondays. She also remembered the baby clothes that had replaced them for so short a time. Another few years . . .

She looked lovingly at the back of David's head as he bent over one of the old magazines they kept over the broken spring in Ben's old chair. That copy of *Picture Post* must have been there since the war. David must have read it a hundred times. It wasn't good for the boy, sitting there, hour after hour, thinking, listening to his Mam and his Gran talk of the past. What else was there for him to do? There was only the pictures – and they were only old nonsense. All those war films. Why did people want to live through all that again? And those old American films – all that shouting and shooting. No – she must start taking a daily paper, a good one. It would be good for him. They could probably stretch to that now and she had seen how he enjoyed the Sunday paper. And – when she had time – she must take him up to the Public Library; there must be children's books up there. It was not as if he was like the other kids in Cory Street – those Evans kids. He was different, her David. If only Ben could see him now – so quiet, always thinking. She saw him sink his fingers into his hair and scratch. He scratched again, harder. She put the iron back on the steel plate above the glowing coals.

'Excuse me, Gran.'

The old lady drew her feet back to allow her daughter-in-law to stretch high on the mantelpiece. With one hand inside an old tea caddy, Megan turned to her son.

'Come on, mister. Come and sit here.'

David took one look at what she had in her hand and drew back.

'Oh, no, Mam.'

'David, come and sit here,' she insisted sharply.

'Sit by there now, like your Mam says, there's a lovely boy,' old Mrs Royall crooned.

Still objecting, David did as he was told, sitting with his back to his mother, trying to concentrate on his reading, his shoulders hunched against what he knew was to come. With firm down strokes, Megan drove the fine-toothed comb through the thick black hair.

'Stop it,' she ordered as David wriggled and squirmed under the comb's sharp points. 'There.'

There was a note of triumph as his mother held the comb in front of his eyes. With a rolling movement of her thumbnail, she crushed the life out of a head louse.

'Have you been playing with those Evans kids again?'

'No, Mam.'

Megan dug the comb in harder as if she did not believe him. 'You keep away from that lot, d'you hear?' Again a dig that made her son squeal. 'You know their father's in jail, don't you?'

'Yes, Mam.'

'And you know what for, don't you?'

'Yes, Mam.'

'Well then . . .'

Her mind full of thoughts of what she would like to do to Handel Evans, she took her time over squashing another louse in front of his eyes.

'You listen to your mother now, David bach.' Gran Royall had taken to rocking gently back and forth in her chair whenever she spoke. 'You stay away from that family. You're not like them.'

'Another few years,' Megan murmured to herself, but David

heard her. He tried to turn his head, but his mother jerked it straight again.

'What d'you mean, Mam, another few years?'

'I mean another few years and you'll be out of the Infants and down in Porth County and then . . .'

'Got to pass the entrance exam first.'

'You'll pass the entrance exam. Mr Griffiths is sure you won't have any trouble.'

'Finished, Mam?' David pleaded.

'Yes, I've finished.' Her voice softened as lovingly she stroked the back of his head. 'Got any homework?'

'I've done it. It's on the chair by there.' He did not take his eyes off what he was reading as he pointed.

'David,' she scolded. 'How often have I told you not to say "by here" and " by there"? It's common. You don't want to speak like a Rhondda boy all your life, do you? When did you do it?'

'Before you got home.' His grandmother answered for him as if to allow him to go on reading. 'Down by there.' She pointed in front of the fire. 'On the floor, where he always does it. Didn't take him more than two minutes. Why he has to go on the floor like that instead of the table, I don't know.'

'Have you got it all right?'

'Yes, Mam.'

'Sure?'

'Yes, Mam.' The words were drawn out in a long-suffering sigh. 'It was easy. D'you want to check it?'

Megan shook her head, a proud smile on her face. 'No, David. I'm sure there's no need. You're not going to have any trouble with any old exams.'

'He'll pass.' Gran Royall nodded sagely as she rocked. 'He'll pass all right.'

And, for the first of countless times, young shoulders felt the full weight of loving hopes and dreams laid upon them.

'That's if we're still here,' Megan Royall said quietly.

David's head came up sharply, but it was the old lady who spoke first.

'What d'you mean, Megan? What d'you mean, "still here"?'

Megan, old rags in her hand to protect it from the heat of the handle, picked up the iron once more. She spat on the flat surface, waiting until the sizzle died away before thumping it into one of David's vests. She spoke over her shoulder, keeping her face from view. 'If we're not down in Cardiff by then.'

'Cardiff? What d'you mean, Cardiff?' Gran Royall made the capital of Wales sound like one of the outer planets.

'Mr Jackson is on at me all the time. He says he could get me a theatre sister's job down at the Infirmary any time I wanted. I've told you; he's the surgeon who comes up to operate at the Miners' every Thursday morning.' Her head jerked backwards as she thrust out her chin. 'He says I'm wasted up here.' She banged the iron down with pride. 'He says he's not coming up any more when I'm on holiday. Says I'm the only one he'll work with in theatre now.'

'What would you want to go down to Cardiff for? That old place. Who would you know down there?'

'We'd soon make friends. Wouldn't we, David?'

David had already learned it was safer to say nothing if he was not sure.

'And it would mean full-time in theatre with a bit more money. And David's old enough to look after himself more now, aren't you, cariad?'

Again – nothing.

'And what about me?' The rocking increased. 'I'm not going down to any old Cardiff. I gave up my home once to help you look after David when my Ben was killed. I'm not going to move again. What's going to happen to me?'

The iron hung in midair as Megan stared out of the window, its spotless glass in eternal shadow, all prospect blocked by the cold stone wall of number 44, ten feet away.

'Don't worry, Gran,' she sighed. 'We're not going anywhere. It was just a thought.'

Reassured, David saw his chance. 'Mam – any chance of us going down to see the shops in Cardiff again this Christmas?'

'Yes, cariad,' she promised, smiling. 'We'll go down to see the shops again this Christmas.'

*

Fatty Griffiths was a two-faced bully of low intelligence. Not that anyone should think any the worse of him for that. How else could anyone hope to teach form three in Cory Street Infants? The children's only hope of a smattering of education in a class that contained someone as disruptive as Maldwyn Evans, was for the master to be an even bigger bully than Mal. This struggle for dominance over the rest of the class was not confined to an intellectual level, however low. It boiled over on occasion into painful physical confrontation between an indomitable eight-year-old, all flailing fists and boots, and a podgy chain smoker who stood his ground only because he was too slow and dyspnoeic to get out of the way. The conflicts were watched by the rest of the class, their mouths agape at such bravery, while teachers from neighbouring classes peered with anxious faces through the glass screens, willing Griffiths on to beat hell out of the little sod, knowing that there, but for the grace of God . . .

A backhander would split Mal's lip, sending him reeling back to his seat with just enough induced respect for authority to allow lessons to proceed. But it would be no more than a truce, and Griffiths was obliged to make concessions to keep the peace. While others kept their heads down out of fear of the cane, never far from Fatty Griffiths's right hand, Mal roamed the aisles, burning off energy with bowling that had Bradman's uprooted middle stump cartwheeling halfway to the boundary or diving catches that saved the crucial penalty at Wembley as the final whistle blew.

David's desk was immediately behind Mal's. The morning had started, as all mornings started, with its mind-numbing routine. Fatty had marched in, the smile, switched on while interviewing an anxious mother, falling away to reveal the permanent scowl beneath. The Lord's Prayer, spoken in unison with hands together and eyes tightly shut, had been followed by the calling of the register. As Fatty had called out the names, Mal had gone from desk to desk, handing out the pens, the slightest thing – a glint of defiance in the eye, a new shirt, a stuck-up girl – resulting in a crossed nib with which to struggle for the rest of the day. Next had come the multiplication tables, always starting with the 'two times table', Griffiths with his cane beating out the rhythm on his desk as he had driven them through the higher numbers. Last of the morning routines had been the period of mental arithmetic, David being forbidden to answer 'to give the others a chance'.

'Right.' Griffiths put the can down and picked up a book. 'Maldwyn, give out some paper. We'll have some dictation.'

The groans around the class lingered as Maldwyn placed one sheet of precious paper in front of everyone including himself. Griffiths dictated as he walked back and forth, amid murmured complaints from the slow-witted at how fast he was going. Mal ignored the whole procedure. He had other uses for his paper. Torn into strips, folded and folded again, the hard V-shaped pellets, projected from an elastic band stretched between finger and thumb, stung as they whizzed behind Griffiths's back. A girl at the far end of the row yelped, her hand to her face, as Griffiths swung round.

'Who did that?' he thundered.

'He did.'

The girl's arm shot out, her fingers pointing. It was only when David looked up that he found everyone's face, including Mal's, centred on himself. On the desk in front of him lay an elastic band. David heard the snot in the back of Mal's throat rattle as he laughed.

'You, David?'

The disappointment in Griffiths's voice hurt, but David said nothing. He felt the rising excitement around him as he was given time to answer. The class had come to know all the signs of an imminent caning.

'Come out here, David. And bring whatever you've got on the desk with you.'

David stumbled over the foot Mal stuck out as he picked his way between the desks.

'Did you do that, David? Is this yours?' Griffiths took the elastic off him and held it high for all to see.

David's face set stubbornly as he glared at Mal. Mal had stopped grinning, his head now cocked to one side as if making a careful assessment.

'I'll give you one more chance, David. Did you do that?'

The silence seemed to satisfy Mal as much as it infuriated Griffiths.

'You disappoint me, boy. I thought you were different. Hold your hand out. Further – out, out, boy. I can't get at you properly like that.'

David had seen hands pulled away at the last moment, desperate efforts to put off the inevitable to the huge delight of the class. There would be none of that. He had seen bitter tears. There would be none of that either. He clenched his jaw as he heard the cane swish, his unflinching eyes taking strength from Mal's strangely compassionate face that stood out clearly against the joyful voyeurism of the other children. The pain of the second stroke David hardly felt through the searing burn of the first.

'Now the other one, boy.'

With a burgeoning pride that there were no tears to blur his view of Mal's face, David spurned the pain in the other hand. The look of disdain he gave Griffiths as he held his hand higher for the second stroke earned him a third.

'And that's for your insolence.' Fatty Griffiths laid his full weight into the last stroke. 'You wait until I see your mother next. Go and sit down, David. I'm very disappointed in you.'

Back in his seat, David did instinctively what he had seen so many do before him, clasped his burning palms around the cold cast-iron frame beneath his desk.

As they tumbled out of the door, lessons finished for the day, Mal caught David by the shirt front and hauled him, sullenly resistant, along the yard. Gran would have his tea ready for him; he should go home.

'Ew come with me.'

On the wall at one end of the yard, picked out in chalk in the crumbling mortar between the bricks, was the nearest thing to goal posts Cory Street Infants was ever likely to possess. The tarmac in front of it sloped steeply from one side to the other, a factor to be taken into account when striking a rolling ball. It was already the scene of noisy, disorganised children's play. Mal went straight to the heart of the mêlée, striding in amongst the chaos, picking up the ball to stand, hands on hips, feet apart.

'Ew lot, bugger off.'

Most needed no second bidding. A few, including the ball's owner, lingered, their faces sad at their own weakness. Mal advanced a step towards them.

'Ew wan' a bloody fight 'en?'

'Can I 'ave my ball 'en, Mal?'

'Ew bugger off. Me an' David wanta play. ' E's my butty.'

With the glow that his first experience of power over other people's lives brought, David watched the other children slink away.

'I'll be goalie. I'm goin' to be bloody goalie for Arsenal when I grows up.'

A big strong boy, David was also well co-ordinated between eye and hand and foot. He knew when to take the ball on his instep in a full-blooded drive, when to play safe against the slope of the ground and use the inner side of his shoe. But, no matter what he did, running across the goal trying not to signal when he was going to shoot, or driving the ball with all his might, or dribbling it to within feet of the wall, somehow, at the last moment, Mal would hurl himself to bring off a save. Fear of grazed knees and elbows seemed not to occur to Mal as he threw himself headlong on to the hard, rough tarmac, bouncing back unscathed each time.

'Ew're no bloody good. Lemme 'ave a go.'

They changed places and, whereas before he had felt merely frustrated, David now experienced the total humiliation of being on the receiving end of natural genius. Nothing he did could stop the ball slapping into the wall just beyond his hand, above his head, even between his legs. The taunting obscenities that accompanied each failure finally drew David out into attack. Grim-faced he charged at Mal, only to flounder in thin air, Mal and ball already behind him, or to lock shins painfully and still not win the ball. He limped away from the first one or two collisions, but found the pain got less and less, the harder he went in. He began to feel a strange exhilaration in the pain of violent human contact, and was giving as good as he received when Mal went sprawling, knocked sideways by a blow to the head from a mother's arm made strong by a thousand washdays.

She bent to pick up the ball. 'I don't buy no balls for ew to play with, Mal Evans. Ew're a bully, that's what ew are. Ew keep ewr hands off my Gareth, d'ew 'ear? End up in quod like ewr father, ew will.'

Mal picked himself up and stood watching the woman's receding back. He waited until he felt safe, then yelled, 'Bloody cow.'

Two happy eight-year-olds, hot, flushed, ragged, bruised and penniless, surveyed each other.

'Ew wait till I get that Gareth Jones tomorrow. Bloody Mammy's pet. I'll knock 'is bloody teeth in f'r 'im.' Mal looked at David. 'Ew got a ball at 'ome?'

David shook his head sadly.

'My Dad,' Mal said proudly, 'used to play with a pig's bladder when 'e was a kid. 'E told me. 'E said they used to go down the slaughter 'ouse. All ew need 'en is a bit o' string. Let's go down the slaughter 'ouse and get a pig's bladder.'

He saw the hesitation in David's face.

'Scared, are ew? Scared of a bit of blood, are ew? I seen 'em lots o' times. Cuts their bloody 'eads right off, they do. I'm goin'. Ew needn't come if ew're scared.'

They made their way through the maze of terraced houses, David close at Mal's shoulder. A small herd of lowing bull calves, their watery, bulging eyes already rolling at the smell of blood, jostled as David and Mal climbed the gate into the slaughter house yard. Just inside the door a man sluiced the concrete floor with a hosepipe. He grinned at the boys as he twitched the jet close to their feet.

David heard Mal make a small noise behind him as the knife was driven into a calf's neck. The slosh of the cascading dark blood, the brisker sound of the bright red jets as they hit the concrete, had little outward effect on David. A feeling not of nausea or fear but of a deep sadness welled up inside him, not so much for the beast that was now beyond all pain but for the next young animal, which stood looking at him with such trusting brown eyes. He turned to share his sadness with Mal. But Mal was gone.

David stayed, reluctant to desert the animals in their last

moments, until one of the men advanced on him and turned him out.

'David, where are you going?'
　'Up the Maindy.'
　'On your own?'
　'Yes, Mam.'
　'What do you do up there on the mountain, all on your own? I don't like you going up there all by yourself.'
　'Where else is there to go?'
　'It's not good for you.' Megan Royall shut out all thoughts of why it should be bad for her son to be all on his own on a mountainside. 'Wasn't there a match today? Wasn't it the last match of the season?' If only Ben was still alive. 'I'd have given you the money.'
　'It's too hot, Mam.' Mal had shown him where you could unhook the fence and get in for nothing anyway. 'Can I go to the pictures tonight instead?'
　'No.'
　Head down, David walked out of the house, closing the door quietly behind him.
　He went across the street and through the deserted school yard, bending forward slightly as he began to climb the hill. A burst of sound from the football field carried to him and he felt a pang of lonely jealousy. When the steepness of the slope defied the terraces and the last of the slate roofs now lay in grey serried ranks below him, the rutted, potholed tarmac gave way to a mountain track. The climb was enough to make a fit youngster breathe hard, and by the time he reached the farm he was glad of the halt to enjoy the cringing welcome of the border collie bitch that slunk out of the yard to meet him. They were old friends, and David had company for the next ten minutes of his climb until deeper loyalties prevailed. Another half an hour and he was above the untidy, haphazard oaks. Now there was nothing but blackened sheep droppings scattered on close-cropped grass amongst a patchwork of scented bracken and spiky rushes. And silence, broken only by the occasional distant clang of trucks

being shunted in the valley far below, and the soft woodwind puff of the winding engine from the Pentre colliery away to his right.

He found the gap in the crumbling dry wall that he had tried to repair the last time he was there. He took up the task once more, the stones heavy and rough in his soft hands. Suddenly bored with his lack of success, he took to the chest-high bracken, forcing his way through the fronds that caught at his legs. He fought his way through a tropical jungle, leaving behind him a trail of dead pygmies with their poisoned arrows, before finding a clearing where, if he was careful, no one would ever find him. Stalking on knees and elbows, he crossed the clearing stealthily to clear a gap in the bracken just big enough for him to look down on the Pentre and the valley beyond without being seen. He lay on his belly, the way he did his homework, his chin in his hands.

Across the valley, shimmering in the heat, the twin chimneys, one each side of the Pentre's winding gear, puffed their steam alternately as the engine lifted the cage between the levels below ground. They started slowly, quietly, building up to a crescendo that died away again as the big wheels came to a halt. It fascinated David to count how many puffs he saw before hearing the first sound, how long the sound went on after the last puff died away. Was it the same length of time? He counted carefully. Why was it you saw things straight away but had to wait to hear the same thing? As the pithead fell silent below him, his eye wandered to the houses beyond and below. He loved his Mam, he loved his Gran, he loved his home, but . . . he rolled on his back, frowning. He tried to overcome an overwhelming loneliness by searching in the blinding sunlight for the skylark that sang somewhere up there above him. It was warm. So quiet. Distant sounds . . .

'Why d'ew come up by 'ere on ewr own 'en'

David jerked awake at the sound of the voice. Faye Evans sat within feet of him with the stillness of someone who had been there for some time. He looked around in alarm, expecting Mal to leap from the bracken at any moment. She read his thoughts.

'Mal's gone to that silly old football match. Why d'ew come up by 'ere on ewr own 'en? I seen you, lots o' times.'

'I don't know.'

'What d'ew think about when ew're up by 'ere 'en?'

'Nothing.' Nothing she would understand.

If David's rebuffs were having any effect, Faye's calculating expression did not show it as she concentrated her gaze for a moment on some point deep inside David's head.

'D'ew like girls?' she asked.

David's cheeks flushed. Nine-year-olds can appear very worldly to eight-year-olds. His throat went dry as he countered with 'D'you like boys?'

'I hate men.' The simple statement was made in the flat monotone of a defeated, degraded adult.

For a while they spoke of important things with the serious, disjointed logic of children. David, conscious of the long muscular legs beneath the skirt, did not look at Faye. She did not take her eyes off him.

'What are ew going to be when ew grow up?' she asked.

'I don't know. My Mam says I'm going to be a famous doctor up in London. She says I'll have a bigger car even than Dr Davies.'

''Ave ew ever been to London?' Faye seemed to have forgotten about men and was a wide-eyed child once more.

'No. But my Mam has promised to take me one day; if I get into Porth County, she said. She said she'd take me on the underground trains, the ones with the sliding doors. She says you've got to be quick or the doors close and cut you in half.'

For a moment, children's minds were filled with scenes of subterranean carnage.

'I've been to Cardiff. My Mam's taken me to Cardiff,' David said, proudly. 'And we're going again next Christmas to see the shops.'

'Must be lovely,' Faye whispered. 'I've never been to Cardiff.' Her face became serious as if something had been worrying her. 'D'ew really want to see my knickers? Ew can if ew want. I don't mind.'

Knowing immediately she had said the wrong thing, she saw

David shake his head. He got up without a word, turned his back on her and walked away. In an adult it would have been an act of bad manners. Between children, nothing seemed more natural. Faye simply got to her feet, regret now mixed with the permanent sadness of her face. She followed him down the mountain in silence, a pace behind him and on the other side of the track. Someone had locked the schoolyard gate, and they had to take the gulley behind the houses on the other side of Cory Street. They turned the corner to find Mal showing a group of children how he would have won the match. There was no turning back.

'Where ew been 'en?'

David chose not to reply, walking on, head down, trying to walk around the group. Faye answered for him.

'Been up the Maindy.'

'What ew been up the Maindy with my sister for 'en?'

Again David said nothing, and three of the bigger children, sensing sport, hemmed him to the wall. Mal took David's arm, forcing it painfully up behind his back, and David felt the rough grime of the bricks on his cheek as he tried to twist away from the pain in his shoulder and his elbow. He winced as Mal gave his arm a sudden jerk.

'My sister don't go up the mountain with nobody.' Mal had spied on lovers amongst the bracken often enough to know what went on up the Maindy.

David felt Faye's body against his as she struggled with her brother. 'Ew leave 'im, Mal. 'E didn't do no harm. I followed 'im up.'

'Ew shut ewr bloody gob.'

Mal made a long scything swing with one foot, and David felt the sickening pain in one ankle as he toppled sideways to sprawl in the black dust. His breath was squeezed out as Mal descended on his chest to lean over and rub David's nose in the filth.

Within inches of his face, a rotting straw mattress, disturbed by scuffling feet, crawled with woodlice. Beans, congealed into a fetid coronet around the jagged edge of a rusting tin can, threatened a soft cheek. A decaying doorpost, falling away from crumbling brickwork, grazed his scalp. All this he noted with a child's intensity of perception and feeling. With the smell of rotting garbage and dog's pee in his nose, the far worse taste of humiliation in his mouth, a sudden revulsion gave David the strength to throw Mall off. Hearing, as from a long way off, the delighted chants of 'Fight, fight,' he got up and hurled himself at his tormentor. For a few moments they rolled together in the dust before finally facing up to each other, their fists small and hard, murder in their eyes. Numbing pain to one side of his mouth only added fury to David's blows as he bored in. Mal was no more than a blur at which he struck and kicked without fear. He gasped at a sickening pain in one knee but knew that, somewhere out there in front of him, he was getting through to Mal too. As the world disappeared for a moment behind a black-red wave of pain, he staggered back, knowing that he was finished, that he could do no more as blood from his nose ran into his mouth.

He turned his back and walked away, expecting the jeers and taunts reserved for losers, only to find he was not alone. The centre of an excited, chattering group, he was escorted out into Cory Street. He felt an arm around his shoulder. Someone offered a grubby handkerchief for his streaming nose. There was a scramble to knock on the door of number 45.

Megan Royall's immediate reaction was that of a mother confronted with her battered and bloody son. She caught her breath as she put out her hand at the sight of the swollen, split lip, the bruised knee, the bloody nose. Then she saw the proud defiance in David's eye and the excitement of the fickle toadies who surrounded him. The strong, capable woman took over. She scanned David's injuries again, this time with the eye of the experienced nurse. It was then she saw the skinned knuckles of his right hand.

'Get in that kitchen with you.' She gave David a push as he passed her and then she slammed the door on yelling, exultant young faces. She followed him inside and there was a firm line to his mouth that had her stripping off his clothes, ignoring his winces. 'Is that that Mal Evans again? Is that who you've been fighting? Yes?' A fly button popped as she yanked his trousers down. 'That settles it. We're going to Cardiff. We're getting out of here. I'll talk to Mr Jackson next Thursday. I'm taking that job at the Infirmary.'

3

David crossed the room, taking a stride beyond the woman, turning her so that the light fell on her face. Any taller and she would have looked ungainly, but she stood her full height, wearing clothes that shrieked of money with the arrogance of some top model strutting down a catwalk. The makeup on her high-cheekboned, lean face was subdued but professional, hardly the hurried daubs of a harassed mother with three kids howling not to go to school. Her hair had the natural appearance that would look perfect indoors or out, but the years had darkened the honey-blonde almost auburn. What the years had not changed was the look in her eyes.

'Good God – Faye. Faye Evans.'

'Right. Except it's Faye Grainger now. The only decent thing my bum of a husband ever gave me. So do me a favour, would you? Forget the Evans. Whoever heard of anyone called Evans making the grade?'

'Oh, I don't know,' David laughed. 'I can think of a few – Sir Geraint Evans, Evans of the Broke, William Evans . . .'

'William Evans? Who's he?'

'One of the very first cardiologists. He . . .'

'Men – all men. You bastards can get away with anything. How's Mal?'

'I still can't believe it.' He looked at her for a long time, the smell of the schoolyard suddenly in his nostrils. Slowly, reluctantly, he allowed thoughts of Mal to intervene. 'Are you trying to tell me that's Mal in there?'

'Don't you look at your patients when you operate on them?'

'One liver looks much like another, and that's just about all I saw of him the day he was brought in. And this morning, he was otherwise engaged behind a screen, answering a call of nature. They tell me he's fine.'

'What on earth made him do a stupid thing like that? He's normally such a good driver. Fast, maybe . . .'

'I can imagine.' David smiled.

'. . . but very safe. And he doesn't drink. So . . .' She showed sudden anxiety, catching her breath. 'He wasn't drunk, was he? He hadn't . . . ?'

'No, he wasn't drunk.'

'And nobody was killed?'

'No.'

'Thank God for that.'

'One or two people who were standing in a bus queue minding their own business are not going to be too pleased with him – fractured base of skull, ruptured bladder, compound fractures, that sort of thing.'

That did not appear to concern her too much. She gave the impression that being mown down on the pavement by a black Porsche was a risk everyone had to take.

'You realise the police are going to be crawling all over him the moment we say he's fit enough,' David added, as if to bring home to her the seriousness of what Mal had done.

'And when will that be?'

'Any time now by the sound of it. Tomorrow certainly.'

'Right. I'll have a word with our legal boys. They'll take care of that.'

David smiled, intrigued. 'Our legal boys'. Most people said 'solicitor', a few spoke of 'lawyers'. But 'our legal boys' – not '*the* legal boys', '*our* legal boys'. Faye read his thoughts.

'Spoiling your day, am I? Thought you were the only success to come out of Cory Street, did you?'

'Not a bit,' he blustered. 'I've basked in Mal's reflected glory many times. There was a time when he seemed to be on television every weekend. I even went to watch him play a few times; told everybody around me I knew him. It's not everybody who can claim to have been brought up with an internationally famous soccer player.'

'But what about the internationally famous soccer star's sister?

Where did you imagine she'd got to? Ever spare a thought for her?'

She allowed him a moment of blank confusion before laughing with everything but her eyes.

'Wer did ew think I'd got to 'en?'

The accent made him cringe. Instinctively he looked over his shoulder to see if anyone was within earshot.

'Back by there in the Valley, was it? Still up the Rhondda, was she? Never gave no thought to wot 'ad 'appened to poor ole Faye 'en? Didn' think no old girl could make it too, did ew? Scrubbin' floors or workin' in Tesco an' goin' down Bingo Friday nights, ew thought, didn' ew?'

They stood surveying each other as Faye smiled the smile of personal ascendancy.

'Poor David,' she murmured. 'You always were frightened of girls, weren't you?'

Without giving him the chance to reply she suddenly tugged purposefully at her coat lapel.

'Now then, d'you think you could use your influence with that old cow of a ward sister of yours and get me in to see my brother?'

'She's not an old cow. She's a first-class sister.'

'You don't have to tell me that. It takes one old cow to know another. I'm thinking of offering her a job. But I haven't come all this way to be stopped over the last few yards.'

'Where exactly *have* you come from?'

'Los Angeles.'

'Los An——? What on earth were you doing in Los Angeles?'

'I live there.' Faye Grainger slowly unbuttoned her coat. 'Now then – are you going to take me in, or do I have to scratch that bloody woman's eyes out?'

Faye walked up to Mal's bed. For a moment she stood back, taking stock. Apparently satisfied with what she saw, she grunted, leaned over and kissed her brother's forehead.

'Bloody idiot,' she growled.

The nose – could it really be Maldwyn Evans? – was pulled to one side by the adhesive strapping that held the Ryles tube in place, twisting the smile the sight of his sister brought to his face. Her tender words of compassion would have had him grinning were it not for a mouth he seemed reluctant to open. Faye pulled out the stool from under the bed and sat as close as she was able, shoulder to shoulder with her brother. Without another word to each other, they turned expressionless faces towards David where he stood at the foot of the bed. *Déjà vu.* So much happened; so little changed.

'Hullo, Mal,' David said lamely. 'I'm so sorry. I had no idea it was you.'

After more than thirty years, Mal could only jerk his head philosophically.

'How d'you feel?'

'Great.' He sounded as prim as a vicar who has just been told a dirty joke, his lips held almost closed. 'When do I get rid of this bloody thing?' His words were pinched out through a taut, ruler-straight mouth. With the thumb and middle finger of the hand not tethered by his intravenous drip, he flicked at the tube disappearing up his nose.

'Depends.' David picked up the notes hanging from the foot of the bed. The feel of the clipboard in his hand was like the touch of solid ground under the feet of a swimmer who had been out of his depth too long. 'Those screens round the bed earlier – were they just for show or did anything happen?'

'God – didn' ew 'ear the windows rattlin'? Thought I was goin' into orbit.' Mal tried to laugh with his mouth shut and paid for it in pain.

'In that case, I'll have a word with Sister. Have you lost your other tubes?'

For the next few minutes, David restored his self-importance mauling Mal around as he examined his wounds and listened to his chest. Faye made her brother comfortable again with a few deft, unemotional movements.

'You'd have made a good nurse,' David said, smiling.

'And have you bloody doctors walk all over me? Do me a favour.'

There was an uncontrollable twitch to the corner of her mouth as David posed with X-rays of Mal's chest held up to the light. The old trick of holding a film at an angle, squinting along it with half-closed eyes, failed equally to impress. Under Faye Grainger's clear blue stare, David felt more transparent than the films he held. Throwing the plates nonchalantly into a slithery heap – whoever heard of a lofty consultant putting them away in their envelope? – he sat on the bed, a little closer to them both, striving to look professional in front of two people who could remember when he did not bath.

'I reckon you'll live, Mal. It takes more than that to knock off a good Valley boy.'

A delighted grin finally spread over Mal's face, bursting through to peel back lips and reveal at last a broad gap in his top teeth. He lifted his free hand to cover it. 'In that case, d'ew think they'd let me 'ave my teeth back now?'

'I don't see why not, Mal. You shouldn't have played such a rough sport.'

'Rough sport, be buggered. Ew kicked the first one out fer me. Remember that scrap we 'ad?'

'I did that?' There was pride mingled with the surprise.

'Not all of them. A bastard of a Chelsea defender kicked the others out fer me. But the first one' – he made it sound like losing his virginity – 'that was ew. One 'elluva scrap that was – one to remember, wun it?'

'Certainly was. I've never forgotten it.'

'I can remember . . .'

'I can remember' – Faye was not going to be left out – 'grovelling on the floor, looking for the tooth, washing it under the tap and trying to push it back in before going home.'

'Yeah.' They were competing now to complete the story. 'And the leatherin' I got when it fell out again into my cocoa.'

Their laughter was cut short as they heard voices from the far end of the ward. Faye watched a ward round make its way towards them as Mal and David began to talk over old times, lowering their voices as the ward round came closer. The gaggle of assorted doctors, nurses and students came to an untidy halt at the foot of Mal's bed.

'Good morning. And how's our VIP patient this morning?'

Brian Pullman, Merton's senior surgeon, had the habit of smiling into space before turning his face towards the person for whom the smile was intended. It was a stock, unchanging smile, one he used to supplement platitude, insult or, on rare occasions, compliment. His eyes blinked several times before they settled on Mal.

'Smashin', thank ew.'

The smile did not waver as Pullman waited to be introduced to Faye, and David waited for him to move on. Faye heard the edge to David's voice as he introduced Pullman as the *senior* surgeon. It failed to register on Pullman, who was too busy putting a price on Faye's leather coat.

'I'm not surprised you've done so well.' Pullman's all-or-none smile swung towards David and back again. 'Not many road accidents are fortunate enough to be operated on by one of the profession's up-and-coming stars. They're usually left to us more mundane creatures.'

Pullman, incapable of paying a compliment that wasn't barbed, always laughed at his own jokes – someone had to. Faye watched David's fists clench as Pullman picked up the clipboard from the foot of the bed, scanning it with the small grunts of approval of a consultant checking his house surgeon's findings. He replaced the notes and looked at Mal.

'Everything seems in order, Mr Evans. I'm just surprised they haven't found a single room for you. Well-known face like yours. Do you still get pestered for autographs?'

'No sweat – this'll do me fine, thanks. I like a bit of company.' Mal looked quickly to each side like a stand-up comic. 'They're not a bad bunch of lads' – he raised his voice – 'even if they are Wimbledon supporters.'

Pullman waited for the laughter that rippled around the ward to subside before allowing his smile to traverse to David, his eyes dipping to focus somewhere below David's chin. 'Mr Evans and I are next-door neighbours, you know.'

'Are we?' Mal's surprise was obvious as he broke in and Pullman's smile swung back.

'Yes. My garden backs on to yours. Not quite in the same league as yours, of course, but sufficient for our modest needs. The world would be a *very* dull place if we were all millionaires, wouldn't it? I've got one of the houses in Orchard Close.'

'Ah, Orchard Close. Ew live there, d'ew? Nice little development that.' Mal grinned. 'I wasn' all that keen to sell that plot, but they finally made me an offer I couldn' refuse. Scand'lous what they'll pay fer good buildin' land these days, init?' Mal's street urchin grin was accentuated by the gap in his teeth.

Pullman saw a man who indirectly, and without lifting a finger, had taken money from him. 'Yes,' he drawled, while everyone read his thoughts, 'very astute of you, I'm sure. Well, must get on.' Pullman's retinue took a step back to give him room. 'Some of us have to earn an honest penny.' For the first time, Pullman looked directly at David. 'On parade tonight, I trust, David?'

'Tonight?' David looked vague.

'Yes. Reggie Bevington's coming down to give a paper on obstructive jaundice.' Pullman winked. 'Surely you hadn't forgotten. Influential man, you know, is our Reggie.'

David felt something turn over inside him. Why the sudden surging nausea? It was the wink, the outward visible sign suggesting they were in there together, co-conspirators in something the others would not understand. It had to be the wink. The smile, the snide, bogus servility, the pompous crap he talked, they were bad enough. But the wink – that drew David towards him, bound him to the slimy creep in the eyes of others. Ample cause for revulsion.

'No, Brian, I hadn't forgotten,' he lied. 'But I'm afraid I can't make it tonight. Perhaps you'd be kind enough to give my apologies.'

'All this mad social whirl, David.' The relief on Pullman's face was obvious. He'd have the great man all to himself. 'That's not going to bring you in any votes, you know.'

'Nothing social about this evening, I'm afraid, Brian. I've got to be in Birmingham. I'm lecturing to the surgical unit at the Queen Elizabeth tonight.' He tried to keep the smugness he felt out of his reply, but enjoyed the knowledge that he was not succeeding. 'I must admit I'm beginning to find this lecture circuit a bit of a chore, but then one's got to take the rough with the smooth, I suppose, hasn't one?'

The muscles that kept Pullman's smile in place twitched painfully. Muttering something about being lucky to be able to get away so often, Pullman turned and left. A few moments later, he was to be heard taking out his fury on a defenceless student.

'There goes one man,' Faye drawled, 'you would be foolish to turn your back on in a dark alley. Why is he so jealous of you?'

'Rubbish.'

'And balls to you too.' Mal sniggered painfully as his sister drove on. 'You know he's jealous *and* you enjoy it. What's all this about votes?'

'Well, it's all very awkward really. Brian tried to get on the staff at his teaching hospital and failed. Then he applied to get on the Court of Examiners and failed. And now we're both up for election to the Council – the Council of the Royal College of Surgeons, that is.'

'And you're going to beat him yet again, that's obvious.'

'I don't know about that. The problem is that most people think this will be his last chance. He's a good bit older than I am.'

'And giving a lecture up in Birmingham is going to canvass more votes than having old Reggie somebody-or-other to give a talk down here?'

'Shhhhhh.' Laughing, David put his finger to his lips. 'That's a dirty word, canvassing. In all fairness, they are pretty strict about that sort of thing.'

Lips on a worldly face turned down cynically.

'All right,' David conceded. 'So people tend to put themselves around a bit in the run-up to the election. No harm in that, is there? Nobody gets elected to the Council just by doing his job and going straight home to dig his garden. Which reminds me' – he looked at his watch – 'if I'm going to get to Birmingham in time, I'd better be off.' He patted Mal's knee through the bedclothes. 'I'm in here three times a week, Mal. I'll pop up to see you, and they know where to find me if they're worried.'

'Nice to see ew again, David – and thank ew.'

David raised one hand briefly as if what he had done was nothing. Faye walked to the ward door with him. He moved as if to open the door, but she lengthened her stride and thrust her way ahead of him. In the corridor beyond, she turned to face him.

'When do you think Mal will be home, David?'

'Difficult to say. Depends.'

'Oh, Gawd. Can't you bloody doctors ever talk straight?'

'It's not that easy.' David smiled. 'We're beginning to wonder whether Mal might have had some sort of epilepsy. We know he wasn't drunk, there were no real signs of a head injury and he has no neurological signs now. So epilepsy has got to be pretty high on the list.' His voice dropped, almost as if he did not want her to hear. 'Or a tumour.'

Though she said nothing, he could see by the look in her eyes that she had heard every word.

'Has he ever had any fits before?' he asked.

'No.'

'Any real head injuries?'

'Apart from you kicking his face in, d'you mean?'

David grinned and nodded, feeling macho.

'Sure – umpteen. He was unconscious once after a kick on the head playing for Juventus in some European cup tie. He was never the same after that. Bloody Wops. The worst thing he ever did, going out there. So – where do we go from here?'

'He'll be handed over to one of the more intelligent branches of the profession who, no doubt, will be doing CAT scans and all the rest of it in the next few days. I'll let you know what's going on. How long before you go back to the States?'

There was more than simple concern over Mal's welfare in the question. It came through in the tone of his voice.

'Not until I know he's all right.' She put out a hand to turn David towards her. Her face looked just as adult as it had when she was nine years old, her eyes just as blue. 'I owe him, David. He's still the only bastard that's ever given me a straight deal.' She opened a large handbag, but there was none of the usual rummaging before she picked out a small card which she handed to him. 'The last time we were alone together, you went home with a bloody nose. Mal won't be around this time. You'll be quite safe.'

*

'How did you come by two young tearaways with a name like Hussein then?'

Digger Drew was just settling the child on a maintenance dose of anaesthetic as David painted the boy's silky brown skin with a bright red antiseptic solution.

'One of the fringe benefits of having a father-in-law in the oil industry, especially if he happens to speak Arabic. That always goes down well in the Embassies.'

'Full of mischief, the pair of them.' Drew ran his fingers through the child's tight black curls affectionately. 'Difficult to imagine them growing up to carry Kalashnikovs and wear scarves round their faces, isn't it? Don't look much different from our kids, lying there.'

Silence fell as David made his incision. Within minutes he had found the hernial sac. Drew knew that it was for David now to decide when he wanted to talk, when to concentrate. Drew had worked with them all – the silent ones, the talkative ones, the bombastic, the blasphemous, the neurotic, the humble instruments of God's Will. He was lucky – he found no difficulty in adjusting. When the surgeon talked, he talked; when things got tough, he kept his mouth shut. He had the good sense not to ask David who he thought was going to win Wimbledon just when a large artery had chosen to slip from a clamp deep inside an eighteen-stone belly.

The sac was small and dissecting out easily. David relaxed. 'Can't remember when I last had bilateral hernias in identical twins. I've had hernias in brothers often enough, but I wonder what the incidence of bilateral hernias in twins is – I must look it up. Must be rare.'

'No doubt you'll charge them twice the fee for a bilateral hernia?' Creases appeared in Drew's cheeks alongside his mask.

'Of course.'

'And what about the poor anaesthetist? Can I charge double?'

'Certainly not, you mercenary beggar. It's still only one anaesthetic,' David chuckled.

The peace of the private hospital's operating theatre descended and the case went smoothly. Half an hour later and they were at the same stage on the second twin. All surgeons have their own peculiar audible reaction to sudden technical difficulty, sounds as specific as a genetic fingerprint. Drew looked up sharply. He saw David's shoulders hunch and his head drop closer to the wound. He stood up, craning his neck to peer beneath David's hands. The gossamer-thin sac had split, the ragged, friable edge tearing at the touch of a forceps. He watched through a quarter of an hour of intense muttering, blaspheming concentration until he saw David straighten once more, blowing his relief silently between pursed lips.

'Nasty, those are. Lose your temper with one of those and you knock off the testicular artery and the poor little beggar ends up a bit lopsided. Do it on both sides of course, and you've got a eunuch.' There was nothing frivolous about David as he turned to Drew. 'If I were to charge more for that one than for the first, I suppose the father would want to know what went wrong. He looks the sort who might ask.'

'He does.' Drew laughed as he watched David calculate the chances. 'Airline pilot, isn't he?'

David nodded.

Drew rubbed the boy's cheek where some of his tubing had left its mark. 'Do they earn enough for this sort of thing? If he's pushed . . .'

David did not let him finish, adding hurriedly, 'No need. Grandma's Lebanese, but gets no closer to Beirut than a modest little pad just off Grosvenor Square.' He pinched his thumb and forefinger together and shook them as if jingling a money bag. 'Mucho shekels.'

Fleetingly, Drew's eyebrows contracted.

Later, they sat, the Clinic's best china in their hands, savouring the best coffee.

'Taking your time this morning, aren't you?' Drew remarked. 'Don't you have to get back?'

'Got a bloody marvellous SR at the moment.' David grinned. 'Coming to the end of his time. He's going to find himself carrying the can out in some DGH very shortly, so I feel the more experience he gets, the better for him, and there's not all that much to go round these days.' He winked. 'I'm only thinking of him really.'

'No wonder Brian hates your guts.'

They laughed as they helped themselves to another cup of coffee, settling happily into silence for a moment. Neither seemed in any hurry.

'How did Brian's meeting go the other night?' David asked. 'Did you go?'

'Yes, I went.' Digger Drew pulled a face, shrugging his shoulders. 'Somebody's got to go to these things. Drumming up people to go to what everyone was calling Brian's Benefit Lecture was pretty embarrassing, almost as embarrassing as the lecture itself.'

'What, Reggie?'

'No. Brian.'

It was what David had been waiting to hear. 'In what way?' he asked. As if he didn't know. 'Brian on about his operation again – correct?'

'Correct.'

'I thought he might.'

'Reggie gave his usual talk on the surgical management of jaundice. Everybody knows Reggie's wined and dined on that one now for twenty years, but he's such a nice old boy, isn't he; and been such a good surgeon in his time. Nobody really minds. But as soon as the discussion started, Brian had them round to discussing his operation in no time at all.'

'The man's totally obsessed with it,' David muttered.

'You could see Reggie was upset, though he was far too much of a gentleman to say anything. I feel so sorry for Brian at times – I've never known a man with less insight. He looked so pleased with himself, quite sure he'd impressed everyone, when all he'd done really was to antagonise one of the College's vice presidents.'

'But how d'you divert a discussion of the management of jaundice to an operation for intestinal cancer?'

'You don't. You bulldoze it, just blurt it out, apropos of nothing. You could hear all the juniors sniggering. It was as if it was just under the surface all the time and he just couldn't contain himself any longer.'

David simply shook his head slowly in disbelief.

'What d'you think of this operation of his, David?' Drew asked quietly, his eyes half closed.

It took a while for David to answer. It was the first time he had been asked the question out loud by someone with whom he could be perfectly honest, not constrained by formal professional loyalties. It was a question he had asked himself many times, only to get vague, disjointed answers, befouled by personal antipathy. Now he must put it into words.

Pullman was a king-sized shit, a pompous, oleaginous creep the very sight of whom made the hairs on the back of his neck stand up. All right – point made, taken, agreed, enjoyed – now set it aside. Did that mean Pullman was incapable of original thought? Or was it jealousy on his part that prevented him from accepting the fact – mean, cramping professional jealousy – nothing to do with money – more to do with something far more precious – fame. That was it – fame. Everyone in surgery dreams of the operation, performed worldwide, named after himself. The Bilroth gastrectomy, the Millin prostatectomy. And Pullman was beginning to be talked about. His name was to be heard more and more frequently now in the 'shop' talked in the corridors of Lincoln's Inn Fields and the RSM. People were beginning to talk of Pullman's operation. David had been asked about it at his lectures as far apart as Manchester and Southampton, extorting from him in empty words the reluctant support considered due to any close colleague. A surgeon in Leeds had told him with pride he had 'done a Pullman'.

Drew was still waiting patiently for his answer. David began slowly. 'I really don't know what to think, Digger. It goes against all the basic principles I was taught, all the methods I use. But – if you can believe his figures . . .' His voice faded away for a moment before returning, full of concern. 'If his figures are right, it means we're all guilty of doing many operations that are far more radical than is really necessary, with higher mortality rates, morbidity rates, colostomy rates, things like that. If everything he claims is true, there's no doubt we all should be doing what he's doing. As I say, Digger' – David raised one hand then let it flop back into his lap – 'it's all a bit worrying if you stop to think about it. In my book, the man is a pompous windbag. But what if he's right?'

4

Steering with one hand, the small white card in the other, David drove slowly along Eaton Place, slowly enough to be harassed even by Belgravia's meagre late-evening traffic. He ran his window down and peered out. It was dawning on him that he must already have passed the number he was looking for when a squeal of brakes was followed by an opinion on his IQ, parentage and driving ability as succinct and as obscene as only a Cockney cabbie could give.

David put his head out of the open window.

'And up yours too, yer great ignorant git.'

His heart racing, his face flushed, he grinned at himself. That had been *his* voice he had heard – coarse, good-humoured, uninhibited. His *real* voice, perhaps? Maybe he *was* a consultant surgeon, a Master of Surgery, a Hunterian Professor, but, deep down, there was still Cory Street, flung to the surface in an unguarded moment. That was not the language expected of him now, someone soon to be engaged in urbane chat with fellow Members of Council, strolling in robed procession. Not the language of the company he kept now – not even the company of his wife. A similar reaction had slipped its leash under almost identical circumstances when Jackie had been in the car with him – and he had seen her face. She had said nothing, lips carved in stone. Did they never let their hair down?

He found the number on his next circuit. He had to go round once more before he could find space to park.

The marbled hall had all the cold, sterile appeal of a disused operating theatre. The security guard, bulging out of his uniform, the chin strap of his smart peaked cap brightly gleaming, put down his crumpled copy of the *Sun*. He breathed through his mouth like an ex pug.

'Good evening, sir. Can I help you?'

'Mrs Grainger, please?'

Without taking his eyes off David, the man picked out a switch from the row on the desk in front of him with the certainty of a concert pianist making an entry. He waited until he heard the hiss of static.

'He's here, Miss Grainger.'

'Send him up, Joe.'

David felt himself being pushed gently into a small lift like some capsule being fed into a vacuum communication system. A button was pressed for him by a man who showed his scorn for someone incapable of doing such a simple thing himself.

'What number . . . ?' David began feebly, but it only intensified the pity on the face that slowly disappeared behind closing doors.

When the doors slid back, David realised the futility of his question. The lift opened on to a small landing from which there was only one door.

It was open.

'Come in, David.'

He had not known quite what to expect. Subdued lights, Nat King Cole, the air heavy with hash, and Faye lying on the hearth rug in tight leopardskin pants?

'You're late,' Faye said.

'I know. I've got that sort of a job.'

She gave a small smile of approval from where she stood, letting him do all the walking.

'And whose life have you just been saving? Some poor old bastard from the East End, or some oil-rich sod from the Middle East?'

'Cut an Arab; does he not bleed?' David spread his arms like some ham actor.

The smile of approval deepened. She bent to turn off the radio, blotting out the sound of an angry woman's voice.

'Whisky?' she asked. 'I imagine you're a whisky man by now.'

'How very astute of you. With water, please. A small one; I'm driving.'

'Sit down then.'

David sank into one of two silk-covered sofas that faced each other across a low marble and gunmetal table. The litter of proofs, transparencies and magazine cuttings that spilled from the table on to the Chinese carpet was for real, with nothing of the poseur's careful display. There was no fireplace, no visible television, but the furniture was arranged so that one would feel in place wherever one sat. Crushed jade in the panels of antique Japanese screens that hung from the walls gave a cool, clear feel to the room. Crystal and jade ornaments had been chosen with care, and David smiled at the sleek bronzes of predatory animals that seemed to snarl at him from every angle. His survey of the room behind Faye's back was brought up short. He rose to walk across the room, attracted by the black and grey enlargement of a photograph in its plain steel frame that stood out, stark and gritty amongst the opulence.

He felt a tightening in his throat as he saw a twelve-year-old boy on his hands and knees in the black filth of a coal mine's spout hole, the sleeves of his grimy flannel shirt rolled up above spindly elbows, a man's cloth cap askew on his head. The thick rope that bit into armpits and nape of neck was ramrod taut with the weight of the sled he dragged behind him.

David took his whisky from Faye, who had come to stand beside him. He pointed with the glass.

'Why?'

'Lest I forget, Davy boy; lest I forget.'

For a moment she watched, searching his profile as he gazed up at the picture abstractedly sipping his drink. She put out a hand and led him gently back to the table, clearing enough space for them to put their drinks down. She sank to the floor opposite him, her back to the sofa. She wore a short Arran jumper over a denim shirt, a Paisley handkerchief knotted at her throat. The top button of her jeans, left undone, had nothing to do with the size of her waist, which suggested a belly as flat as a teenager's. She wore no jewellery and her feet were bare.

'Well, David Royall, late of 45 Cory Street, tell me about

yourself.' Unchanged was the unblinking stare that had stirred up vague feelings of guilt in an innocent eight-year-old boy. Thirty-five years later, she still had little difficulty in staring him down. 'I'd heard you'd made the big time in the surgical racket up here in the big city, but I hadn't realised just how big. How did you manage it?'

'God knows, looking back. Nothing to it really.'

'Awwwwwww – shit.' Her head pecked to give the word greater impetus. 'Don't tell me you've become one of those lah-de-dah pseudo-amateurs who give the impression that any kind of achievement is an awful bore.' She drawled maliciously. 'All right, so you live amongst them, take their money off them, lay a few of them by the look of you – that doesn't mean you've got to become one of them. It's Faye you're talking to now – remember? So cut the crap, will you?'

'Faye.' David put his head back to roar with laughter. 'You're like a breath of fresh air.'

'Balls. If I remember correctly, it all started with some sort of scholarship, didn't it?'

'Yes, a choral scholarship. For three years I was a rosy-cheeked, angelic cathedral chorister.'

'I can see you.'

'From there I got another scholarship into the senior school. And my mother found herself locked into a system she couldn't really afford and would have died before admitting defeat and taking me away. Nobody knows just how tough that must have been for her – and I include myself in that. God only knows what she went without.'

'How *did* she manage?' Her voice had the edge of a hard-nosed interviewer.

'She had her job as a theatre sister, of course, but that wasn't enough. She earned money on the side as housekeeper cum receptionist cum nurse cum cook to one of the old bachelor surgeons. It also meant we had our flat rent-free. And, no' – he raised his hand angrily – 'I know what you're thinking. There was nothing like that. But she was never exactly the best-dressed woman in town, and I rather suspect there were times when she didn't eat too well either.'

'I'll always remember your mother.' Faye looked into her glass. 'Bathed more than one black eye for me.' She glanced up at him. 'Is she still alive?'

'No. She died last year. She'd retired long before, of course, but still lived in the flat, thoroughly enjoying herself looking after a bunch of consultants to whom she rented out consulting rooms below.'

A non sequitur registered, sending one of Faye's eyebrows aloft.

'Old Papa Jackson left everything to her when he died.'

'Ah' – the eyebrow dropped once more – 'and, of course, all that will have come to you now,' she said quietly to herself, adding, more briskly, 'but she never married him?'

'No.'

'Good for her,' she growled. 'And what about your Gran?'

Their voices rumbled on as they filled in the gaps. Gran Royall and her stroke – Faye's father with his broken neck, lying askew at the bottom of the stairs – her Mam and her death bathed in summer sun streaming through an asylum's tall windows. Two ex-children wondered whether Fatty Griffiths, the sadistic old sod, was still alive. Cory Street ghosts came and went, uncomfortable in the luxury of a Belgravia apartment, before Faye got back once more to David Royall's climb away from the Valley.

'So that got you to being a medical student, I imagine. What then?'

'Pretty standard from then on. Qualifying was no great sweat. After that, I just fed myself into the system and made sure I didn't miss any opportunity to kick my competitors in the crotch. And, of course, like everything else, there was the question of luck. And I got lucky.'

Through Faye's mind went vague pictures of the right jobs coming up at the right time for a bright, ambitious, hard-working young man. Rather different scenes flashed through David's.

A registrar working on rotation out in a DGH, next in line for a senior registrar's post back in Queen's, everyone's odds-on bet for ultimate appointment to the teaching staff there. The most promising young surgeon Queen's had had in a decade. Sir

Geoffrey thought the world of him, everyone knew that. And he'd almost blown it. David still came out in a cold sweat every time he thought about it.

The staff nurse had been elegant, rather aloof – a challenge – and she had played him well. But a Sunday afternoon visit to the terraced house in Acton had found him back in Cory Street, sitting down to high tea eaten with a knife held like a pen by a fat old man who had sat at the top of the table in open-necked shirt and braces, pontificating on the evils of capitalism. Breaking away had been painfully brutal – better that way. He had weathered several such bitchy storms before. But then had come the torrential haemorrhage – almost as fatal to a young man's career as to his foetus. She could have gone to another hospital for her miscarriage, been discreet. There had been no need to be *that* bitchy. He'd have gone to see her. As it was, for weeks he had hardly dare breathe as he waited for his chief's reaction which would decide his future. That was when he had got lucky. They had been alone in the theatre changing room when the old man, Sam McClusky, had taken him aside.

'You, David, have been a bloody idiot, have you not?'

'Yes, sir.'

'Nurses don't bleed nigh to death in their own hospitals without someone noticing.'

'No, sir.'

David had seen the tilt of the head, had heard the subtle change of tone that normally goes with an old man giving a young man advice. Normally, he would have sighed inwardly with boredom. Then, he had found himself moistening his lips.

'It's a strange relationship, doctor and nurse, in many ways. You would do well to remember that.'

'Yes, sir.'

'We expect to dominate them, to exploit them, but we are also expected to protect them – and the older we get, the more protective we get. And those who sit on senior registrar and consultant appointment committees are very, very old doctors indeed. Am I making myself clear, David?'

'Yes, sir.'

'Besides which . . .' Old McClusky's gaze had been centred

somewhere between David's third and fourth shirt buttons, downcast, as if he too might have had something to hide. The look in his eyes as they flickered up to David's for a moment had given him his first hope of survival. '. . . The last thing you want around the place when you've just made a balls of a case is a vindictive nurse.'

David had wondered whether he dared smile but had decided against it.

'So – I've no intention of letting one bloody fool mistake ruin a brilliant career.' Another flicker. 'We were all young once. But – anything like that again, David, and you can take it from me, you can kiss Queen's goodbye and everything that goes with it.'

McClusky had not allowed David to thank him, adding a word of advice that had been valued and respected ever after.

'Only a fool shits on his own doorstep, David.'

'And you're married,' Faye said. 'Any children?'

'One daughter, Debbie. She's seventeen and in the sixth form at Marlborough; giving as good as she gets, I imagine. The light of my life.'

'Does your wife do anything?'

'What d'you mean, "do anything"?'

'Work.'

'Yes, she does. Jackie works very hard.' His mouth hardened in resentment as he thrust his empty glass in Faye's direction. She got up from the floor in one long sinuous movement. 'She's in publishing.'

'Oh? That's interesting. Who with?' Faye asked over her shoulder.

'She's with Janssen and Paul.' He made it sound offhand.

'Janssen and Paul?' Faye turned to face him. 'You said Jackie. You don't mean Jacqueline Lee?'

'That's right. She works under her maiden name. She's over in New York at the moment, helping launch some book or other.'

'Daughter of Sir Marcus Lee? You're Marcus Lee's son-in-law?'

David's grin was answer enough.

'Now I *am* impressed.'

'You'd heard of Jacqueline?'

'Yes. We've not met, but I've heard of her.'

'Now how would you have heard of Jacqueline Lee?' he asked. But Faye ignored the question. He asked again and was ignored once more, leaving him no option but to change the subject. 'And what of you? Where is Mr Grainger?'

'God knows. The only real mistake I've made, so far. When I think of the hard-earned money it took to buy him off . . .'

David laughed at the venom in her voice. 'You said you worked in the States. Whereabouts?'

'Los Angeles.' She smiled, and he wondered why she did not do it more often. 'It's a long story.'

'I'm in no hurry. There's no one waiting up for me, watching the clock.'

Faye now sat on the sofa opposite him, her legs outstretched. She wriggled her toes in his direction.

'It began even before we left Cory Street. I had a job washing hair in Annette's. D'you remember Annette's, next to the Co-op? No? Well, I started nicking rollers and shampoo and earning a few bob around the houses.' She had a small private laugh at fleeting memories. 'Mal used to find the market for me, offering to get the old dears' coal for them, doing a bit of shopping for them, that sort of thing, and then talking them into letting me do their hair for them instead of tottering down to Annette's. The day after pension day was the best – when they were a bit flush.' She laughed. 'I was always off work, sick with something or other, that day.'

'Then a Cardiff City scout saw Mal playing for the local club side and signed him on as an apprentice. That meant a move to Cardiff, where we rented two rooms in Grangetown and I set up shop.' She paused, her eyes focusing somewhere in midair. 'My first chair was an old dentist's chair Mal bought from a scrap yard for five quid. Neither of us smoked or drank in those days, – Mal still doesn't – we worked hard and shared every penny. I went to night classes and picked up a bit of accountancy and management and lost my Valley accent. By the time Mal moved to Arsenal, I had two shops and eight people working for me. I sold up and came up here with him.'

'No Mr Grainger yet?'

'No. That bastard came much later. It wasn't long before I had a string of hairdressers and Mal began to make real money. Half a dozen teams were after him and Arsenal were not keen to let him go. He was beginning to have a finger in a few pies too; started off with an interest in a club in Manchester – he owns it now.' The only time her face softened seemed to be at the mention of her brother. 'It was round about this time that Mal learned to read a balance sheet.' She chuckled. 'The *Beano* didn't get a look-in after that.'

They both laughed.

'I began to sell cosmetics and, before I knew where I was, my hairdressing shops had blossomed into beauty salons. Then Mal went to Juventus for more money than we knew what to do with, and we added saunas and massage, hair clinics – all with the best staff and equipment money could buy. It's so easy for those places to look sleazy. After that, Soigné just seemed to take off on its own.'

'You own Soigné?' David spluttered.

'I did. I've still got an interest in it. But it just got too big. It had been too easy. With a shop in every sizeable town in the country, I had to have an army of managers and accountants and designers and marketing experts. I got bored. That's when I got married. Just imagine' – she shook her head slowly in disbelief – 'I think I got married because I was bored. I must have been bloody crazy.'

'How long did that last?'

'Three months.'

'Three months? That's all.'

'Doesn't take long to find out you've made a mistake. The bastard didn't have a day's work in him. That's why I pushed off to the States.'

'Why the States?'

'As I said, David – I was bored. I tried to analyse why. Normally I'm never bored. And I came to the conclusion it was because everything had become too easy. Women are so bloody vain you can sell them anything.' Her forehead creased as if putting something into words for the first time. 'At least that was how I explained it at the time. I almost wished I was back with a dentist's chair and cash in a tin box. It was a long time after . . .' Her eyes screwed up as she struggled to decide exactly when it had happened. 'I'm not sure now just why I lost interest. Yes, I am.' A twitch of irritation at her own indecisiveness jerked her body into a new position. 'I couldn't stand it any longer – pandering to fat old cows with podgy hands and boobs like bloodhounds' ears.'

David laughed, looking at the lithe body stretched out before him.

'What are you sniggering at?' she asked.

'Who was it, in the Bible, who had a dream where he saw seven lean kine devour seven fat kine and remain just as lean afterwards?'

She stuck her tongue out at him. 'They weren't all like that. We had the others, in a hurry, competing in a man's world. They were great. It was the ones who were quite happy to spend money they had not earned that bugged me – you know the type – a couple of hours to kill between the Savoy Grill and the Ritz?'

'What, in Leeds?' he laughed.

'You'll find them in every big city, you know that as well as I do,' she said, looking down sadly into an empty glass. She reached out her hand. 'Let me have your glass. I never drink alone, I'm too frightened. Ergo – this is a rare occasion for me. Drink up. I imagine you can afford a taxi these days?'

Ergo? *Ergo?* Faye Evans and *ergo?* Where the hell had *ergo* come from? He watched Faye's back as she poured the drinks, shaking his head as he tried to see Fatty Griffiths, cane in hand, beating time – ante, apud, ad, adversus, circa, circum, citra, cis . . . Cory Street, Faye Evans, *ergo*.

She returned to sit at his feet, her legs tucked under her on the carpet just as they had been in the bracken.

'So I decided I'd like to work for a women's magazine.'

'Just like that?'

'No. I thought about it.' Faye's eyes narrowed. 'I decided I was fed up with working with women of both sexes. I felt I'd made it, but in a woman's world. I wanted to compete in more of a man's world. The thought of journalism attracted me, but what had I got to offer? How could I get a foot in the door? All I knew was business and fashion. Then it all took on a certain urgency when I suddenly found myself revolted at the sight of the naked female body. David – ' she paused; and a lark sang above them, the bracken around them moved in a gentle summer breeze and the Pentre puffed slowly in the valley below ' – do you think I'm a bit of a lezzie?'

He lowered his glass from his lips so that he could laugh – but didn't.

'You've no idea how relieved I was to find I never wanted to see another boob again. I was getting quite worried.' Her chin jutted as her tone became defensive. 'You haven't *got* to be a lezzie to fight for women's rights, you know.'

'I know that. All I can say is, if you're a lesbian, you're the most attractive one I've met.'

'And that's another of my problems. I'm not over the moon about the naked male form either. Never have been. My experience of men, starting from a very early age, has not been of the best.'

He heard his mother's voice. 'You know their father's in jail, don't you?'

'Yes, Mam.'

'And you know what for, don't you?'

'Yes, Mam.'

He felt an urge to reach out and touch Faye's hair. 'Yes, I know,' he murmured.

'So I spent a couple of weeks looking round the States, making a few enquiries. I found a magazine, with their offices in Los Angeles, that was struggling at the bottom of the pile, one I thought would not be too choosy who worked for them. So I marched in, told them my background, and asked for a job working for the beauty and fashion columns. I offered to work for three months for nothing as a trial period.'

'And got the job, obviously.'

'They told me to get stuffed.'

'So?'

'So I came home, sold ninety per cent of Soigné in this country, went back, bought the magazine and changed its name to Soigné too.'

David caught his breath in mid-swallow, and tears rolled down his face as raw whisky fumes seared his trachea.

'And the first thing I did was sack the bitch who didn't give me the job.' She rubbed her hands together, vicious delight on her face. 'It was worth every penny. Marvellous feeling.'

She waited for his laughter to subside before pointing to the litter on the table. 'Hence my need to get back. There's half next month's copy there. But Mal comes first.'

'He's all right. I'll keep an eye on him. But how's the magazine doing?'

'Nearly doubled our circulation in the first year and still climbing.'

'How did you manage that? Without experience, I mean.'

'Not difficult. Applied what I'd learned in the early days with Soigné. I picked out the compulsive workers like myself and read them the riot act. If you work sixteen hours a day, you produce a lot of material – all crap. Cut that time in half and you treble the quality.' She nodded her head like a wise old man. 'So I turned everyone out at seven, locked the doors and said I'd sack anyone I saw taking work home. I told them there were to be no calls in the middle of the night with bright ideas and that they would be judged on the work they turned out, not the hours they put in. In a few weeks they'd changed from a bunch of tense, knackered neurotics into an absolute hornets' nest.'

Her voice dropped.

'Had to get rid of some dead wood in the process, of course. Some of them didn't seem to get the message that dysmenorrhoea and acne were now taboo subjects. They didn't seem to understand that I was not interested in the pimply, skinny teenage kid obsessed with her virginity but in the mature woman who enjoys her own orgasm, however she might choose to bring that about. I'm after the woman who wants her own bank account with her own money in it. And by that I don't mean ending up a rich, solitary bitch like myself. It's not about achievement – not every woman envies Maggie Thatcher, you know. It's about someone with an identity of her own – a partner, not a serf – someone who can bring up a couple of kids, run a small business on the side and still cook a good meal in the evening now and again.'

David watched as she stopped to catch her breath.

'But Faye, can you write this sort of stuff?' he asked.

'No. I can't string two sentences together – but I sure as hell know what I want written, and I can recognise good stuff when I read it. And I've left them in no doubt where they stand. If they don't like what I want in my magazine, they can go and work for someone else. I've put up a big red sign on my desk – EDITORIAL FREEDOM STOPS HERE.'

She gazed into the bottom of her glass, swirling nonexistent drops inside it. Then she threw her head back, holding the glass to her lips as if to convince herself it was empty. Reluctantly, she put it down.

'But apart from that,' he asked, in the tone of someone still not totally convinced. 'What about the day-to-day running of a vast organisation like that? How did you learn that?'

'Three-quarters of the top executives in this country have had no formal management training, and there's nothing like twenty years in the retail business to teach you enough to walk into any boardroom. They like to give the impression that there's some mystique about it, but there isn't really.'

She straightened her back so that she could shake out her hair.

'So – there it is. We've both made it. Doesn't sound much though, does it,' Faye said quietly, 'said like that? Difficult to describe thirty years' bloody hard work in a few words, isn't it?'

They stared at each other, small smiles lurking at the corners of their mouths.

'Happy, Faye?'

She thought for a moment. 'I'm enjoying myself, if that's what you mean. In fact, I'm having a ball. A challenging job in LA with more money than I need. This pad in London with an interest in half a dozen companies here, one of which owns a house and a boat on the Med we never see. Mal's on the board of a small commercial airline specialising in charters for pop stars and famous sportsmen, so I get cheap flights anywhere in Europe. I hate kids and animals, so I can go anywhere I want, any time I want; I don't have to ask anyone. Could be worse.' She looked closely at David. 'What about you?'

'Yes – I think I'm happy. Still got one or two things to do, but I'm working on it.' He leaned forward, reaching across her to flick through some of the papers on the table in front of them. 'What's this?' he asked. 'I thought anyone taking work home got the sack.'

Faye laughed, watching his expression change as he picked up a transparency, holding it up to the light.

'God – who is *she*?' He turned it over and over, examining the mount as if looking for a name. 'What a striking-looking woman.'

'Her name's Jo Logan, an appellate court judge – sits on the District Court of Appeal in Los Angeles. And – ' she began to thump his knee with a clenched fist – 'don't be put off by the word "district". They're federal courts, only eleven of them in the whole of the US, and only the next tier down from the US Supreme Court itself in Washington. In fact, Jo Logan is tipped as being only the second woman to be appointed to the Supreme Court.'

'Is she, by Jove.' He picked up the print to look at it afresh, but Faye took it from him and peered at it closely herself.

'She is also the wife of the next President of the United States of America.'

'And you've met her?'

'I have. Maybe I can't write, but I find no difficulty in interviewing.'

'That I can believe,' he laughed.

'She'll be the *real* President, you wait and see.'

'An *éminence grise*, you mean?'

'An em——? A what?' Faye's face screwed up, sharp and intent.

'A power behind the throne.'

'How d'you spell it?' She rummaged for a pen and a scrap of paper. 'That sounds good.'

He spelt it out, grinning as he saw the capital letters pressed deeply. Hence ergo?

'Yes, I've decided' – Faye put the scrap of paper where it would not be lost – 'that Jo Logan is the sort of American woman we want all our readers to become. They don't know it yet, of course,' she laughed, 'and we will have to lace the mixture with enough advice about baby clothes, laxatives and how to cook *poulet chasseur* to keep the punters interested. But you might say we're hitching our wagon to Jo Logan's star. She'd better not let us down. Mind you, we'll have to be careful. Most of our readers at the moment stay home, take the kids to school in the family station wagon, stand at hubby's shoulder when he's not playing golf or letting it hang out in some out-of-town convention. What's more, most of them actually seem to enjoy the existence, God damn them. So – somehow, we've got to make it sound like their idea, not ours. It's not going to be easy.'

'And are all the Jo Logans of this world happily married?' David smirked.

'You should know.' The reply was quick and sharp. 'After all, you're married to one. Is your wife happily married?'

He did not answer, neither did he smile.

'And children?' He found himself wanting to hurt. 'Where do they fit into this scenario of yours?'

'Chauvinist sod,' she growled. 'You managed, didn't you?' A note of envy brought a petulant tone to her voice. Her face reflected her sudden change of mood. The whisky was beginning to have its effect on both of them. 'How *do* you manage?'

'What d'you mean, manage?'

'You and your wife. What I mean is, how does a horny male like you manage if you're married to a busy, professional wife who just hasn't got time for it? There's got to be the female equivalent of the barrister's droop, hasn't there? Let's be honest – there's been many a time when I've got home late, bushed after a long day, and thanked God that at least I didn't have to turn on my back, close my eyes and think of England. As I said – how *do* you manage?'

As if to confirm an advantage over him, Faye stood up to look down on him. 'You don't look the sort of man who has to pay a penny to see a pair of knickers any more. What *do* you do for sex?' she asked.

There was no particular emphasis in the question, and it took a moment for David to come to terms with it. Frowning at the irrelevant regret at heeltapping on a good whisky, he took great care over laying down his glass before standing up to confront her. He wobbled, having to take a step to steady himself – he had not realised he had drunk so much – and found a face so close to his as to be blurred. Befogged by whisky whirling around in a bounding circulation, he was puzzled by the two Fayes he saw come and go in the blur. He saw one Faye, lean and pantherlike, warm and vital, infinitely desirable. He also saw the other, the flint-minded predator. His hands felt clumsy as he took her face in his hands to kiss her gently. He frowned as she swivelled her head, disengaging her face from his hands before their lips met. This didn't happen to *him*, David Royall, Master of Surgery, Hunterian Professor.

'I rather think it's time I went,' he said.

'Where?'

'Home.'

'Home? And where's home? The regulation one daughter, packed off to boarding school, and a hard-headed, jet-lagged career woman of a wife who may be in New York today but where tomorrow, Frankfurt? Is that what the Valley boy expected for a home then? Someone who was born into a culture where the man expected his bath ready and his meal on the table when he got home? Where a man's pride was in his sons, not his daughters? Come on – be honest. Don't you miss all that? Somehow I don't see you consoling yourself with the myth that you don't miss what you've never had. So what *do* you do in Harley Street when your daughter's in school and the dearly beloved's in Tokyo? You can't be seeing patients all day and all night.'

The blue ice melted a little.

'And you always had that buzz about you, David Royall, even as a kid. You turn women on and you know it – you make 'em growl inside.'

Blue irises froze over again. *Women* she had said, not to be confused with any one woman in particular.

'So, I repeat my question – how d'you manage?'

Goddamn bitch. So maybe his home life was not perfect, but it was there – something *she* did not possess. Perhaps that was what bugged her. Perhaps that was the one thing that would always be missing from *her* success, the admiration of others at her ability to achieve it in spite of the millstone of a husband, and a home to run, around her neck. Not for her the joy of the husband on the fringe, listening to the conversation centred around *her* ability to cope, with no one bothering to ask *him* how *he* managed. Was she missing that? If she was, didn't she realise how lucky she was? For every one who saw him as David Royall, Master of Surgery, Hunterian Professor, there were two who saw him as Jackie Lee's husband, Sir Marcus Lee's son-in-law. *Her* success was hers, all hers. Easy enough then to stand there, so cool and self-possessed, when she did not have anyone else to worry about but herself. She could come and go as she pleased, sleep where . . .

Sod it. He was not going to be the next in line. His face hardened as he was suddenly overcome by a desire to hurt.

'So I'm no saint – I admit it – but then you don't meet many of those on a day's march, do you? And, if I need to satisfy my animal needs away from the home now and again, that's no reflection on Jackie and no business of yours. If you're a wanderer, you're a wanderer – full stop. Some need it more than others. But when I do, I like to think I perform with a certain amount of tenderness and affection, with panache if you like, at least with a bit of style. Sham affection it may be at times, I admit, but I suspect that some of us are not even capable of that.'

He could hear a slur in his voice that he could not control. It took time to bring Faye's features into sharp outline, but what he wanted to see was still not there.

'So, if you had any fancy ideas that I've come here to climb into bed with you, you can forget them. Because it's too cold, too calculated. When I walk away from something like that, I like to feel I've left behind something more than just a scalp hanging from someone's belt.'

He thought that sounded rather good.

Now, as they stared each other down, David saw the hurt in her eyes he had been striving for. Now, he felt, he could leave, his head held high, his virility intact.

They walked to the door, in silence, Faye one step behind just as once they had descended a mountain together. Inside his head, one voice told him to apologise, another, slightly slurred with drink, said she had had it coming to her.

5

David fumed at the Jaguar, dawdling along at ninety in the fast lane. The driver ahead, who never seemed to look in his mirror, finally pulled over, and David watched his speedometer climb above the hundred mark once more. It was a glorious Saturday morning in early June, and all London seemed to have decided to go west. It was as if the city had festered for a week in the summer heat, finally bursting to discharge its contents along the sinuses that radiated from it. The M4 streamed more than its fair share of evil-smelling contagion. He braked hard, swearing as a red Golf GTI, crammed with brawny young men, pulled out in front of him. Cocky young bastards. That was not the respect due to a Master of Surgery, a past Hunterian Professor, a future Member of Council. To show his displeasure, David drove to within a few yards of the Golf's hatchback, his lights flashing. He got close enough to read the maker's name on the sailboards on their roof rack, hoping, quite dispassionately, they had made a good job of tying them on. He grinned back at their two-fingered salutes as they let him through. Perhaps the generation gap was not as wide as all that; he was, after all, going to be the youngest Member of Council. The brief encounter with macho virility gave him a boost that evaporated at the next hold-up.

He was late and had no illusions about the reception he could expect. The M4 got longer every time he drove it, and it seemed an age before he reached the Marlborough exit. Held up for miles by a wide load and its police escort, by the time he reached the College he was shaking with frustration.

So was his daughter.

Debbie Royall threw open the car door, hurled a bulging sports bag on to the back seat and flung herself in beside her father. He leaned across towards her in the vain hope of a kiss.

'Daddy, you are vile. You're so late. Where on earth have you been?'

It would have been pleasant, a short time at the school, perhaps a few minutes' walk around the grounds, absorbing the atmosphere in which his most precious possession now spent most of her time. No chance of that now.

'Everybody else has gone, long ago. I've felt such a wally. *Everybody's* seen me standing here like a tart in Shepherd Market.'

'What do you know about tarts in Shepherd Market?' He smiled as two young men trotted by, tennis rackets in hand. Nice-looking lads, a few pimples but with strong limbs and broad shoulders, their conversation languishing as they smiled Debbie's way. She did not spare them a glance.

'All my friends went yesterday. Why couldn't we have gone yesterday?' She stamped one foot, glaring ahead through the windscreen.

'Because I was working. I had a couple of cases in the Wellington late last evening. That's why I'm a bit late this morning – I had to go and see they were all right before I left. Somebody's got to pay for all this.' His hands waved vaguely.

'Where's Mummy? Isn't she coming?'

'Yes, she's coming. She's gone down on her own. She had a late night too; one of her dinners somewhere.'

'Don't you two *ever* go *anywhere* together?'

Straight for the jugular. The bite in the young voice left them both staring silently. He tried to think of an answer and decided there was no answer. With a shrug of the shoulders, he put the car in gear and moved off.

The road south was busy. It seemed narrower and more tortuous than ever, and his inability to use the car's potential only deepened David's frustration. He snatched sideways glances at his daughter. She was always her mother's daughter but, in this mood, her lips compressed, the gap between her eyebrows pulled tight, the likeness was uncanny. She would never be tall, but was far too slim and athletic to worry about looking stocky. But her hair, her beautiful, thick, black hair. Did she have to have it cropped so short, so no-nonsense, so businesslike – so like her mother's?

'Where are we going, anyway?' She finally broke the silence.

'I don't know.'

He heard a snort of irritation and tried to justify his remark.

'I thought I'd better leave that to your mother.'

That only produced an angry tug at her seatbelt and a vicious jerk of her foot.

'Your mother's not all that fond of sailing, you know that. Though that's not quite true. She enjoys sailing, but she always gives me the impression there are more important things to do, that she would rather be somewhere else.' Why didn't he say it? – 'and with someone else'.

'Couldn't we get a boat of our own, Daddy?'

Laughing, David took his eyes off the road for a moment. 'What d'you mean? We've *got* a boat of our own.'

'No we haven't. It's Grandpa's boat. It's not really ours. We just use it.'

'Same thing.'

'It's not. *Sally Anne*'s a lovely boat – it sails beautifully – but it's, it's . . . It's so big. It's like going to sea in the Dorchester. And what does it do – tied up to a pontoon all the year round? Helps entertain some of Grandpa's cronies now and then with a potter around the Solent in a force zero, gin and tonic in hand. But that's about all.'

'We've been to Cherbourg, darling,' David pointed out proudly. That had required a bit of navigation. They had been out of sight of land for hours. And things happened suddenly in the Channel.

'Once – in perfect weather.' Debbie turned towards her father, her voice softening. 'Couldn't we get something a bit smaller, Daddy?' she coaxed. 'Something a bit more exciting. There are a couple of the boys in school who'd love to come and crew. One of them has done quite a lot of it.'

'Why didn't you ask him to come today then?'

His daughter's look of disbelief had all the appearance of being genuine.

'You've got to be joking,' she said.

Because of the boat or the parents? Better not push that one. 'But those racing cruisers take a bit of handling. I'm not that much of an expert, darling.'

'Only because you're so busy making money, Daddy. Haven't we got enough yet? We could enter for one or two races. Round the Island, that sounds fun. What about entering for Round the Island this year, Daddy?'

'It would be fun,' David murmured, more to himself than to Debbie. He turned to smile at his daughter. 'We'll see,' he said. 'We'll see. Maybe next year.'

'That's what you always say.' The manipulative woman changed back to the petulant teenager as she slumped back in her seat. 'But you never *do* anything, do you? All you think about is making money.'

It was well past one o'clock before they reached the Hamble and felt the motion of the pontoon under their feet. They looked expectantly for Jacqueline. The big Moody creaked gently against its fenders, deserted. Hungry, bad-tempered, they threw their bags into the cabin, walked back to the car and found a pub. By the time they got back, Jacqueline's head was framed in the companionway. Her voice carried over the water, sharp, incisive, as she asked them where on earth they'd been. Hell of a start to a weekend.

The fairway down the Hamble was a nightmare of cruisers and dinghies, Southampton Water little better. They switched off the diesel and hoisted sail, only to lie dead in flat water under a hot sun. Debbie pouted, pretending not to notice, as a lightweight racing cruiser, heeled by a row of grinning young men sitting over the rail, glided past. Jacqueline sat with her back to the bulkhead, manuscript and pencil in hand, her surroundings switched off. David held the wheel as if it was serving some purpose, trying to give the impression of being in total control of a boat that drifted gently with the tide. After a while, without asking her father, Debbie rolled up the foresail, stripped to a bikini and lay to sunbathe on the deck. Reluctantly, he started the motor once more and headed out into the Solent.

Off the Needles, Jacqueline dropped her manuscript on the cockpit seat besides her. She looked round.

'Where are we going?' she asked.

'I was just about to ask the same thing,' David replied.

Jackie glanced at her watch. 'What about Buckler's Hard?'

'But that's halfway home again,' said a plaintive voice from the foredeck.

'At least we can be sure of a decent meal there.'

Jackie was obviously not to be gainsaid and, with a shrug of the shoulders, David swung the wheel over. 'It means we'll have to get the dinghy out,' he grumbled.

'Do you good.' Jackie took the wheel. 'About the only exercise you'll have had in a month.'

With something constructive to do, their tempers improved as they took turns to use the foot pump, under Jackie's critical eye. Their appetites sharpened as, towing the dinghy, the Moody nosed its way up the Beaulieu River. The little outboard engine started first time and they chatted happily as the dinghy headed for the slipway.

The restaurant was fully booked. The head waiter was polite but firm – there was no hope of a table. Jacqueline did not fancy a bar meal in a crowded pub and, half an hour later, they were back afloat, a three-cornered family feud, making the best of what food Jacqueline had brought with her. Before it was fully dark, Debbie was in her sleeping bag with a paperback, Jacqueline lay on her back, staring at the cabin ceiling, while David took the whisky bottle out into the silent, warm night air.

The next morning, they had not left the river before Jackie had informed them that she must be ashore by lunchtime. There was a fresh breeze and, after reaching up and down the Solent for a couple of hours, they made their silent, hangdog way back up the Hamble. Everyone seemed to be going the other way, obviously enjoying themselves enormously. Neat, quick and competent, Jacqueline had tidied the boat and gone with scarcely time to kiss her daughter. Ashore, David sat and watched while Debbie picked morosely at the most expensive lunch he could find, and the sun was still hot when they drove back to Marlborough.

David switched off the engine and leaned back against the headrest. What the hell were they doing there? He should be driving her home. As it was, he was sitting in his own car, alongside his own daughter, feeling a stranger, fighting off the desire to get it over with, push his daughter out, drive away with his own thoughts. He ran his window up as if to shut out the paralysing inhibition floating in a public school's ambience. A charade, that's what it was – play-acting in front of his own flesh and blood. A parody of a family. Three lives overlapping here and there – rather like those sets in the new maths Debbie had had to learn for her O levels. All three shared a name and an address. Apart from that?

'I'm sorry, Debbie. Not much of a weekend for you, was it?'

'That's all right, Daddy.'

He looked around. The school really did look deserted now.

'What will you do for the rest of the evening?'

She shrugged. 'I'll probably find someone; perhaps play tennis. There's usually someone around whose parents are working in some former outpost of our far-flung empire.'

'Like Harley Street, you mean?'

His daughter did not laugh; she did not even smile.

'Are you all right for money, darling?' he asked.

She didn't seem to hear him as she leaned across to kiss him. 'I'll be off then, Daddy. See you.'

'See you, Debbie. I'll make it up to you, I promise. We'll try again soon, shall we?'

Half in, half out of the car, Debbie turned. Her words were hesitant, but there was nothing held back in the wide-eyed look she gave him.

'Daddy, would you mind . . . ? There's this boy, Richard. He sails a lot with his Dad, and he's after me all the time to go along with them. They were down there today. Would you mind . . . ? I mean, next time . . . ?'

He felt his smile begin to ache as he fought to hold it.

'Of course not, darling.'

'Thanks, Daddy.'

There was a flurry of youthful energy as she clambered back to kiss her father once more. He felt her relief.

'I . . .' David began, and he sensed her look harden, her body tense as she expected some family condition about to be applied. 'No – there's no problem.' He saw her relax once more. 'I . . .' Again he hesitated, gauche with the only person he was sure he loved. 'I've been elected to the Council of the Royal College,' he blurted. 'I thought you might like to know. I heard last week.'

Debbie put a hand gently on her father's shoulder. Her face lit up with genuine pleasure.

'I'm so pleased for you, Daddy. You wanted that, didn't you?' She looked at him, smiling through half-closed eyes. 'You're a clever old devil, aren't you?'

Suddenly the car was empty and David Royall, Master of Surgery, Hunterian Professor, the youngest Member of Council, rich and successful, was alone.

'Did you get her back safely? I suppose you'll want some supper.'

'Yes. Yes.'

Jackie Royall looked at her husband blankly, her forehead furrowed with the irritated look of someone whose mind is being prised away from what it really wants to be thinking about.

'Yes, I got her back safely. Yes, I would like some supper,' he explained laboriously.

Jackie was not impressed. She took her time arranging into some sort of order the papers strewn over sofa, table and floor around her. She sighed as she stood up, brushing erasure dust from her skirt.

'What d'you want? Both Mrs Baker and Maria are off for the

weekend. I wasn't expecting you back so soon. I'm not too sure what we've got.'

'Anything will do. Whatever's easiest.'

The first whisky David hardly tasted. He drank it where he stood, within reach of the decanter, the object simply to prime the pump. He waited until Jackie had left the room before pouring the second – her eyes always seemed to follow the level as it rose up the glass. He took it with him into the kitchen and raised it towards her.

'Want one?'

She shook her head in a way that conveyed the message *she* neither wanted nor *needed* it.

Sitting on a stool, he watched her throw things into a wok with the careless expertise of the talented cook, conjuring a meal out of nothing. He saw her frown as she sensed he was looking at her. She was an attractive woman, one of those fortunate women, he thought, who seemed to become more beautiful the older they got. She was much more physically attractive now than when he had first met her. Then she had been thinner, tenser, the neurotic, competitive academic with little time for the disruptive triviality of sex. The driving ambition remained, but success had suited her, had brought a certain serenity that had allowed her body to fill out, become more rounded. And therein lay the paradox, for his sexual attraction towards her had waned as her physical attractiveness had waxed. It still surprised him how dispassionately he could look at her now. No, not dispassionately – that was how he tried to look at his patients. He did not look at Jackie clinically – just without passion. Apassionately. That would be nearer the mark. Was there such a word? If there wasn't, there should be.

It was crazy really. She was sexy – yes, *sexy* – plain, honest, earthy sexy – though she would deny it with her dying breath. And getting sexier year by year despite the drive to suppress it with more and more work. The only problem was, he was married to her. Why should that result in the passionless, jerking, groaning failures when he had no complaints elsewhere? That had to be in the mind – he grinned to himself – like other beautiful things, such as music and poetry.

He sighed, looking round at the rows of fitted cupboards, the split-level cooker, the microwave, the mixers, the gleaming stainless steel. He remembered the warmth of the kitchen in his first three-roomed flat.

David had been senior registrar at Queen's when he had been asked to rewrite a chapter for the new edition of Mallory's *Operative Surgery*. That had ruffled a few feathers amongst the establishment. Someone not of consultant status being asked to be co-author of what had been a surgical bible for more than fifty years? What could Janssen and Paul have been thinking of?

A Miss Jacqueline Lee, he had been told, would look after him at Janssen and Paul's medical and scientific section. She had been much younger than he had expected, probably younger than he. A first-class honours graduate from Oxford, she had been brisk and businesslike, explaining that, one day, she would be a fiction editor, that she was only in the medical and scientific section to learn the nuts and bolts of publishing. She had spelled out in no uncertain terms what she wanted, and his immaculate early drafts had come back covered in crimson slashes. An argument had developed over layout and he had asked her out to dinner to resolve it. Jacqueline Lee had taken a long, hard, analytical look at David Royall – and had said 'yes'.

David shifted his position on the kitchen stool as his memory failed him. There must have been some discussion about Jackie moving in with him. The pros and cons must have been gone over in detail, looked at this way and that, probably sandwiched between differences of opinion over an index or a graph – but he just couldn't remember any. What he could remember was feeling no surprise on discovering her virginity at her tense, tentative, stop–start defloration.

Looking back, that had been their happiest time together, those precious first few weeks and months, with freedom to go their own ways in the morning, their evenings filled with comparisons of steeply upward paths. Both mentally agile and competitive, his physical energy had acted for a while as the perfect foil for Jacqueline's bookish reserve. That had been before propriety had reared its ugly head. David had woken one morning to find they had agreed to marry, something he could not remember proposing. He had found he had an appointment at ten o'clock to meet Jackie's father, who had always been kept firmly in the background, simply dismissed as being 'in business'.

The labels on Jackie's clothes and a few chance remarks about Caribbean holidays had gone some way to put his mind at rest about the financial consequences of their merger of energies. Any lingering doubts about the wisdom of his choice had been swept away by the towering office block, the security check, the personal secretary with the office bigger than his flat, the wait of studied duration, the announcement that Sir Marcus would see him now.

The interview had gone well.

'Your father still alive? No – Jackie told me – he's dead. What did he do?'

'He was a miner. He was killed before I was born.'

That had scored a few points.

'My father was drowned at sea and my mother died of consumption in a Lancashire cotton mill. Your mother?'

'A nurse.'

'Alive?'

'Yes.'

'Hmmmmmmmph – must bring her up to meet Jackie's mother – if she ever gets back from bloody birdwatching in the Himalayas. You a thinker or a doer?'

Things had gone from good to better.

'Are the two mutually exclusive?' he grinned. 'I'd say I was a doer who has been known to think now and again.'

'Thank God for that.'

The half-hour had passed quickly. Sir Marcus had actually put his arm round David's shoulders as they walked to the door together.

'I never really thought Jackie would bring home one of those Hooray Henry fops you see around the place, but I was worried she might go for a writer – you know the type – beard, thick jumper, sandals, halitosis. But she's obviously a chip off the old block – knows a man with potential when she sees one. Only natural to worry though, isn't it, when it's your only daughter?'

'And she'll be my only wife, I promise you, Sir Marcus.'

That had been his one mistake, the glib, snide reply that still made him cringe every time he thought about it, the reply that had brought sudden doubt to Sir Marcus's eye.

What he did not realise was that it, above everything, had earned for him Sir Marcus's respect, the respect he kept for those he would never trust completely.

Jackie swept some of the contents of the wok on to a plate and slid it in his direction. She poured herself a coffee and sat across the table from him. Her nose wrinkled at the smell of the whisky alongside David's plate. For a moment Debbie, one of their few real bonds, allowed affection to jump the gap.

'Not much of a weekend for her, was it?' David spoke with his mouth full.

'Who – Debbie?'

He nodded.

'I don't see why she should complain.' Jackie leaned over to pick from his plate before putting her head in her hands, her elbows on the table. 'Lots of girls would give their eye teeth for the chance to go sailing like that.'

'Call that sailing? But that's not the point, is it? She'd probably prefer to go sailing in a Mirror dinghy than a thirty-five-feet Moody if it was with a couple of her friends.'

'There was nothing to stop her bringing someone. There was plenty of room. Why didn't she bring someone?'

'Are you serious?'

'Yes. Why not bring someone?'

'Oh, come on.' David stopped chewing for a moment, his voice scornful. 'Think back. Would you have asked anyone to spend a weekend in a boat in *that* atmosphere?'

'Why not? What was wrong with it?'

He raised his head, food halfway to his mouth, to look at his wife in disbelief. Had she meant that? He looked again – she *had* meant it. Stupid of him – had he ever known her say anything she did not mean?

'You mean that was your idea of a weekend's sailing?'

'Better than a lot of girls her age could look forward to.'

'Be fair – how could she ask anyone to come when she couldn't even depend on both of us turning up? Why did you have to get back so early?'

'Because I've got a meeting at ten o'clock tomorrow morning. I bought this book when I was in New York – it's brilliant. They've closed the autumn list, but I want them to include this one. It deserves to go on sale just before Christmas. I had to go through it again. It needs a few changes here and there for the British market.' She swivelled on her seat, reached for the wok and emptied the rest of the contents on to his plate. 'I told you I had to get back early, but you probably weren't listening, as usual. If it was going to mess up your weekend, you should have said so. I'd have stayed at home.'

'That would have been just as bad. Debbie said we never seem to go anywhere together.'

'If you had someone very sick in the Clinic or in the Wellington, someone you were *really* worried about, would you have gone sailing?'

'That's different, Jackie. It's got to be.'

'Different? Why is it different?'

They had been there so often, they hardly noticed the gulf. Out of habit, subconsciously despising himself for doing so, he backed away.

'You bought this book off your own bat?'

'Yep.'

'What if the others don't like it?'

'They'd damn well better.'

He laughed at the jut of her jaw. 'No chance you might be wrong?'

'Not on this one.' She stretched and yawned before settling back, her head in her hands once more. 'What have you got on the stocks this week? Anything interesting?'

'My first Council meeting.' Try as he might to prevent it, a smug smile spread over his face.

'I'm delighted for you, David.' There was no doubt Jacqueline still meant every word. 'You deserve it.'

'I must admit I am rather pleased.'

'You did so well in the election.'

'I'm not looking forward to the next time I meet Brian

Pullman.' Mock fear replaced the smugness. 'Bit embarrassing that, the number of votes he got.'

'I'm not surprised – horrible man. And that dried-up prune of a wife of his. What was her name, Iris?'

'Not was – is.'

'Remember when we had them to dinner? Even worse, when they had us back? Ghastly, wasn't it? Remember them apologising all the time about the sherry and the silver?'

'Which reminds me.' David lifted his empty plate on to the draining board. 'Can you face a bit more entertaining? Now that I'm safely on the Council, I think it would be in order to have a few people to dinner again – one or two of the old guard I thought might take offence if I'd asked them during the run-up to the election. Can you manage it?'

'Delighted. Just give me plenty of notice. It's important you keep pressing on. Nothing succeeds like success.'

6

The question rarely asked of a candidate being interviewed for a consultant post at a teaching hospital is – 'Can you teach?'

The applicant's qualifications and list of publications are examined in detail. References extolling his skill and knowledge are nodded over, particularly if they report impeccable behaviour towards the nursing staff. Club ties and Masonic signs are taboo, and it helps if he dresses for the interview in a manner unlikely to raise suspicions that he might eat his peas off his knife. But no one is ever detailed to stand behind him at bedside or clinic and report back on his ability to pass on his knowledge to the next generation. No one asks to hear him lecture. His technique in coping with a bunch of bright, iconoclastic twenty-year-olds is never put to the test. No one ever asks a student for a reference.

David loved teaching almost as much as making money. In his outpatient clinic, the compulsive tyranny of his private practice permitting, and with an able senior registrar in the next room coping with the bulk of the work, he was in his element. Whereas in his outpatient session at the Merton, with little help from junior staff, he had to take what came, at Queen's he could choose what he saw, picking out the notes that looked as if they would provide 'lumps and bumps' on which to teach. It always helped to find one or two pretty girls amongst the medical students at his back. He was enjoying himself, gently teasing answers out of one who did not look much older than Debbie, when the door opened.

'You wanted to see this man yourself, Mr Royall.'

The SR slid a thick file and a large brown envelope of X-rays on to the desk in front of David. 'He's the man you did the colonoscopy and biopsy on last week. The biopsy result is in the notes. He's sitting outside.'

The man who entered and sat at the desk alongside Royall would have been described in the Rhondda Valley as a 'tidy old chap'. His hair was close cut, his shirt clean, his tie Sunday best, his suit cleaned, pressed and shiny. David gave him a long quiet smile before saying anything.

'Good afternoon, Mr Lever. How are you feeling?'

'Not so bad, Mr Royall, thank you.'

David looked at the collar that was just a little too loose, the skin that was just a little too grey, the eyes a little too small for their sockets.

'And not so well, either, perhaps?'

'Not so good, no.'

'Still having bowel troubles?'

'Bit constipated, Mr Royall, but then, I'm not eating much. My appetite's gone completely. Don't eat so much as you could put in your eye.'

'Still bleeding?'

'Now and again.'

Flicking through the file, David found the page of pathology reports. He ran his finger down until he found the one he wanted, the result of the biopsy he had taken from Lever's tumour the week before. It was a long report – the pathology department at Queen's was a centre of excellence that prided itself on its attention to detail. He ignored most of it, searching quickly for the crucial words. They were not hard to find – 'well-differentiated adenocarcinoma'.

Closing the file, David stared at its cover long enough for the students behind him to glance at each other in surprise. It was not like him to be so hesitant.

'Mr Lever, I . . .' He stopped and took a deep breath. 'Would you mind coming back to see me again next week, Mr Lever?'

'Of course not, Mr Royall.' Lever hesitated, unsure whether or not it was permitted to question a consultant. 'Is there some problem?'

'Not really. I need to have a word with someone about one of your reports.'

'Is it going to mean an operation, d'you think, Mr Royall?'

'Yes, almost certainly, Mr Lever.'

'Then . . . ?' The patient glanced at the students and saw the same enquiry in their faces. 'If . . .'

'It's very difficult to explain, Mr Lever. Will you trust me? Come and see me next week, and I promise you all will be sorted out by then.'

He watched the door close on Lever before turning to the students behind him.

'Well-differentiated adenocarcinoma – what does that mean to you?'

'A cancer of the bowel of low-grade malignancy.'

The tone of the answer suggested the simplicity of the question had given offence.

David had noticed him earlier – an arrogant young buck with a pink shirt and a crew cut – one of the 'tell the patient everything' generation, a 'black and white' cocky young bastard to whom doubt was the eighth deadly sin. He had refrained from answering any of David's previous questions as beneath his dignity. But a cancer of the large bowel, one that had a consultant surgeon in two minds – that was more in his line. There was the rustle of expectation amongst the other students. The lad obviously had a reputation to keep up. David focused on him.

'And what would you do with it?'

'How big is it?'

Medical students do not reply in the form of another question. They answer politely and wait, trembling, for the next. This one's voice rang with the militancy of the indoctrinated.

'Very small; less than an inch across.'

'And whereabouts?'

David pushed the colonoscopy and barium study reports into the student's lap. That usually threw them, but not this fella. He took his arrogant time to read them before tossing them back.

'So, I repeat,' David said, 'what are you going to do about it?'

'What would *I* do about it, or what do I think *you* will do about it?'

David ignored the suppressed sniggers from the group of students.

'What would you do about it?'

'For a tumour like that? I would do a wide local removal.'

David smiled slowly. 'Something tells me you've worked at the Merton at some time or other.'

'I did my surgical block on Pullman's firm.'

'I thought you might have. And you were impressed, obviously, with *Mr* Pullman's operation.'

'Very. In *his* hands.'

'No need to ask you, then, what you think of the old argument that the smaller the tumour, the better the chances of success with a radical operation?'

'Like doing a radical mastectomy for a tiny carcinoma of the breast?'

David would have cried '*touché*' had it not been for the smug look that spread over the student's face. 'And there are no doubts at all in your mind about what I should do for this man?'

'None.'

'I envy you.'

David swung round in his swivel chair, turning his back on smug satisfaction. When the next patient walked in, his trousers bulging around a massive scrotal swelling, David was tempted to use the man to take the piss out of one prime bastard medical student. It was easy enough to do, and he'd often done it before.

They didn't really have any defence, even the brightest of them, if you really decided to get in there and take their balls off. Some consultants did it all the time – loved doing it. He laughed inwardly. Pullman and the youngster must have got on famously. What the hell; let the snotty-nosed little bastard have his moment. Life was too short.

But the young man's mocking face returned time and time again, his smirk reflecting back from X-ray viewing box, car windscreen, TV screen, bathroom mirror. David saw him again as he stared into the darkness, listening to Jackie's even breathing alongside him. It might have been better if he had kicked him in the teeth – got him out of his system. The face melted into a mocking grin as it challenged him to spell out the true reason for his hesitation over Lever's cancer, to admit why he loathed the idea of referring the case to Pullman. Was it really genuine doubt about the operation? Or was it that he could not bring himself to admit openly that Pullman was better at something than he was, or – even worse – help Pullman become more famous than himself?

The next time he was at the Merton, Lever's notes and X-rays under his arm, David found Pullman on his ward round.

'Can I see you a moment, Brian?' he asked, beginning to turn away.

But Pullman showed no sign of moving, and students and nurses parted to let David into their circle. Pullman nodded at the notes in their distinctive Queen's colour. 'Something for me?' he said.

'Yes, Brian. Would you be good enough to see this man for me? Age fifty-five, with a small, well-differentiated adenocarcinoma; right up your street, I think.'

Pullman used the same smile for the students as he turned his head towards them. 'If you lads cherish any hopes of doing surgery, this is the man to keep on the right side of. You realise you're in the presence of a future President of the Royal College of Surgeons, don't you?'

Embarrassed young men glanced nervously in David's direction, worried that Pullman was already getting them off to a bad start.

'But it's nice to know' – Pullman's head and shoulders were still turned away from David – 'that even the mightiest in the land need the help of a poor lowly general surgeon in a DGH now and again.'

David suddenly realised just how much he hated Pullman's guts as Pullman turned his smile in his direction once more. He had never seen the bastard look so happy. He handed Pullman the notes. 'I'll be seeing him again next week. Shall I tell him you'll be sending for him?'

'Please do. Perhaps you'd better warn him too that he'll have to have all his investigations repeated. No reflection on Queen's, of course, but you know how it is. You always feel better when you've looked at these things yourself.'

David did not trust himself to speak, but turned to walk towards the door. Words floated up from the deep – creep, shit, oily, poisonous, Uriah Heep, Obadiah Slope, oleaginous, unctuous, greasy, slippery. 'Greasy shit' broke the surface, hissed between clenched teeth as he felt Pullman's eyes on his back. Never again. Sod the patient *and* his cancer. Never again.

The towering, ornate steel gates, set in unscalable, spike-topped walls, would have stopped a tank. High on Wimbledon Hill, the gates were themselves hidden in a shady, tree-lined lane, fifty yards from the purring Jaguars and Volvo Estates. There was no sign of life, no bell to ring, no brass knob to turn. No need for any 'Keep Out' sign. David drove to within a few feet of the bars and opened his car door to investigate. Half out of the car, he heard his name hissed somewhere above his head.

''Ullo, David. Come on in.'

There was a click, the gates swung noiselessly open, and his wheels spun in the fine gravel as a vision of his car crushed in their vice-like grip flashed through his mind.

The house had been built in the style of a small country manor. Plain-fronted, with long shuttered windows, its white walls festooned with wisteria, it was of perfect proportions, the porch over what had been the front door now opening on to a wide, paved verandah. Tiers of formal gardens led down to a tennis court on one side, a lavish swimming pool on the other. Below these, a paddock fell away towards the golf course and the park with its lake beyond.

The drive led David to the rear of the house, where an entrance porch had been added. As he climbed out of the car, he saw a walled kitchen garden, a small cottage within its walls.

Mal Evans, propped up on crutches, stood in the doorway.

'Good of ew to come, David.' He wedged one crutch under an armpit as he held out his hand.

'No problem, Mal. I intended coming to see you shortly if you hadn't rung. It was no great distance to come, and I was at the Merton today anyway.'

'I know,' Mal grinned, 'but time's money, init? At least now ew'll be able to send me a proper bloody bill. And I don't want no bloody nonsense, d'ew 'ear me now? I know ew're not allowed to charge for all what ew did fer me in 'ospital, but I'm expectin' ew to add that on now to whatever ew charge fer this visit. Nothing to stop ew doing that, now is there?'

'You'll get no bill from me, Mal Evans. We've known each other too long.'

'Well.' Mal looked at him out of the corner of his eye as he turned to lead the way into the house. 'We'll 'ave to see about that, boyo, now won't we? We'll 'ave to make it up to ew some'ow.'

'Don't give it another thought.' Polished oak flooring creaked beneath their feet. How the hell had Mal come by such a place? 'What's the trouble?' A flower arrangement in a silver punch bowl on a small oak refectory table. Mal and flower arrangements? That had to be a woman's touch. 'You seem to be getting about pretty well.' A portrait in oils against oak panelling. 'What d'you need me for?'

'Got somethin' stickin' out.'

A tapestry hung from the wall alongside the broad staircase. It was difficult to look at it, to measure it as a criterion of wealth, and, at the same time, appear interested in something sticking out.

'Where from?'

''Ere.' A thumb was released from gripping a crutch to point to his stomach. 'An' I'm getting bloody fed up with this too.'

Mal recoiled his thumb to grip the crutch once more so that he could use it to give his leg plaster a whack that made David wince. 'Why won't the bastards let me put any weight on it yet? Never 'ad this trouble when I cracked my fib'la.'

'You behave yourself, Mal Evans,' David grinned. 'You do whatever the orthopods tell you. You did rather more than crack your fibula this time. But what's wrong with my side of the business?'

'It's still dischargin' in the middle, an' now there's somethin' stickin' out.'

Mal led him into a room redolent of polish, leather and books. A full-length window was open. Through it drifted the faint sounds of distant children's voices. Mal dropped his crutches and sank into a vast, worn hide chair. Unbuttoning his clothes, he tugged at the bulky dressings beneath. Kneeling beside the chair, David pushed Mal's hands aside to expose the incision. An inch or so of the wound had broken down. A length of blue nylon suture curled between the skin edges.

He laughed. 'We had to cut your rib margin to get at the bleeding,' he explained. 'My registrar obviously must have used nylon to stitch it together again.'

'Ew mean *ew* didn' stitch me up?'

'How was I to realise it was such an important ribcage?' David laughed. 'Of course I'd have done it myself if I'd known. But that wound is not going to heal until that nylon's out, I'm afraid.' He curled the loose end around his index finger. 'Can I give it a bit of a pull?'

'If ew must.' Mal clutched at the leather arms of the chair.

'Ready?'

Mal nodded grimly.

David gave a short, sharp tug, the wound tented outwards and Mal howled.

'Ew bastard. Ew great bleedin' bastard. Why didn't ew warn me it was goin' to 'urt like that?'

'You wouldn't have let me try if I had, now would you?' David grinned at the nylon loop. 'Doesn't want to come, does it?'

'Bleedin' 'ell.' Mal still squirmed and wriggled as the wave of pain receded. 'So what 'appens now?'

'Ask the nurse to give it a pull every day when she does the dressing. If I could see a knot, I'd cut it – but I can't. So – if it hasn't come out in a week or so, we'd better have you back in for a day to remove it.' He laughed as he watched Mal cover the wound once more. 'I've been waiting more than thirty years for that.'

'What d'ew mean?' Mal growled.

'To get even for that beating I took for you from Fatty Griffiths. Remember?'

'Made a man of ew, my son. S'wot they don't teach ew in school no more, 'ow to cope with a bit of injustice.'

They both chuckled. David raised his hands to show he wanted a wash.

'The bog's down the corridor on the right.'

Aged plumbing and spotless white towels that would have graced an exclusive golf club. When David returned, he sat opposite Mal.

'Drink?' Mal asked.

'Too early.'

'Coffee?'

'Just had one.'

A large Adam fireplace was no interior decorator's trendy feature but the well-used focal point of a room as mature as vintage port. Logs overflowed from a vast brass scuttle. One wall was covered with glass-fronted, carved oak bookcases, their shelves neatly filled with rows of leather-bound volumes. Another wall supported massive landscapes that looked as if they had hung there for a hundred years. Long windows in the fourth wall were bracketed with foldaway shutters that led down to carved oak window seats at their bases. The furniture was a comfortable blend of mahogany, dark oak and old worn leather, the oak strip floor strewn with Persian rugs.

David laughed.

'What's so funny?' Mal asked, smiling.

'I was looking for the tiger's head over the mantelpiece.'

'Not what ew expected?'

'Frankly, Mal, no.'

Mal chuckled as if he were glad.

'Don't get me wrong, Mal; I think it's beautiful, the whole house. But how did you come to buy it?'

'Always dreamed as a kid of 'avin' a 'ouse like this. Like the colliery agent's 'ouse back 'ome, remember?'

David nodded.

The face with which Mal scanned the room beamed with pride.

'It used to belong to an old bachelor who was a director of Arsenal. 'E used to 'ave us out fer parties, an' the first time I saw the place I knew I must live 'ere sooner or later, whatever it cost. When the old boy died, I bought it lock, stock and barrel. An' I 'aven't changed a thing. I know class when I see it.'

David took a second look. 'What about Faye? Didn't she have a few ideas?'

'Sure. She wanted to do all sorts of things, but I didn't let her. She even tried to get me to buy one of those 'orrible 'ouses up 'Ampstead way, but I've never fancied that sort of place. But then, what d'ew expect? Faye's got no class.'

'Come on, Mal, that's not fair. You must have seen her flat.'

'So ew've been there, 'ave ew? Ew don't 'ave to climb up no mountain to meet now?' Mal laughed. 'Faye's got style all right, no doubt about that; right down to 'er fingertips she's got style – but no class . . . just like me.' He laughed, easing his plaster into a more comfortable position. 'The only time I 'ad any class was on the football field. No style – I was all bloody knees an' elbows – but plenty of class. I knew a lot of players who were all style and no class; they never lasted long when the shit really 'it the fan. And, of course, there've been a few with both – Stan Matthews, John Charles, Bobby Charlton – but ew don' come across those sort of people very often, do ew?'

'I wonder where I fit into your classification,' David murmured, raising his voice as he saw Mal about to tell him. 'And d'you live here alone? Faye didn't tell me whether you were married. I seem to remember reading something in the newspapers, years ago . . . ?'

'Probably. They gave me the usual runaround – one slip an' they never let ew go. If they don' 'ave no story they'll make one up. Ew know the trick – they ring ew up an' ask if it's true ew've been screwin' some bimbo – ew tell 'em to get stuffed – an' there are the 'eadlines the next mornin' – "Mad Mal denies affair with topless dancer". 'Appens to everyone. There was a time when I wouldn't have been surprised to wake up to find a cameraman in bed with me.'

'And were you?'

'Was I wot?'

'Screwing some bimbo?'

Mal grinned. 'Normal 'ealthy male, wun I?'

'But you *were* married.'

'Yes, I was married – twice.'

'Was? Twice?' David raised an eyebrow.

'The first one, Sammy, she was a girl and a 'alf.' Mal stopped to chuckle to himself. 'A laugh a minute, she was. Trouble was that, when I was playing abroad – European Cup or fer Wales, somethin' like that – she was playin' away from 'ome as well, if ew know what I mean. Still, there were no 'ard feelings – I can't say as 'ow I was any saint. I still see 'er now and again. She's got two kids now. I'm godfather to the boy.' His face suddenly lost all expression. 'An', of course, my second wife, Rachel, she committed suicide.'

David closed his eyes for a moment. 'I'm sorry, Mal,' he said. 'I should have known. Now I remember . . . I'm sorry.'

'S'all right, David. She was quite a few years older than I was. I 'ad money, she 'ad class. Just like I bought this 'ouse, p'raps I thought I could buy 'er too. Lookin' back, it was never goin' to work out. She was very depressed for some years before she died. I thought she might get better when we bought this place – I thought it would be just 'er sort of 'ouse – but she didn't.'

'And you've gone on livin' in' – David waved his hand vaguely – 'this great big house – all alone?'

'Not always alone,' Mal smiled. 'I 'ave the occasional lodger, but they don' usually stay long. The peace an' quiet seems to get to 'em sooner or later – seems to drive some of 'em mad.'

'Not quite like Cory Street, I imagine, with people in and out all day. I don't suppose you can leave the front door on the latch any more. Who are your neighbours? Do you *have* neighbours on Wimbledon Hill?'

'D'ew 'ave any in 'Arley Street?'

David said nothing.

Mal waited long enough for the point to be taken before jerking a thumb over his shoulder. 'Arabs that side – never met them.' He pointed ahead. 'That side – Godfrey Strait. Tidy chap.'

'*The* Godfrey Strait?'

'I've only met 'im a couple of times. First time was when 'e ran into the back of me at a traffic light. Not a bit like 'e appears on 'is show. 'E's another old bachelor like me. All 'e seems to want is to shut 'isself away when 'e gets 'ome. I let 'is niece run 'er pony in my paddock.' He used his head this time to indicate the back of the house. 'An' I've got the Parkers; they live in the cottage. Mary cooks and is generally the boss while Daniel looks after the garden with whatever 'elp 'e can find. I've 'ad a succession of maids – Portuguese, Korean, Welsh, Irish; ew name it, I've 'ad 'em.' He grunted as some memory amused him. 'But they don't stick Mary for long. Mary kinda mothers me; I think she worries I'm gonna up an' marry some flea-bitten trollop. I reckon she'd hire an' fire my lodgers too if I gave 'er 'alf a chance. But, chwarae teg, boyo – a man's got to be master in 'is own 'ouse, 'asn't 'e?' A trace of the Rhondda backstreet grin crossed his face. 'I work 'ard. I've never smoked. I don't drink and I 'ate gamblin' 'ard-earned money. I got to 'ave some vices, 'aven't I?'

He winked. 'That reminds me.'

'What?'

'When d'ew reckon they'll take this off?' He rapped his plaster, grinning. 'It's all right when they're up there doin' all the work, but it's when ew try to get on top. Makes it bloody awkward. Complain like 'ell, they do.

'An' another thin'.' Mal waited for David to stop laughing before lifting his plastered leg. 'Are they goin' to let me drive when I get out of this?'

'You'll have to ask the physicians that, Mal. I'm no expert on that. Have you had any more blackouts since?'

'None. I feel perfectly fit. Bloody nonsense, is all that.'
'Have you had your EEG done?'
'That thin' where they put them wires all over ewr 'ead?'
David nodded.
'Yes.'
'And?'
'They won' tell me. Typical of ew bastards. But I need to know. If I can't drive, I'll 'ave to get a chauffeur – which I'll 'ate. Daniel is driving me around at the moment, but 'e's bloody awful – and I need to get about. I'm in the sort of business where it pays to keep an eye on thin's ewrself. Rob ew blind, they will, if ew don' watch out.'

'What sort of business are you in?'

'I got this club up in Manchester – been there a long time – runs itself more or less now – I don' 'ave to go there very often. But I've got a couple of places down 'ere, south of the city, in what I call London's soft underbelly. Old country 'ouses – ew know the type – green fields all round, nine 'ole golf course, bloody good food and a good cellar with a 'ealth centre and ritzy-looking masseuses, know what I mean? Fatten 'em up one end of the 'ouse, sweat it off the buggers the other end, and they pay through the nose for both. Good place for some soccer manager to take 'is team to relax before a big match; better 'an Spain – no chance of losin' 'alf your team with the squitters. Useful, too, fer entertaining business colleagues with no questions asked. Know what I mean?' The expression on Mal's face changed. 'But it's the snooker 'alls what need watchin' at the moment. I could see the snooker boom comin' a mile off and I got a string of 'alls now, strung out in the council estates. I picked the towns with 'igh unemployment; you know – plenty of time on their 'ands – young kids 'opin' to make the big time? Not too big, you know, the 'alls; just three or four tables in each. I'm goin' to sell up before the bubble bursts, but they need watchin' like a bloody 'awk at the moment. There's a few 'ard boys around in that business. Got to keep ewr wits about ew. An' I'm goin' to be stymied if I can't drive.'

'I'll see if I can have a word with one of the physicians, find out what's going on. I'll give you a ring.' David stood up. 'It's time I was off.'

Mal Evans struggled to his feet. 'Ew must come to one of my parties sometime, David. Bring the missus – I'd like to meet 'er.'

'She's not much of a party girl, I'm afraid, Mal.'

'No?'

'Literary lunches are more her style.' A far less astute mind than Mal's would have heard the edge to the voice. 'She's a director of a big publishing firm. Spends half her time in the States.'

'That so?' Mal seemed to be considering the implications. 'Let me know the next time ew're a bachelor then and we'll 'ave a party. 'Aven't 'ad a party f'r ages. If ew won' send me a bill, the least I can do is 'ave a party f'r ew. Might do ew a bit o' good. All the men I know 'ave made so much money they're shit scared they're goin' a die tomorrow an' not enjoy it, an' their wives'll pay the earth to 'ave some good-lookin' doctor like ew run his 'ands over them. I'm sure ew can always find some lump to massage f'r 'em.'

'There's no need, Mal.' Members of Council did *not* do that sort of thing. 'There really isn't.'

Mal, grinning, ignored the prissy tone. 'An' ew'd better stay the night. We don't want no famous 'Arley Street specialist breathalysed, now do we? Ew leave it to me.'

7

It was beginning to get dark. Twilight promised a gorgeously hot summer evening. This time the gates were open, but a squat, powerful-looking man, all shoulders and no neck, barred his way. David ran his window down and was about to explain who he was when the man, after a cursory look at him and his otherwise empty car, stood aside and jerked his head backwards towards the house. It could have been the man's twin who wandered, humming quietly to himself, amongst the parked Porsches, Mercedes and Rolls.

'Good evening.' David smiled weakly at someone he decided would make a better friend than foe.

Watery eyes, bulging from their sockets, looked the car up and down like a second-hand car dealer being offered an old banger in part exchange. He did not seem unduly impressed with a six-month-old BMW. Its owner, a mere consultant surgeon, could be safely ignored, leaving him to find his own way into the house. David followed the sound of a party that had obviously been going for some hours. He stepped aside smartly to avoid being bowled over by a curly-haired young man who dragged a squealing girl after him towards the open door and the floodlit verandah beyond. He edged his way into the room, stone cold sober, deafened by a drunken babel as red faces, inches away from each other, roared their meaningless trivia. One or two heads turned his way but not for long. He was about to cut and run when he was spotted.

'David, ew bastard. I'd given ew up.'

Mal Evans, hobbling now on a short, weight-bearing plaster and walking stick, forced his way out of the scrummage, turning sideways to squeeze between the groups. A blonde head turned, radiant appreciation lighting an otherwise sullen face as his free hand slid over a rounded silk-clad buttock. 'How're ew doin' darlin' – awright?' – the witticism that went with the act – was equally well received. He limped his way over to David.

'What kept ew? I wouldn't 'ave asked this bunch of bloody crooks if it 'adn't been f'r ew.'

'I'm sorry, Mal. Something unexpected came up.'

'As the bishop said to the actress. Never min'. Better late than never. 'Ere, everybody.' Mal shouted above the bedlam and waited until the noise level dipped. 'David Royall, OK? Guest of honour. Saved my life.'

There were a few faint smiles before an upsurge of conversation once more.

David tried to reconcile Mal, the genial, wisecracking, bottom-pinching host, with Mal, the shy recluse, content to live quietly, alone in the old house. This must be Mal in his working mode, a façade to be discarded the moment the last car drove away. To Mal, this must be what a meeting of Council was to him: a time to conform, put on distinctive robes, blend vocally.

'Daniel,' Mal roared, and an elderly, respectful, respectable-looking man in a short white coat appeared, carrying a silver salver. 'Give the guy a drink.'

David found he had no choice. He took the champagne served in large crystal glasses. By the time he had drunk thirstily and belched politely, Mal had deserted him. He turned, with the smile of someone walking into a dentist's surgery, to the couple to his right. They did not smile back, leaving him in no doubt that he had interrupted a very important conversation. The woman was tall and beautiful, wearing both the look and the makeup she judged best suited to the most expensive clothes money could buy. She had fine, smooth shoulders with just that little too much décolletage, and David glimpsed a nipple as she bent to stub out a long, hardly smoked Turkish cigarette in the remnants of a plate of smoked salmon. The man wore a dark blue velvet jacket and pale blue trousers. The gold medallion, nestling in the hair that curled through the open neck of his white silk shirt, went with the heavy gold bracelet, the signet ring and the buckles on his shoes.

'You known Mal long?' The man managed to get the four words out without disturbing the phlegm that rattled in the back of his throat.

'We were kids together.'

'Hmph.' Calculating eyes ran over David like an electronic scanner, inducing in him an irresistible urge to put his hand over his wallet. 'What's your racket then?'

'My racket?' David laughed. 'Surgery. I'm a surgeon.' Suddenly, he felt more at ease, relieved as the weight of pretension fell from his shoulders. 'What's yours?'

The man blew in David's face, putting up a smokescreen.

'Are you now?' he said, from the other side. 'Where?'

'Harley Street.'

'Are you any good?'

'The best – in my line.'

The look in the woman's eyes changed as if she was seeing him for the first time, but she said nothing – which was a pity. David was dying to hear her voice – it might help him decide whether she was someone on the way up or someone on the way down. He grabbed another glass of champagne as a tray went by.

'My quack sent me up to see one of your boys in Wimpole Street a couple of months ago. You must be making a bloody fortune, judging by what he charged me. Still' – he leered at the woman – 'made a new man of me, didn't he, darlin'?'

'Glad to hear of at least one satisfied customer. That's always good for businesss. We can't always guarantee success, you know. And, of course, there's no consumer protection act to cover you. You don't get your bits back if you're not satisfied.' Stupid crap. Why talk like that? Why let them drag him down to their level? They were nothing to him, a Member of Council.

David had decided the man probably owned a string of massage parlours or porn shops, but he was never to find out. The rattling phlegm, finally dislodged, induced a fit of bubbling, vein-bulging coughing, and, by the time the man could breathe again, someone had elbowed David out of the way, spilling champagne over his jacket. He turned sideways to see, in the adjoining group, a tall, pale young man, staring over his neighbour's shoulder out into the night. A soul mate? He looked bored enough. Just sat his A levels perhaps? Waiting to go up to Oxford?

'You look as much a stranger as I feel,' David said, smiling.

'Eh?'

The young man turned to face him. He had a Stan Laurel haircut and boils, some so pustular he'd had to shave between them, leaving dark stubble around septic craters. Blood and pus spotted the high collar of his designer shirt.

David tried to take his eyes away from a particularly painful-looking pustule on the side of the nose. 'I always find it difficult, walking into a room full of people I've never met before – don't you?'

'Fraaankly, I couldna gi'e a fuck.'

David blinked and found his lower lip hanging. Slowly he closed his mouth.

'I take it then they don't frighten you?'

'This fuckin' lort? Do me a favour, won't ye.'

'Why do you come then?'

'Same bleedin' reason you probably came – fuckin' money, wha else? Wha else would anyone stan' roon wi' a bunch a piss artists like these? When your fuckin' manager says "make a fuckin' appearance", you make a fuckin' appearance. An' o' course, there's Mal. I owe him. He was ma furst sponsor. Only wee sod who's ever gi'en me anythin' wi'out wantin' somethin' baaack.'

'Sponsor. You mentioned a manager. What exactly do you do?'

The young man looked disappointed.

'Didya no see me?'

'I'm sorry?'

'Orn TV.' The look of disappointment deepened to resentment. 'I got to the quarter finals o' the Rothman's this year.'

'Rothman's.' David thought for a moment. 'That's snooker, isn't it?'

'Fuckin' 'ell,' the young man whispered, his resentment now overcome by awe at the extent of someone's ignorance. 'Wha' sorta fuckin' wurld d'ye live in?'

Intrigued, David probed the background of someone, not yet twenty, who probably was already earning more than he was. It did not take long. There was no lengthy catalogue of academic and social achievements through which to sift. 'The only fuckin' O level I got was in glue sniffin'.' It was difficult to tell who lost interest in the other first – probably one of snooker's rising stars, who found himself talking to someone who didn't know a stun from a screw. By tacit mutual consent, they gave up trying to communicate, and David now knew what the young man found so all-absorbing as he returned to gazing out of the window – vacant space.

He moved on, to hear how much someone had lost that week at backgammon. He was foolish enough to let slip once more that he was a surgeon, and paid the price, being regaled for the next half-hour with someone's detailed gynaecological history. Relief came in the form of realisation, finally dawning through the alcoholic mist, that he was not expected to pay attention, let alone to reply, and, fascinated, he stood back, listening to the champagne take its toll as accents reverted and profanity multiplied. Another hour of the crude boasting of the vulgar rich, and he found himself leaning against a wall, light-headed and exhausted, certain in his mind he had made a mistake he would never repeat. From somewhere the other side of the room came the sound of a smashed glass, and a cheer went up. Someone shouted to Mal, asking if he had a piano.

David was suddenly overwhelmed by a desire to be at home – even an empty home. If that meant he was an intellectual snob, so be it. But – he looked around him. Was he really any different from them? Was he any less amongst his peers here than in the Royal College or the Royal Society? Was he doing anything more laudable than they were, pursuing fame and money with what talent had come his way at birth in that all-important providential lottery? They might even have had to make the grade without the relentless drive of an ambitious mother to help them. He pulled a face. Hell – yes. There had to be a difference. No one there looked likely to get himself a knighthood.

Home. But how to get there, half pissed? Food. It would help if he could find some food. Looking around, he saw, for the first time, the long table at the end of the room, a totally bored, half-drunk chef, his hat askew, standing behind it.

The table was a shambles. David turned away from what was left of the smoked salmon – he could still hear the hiss of the woman's cigarette stub being crushed into extinction – and the caviare was all gone. He picked up one of the dishes, looking ruefully at a few sad, isolated black eggs. He ran his finger around the edge and then sucked it.

'I'm sure there's some more somewhere. It's not like Mal to run out of caviare like that. Would you like me to go and look?'

She came to about his shoulder. As he swung round, his first impression was of soft brown curls – horse chestnuts just out of their burs – and brown eyes set in a tranquil face upturned towards him. He put the dish down hurriedly.

'Of course not. It's just I didn't have time to eat before I came and I was a bit late arriving.'

'You were rather, weren't you – and you the guest of honour.'

He picked up an empty plate and looked indecisive.

'Here, let me help you.' She took the plate from him. 'I can recommend the lobster – it's gorgeous. Would you like me to salvage some for you? Are you hungry?'

Five minutes later, he stood, a laden plate in one hand, a knife and fork in the other. Someone's elbow almost spilled the lot. The sound of someone thumping a piano came from the next room.

'Why don't you go out on to the verandah?' she said softly. 'There's more room out there and it's a bit cooler. I'll bring some more champagne.'

She walked across the verandah towards him, the swing of her hips accentuated by the stillness of her upper body as she held two glasses out in front of her. She wore a full-length skirt of embroidered material that looked to David like some kind of linen. Her silk shirt had long sleeves, ruffed at the wrists. A waistcoat matched the skirt, and a silk cravat was tied at her throat. She put one of the glasses down beside him and sat on the low stone balustrade to watch him eat.

'I'm Gemma Ainsleigh,' she said, holding out her hand.

Caught with his hand halfway to his mouth, he tried to stand, dropped his knife, sat back in confusion and laughed. Finally freeing his hand, he shook hers.

'David Royall.'

'I know.'

He looked surprised.

'I was there when Mal introduced you – remember? And he'd told me all about you before. You've known each other a long time, haven't you?'

'Brought up in the same street. Born a few doors from each other.'

For a while, she sat, quiet and considerate, and let him eat.

'Must have given you a nice feeling then, saving a friend's life like that.'

His mouth full of lobster, David shrugged his shoulders. He swallowed. 'I didn't even know who he was when I operated on him – just another abdomen. Anyway, it's a bit overdramatic, putting it like that.'

'Would he have bled to death if nothing had been done?'

'I suppose so.'

'And it was you who stopped the bleeding – no one else?'

'Yes, but . . .'

'So why don't you accept that you saved his life? You do, deep down inside you, don't you? So why not be honest and say so?'

They looked levelly at each other long enough for David to feel an excitement beginning deep in his belly. The hand she stretched out to take his empty plate looked cool and slim.

'And now I suppose you'd like a real drink. Whisky or brandy?'

'Whisky.'

He began to stand.

'Stay there. I know where to find it. I'll bring it out.'

The whisky was perfect but, as she sat once more, he noticed she had not touched her champagne. They both looked round as screams came from the swimming pool. There followed loud, splashing sounds that rose for a moment above the noise of the singsong now in full swing inside the house. Flashlights lit the night sky. David had noticed them before. He frowned.

'Paparazzi,' Gemma explained.

'Paparazzi?' Princess Margaret, Mustique and mammoth zoom lenses. 'Here?'

'Mal's got some of his boys patrolling the grounds, but you can never keep them away altogether.'

'But what are they doing here?'

'Danny Harland.' She saw him frown again. 'You must have heard of Danny Harland?' She watched the slow shake of the head. 'The biggest transfer fee United's ever paid?' David's polite nod did not fool her. 'D'you live your entire life in that operating theatre of yours?'

He laughed and she raised an eyebrow.

'That question has been put to me already tonight,' he explained, 'though not quite so charmingly.'

'He's here tonight,' she explained. 'Down by the pool, by the sound of it. You know what they say about a fool and his money. The problem is that his manager is just about as bad as he is. They're not all like Mal, unfortunately. He was the exception that proved the rule. He's tried to talk some sense into the boy, advise him what to do with his money, but he just won't listen. It's like a death wish some of the more talented ones seem to have. No self-discipline. He does nothing to control his talent – perhaps that's why he's so exciting to watch. They say defences don't know what he'd going to do next; *I* don't think Danny himself knows half the time.'

'You go to soccer matches much?' He tried to imagine someone so elegant in a striped muffler and woolly hat.

'Now and again.'

'How long have you known Mal?'

'Long time. He's one of the nicest men I know. Why he doesn't cut himself off from this bunch of hoodlums, I don't know.' David found himself looking away from her as she put her hands behind her on the rough stone, bracing her shoulders as she leaned back slightly. 'But then I suppose he's got to do this sort of thing in his line of business. I imagine it's the same in your business – sorry – profession?' She seemed to be daring him to hold her cool, level gaze as she smiled.

He nodded. 'True,' he said.

'And do *you* enjoy it?'

'Not really. We just feel we must. It's part of the system.'

'Exactly.' There was silence for a moment. 'And I doubt if Mal enjoys it either really,' she said firmly. 'I think, basically, Mal is a very quiet, contemplative man. Why else would he choose to live in this great big house all alone?'

'Maybe you're right,' David conceded. 'How did you come to meet him?'

'I work for him now and again up north. I'm in the entertainment business.'

She wore no wedding ring. David, his mouth dry, found he

still could not look at her as he asked. 'And your husband? Has he come down with you?'

She disengaged her hands from behind her, leaning forward towards him to clasp them around her knee. Again there was the quiet, seductive laugh before she answered. 'There's no husband; just a fifteen-year-old son who's soccer mad and doing his O levels.'

Now he *could* see her in that muffler and hat. 'You don't look old enough,' he smiled. 'I have a daughter, a bit older . . .'

There was talk of careers, and hopes and fears for only children, until he found himself looking into an empty glass. Gemma Ainsleigh stood up and put out her hand.

'Don't drink anymore. Let's walk down through the garden. It's a beautiful night.'

She took his arm, her shoulder against his, her skirt swishing slowly and rhythmically as they strolled over lawns and along flowerbeds where, all thoughts of escape forgotten, he felt his ignorance as she spoke of the flowers and shrubs.

'D'you have a garden?' he asked.

'I couldn't live without my garden. I don't know how you survive in the middle of London. Wouldn't you rather live out here than in Harley Street?'

They passed out of the floodlighting and into the shadow of some trees. Without stopping, he bent over to kiss her – it seemed the natural thing to do.

'Thank you, sir,' she murmured, stopping and turning him towards her. 'More, please?'

She broke away, taking his hand, as she felt him begin to grind against her.

'Come on. Let's see what they're up to over at the pool.'

The floodlights around the pool had them squinting through narrowed lids as they came out of the shadows. Flashlights from somewhere out in the darkness now hardly registered. They joined half a dozen others at the pool's edge, watching the antics of the swimmers, dodging back as flailing arms and legs sent arcs of water sluicing their way. Wet, glistening bodies on a still, warm night. They watched the face of a fat man float past, a cigar clamped in his teeth, his belly trailing behind like some adipose iceberg. Convulsive, frog-like jerks of his legs propelled his cigar out of range of the splashes as three young girls, screaming, naked and nubile, wrestled with and were chased by a handsome, curly-headed young man. One swam to the side, holding out her hand to David who, laughing, hauled her to safety. She bent over by his side, dripping, howling for his help as she tried to pull another of the girls out. When he took the second girl's hand, however, it became clear that they had other plans for him, and it was only with Gemma's help that he did not end up in the pool with them.

They strolled back to the now silent house, as slowly as David could manage. Each room they went into was an empty shambles. They drank a mug of coffee where they stood, touching close, in the kitchen. David looked at his watch.

'My God, it's after one o'clock. I had no idea. I wonder where I'm supposed to sleep.'

'That needn't be a problem.' She stood in front of him. 'That's if you want to. You don't *have* to,' she said with a smile. 'It's not an essential part of the system. You don't *have* to conform.'

In the bedroom, Gemma turned out the lights and opend the windows wide. As she stood in the warm night air to let him undress her, there was an ache inside him he had never known, a wish to be gentle and at peace with someone, at peace with himself, that took any trace of violence out of a passion that was intense. He wanted, not to possess her, but to be with her, of her, inside her. In their lovemaking, she drew from him, in gentle and subtle movements, a climax so deliciously delayed, so excruciatingly intense, as to be almost unbearable.

He lay for a while, gasping at the shadowy ceiling, Gemma's head on his shoulder. It took a while for his tumbling senses to stabilise. Gemma waited patiently, smiling quietly, a private smile, until his gasps subsided.

'Did that really happen?' he asked breathlessly.

The head on his shoulder moved. 'D'you want me to make sure?'

He laughed, holding her closer, wanting still to feel the length of her body. No remorse. No guilt. They murmured affectionately as they drifted off to sleep.

It was light when she woke him to make love once more, rousing him to the same tender intensity that brought in its wake profound, dreamless sleep. When he finally woke, the bed beside him was warm – but empty.

Partly dressed, unwashed and unshaven, still carrying within him a deep craving, he searched the house, but there was no trace of her. All he found was a housekeeper with a martyred look, some bleary-eyed girls, and United's young soccer star with a hangover. Mal sat grinning at the kitchen table.

'Mornin', David. 'Ad a good night, 'ave ew? I didn't see much of ew. Breakfast?'

'Where's she gone?'

'Who?'

'Gemma. Gemma Ainsleigh.'

'She 'ad to get back. She left early.'

'Did she leave any message?'

'Message?' Mal grinned. 'What sort of message?'

'Don't be so bloody infuriating, Mal. She can't just walk out on me like that. How am I going to see her again?'

'No problem. I can fix that easy.' He watched the relief spread over David's face. 'But ew can pay next time, boyo. She costs a bloody arm an' a leg, that gel.'

'How . . . ? What d'you . . . ?'

Mal's grin only deepened as shock and confusion took their grip on David. 'I mean a rich 'Arley Street specialist like ew – ew can afford to pay for ewr own pleasure.'

'You don't mean she was . . . ? She's a pro——?' David's first complete sentence emerged as a shout. 'D'you mean she's a *hooker*?'

'Just about the best there is. It's all ewr fault fer not sendin' me no bill. I 'ad to find some way to pay ew.'

Slowly, David began to laugh in short, staccato explosions of sound.

'They don' all walk the streets with short leather skirts an' poodles, ew know.' Mal began to laugh too. Soon, both men were roaring. Mal leaned over to tap David on the leg. 'Now p'r'aps ew know what I mean about someone 'avin' both style an' class.'

8

The goitre was a big one. It was also very vascular. It was a very hot day, the air conditioning in the Merton's theatres had broken down and a rivulet of sweat trickled down David's back. It was an operation designed to bring out the best in any surgeon. A character-builder; a sorter of men from boys. One that brought a ring of justification to some of the hackneyed, age-old surgical aphorisms: make your incision twice as long as you think it ought to be and then you will not have to enlarge it much; don't go on to the next stage until you have finished the one you are doing; do it slowly, do it once. Bedrock technical principles that were standing someone even of David's experience in good stead as he bent his shoulders a little lower, intensified his concentration.

The right upper lobe was grossly enlarged – that was how it would go down in the operation notes. David's mental notes read rather differently. Sod, bastard, sodding bastard ran round behind the mask-like face. He had already divided the strap muscles to give himself maximum access, but his dissection up into the neck was still partly blind, depending on touch, on experience, on luck, on his ability to concentrate, not think of other things like a wife's parting remark or the most satisfying one-night stand he'd ever had. It was just him now and the patient, and her sodding goitre with its bastard of a superior lobe. So far, he had been able to keep the operation a controlled, methodical procedure, but he knew that one rash, hurried movement and . . .

'They can be tricky, those superior thyroids, can't they? It's all a question of getting in the right plane, you know. No problem then.'

David pushed a swab in the wound and slowly, meticulously

put his instruments down. He swallowed hard, afraid to speak. When he spung round, Brian Pullman's smile was inches away.

'I've just done that man Lever for you,' Pullman went on. 'Quite straightforward. Should have a good result.'

'Good.' David had to unclench the muscles of his jaw to speak. 'I hope he does well. He's a hell of a nice old boy.'

'Any more like him you have referred to you at Queen's, don't hesitate. Only too glad to look after them for you. I've already got enough for my paper to the RSM, but the more the merrier. Mustn't stop now, must we? This man Lever will certainly go into the series, but I'll have to call a halt soon so that I can draw up the figures.' He pointed at the woman on the table. 'But don't let me hold you up. I know how anxious you must be to get away.'

David now found the dissector in his hand shaking as Pullman stayed to stare pointedly over his shoulder. Why didn't the swine piss off? He began to scratch where, before, he had dissected.

'I don't believe those people who talk about the thyroid being stuck down – do you?' The raking voice behind him goaded him on. 'Usually means they're in the wrong plane of cleavage, doesn't it?'

A vein split and the wound filled with blood. The sodding creeping bastard. David snatched with an artery forceps, only to make things worse. Bugger off, you sanctimonious twit. Pullman stood silently throughout ten minutes of undignified, bloody scramble, exuding a subtle aura of disappointment as he saw David finally regain control.

'Not the sort of case to tackle the day after some wild party,' Pullman growled, turning on his heel and walking out.

The operation completed, David, still fuming, stood beside Digger Drew as he disconnected his machine.

'I've a bloody good mind to resign my sessions in this place.'

Drew never swore – a man at peace with himself. Normally David refrained out of courtesy, but Pullman had driven him too far.

'I don't know how much longer I can go on working here, Digger, without kicking that bastard in the balls. If I worked here full time, I'm sure I would have done it long ago.'

Although now a pillar of the church, Drew never had the patronising air of someone praying for your soul, but there had been times when David, wallowing in a trough of alcoholic or sexual remorse, had hoped that Drew did just that – pray for him, that is.

'I trust you're joking,' Drew laughed. 'About resigning, I mean. I would be very sorry to see you go.' He paused as, gently, almost reverently, he withdrew the endotracheal tube. He did not take his eyes off the patient's face as he added, 'And I don't mean just because of the private work.'

'I know that, Digger.' David joined in the vigil over the semi-conscious patient. If he had damaged the recurrent laryngeal nerves during the operation, paralysing both her vocal cords, now was the moment of truth. For a short period they held two conversations simultaneously.

'Want me to look at them?' Drew asked.

David watched a few more quiet breaths. He had heard, as an impressionable young man, the terrifying stridor of paralysed cords, witnessed the horror of the permanent tracheostomy in a young woman. He shook his head.

'Sounds all right. I don't think I got anywhere near them really. But I must admit, jacking in my sessions here has crossed my mind.'

He had more private work now than he could handle. He was caught in that much-sought-after dilemma; how to cut his private practice down to reasonable proportions without running the risk of losing it altogether; how to cut out the middle class, the ones with the building society accounts and a few unit trusts, who liked to say they'd been seen in Harley Street but couldn't afford the operation privately; how to distil the brew down to the vintage stuff – Mayfair and the Middle East, Belgravia and the board room, Ascot and Mustique. Should he double his fees? The old hands had warned him against that; that could double his practice. It was difficult. What *was* certain was that the cases sent him by the local GPs around the Merton, so useful in priming the pump, would be no great loss to him now.

If Drew could read his thoughts, he did not show it.

'Don't do that, David.' He leaned forward to shout in the

patient's ear – a few words in reply would be added proof of functioning vocal cords. All he got were low groans. They would have to do – anything was better than stridor. 'You're our last real link with the teaching school now and we wouldn't want to lose that. Brian's all right, really. A bit paranoid, perhaps, but he's a good operator. You can forgive a lot then, can't you? It's a pity you both work in theatre the same day. Would you like me to see if we can change things round a bit?'

'Just not possible, Digger. Far too complicated. Let things stand for now. But that's the last case he ever gets from me, the pompous bastard, RSM or no RSM.'

'Poor Brian.' Drew was a generous man. 'You can't help feeling sorry for him. Try and see it from his angle, David. To him, you are everything he would have liked to be. To him, you epitomise success. And for him? Well – now that the College is finished as far as he is concerned, President of his section of the Royal Society of Medicine is his last chance of fame. Heaven forbid anything should go wrong with that. I just don't know how he'd handle that.'

Drew, his eyes half closed, looked sideways at David.

'What was Brian on about, wild parties? What does he know about wild parties?'

David shook his head.

'Can't imagine,' he said.

David always knew when he was frightened – really frightened. Sudden fear always produced the same reaction, a mass contraction of his large gut which had him looking for the nearest loo. It had been like that since early childhood. Others might find their mouths going dry, or vomit, or cringe to the throbbing, thumping pain at the base of their skulls, but to David, fear was the purgative above all others.

His appointments were already running ten minutes late, his next patient was from a family named in the Doomsday Book, and it was difficult to feel one's suavest with a loaded bowel.

It would have helped if he had known precisely why he was suddenly so scared. The voice had been friendly enough. Perhaps it had been the brevity, the overtones of senior and junior, the routine jargon used in a call anything but routine. He stared for a moment longer at his desk top before picking up the phone. It was a day when Jackie worked at home – happiness was peace and quiet and a big fat manuscript. He rang the upstairs extension.

'Yes?'

Quick, sharp, businesslike. He felt like a temp who had got through to the managing director by mistake.

'I've just had a phone call from Reggie Bevington asking if he could come and see us this evening. I said seven o'clock; is that all right?'

'Not really. I've arranged to eat about then. Can't you see him down there?'

'He wants to see both of us.'

'Both of us? What on earth for?'

'I haven't the remotest idea.'

'But they're due to come to dinner on Saturday night. What can he possibly want that can't wait until then?'

'He didn't say.'

'But he's coming at seven – you've fixed that?'

'Yes.'

'Nothing much we can do about it then, is there?'

The phone lay dead in his hand for some seconds before he put it down. His face crinkled as another wave of rumbling contractions sped across his lower abdomen. Did he have time? No. He rang Martha, asking her to show the next patient in.

At ten minutes to seven, David stood in his own waiting room, listening. At five to seven, he heard the doorbell ring. An ex-naval man, bluff and erect in his double-breasted dark blue suit, Reggie Bevington, President of the Surgical Section of the RSM, stood four-square on the doorstep. Upstairs, he blushed with pleasure as Jackie kissed him. Disconcertingly clear blue eyes beamed from under shaggy eyebrows at her show of affection. He huffed and puffed his way to the most comfortable-looking chair.

A drink? A bit too early – which it was not. Had he eaten? A sandwich perhaps? Most kind – but May would have something waiting for him.

He was always difficult to talk to before his first gin and tonic, and a conversational chasm now yawned. He sat, obviously embarrassed, searching for something to say. Jackie shot enquiring glances at her husband across the silence.

'Real reason for coming to see you . . . Bit embarrassing really . . .' One hand fumbled with a College tie. 'It's not for me to pry into family matters but . . . How can I put it?'

Bevington's shoulders came back and he looked fearlessly at them both.

'A week last Saturday night,' he blurted. 'I imagine you would have been together somewhere? Opera perhaps? Out to dinner together?'

Eyes half closed, Jackie searched the old man's face. 'Yes. Of course,' she murmured vaguely. To David, the rumbles now sounded deafening as contractions complained at the thrice-emptied bowel.

'Difficult to explain . . . Rather you didn't press me. But I have my reasons for asking such a personal question. I would quite understand if you told me to mind my own business, but it would be a great comfort to me to know you were together that night.'

'Of course.' David, struggling to keep a look of surprised, innocent enquiry on his face, heard Jackie's crisp, confident voice as if from afar. It was Jacqueline Lee once more, competent, taking charge, her mind quicker, less fuddled with vague passions than his. 'That was the weekend we went sailing, wasn't it, darling?' He heard her leading him. He felt himself nod his head. 'We went round to Poole; tied up for the night there.' She glared furiously at her husband, looking for support that was not forthcoming.

Relief spread over Reggie Bevington's honest face. 'I'm so pleased to hear that. And I'm grateful to you both for not nagging me to find out why I wanted to know. There has obviously been some misunderstanding and I really think the rest is best left unsaid. Will you trust me?' He stood up, the avuncular doyen of surgery once more. 'Least said, soonest mended, as they say, what?' He radiated genuine affection as he walked beside Jackie to the door – the headmaster and the parent leaving the room, the naughtiest boy in the class following behind.

'And, of course, you've kindly asked us to dinner on Saturday. May and I are looking forward to that so much. We still talk of the meal you served the last time we came. How you manage to do it all, Jacqueline, with a busy career of your own to contend with, May and I can't imagine. We were only saying the other night . . .'

Jackie went back into the apartment, leaving her husband to walk down the broad stairway beside Bevinton.

'Where have you left your car, Reggie?' he asked.

'It's round in the mews.' Bevington's smile had lost some of its warmth. 'Parking's always a problem here, isn't it? Perhaps you'd walk round with me.'

The immaculate, twenty-year-old Rolls stood gleaming in the evening light. Sitting behind the wheel, Bevington wound the window down. He then leaned across to unlock the glove compartment and extracted some photographs, big, black and white, unmounted, slightly curved, professional looking. Without a word, he handed then to David through the open window. To one was stapled a scrap of newspaper bearing the date, nothing more. One picture would have been enough. There had been no need to take so many. Even at that range, there was no doubting the beauty of the woman in the long evening dress, holding on to the man struggling against the attentions of two naked girls.

'Came addressed to me at the College, in a plain envelope with a London postmark. They were inside this.'

Bevington handed David a folded sheet. He saw the College notepaper, the list of Fellows who had been eligible for the last election to the Council, the red question marks that bracketed his name.

'So we must accept you've got a double,' Bevington said drily. 'But what is blindingly obvious is that you also have someone who hates your guts. That could be awkward. You need to be careful.' He nodded to the prints. 'I don't know if there are any more of those around the College, but I'll make discreet enquiries and put minds at rest if there are. There would never be any question of official action, of course, unless someone came out into the open and made a specific allegation. But this sort of thing never does anyone any good.'

David hung his head. 'Thank you, Reggie,' he murmured.

Bevington reached for the starter and changed his mind.

'That's one hell of a fine girl you've got up there, David. You realise that, don't you?'

'I do.' Hadn't he been told so often enough?

'You are both so successful in your own fields, I would hate to see things go wrong for you. And you could go all the way, David – you have it in you. You have the knack of being in the right place at the right time. I'd hate to see you make a mess of it.' He looked at his hands for a moment, giving a short, bitter laugh. 'I know what people think of me. Good old Reggie; bloody good surgeon in his days, but a bit thick, a bit pompous. But I wasn't always an old man.' A distant expression changed his face. 'I came *this* close to coming a cropper myself once.' A stubby forefinger and powerful thumb were held up, microns apart. 'Would have done if it hadn't been for the generosity of spirit of a very wonderful woman. One word from her and I would have been struck off – probably have ended up a rep peddling pills in your outpatients. So, David – ' this time he did start the engine – 'you don't have to have been an angel all your life to be on the Council. Come to think of it,' he laughed, 'there'd be damn few of us there if you had. But now you are on, and if you have a problem you can't control, all we ask is that you should be discreet. It would be foolish to take it for granted that everyone would rally round a second time. Goodbye now, David. Look forward to seeing you on Saturday.'

'Thank you, Reggie. I'm grateful to you,' was all David could say before the car purred away.

He stood in the deserted mews, looking at what he held in his hands. What should he do with them? The nearest dustbin – his mind sketched in the picture of some bum picking amongst the garbage with enough intelligence left in his pickled cortex to recognise the value of such candid camera work. Burn them – where the hell, in central London, in an oil-fired, centrally heated apartment with no garden, does one burn incriminating evidence? A few minutes later, he was locking them in his desk drawer.

A sticky time waited for him upstairs – he knew that – but it was not a desire to put off the evil hour that kept him in his seat. With the slow movements of some hideous compulsion, he unlocked the drawer again, laid the photographs on the desk in front of him and stared at them. He looked up for a moment, wondering whether he should lock the door, deciding there was no need. Jackie never put a foot in his rooms. Only when duty-bound did she enter in any way into his professional life.

He had been a bloody fool. He had come close to ruining his career – again. He was not going to be asked to resign from the Council, that much was obvious from what Reggie had said. He closed his eyes and shivered at the thought. But the Presidency. What of that? Who was to know how many more of those photographs were being passed from hand to hand. He imagined the sniggers.

But it would be several years before he could hope to appear in the frame for the Presidency. Memories faded. There was always plenty to gossip about in the macho branch of the profession. He simply must be more careful from now on. Looking back, it had been a seedy, sordid business. He had not really belonged amongst that uneducated rabble of *nouveaux riches*. The most sophisticated person there had turned out to be a hooker. He could do better than that. So – the photographs. Wait until he was alone, tear the shiny print into small fragments, and slowly, methodically, flush them down the loo. Cut across young breasts, firm thighs, rip through hair he knew was the colour of chestnuts – that was the thing to do. Why then was he going to risk the chance of their discovery by locking them away in the drawer again as he knew, in his heart of hearts, he would? Because – he leaned closer over the top of his desk, screwing his eyes up as he fought for the last detail in a face, the curve of a hip – because he was honest enough to admit that, if Gemma Ainsleigh were to walk through the door at that moment and crook her finger, with the sound of Jackie's footsteps on the floor above, there would be nothing he could do about it. He gave a tiny laugh within himself as he felt the first embryonic kick of excitement. He had to have it. Another laugh just broke the surface. Let's face it, it was his 'little weakness'. In the years ahead, there would be plenty of others only too ready to crook their finger at one of the most successful surgeons in London. 'All we ask is that you should be discreet,' Reggie had said. Half the thrill was in getting away with it, kidding yourself people did not know.

A few minutes later, he faced his wife.

'And what the hell was all that about?'

He denied himself the beckoning decanter – better keep his wits about him.

'Not too sure, Jackie. Reggie was a bit vague, wasn't he?'

'Having just lied through my teeth for you and having had someone I respect know perfectly well I was doing so, you are going to have to come up with something better than that. The weekend before last, I was in Edinburgh. Where were you that Saturday night?'

'At a party – a rather wild party. Things got a bit out of hand.'

'Where?'

'In Wimbledon.'

'Where in Wimbledon?'

'At Mal's'

'Who?'

'Mal Evans. I've told you about him.'

'Oh, *him*.'

She let the scorn in her voice sink in before going on.

'Were the police involved?'

'Don't be ridiculous. Of course not.' He made the very idea sound inconceivable.

'So what was it then? No,' – she held up her hand as he prepared to fight his rearguard action to the bitter end – 'let me work it out. It's got to be a woman. Though you drink far too much, you're no lush, I'll say that much for you; you usually manage not to make a fool of yourself that way. Cards, I know, bore you to the back teeth, so it's not gambling. You're not into drugs – are you? – so it's *got* to be a woman. But why Reggie? You're not at the same hospital – so it's got to be something to do with the College. And, if the College is involved, that means someone at the party must have spilled the beans. Were there any other doctors there?'

'Not that I know of. It wasn't that sort of party. They were a pretty rough lot, looking back. As I say, things just got a bit wild. I don't see why you say it has to be a woman.'

'Don't you? Because I know you, David Royall, better than you think I do. Women are your weakness. They're your addiction, and I can understand that you have to have your fix every now and again to keep you going. I came to terms with that a long time ago. Don't imagine I haven't smelled them on you often enough.' She tilted her head to one side, a sure sign she was intrigued. 'Funny, isn't it?' She laughed. 'If it was booze or drugs, it would be quite simple. I could nag you into going to AA or Narcotics Anonymous. But there's no such organisation for you poor sex addicts, is there?'

She held her hand up again as he made a show of objecting. He had already decided there was no percentage in a stand-up, knock-down slanging match. He had lost out to her, arguing from far more favourable positions. Better to let her run her course; get it out of her system.

'Don't worry, David. I'm not bothered. If you want to prance all over Mayfair and Belgravia like some rutting stag, that's your affair. Your one-night stands don't concern me as long as they do not involve me. And, if I was to be completely honest with myself' – there was a catch in her voice – 'perhaps I should take some of the blame for your behaviour anyway. But' – the cutting edge returned – 'I am not lying for you again. Is that clear? And, one other thing.' Her voice dropped as her jaw jutted. 'If I were to find that you were having an affair with anyone, a real affair, that would be different. We've got Debbie to think of. She is at a stage when she needs a home and a mother *and* a father. For her sake, and her sake alone, I'd have any woman's *guts* who tried to come between us. And don't forget.' She gave a short, barking laugh. 'An ambitous Member of Council, with a President coming to the end of his term, needs a divorce like a hole in the head.'

David looked at his wife's face. It was composed, almost

serene. Violent emotion had been one word long, no more – but all the more dramatic for that fact. She probably looked and sounded like that when giving her opinion on a manuscript at an editorial meeting. He would have preferred fury, even controlled fury; something that hinted at some slight feeling of insecurity, some vulnerability that, once the storm was over, might reach out towards him. How can you love someone who does not need you, not even now and again? After all, some of the fiercest fights often ended in bed.

'And what about Frankfurt?' he sniped. 'When was it – two, three years ago?' Mean bastard. He had been waiting for years for that one, longing for the moment when she overstretched herself, left herself open for the knife thrust.

'What about Frankfurt?' She didn't back away, simply going on the defensive as a flush spread upwards from her neck.

'You forget, darling – I spend half my time observing people. It's my job and I'm good at it. You deal with words, written on dead trees. I deal with living people. You were on cloud nine, coming back from Frankfurt that time – you didn't need an aeroplane. You were in love, Jackie. One didn't have to be the best diagnostician in London to see that – the postman could have told you.'

It took a few seconds for Jackie to think about lying for the second time that evening.

'That was over almost before it started.' Her mouth hardened. 'I saw to that.'

9

Snugly cocooned, David eased his car confidently through the traffic swirling around the Elephant and Castle. It looked like being a hard winter. He could not remember it so cold in late November. He spared a pitying glance for the pinched faces in the bus queues, wizened by the piercing chill of an east wind.

Poor sods – but then, it would be a dull world if everyone drove around in BMWs.

A few minutes later, he was in amongst the narrow suburban streets that surrounded Queen's College Hospital, their pavements deserted in the lunch hour. Rusting cars listed into littered gutters outside run-down houses converted into bed-sits. Here and there, secluded, intimate squares showed the gloss paint, wrought iron and XR3Is of early metastatic yuppiedom, but the predominant colour was dusty grey, the midday gloom only accentuated by the glimmer of coloured lights from pub window or corner shop.

They had been digging up the same gas main for months, long enough for the man operating the temporary traffic lights to have perfected his art. With the precision of a knife thrower, he let a lorry and an ambulance through before bringing the rich bastard's car to a halt. Power to the masses. He thrust his head forward, ready to stare David down, grinning, oblivious to the cold in his filthy T-shirt, rippling the tattoos on bulging deltoids and triceps. He saw the drumming fingers on the steering wheel and took to himself the full credit for the sign of frustration. He was mistaken – but how was he to know that Digger Drew, of all people, had let David down?

A total gastrectomy, a gall bladder and a veins – not to be sniffed at. And to have let him down at such short notice. Not that there had been any difficulty in finding a replacement, there was always someone poised, ready to pounce where another had faltered. It had been Drew's attitude that David had found so irritating – as if there were more important things, that he hadn't had time to explain. He knew Drew was not *that* concerned about money – but, hell, a total gastrectomy, a gall bladder and veins.

He stared ahead as he drove past the man controlling the lights. He clucked his annoyance as, turning in at the hospital gates, a student in a rusting red Spitfire cut in ahead of him, making him brake sharply. A medical student waving like that to a consultant surgeon. There was no respect any more.

Queen's College Hospital was basically an old Victorian workhouse, its high surrounding wall still intact. Just within the walls and encircling the central modern development was a ring of the original three-storey stone buildings, standing like prison cellblocks with their ugly external fire escapes and narrow grimy windows. Buddleia, blackened and withered by frost and exhaust fumes, sprouted from the crumbling walls where two of the blocks lay derelict, awaiting demolition. In stark contrast, the central building, all gloss and sharp edges, towered high above them as befitted the more prestigious disciplines housed within it, the specialities at the top of a pecking order forged out of generations of feudal conflict between the barons of the profession. The physicians, top of the heap on account of their self-confessed intelligence; the surgeons, the prima donnas of the other theatre, snapping at their heels; the obstetricians, their case torn between the dignity of motherhood and the indignity of parturition, a close third. To the peripheral blocks, with their Nightingale-style wards, had been banished the less glamorous departments, the ones with least political clout – Dermatology, Geriatrics. And the bottom line had been drawn – Psycho-geriatrics had not 'made the cut'. It was out there somewhere, outside the wall, in decent obscurity, together with all other kinds of mental illness. Back within the walls, fighting for every bed and office in the hotchpotch of temporary buildings that filled every inch of space between these architectural extremes, came the rest of the innumerable departmental subdivisions that go to make up a modern teaching hospital.

All turned jealous eyes on the Merton, only a few miles down the road. How the hell had they managed it? – a spanking-new hospital, purpose-built on a virgin site. All that money going on a non-teaching hospital. A good DGH as DGHs went – no one would deny that – but . . . but . . . competent, that was the word. Good, solid competent staff, but with no real stars. No one at the Merton was likely to win a Nobel Prize, whilst they, at Queen's . . .

And yet – those run-of-the-mill competents at the Merton still seemed to attract all the good clinical material. In his outpatient clinic at the Merton, David found the occasional student an added burden as he strove to cope with the stream of surgical pathology that came his way. At Queen's, he found himself scratching for physical signs to satisfy the eager minds that seemed to be perpetually at his back.

The afternoon had been no exception. He had done his best to teach on what the sister had led in through the door. He twisted uncomfortably in his seat to face them once more in his struggle to rouse their interest. Surgery in the abstract. Anecdotal. Laboured. Young faces looked back at him, their features spelling it out. Couldn't he do better than that? Was that all he had to offer? They would have been better off in the library. David gave up. Sod 'em. No skin off his nose. He turned back to his next patient, sitting meekly beside his desk.

His smile hardened at the sight of the man. His forehead furrowed as two things registered: one, this guy was ill; two, he'd seen him before.

'Good afternoon, Mr . . .' He looked down at the thick folder stuffed full of multicoloured forms. He flicked it open, anywhere, to read the man's name. 'Of course – John Lever. I remember now. How are you, Mr Lever?'

'A bit rough, sir.' Lever smiled a slow, brave, philosophical smile.

'And what's the trouble?' As if he did not know. The yellow-grey skin, the Auschwitz face with the big appealing eyes.

The only answer he got was a shrug of the shoulders.

'Any pain?'

'Bit.'

'Where?'

A vague sweep of the hand.

'And how's the appetite, Mr Lever? Are you eating well?'

Lever's face showed compassion for someone who could ask such a stupid question. 'Not so much as you could put in your eye, Mr Royall.' He'd said that the last time they'd met.

'And your weight? How's that keeping?'

'Falling off me.' He pulled back a sleeve, sending waves through folds of skin hanging from his forearms.

'We'd better have a look at you then, hadn't we?' David saw the weary glance that flickered at the students. 'Don't worry, Mr Lever – just me.'

Lever began to rise, but David put out a hand to stop him.

'When did you see Mr Pullman last, Mr Lever?'

'Not since the operation, Mr Royall.'

'Have you not seen anyone?'

'I saw one of the doctors in the clinic about three weeks after I left hospital.'

'Nothing since then?'

'No.' The smile returned. 'How is Mr Pullman? All right, is he?'

'Yes; he's fine.'

'Wonderful man, Mr Royall; wonderful man. I will always be grateful to you for sending me to see him.'

'Ye-es.' The drawl was there for everyone to hear. Why not? David felt he was allowed it. Lever was a gentle man, a polite man, but, in his gentle, polite way, he had given everyone the clear message that he was seeing David only because he was too gentle and polite to buck the system. His GP had sent him to Queen's and Mr Royall – so Queen's and Mr Royall it had to be. The Levers of this world do what they are told.

'Go along with Sister, Mr Lever. I'll come and have a look at you shortly.'

The examination was carried out in silence. The flat of the hand pushing lax skin across a wasted abdomen, the tips of the fingers probing up under the rib margin, the head cocked to one side, listening to the tapping fingers. Nothing. No liver. No fluid. The glove, the lubricant, the murmured, hypnotic words – and the truth. The gritty, fixed, iron-hard mass – a pelvis set in malignant concrete.

By the time Lever had rolled on to his back once more, David had pulled on a bland, mask-like look as easily as slipping a car into neutral. He tried not to notice the appeal in the man's face.

'Well, Mr Lever. I think you need a few tests done to find out exactly what is going on.'

'That means *you're* not quite sure what's going on, Mr Royall?' Translation – Mr Pullman would know.

'Well . . .' What the hell. Why bother? There was no joy in this guy for anyone. Why not let Pullman look after his own cockup? It was only right, that he should see what he'd done to the poor old devil. After all, Lever was included in the famous series. Pullman would not be pleased. Lever was going to spoil the figures somewhat. 'How would you feel about going back to see Mr Pullman at the Merton again?' Something inside David cringed as he saw the hope in a face transformed. 'He'll have all your notes over there.' Let's hear the bastard talk his way out of this one. 'He'll remember exactly what he did to you.' That'll take the oily grin off his face. 'How would you feel about that?'

'I'd appreciate that, Mr Royall. I didn't like to ask – you know . . . But my wife and I have such great faith in Mr Pullman. No disrespect, Mr Royall, but think the world of Mr Pullman, we do.'

David nodded. Idols with feet of clay. No problems there with Pullman – clay all through.

'I'll fix that up then, Mr Lever. You dress up now and wait outside while I have a word with your wife. She is here, is she?'

'Sitting outside, Mr Royall. And' – he held out his hand – 'thank you.'

The gentle, trusting man had a gentle, trusting wife, the type who left it all to the important man in the white coat, the type so impossible to talk to, so happy was she to leave it all to the experts. No discussion, no feedback, no demands for the truth. Damn sight more difficult to handle than the belligerent ones, the intellectuals, the searchers after truth, those that argued from the premise that there must have been a cockup, that someone else could have done better. What should he say to her, knowing she would accept whatever that was without a single doubt? Sod it – why didn't she say *something*, give him *something* to work on? Your husband is going to die because a colleague of mine has done an inadequate operation on him and I asked him to do it. How about that for starters? And, if I had done my usual operation, the chances are that he would have been good for the next ten years. But was that true? Had he never had a similar result? Could he guarantee no case of his would come back with a pelvis full of tumour in the future? Would he never have cause to hope that some surgeon, in some other hospital, would not let him down, criticise his management in front of the patient? Surgery was rough enough without jealous colleagues pulling the rug out from under you. Didn't they all *have* to close ranks around each other, even around such pompous shits as Pullman? He switched on the charm.

'I've just seen your husband, Mrs Lever.'

'Oh.'

'He's a very sick man – you realise that, don't you?'

'He has been a bit peaky, Doctor.'

Peaky. You stupid bloody woman. Your husband's going to die, in all probability unnecessarily, and I had a hand in it.

'I think it's rather more than that, Mrs Lever.'

'Oh.'

The calibrated smile, the carefully graduated sentences that went with breaking bad news, all projected at someone with the reflective powers of a lump of dough.

'I can't be certain – he will need to be examined more thoroughly – but I think . . .'

'Mr Pullman said he'd be a new man. That's what Mr Pullman said before the operation.'

At last – *something* – something to latch on to. She'd thrown him the lifeline he'd hoped for. Let Pullman talk his way out of his own particular load of crap.

'I was just going to say – Mr Lever has agreed to go back and see Mr Pullman again. I've told him I'll fix it up as soon as I can.'

Did she *have* to look so relieved?

'Thank you, Doctor – Mr Royall, sir. No disrespect, but I know John has such faith in Mr Pullman. You understand. No offence, like.'

An hour later, his secretary sat at the desk with pad and pencil – David had an aversion to all forms of recording machine. The clinic was over, the sullen, ungrateful students dismissed. After more than five years of working together they were still Mr Royall and Mrs Spencer, and that was the way both liked it. When it came to Lever's notes, David weighed them in his hand thoughtfully. He dictated a short note to the GP and then hesitated. Mrs Spencer looked up, raising one eyebrow.

'I'd better keep these notes. I'll fix that poor devil's appointment with Mr Pullman myself the next time I'm in the Merton.

I'll make a point of seeing him. I think that's the safest way to do it.'

'In other words, you lose the notes and I get the blame for it.' The corners of her generous mouth twitched. ''Twas ever thus. Let me have the front sheet for his details then, if you don't trust me to make a simple appointment after all these years.' She looked him straight between the eyes. 'Or is it that you want to deliver the *coup de grâce* yourself?'

'Mrs Spencer,' he laughed, 'you've been in this job too long.'

'I wouldn't argue with you there, Mr Royall.'

Once more, David hesitated. Why? Why was he going to the bother of making the appointment himself? Out of consideration for Lever? Or was she right? Was it just to see the look on that bastard's face?

'Perhaps you're right. Life's too short.' He handed the bundle of notes over. 'Perhaps you'd be kind enough to do the necessary.'

Swiftly, efficiently, they sped through the rest of the paperwork. Before bundling the notes together, ready to leave, she tore a sheet from her notebook and slid it over the desk towards him.

'What's that?' he asked.

'Dr Drew from the Merton. He rang earlier; said not to bother you during your clinic, but could you ring him the moment you'd finished?'

'Where?'

'The number's there.' She pointed to the paper. 'His home number, I imagine. It isn't the Merton's.'

David sighed. A total gastrectomy, a gall bladder and a veins demanded a visit before he got home.

'All right. Thank you, Mrs Spencer.'

'Thank you, Mr Royall. Don't forget to call Dr Drew, now.'

'Go home,' he grinned. 'Haven't you got a husband to nag? I won't forget.'

Forget to ring the man who had let him down that morning?

'Thank you for ringing, David.'

The hard edge to the voice was the same as when he had rung to cry off from the private cases, only more marked. David now recognised it for what it was, anxiety.

'Sorry to bother you like this. You've had a busy day.'

'No problem. What's the trouble?' David's tone was neutral, a decision on forgiveness deferred pending further information.

'Can I ask a favour?'

A total gastrectomy, a gall bladder and a veins, all with a strange anaesthetist, and now he asks a favour.

'Yes, of course.'

'It's John, I'm worried about him, David. Could I ask you to come and see him? I know how busy you are – normally I would have brought him up to hospital – but he can be a bit awkward at times, particularly when he's not feeling well. He tends to have the odd tantrum that can be a bit embarrassing.'

Shit. 'Of course. I'll be there in twenty minutes.'

Drew's home was a private place, rarely spoken of. David had often tried to visualise it.

The small detached house was set in a garden, immaculate even in midwinter and surrounded by neatly clipped privet. It was the end house of a long avenue, and alongside it was a large rectangular single-storey building. An old petrol station and garage – Royall could see the rusting bolts, standing proud in the oil-stained concrete forecourt, where the pumps had been. Parked in front was a spotless white minibus. The front door to the house opened before he had a chance to close the garden gate.

'Thank you for coming, David. He's upstairs.' No mention of total gastrectomies or gall bladders or letting surgeons down at the last minute. 'There's something wrong with him – I'm sure of that. He's got no temperature, but normally he's got a good appetite, and he hasn't eaten a thing for two days. We're pretty sure he was sick in the bathroom this morning – you could smell it – but he must have cleared it all up himself. And he's very agitated. You won't find him easy, David.'

'How old is he, Digger?'

'Twenty-two. It's probably nothing, but I'd feel happier if

you'd put a hand on his abdomen.' Drew paused, embarrassed. 'He's very precious.'

At the top of the stairs, dressed neatly in plain jumper and skirt, stood Drew's wife, Mary, the concern on her face giving way briefly to a welcoming smile. Inside the bedroom, David was confronted by a hefty young man, pacing restlessly from one end to the other.

'This is Mr Royall, the surgeon, John.' Somehow, David had expected Drew to shout and he was surprised just how quietly and gently he spoke. 'I told you he was coming to see you, didn't I?'

'Mr Royall, the surgeon.' John Drew stopped his pacing for a moment to see what a surgeon, called David Royall, looked like.

David saw the keloid scars on the left cheek and temple of a face that would have been handsome except for the out-of-focus look that his mental handicap had given him. Though stooped, he was still tall, with the wide shoulders and narrow waist of an athlete. It was his arms and legs that seemed out of proportion, long and gangling, with tiny hands and large, flat feet.

'You must tell Mr Royall if you feel anything wrong now, John.'

'I must tell Mr Royall if I feel anything wrong.' The pacing started again, his arms jerking and waving.

'Have you got any pain, John?' David asked.

'Pain. Mr Royall, the surgeon.'

'He's not normally like this,' Drew said. He turned to his son. 'Life and soul of the party usually, aren't you, John?'

Deciding there was no future in trying to get a history from him, David looked enquiringly at Drew. 'What are the chances of having a look at his abdomen?'

'Mr Royall would like to have a look at your tummy, John. Pop up on your bed for a moment.'

His son jumped on the bed so violently as to bounce on the springs.

'He's moving freely enough, Digger,' David muttered.

'Doesn't feel much pain,' Drew said. 'He broke his wrist when he was a kid and we didn't realise it for two days; just thought he'd sprained it.'

Drew sat at the head of the bed, taking his son's head on his thigh as David laid his chest and abdomen bare. Only then did he appreciate the true extent of the burns down the left side of John's trunk and buttocks. Drew must be seeing them also. How often did he see them – every time he felt like having another drink? Cheaper and quicker to lift his son's shirt than put a call through to AA. David concentrated on trying to examine a constantly writhing abdomen, searching John's face as he did so for the slightest reaction. Shrugging his shoulders, he covered John up again.

'Impossible to say, Digger. I should do a rectal really, but I imagine that might be a bit difficult.'

Drew nodded.

'Let's wait and see. If anything happens, anything at all, let me know and we'll admit him and keep an eye on him.'

Relieved, Drew ruffled his son's hair. 'There you are, John. You wouldn't mind going into hospital with Mr Royall if you had to, would you?'

'Mr Royall, the surgeon. He's a nice man.'

'But you'll probably be all right again tomorrow. And we've got all those breeze blocks to move, haven't we?'

'And who's going to mix the cement?' John Drew tucked his shirt in hurriedly as if he was late for work.

Downstairs again, David found himself gently but insistently diverted into a room where a table was laid. A smiling Mary Drew pulled back a chair.

'Sit down. You've had a long day. No time for lunch, I expect? No? I thought not. You shouldn't go so long without food. What time did you leave home this morning? Eight? You started *operating* at eight o'clock?' She clucked her tongue disapprovingly. 'You work too hard. You're all the same.'

For a brief moment, David thought of all the usual excuses but, with a sense of relief that surprised him, he sat down with a sigh. 'Thank you,' he said. 'That looks marvellous.'

Plates of sliced cooked ham and cold beef. Dishes of salad surrounding an assortment of chutney and pickle bottles. Butter melting in the clefts of hot jacket potatoes. An old-fashioned cracker barrel standing beside the cheese board, a large circular fruit cake proudly bringing up the rear. A Cory Street birthday treat. David was about to reach for a plate when, just in time, he saw Mary Drew's head bow. Hesitating, he snatched his hand back as he heard Digger say grace. There was something comforting to the soul about the way Drew stood at the head of the table for the ritual of breaking bread.

There was little time for conversation – he had not realised just how hungry he had been – and he was balancing some crumbly Stilton on a biscuit before he found the chance to tell them the news that had been bursting inside him all day.

'I must admit I've found it rather difficult to keep my mind on my job today.' He waited until he held their full attention. 'I had confirmation this morning – I'm off to the Middle East next week.'

Bingo. Bull's-eye. His sudden statement, timed to perfection, had the desired result.

Drew put down his cup of tea. 'Good heavens – where?'

'The Middle East.'

'Yes – but where in the Middle East?'

'Secret,' David grinned, enjoying himself. 'I'm not allowed to tell you. They're anxious to keep it as quiet as possible. The man from the Foreign Office made that point very strongly.'

'Foreign Office.' Drew nodded slowly, his mouth downturned to show he was impressed. 'Someone pretty important then.'

'Their crown prince, no less.'

'Oh, my goodness.' Mary Drew's gentle voice came from his left. 'That really is a feather in your cap, David. I'm so pleased for you.'

'That's going to turn a few faces green in Harley Street,' Drew chuckled. 'You can't do much better than that, short of our own royal family. What's the matter with him, d'you know?'

'Difficulty in swallowing.'

'And how old?'

'Fifty-one. His father's a very old man.'

'Oh.' Drew pulled a face. 'Not so good.'

'Why do you say that?' Mary Drew asked.

'Most likely a cancer of his gullet at that age,' Drew explained. 'That's right, isn't it?' He looked to David for confirmation.

''Fraid so.'

'Poor man. Can it be cured?'

With a movement of his head, Drew referred the question to David.

'Let's put it this way – by the sound of it, he'll be lucky to be around to succeed his father.' David pushed his chair back, giving himself room to cross his legs. 'How d'you fancy anaesthetising a crown prince then, Digger? Because one thing's for sure – I'm not opening any chests over there. I'll endoscope him out there if necessary, but if he needs anything major done he'll have to come over here or they can find someone else.'

'They're all the same to me, David.'

'You'll be able to build that place of yours with gold bricks then, not breeze blocks. Get him home in one piece, swallowing again, and perhaps they'll build the whole thing for you.'

'And defeat the object? No, thank you. Breeze blocks will do John and me fine. But I'm delighted for you, David; I really am. The only problem is, of course, where do you go from there? Not much left after that, is there?'

'Well – as you say,' David grinned. 'That only leaves the royal family. Perhaps, one day . . .'

He stood up, smiling gratefully at Mary Drew. 'Mary – I haven't had high tea like that for many, many years. All I can say is what my mother taught me to say as a very small boy – "thank you for my lovely supper".'

Out in the hall, they paused, tilting their heads to the steady thump of heavy shoes pacing the floor above, and David felt again the Drews' anxiety, put aside so hospitably during the meal.

'As I said – any development there, Digger' – he pointed up the stairs – 'and you know where to find me. Any time, now, d'you hear? Night or day. Don't hesitate to call me.'

Vast undulating deserts, bubbling, bottomless pools of black oil, gold bricks and Cadillacs. Tired and excited, David stared vertically upwards, trying to empty his mind so that sleep could pour in. Consciously, he strove to blot them out, one by one, to leave the blackness void. With success within his reach, came tinkling fountains and concubines, white flowing robes and curved, bejewelled scabbards. The final, precipitous plunge into sleep was deep and, ten minutes later, he was deaf to the phone less than two feet from his ear, half waking only as Jacqueline shook him, stretching her body across the gap between the beds to do so.

His fumbling grasp sent the phone thudding into the carpet, but an Australian accent, sharpened by anxiety, cut through the thick pile.

'Hullo, David. Are you there?'

One or two vague gropes and David was asleep once more. The phone, picked up and thrown – Jackie's flight from Heathrow was at eight-thirty – rapped his skull.

'Yeah.' The phone now wedged between ear and pillow, he pulled the bedclothes back over his shoulders.

'David? Is that you, David?'

'Yeah.'

'Are you awake?'

'Yeah, Digger. What's the problem?'

'John's much worse, David. He suddenly got crook about an hour ago. He vomited some pretty foul stuff and he's lying quite still now with a belly like a board.'

Silence.

Belly like a board – belly like a board – belly like a board. Drew's voice echoed in David's mind, rolling away ahead of him, leading him on with an awful inevitability. Belly like a board – to a layman, four words to wonder at, to ponder on; to a surgeon – ? David could visualise already the red thickened peritoneum, hear the fluid rattle up the sucker, smell the pus.

Bloody fool. He should have taken him into Queen's, let the boys there keep an eye on him, see him again in the morning. No registrar with an eye to his next reference would have dared ring him at three in the morning. Shit. Send him into Queen's, that's what he should have done, would have done for anyone else's son. Serve him bloody well right.

'David? Are you there?'

'Yeah, all right, Digger; I can hear you.' Jackie must have switched his bedside lamp on judging from the sudden dull glow that crimped eyelids failed to extinguish. 'If he's that bad, you'd better take him into Queen's. I'll see him there in twenty minutes.'

'I'm sorry, David, but I can't do that.'

'What?' Irritation forced his eyes open, pain closed them again. There was something, deeply embedded inside both eye sockets that refused to be convinced that ten minutes' deep sleep at three a.m. was enough. 'Why not?'

'I'm afraid it's got to be the Merton, David. I've explained to John we'll have to put him to sleep for a while to make him better, and he says he doesn't mind as long as I do it. I don't fancy it, as you can imagine, but I think anybody else might have an awful lot of trouble with him.'

'All right, Digger.' Opening his eyes separately left him with blurred double vision but seemed to have fooled the pain within. 'I'll be there as soon as I can. Will you warn them? Ask them to take him straight to theatre. I'll see him there.'

'Will do.'

His clothes, thrown on, felt uncomfortable – bespoke tailors can hardly be expected to cater for men who go to work in the early hours. His tongue seemed twice its normal size. He felt cold with the car heater on full boost, and he shivered as a prowling police patrol eyed him suspiciously as he drove across an otherwise deserted Vauxhall Bridge. The normally bustling hospital corridors were shadowy, deserted and silent. The theatre corridors, brilliantly lit, made his eyes ache.

One look, a hand on a rigid abdomen – that's all it took – and he nodded to Drew, tense at the end of the trolley. He turned to smile at a trusting face.

'Don't worry, John. Your Dad's going to put you to sleep now for a couple of minutes. When you wake up, you'll still have a bit of a sore tummy but you'll soon be better.'

'Mr Royall, the surgeon. He's a nice man. He's going to make me better.'

The smell of the perforated appendix is like no other. The

peritoneum opened, David felt Drew's eyes on his every movement as he sucked out the pus, delivered the appendix and removed it. Pop a drain in, fill him up with antibiotics, give him some intravenous fluids – big strong boy – piece of cake. With *his* pain threshold, he'd be running around in five days. Without surgery, he would have been as dead as a dodo long before that.

'Still the best operation we do, Digger.' Time to talk again. 'I've left a drain in just for safety. A Ryles tube and a drip for a day or so, fill him up with antibiotics, and he'll be fine. Don't worry. He's a big strong boy.'

'Thank you, David. I'm very grateful.'

'That's all right,' David said, relief and relaxation in his voice. 'I don't get to do these very often now. I hope I didn't look too rusty. If you'd been thinking straight, you'd have got one of the registrars to do this; they're doing them every day.'

'You'll do me fine, thank you, David. Only surgeons who operate on crown princes are good enough for my son.'

10

'Is Mrs Grainger at home?'

'Miss Grainger might be, sir. On the other hand, she might not.' The security guard obviously did not recognise a Master of Surgery when he saw one. 'Would she be expecting you, sir?'

He looked down his broken nose at what David held in his hands. His eyes did not move, neither did their expression of disdain, roused by the sight of a grown man carrying a bunch of flowers, change as he pocketed the note David slid across the desk.

'Still doesn't make me any the wiser whether Miss Grainger's at home or not, sir. But I could find out for you?'

His hand reached for the switch, but David stopped him.

'What are the chances of my going up to find out for myself?'

'None, sir . . .'

The mental processes triggered by the colour of the second note were painfully protracted. David stood waiting patiently. That the outcome was in his favour was signalled by the gargantuan shoulders and the battered head, so rigidly wedged between them, slowly turning towards the lift doors.

This time the man went up in the lift with him. He stood with his back holding the lift doors open as David rang the bell. Raising the flowers to hide his face, David waited until he heard the door to the flat open before slowly lowering them again.

Faye Grainger looked hard and long. The millisecond of weakness as her eyes flickered towards the flowers obviously irritated her, intensifying her scowl.

'You bastard,' she growled, then looked over his shoulder. 'It's all right, Joe. Nothing I can't handle. This one's just a pussycat really. He only thinks he's a tiger.'

As she turned her back on him, David heard the lift doors close behind him. He followed her in, holding the flowers in front of him like a mace bearer. When she turned, he confronted her with them. Hesitating for a moment, she snatched them from him angrily.

'You're a swine, David Royall.'

'I know.'

'A thoroughgoing, unmitigated swine.'

'I couldn't agree with you more.'

The flowers she now held obviously disturbed her as she struggled with the conflict between strength – which told her to throw them in his face – and weakness – the desire to bury her own face in them. Fascinated, he watched the battle of her hormones.

'What are you doing here anyway?' she asked as she looked round a room in which there seemed no place for cut flowers. She did not wait for an answer before taking them into the kitchen. 'How did you know I was in London?' he heard above the sound of running water.

'Mal told me. So I thought I'd better come to apologise.' Hearing no reply he followed her into the kitchen. 'I had no right to say what I did when I was here last. I'm sorry.'

'And so you damn well should be. No doubt you've got the idea that half the women in London are after your body. Well,

I've got news for you, Davy boy.' The stem of a red carnation snapped as she jabbed it into a vase. 'This woman is not. Understood?'

'No, Faye. I mean, yes, Faye.'

'Let's get a few facts straight, shall we? I could have sex seven days a week without having to cross the Atlantic and chase round after some ponced-up Harley Street specialist for it. Got that?'

'Yes, Faye.'

'And we might understand each other a little better if I were to tell you that, in my book, sexual intercourse is a grossly overrated pastime, not in the same street as beating a man in a man's world. Are you so goddamn macho you can't believe that?'

'No, Faye.'

'And can you also bring yourself to believe that it *is* possible for someone born in a Rhondda backstreet, with no education, to resist your fatal charm?'

'Absolutely, Faye.'

'And . . . And . . .' She shook the vase viciously, slopping water on the draining board. 'And . . . I never could arrange flowers.'

'No, Faye.'

Slowly, the anger left her face. She pouted at the chaotic shambles she held in her hand.

'You wouldn't believe it, would you, but it's less than six months since we ran a series on flower arranging. Didn't teach *me* much, did it?'

'Not your fault. Your flower editor – or whatever you call her – must have done a lousy job. You'd better give her the elbow when you get back and try again.'

'You're nice,' she said softly. 'But you're still a bastard. I suppose you want a drink now?'

'I'll settle for a coffee; it might be safer, remembering last time.'

He sat, watching the spasm in the muscles at the corners of her jaw as she ground the coffee.

'By the way,' he said, 'what am I supposed to call you? I ask for Mrs Grainger and Joe the Pug down there takes great delight in referring to you as *Miss* Grainger.'

'Don't talk about Joe like that. I think he's quite fond of me. Why do I have to be either? You don't have to label yourself in public to show whether you're married or not. Why should I? Why should I go round telling every roving, predatory male whether I'm available or not?'

'Oh, God. Another one of those. Will Ms do then?'

'Why do I have to be that either? Like some neutered cat.'

'Because you've got to be called something?'

'Why? My name's Faye Grainger – what's wrong with that? Take it or leave it.'

'But I can't just walk up and ask if Faye Grainger is at home?'

'Why not?' She slid a cup towards him.

'Because that's just not the way I've been brought up, I suppose.'

'Tough titty.'

He looked at her afresh, sober now, able to see her clearly.

'God,' he said, 'I'd hate to cross you in business. God forbid you should ever be a patient of mine.'

'I'll second that,' she retorted. 'No doubt you want your female patients to be like all the women in your fantasies, submissive, adoring and flat on their backs in bed. That's not my style, David. You should know that by now.'

They both laughed.

'Just look at you, sitting there,' Faye said. 'Typical spoiled brat. Obviously used to being waited on hand and foot. I bet you'd happily sit on your backside there watching your wife cook your meal. Do you ever cook *her* a meal?'

'Something tells me I'd better change the subject,' David said, grinning. 'What are you over in London for this time?'

Faye took her time in answering, obviously reluctant to abandon a subject where she had felt herself going forwards.

'I'm looking for a book to serialise, if you must know.' She returned to the flowers, giving them a few petulant prods, and scowled at the result. 'There are one or two I'm interested in. What about you? Anything exciting happened to you since I saw you last?'

'Yes.' He paused, enjoying the moment as he waited for her to hand him the initiative.

'Well?'

'I'm off to the Middle East in a few days' time; by kind invitation of an Arab prince. Care to come with me?'

Her eyes narrowed as she ignored the fatuous question.

'That's no big deal. Arab princes are two a penny. Ask any hotel doorman in Park Lane.'

'Crown princes?'

That slowed her down. She took time to come back at him though still managing not to look impressed.

'What's the matter with him?' she asked.

'He's in big trouble, I'm afraid.'

'Which means cancer, I imagine. Which country? Which crown prince?'

'I can't say.'

'Shouldn't be too difficult to find out.' She frowned as if already working out how to do it. 'Are you going to operate on him?'

'Not out there I'm not.'

'But back here?'

'Possibly. Probably.'

David began to wonder whether he had already said too much. Men were the real gossips. He could sense a shrewd intellect weighing up every syllable. He had a mental picture of Faye at a vast desk, making phone calls. They had stressed he should be discreet.

'What are the chances of your getting me an interview with him?'

'None – or is it "zilch" these days?'

'You could if you tried.'

'There is absolutely no way you are going to get to him through me, Faye. You can forget it. I'd never use a patient of mine in that way.'

'Crap. You wouldn't hesitate to use him for your own advantage. Don't tell me you're going to keep it a secret around Mayfair afterwards that you've just saved Crown Prince Ali Baba's life.'

'That sort of information does tend to leak out sooner or later,' he agreed, grinning. 'Not that there's much hope of that, I'm afraid – saving his life, I mean. Not by the sound of it.'

'Bad as that, is it? Not even in the hands of the Crown Prince of British Surgery?' The regret on Faye's face was not for the Arab prince so much as the ebbing chance of an exclusive interview. 'Pity. It's just the sort of thing we need.'

David saw the clenched fist.

'Meaning?' he asked.

'I'm in a rat race, David.' She raised one hand. 'Don't get me wrong; I'm not complaining. I love it. Catching up with the pack, even getting up amongst the leaders, was no great problem – just a question of good management and making proper use of other people's talents. There's plenty of it around if only you know where to look. But there are a hell of a lot of good women's magazines about, and the problem is how to break out ahead of the pack. Just another magazine, even a top-flight one, is not going to be enough for me.'

'What about that series on Jo Logan? How did that go? I was impressed.'

'You read it?'

'The first one, yes.'

'How did you get hold of a copy?'

'With considerable difficulty,' he admitted. 'Wasn't it a success?'

'At first. Jo was delighted – rang up – said how pleased she was with it – punchy, balanced, reasonable. Wished us luck with the rest. Then it ran out of steam. After Joe, they just seemed to lose interest. I'm beginning to wonder whether women who have the time don't like reading about other women's success because it makes them feel inadequate, while the women who *have* made it to the top don't have the time to sit around reading magazines.'

He watched her recede from him. She began to murmur quietly to herself, her hands constantly on the move, writhing, caressing.

'We need something big.' She half closed the palm of her right hand, the movements changing to short, sharp chops. 'Just –

one – biggie. And that would be just the thing. An exclusive interview with a dying Arab crown prince. Just think of it . . .' Her hand came to rest and she gave a little shudder, her eyes hooded, unfocused. 'Are you sure? Couldn't you . . . ?'

'Faye – no. You can forget it. This one's not for you,' David laughed. 'You'll have to find your own crown prince.'

David slammed the car door and inserted the ignition key. Leaning forward to start the engine, he suddenly stopped, his hand falling away into his lap as he sat back to stare through the windscreen.

Why? Why the sense of excitement?

If success was his guiding star, then women lit his way. Women were his passion, he admitted that. Some might even say his weakness. He smiled to himself. He was a pushover for expensive perfume and a plunging neckline. As a result, he had sat in a car outside an apartment pumped up with smug self-gratification often enough.

So – what was so different this time, having left a woman he had not even touched? Could it be sexual – with a woman with a whipcord body and flint-hard mind? Or was it just another manifestation of that thrusting competitive urge, roused at the sight of someone he knew had started several rungs below him and now had limitless opportunities ahead of her while he must soon have achieved virtually everything possible in his field?

Was it envy then? David shook his head. He honestly did not think it was. He thought about it and decided that other people's success was no more to him than a yardstick for his own and no cause for envy, merely a spur.

So why the sense of excitement in Faye's company?

He laughed to himself, shrugged his shoulders and started the engine.

The heater in the taxi from Heathrow gave out more noise than hot air. Outside, a fine dusting of snow had frozen where it had been driven by the wind. David pulled at the lapels of his coat as he tried to snuggle away from a draughty window. He was too cold to concentrate – and he needed to concentrate. He needed to practise a long and complicated lie until, in his mind, it was word-perfect. Without that lie he ran the risk of being the laughing stock of Lincoln's Inn Fields. At the moment, he was the only one to know the truth. Better keep it that way. And Jackie? Did it matter what he told her? She would take her usual polite interest, but only with that part of her mind she was prepared to make available to him at the time. She would not be *really* interested. She wouldn't see the funny side. Faye now – she would.

He laughed to himself.

Superficially, the trip had had all the trimmings he had expected: the first-class travel, the Old Wykehamist in the embassy car to welcome him on the sweltering tarmac, the waiving of Customs, the suite of rooms. The investigations, carried out on the crown prince with the finest equipment oil could buy, had been more comprehensive than he had expected, their very excellence posing a problem of its own – how was he to justify repeating such lucrative procedures back in London? The radiologist, a perceptive, raw-boned Scot, long experienced in seeing through people, had laughed as he had read David's thoughts.

'Dinna fash yesel, laddie. Screw the auld bastard fur every cent ye can.'

But it was the truth about the consultation itself that must not be told. It had been days before David had been summoned to the Palace. The Prince's private secretary had been urbanity itself, rapport had been immediate, but David felt he had made as much impact on the Crown Prince as if they had both been floating weightlessly in celestial space. Obese, morose, monosyllabic, the heir apparent had refused to allow David to lay a finger on him, dismissing him in midsentence with a wave of a bejewelled hand. David's final protestations to the private secretary as to the urgency of the condition had also been waved aside, though somewhat more politely. His Highness's arrival in London would be governed by one factor only, the earliest availability of his usual suite at Claridge's.

David grinned, hearing again the words 'screw the auld bastard'.

Which raised the question – how much *was* he going to charge? How much *do* you charge a crown prince? Not the sort of thing you can discuss with a colleague who probably hates your guts for getting the case in the first place. The travelling, the days being kept waiting, the loss of the best part of a week's private practice in London. The endoscopy, the twice daily visits while in London, the removal of a cancer of the oesophagus, perhaps the most major operation in his repertoire – how much was all that going to be worth? And how should he ask for it? Dollars? Gold bars? Had the time come at last for a Swiss bank account? The problem for someone born in Cory Street was to think big enough. Mal had obviously learned – and Faye. He must teach himself. It was important.

And it was not only a question of how much but when. Timing in these matters was as important as the bottom line. *Before* the operation – when patients would pay a surgeon anything? What price another ten years of life during those sleepless hours before the fateful morning? It was notorious how the intensity of gratitude diminished in inverse proportion to the feeling of well-being afterwards, and it was often the case that the richer the patient, the shorter the memory. The most unexpected patients had been known to do a midnight flit as soon as they could stagger unaided to a taxi. Or *after* the operation? Then one ran the risk of a poor result and a disgruntled patient or, worse still, a tight-fisted executor. Or take the grandiose line – gamble it all? 'Tut, tut – no question of a fee. Consider it an honour to have been of service to His Royal Highness.' Surely no crown prince would entertain the thought of charity and, perhaps, who knows, the scale of a royal household's generosity might be beyond the wildest dreams of a poor boy from Cory Street.

The wind, scouring up Harley Street, had him running up the few steps to put his key in the door. In the hall, he stopped, suddenly halted by a stillness, a silence over and above the usual quietness. The days of 'cooee' were long gone. He still remembered the sound of his mother's 'cooee', warm and comforting in the tiny Cory Street hallway, on her return from work.

No one calls 'cooee' in the grand halls and broad stairways of Harley Street. Even so, it was still enough of a home to have its own unique atmosphere. For some reason he felt his scalp tingle and the muscles of his back contract. Something indefinable made him drop his suitcase and run up the stairs. His immediate relief at finding Jackie in her usual armchair was short-lived as he saw her staring at the TV. He glanced at the screen. Jackie and a soap? To Jackie, TV was something to be used, with programmes selected that would feed an active mind. Jackie used TV as a stimulant, not a sedative. The sound had been switched off and there was something macabre about the way she stared at the inane mime. She did not turn her head as he crossed the room to kneel beside her chair.

'Jackie – are you all right?'

'Yes.' She spoke with robot-like automatism without taking her eyes from the screen. He reached for the remote control, blotting out the picture. Jackie stared at the dead screen, frowning as if she had been interested.

'No, you're not.'

'I'm all right, I tell you.'

'Something's wrong. What's happened?' His next word was borne on a sudden wave of panic. 'Debbie?'

Jackie faced him for the first time. She shook her head, her lower lip beginning to tremble. 'No, it's not Debbie.'

'So?'

'We had a break-in last night.'

'The bastards. Did they take anything?'

The antique silver, the porcelain, the crystal. Colleagues, colleagues' wives and their children. Some were embarrassingly generous after their operations. Most of the small stuff he knew to be in the safe deposit – but that watercolour, that gorgeous little watercolour. And that Sèvres clock. That Sèvres clock after Sir Geoffrey's rupture. It would have been enough simply to have been asked to operate on your old chief – but that clock, it was priceless. He looked round the room. Nothing seemed out of place.

'Nothing much. We'll survive.'

'Why did . . . Oh my God.' He closed his eyes. Oh for the

chance to go out, come in and start again. 'Were you here at the time?'

'I was. Yes.'

The monotone now had the painful insistency of a thumping headache.

'Did they . . . ? I mean, did they . . . ? They didn't do anything to you?' It was as if he did not want to hear the answer to that as he hurried on. 'What about Mrs Baker – and Maria?'

'It was Mrs Baker's night off. She was staying with her sister as she always does. And Maria has gone.'

'Gone? What d'you mean, gone?'

'The police think she must have let them in; the alarm downstairs had been turned off.'

'The little bitch. But . . .' It was a question that had to be faced sooner or later. 'What about you? They didn't do anything to you, did they?' Again he prevented her from answering that. 'How many of them were there?'

'Two.'

David reached out to take her hand, but she shrank away from him. They never held hands. It was a bit late now.

'They made me get out of bed and take my nightdress off. One of them had a gun.' The only difference from reading aloud from a very dull book was the brittle courage in her voice. 'They tied me to the chair with my tights and they . . . they touched me. With their fingers and with . . . with the gun. They laughed; said they'd "be back for a bit of that later".' Jackie's body shuddered before she went on. 'They took my rings' – she held out a strangely bare-looking hand – 'and most of my jewellery, and a lot of silver has gone from the dining room. Maria couldn't have known about the safe down in your rooms, but I heard them for a long time – it seemed like hours – laughing together in the kitchen. It didn't take them long to find the drinks cabinet. And, all the time, I was waiting for them to come back.'

As Jackie finally broke into dry-eyed sobs, they struggled to make physical contact across the arm of the chair. Awkwardly, jerkily, he managed to get his arm around her shoulders. Shyly, his wife, the mother of his child, let him do so.

When David finally managed to bring out the ultimate

question, he found within himself the honesty to wonder whether he was asking it out of concern for Jackie or for himself.

'And did they . . . ? Did . . . ?'

He felt the head on his shoulder shake but, for a moment, could not be sure in which direction.

'No. Suddenly, everything was quiet. They were gone. I have no idea why, but they'd gone. Something, somebody, must have disturbed them – thank God.'

'As you say – thank God.'

Thank God for what? That they had not raped his wife? Was that such a big deal? After all, the Sèvres clock was safe. What had they done? No more than run their hands over his naked wife – and the gun. It could have been worse. Now – if they'd slashed the watercolour . . .

He held her closer. Her hair was much softer than it looked, than he remembered.

'And you say Maria went with them?'

'Yes.'

'So what did you do?'

'Nothing. I couldn't. I didn't have the strength. That's how Mrs Baker found me this morning.'

She began to shake uncontrollably as her voice dropped to a stuttering whisper.

'And I'd wet myself.'

David closed his eyes. Jacqueline Lee, crisply chic, briskly competent, unassailably independent, naked in a pool of urine. How much more vulnerable did he want her?

'And how long were you there, like that?' he asked quietly.

'Six, seven hours.'

He stood up and pulled her to him, feeling her shudders as they held each other close. He looked down at a face he had never seen before. A small, curious smile played around a softer, more appealing mouth.

'They say, don't they,' she said, shivering as she did so, 'that in a drowning man's last few seconds his life flashes before his eyes. Well – you can take it from me – that's got nothing on a woman waiting a couple of hours to be raped and murdered.'

'Don't worry, darling. It's all over now. No harm done, thank God.'

'But' – Jackie burrowed her hand up between them – 'my wedding ring.'

'That's the least of our problems. We'll go out and get another one today.'

'That's not the point. It won't be the same. It's strange, but it suddenly came home to me how much that meant to me. Looking down at my hand was the one thing that made me feel *really* naked.'

11

David looked at the bottle of twelve-year-old Scotch, a gift from a grateful colleague, then at his empty glass, then at the bottle again, weighing in the balance the peace and warmth and the price to be paid. The last thing he would want the next morning would be to wake with a headache. It had happened. He had never operated when drunk; somehow he had always managed to avoid that. But a surgeon with a thriving private practice must be on immediate call night and day, seven days a week, Christmas and Easter. Especially early in a career when an unattended phone does not ring a second time or, worse still, when an emergency turned down because of that one drink too many means, not just the loss of the patient and his fee, but also the loss of the practitioner who had referred him. Somehow David had survived that period.

But there had been those mornings when the theatre light had bored into aching eyeballs like a laser, when registrars and theatre sisters had kept their own counsels while praying for the coffee break. But even that had been confined to lists of routine, mind-numbing stuff. He would never dream of drinking too much the night before anything as major as a thoracotomy. Or operating on a crown prince. As for the night before a thoracotomy on a crown prince . . .

He reached for the bottle, the trace of a smile on his lips. Just a small one. He was now, after all, no mere Master of Surgery and Member of Council, but an Operator on Crown Princes.

A fresh drink in his hand, his favourite current affairs programme on TV, he sighed contentedly through the aftertaste of the evening meal Jackie had cooked. He looked back over his shoulder as she came into the room, a book in her hand.

'I'm going to bed, David.'

A short time before and that would have been no more than a bald statement of fact. Now she crossed the room to stand behind his chair, putting her free hand on his shoulder. For a while they watched a smiling politician evade every question put to him.

'Tired?'

Normally her question would have irritated him as it distracted him from something in which he probably had no real interest. Now he shook his head, turning to look up at her.

'Not really.'

'I hope everything goes well tomorrow.' Jackie stared blindly at the screen as she spoke. 'Do you get nervous before a big case like that?'

'Nnnnoooo,' he answered, slowly but honestly. 'It gets the adrenaline going a bit – but nervous? No. The abdominal part of the operation might be a bit difficult – he's still a great fat man even though he's lost a lot of weight. The chest part depends entirely on how extensive the growth is when you get inside. You can never be absolutely sure beforehand, but at least his being fat is no problem there – that doesn't affect exposure in the chest nearly so much.'

He felt her give a little shudder.

'Sounds absolutely ghastly,' she said. 'How long will it take?'

'I don't seem to be able to do one in under about three hours.'

They fell silent, turning back to the TV, quietly content as they watched Christians and Muslims kill each other amongst the rubble of a Beirut suburb.

'What goes through your mind when you're operating? I've

often wondered. Three hours is a long time. You can't hope to concentrate absolutely all that time; it's not humanly possible. What d'you think about?'

David gave a short chuckle. 'The theatre sister's tits mostly.'

'David.'

He ducked his head, holding his drink aloft to prevent it spilling, as her hand shook his shoulder.

'I've never heard you speak like that before.' The hand gave another, gentler nudge, edging deeper into the angle between shoulder and neck. 'Members of Council don't talk like that.'

'Don't you believe it,' he grinned.

'Seriously, David – what *does* go through your mind?'

He would have shrugged his shoulders, but she might have taken her hand away. A few square inches of precious contact after so many years.

'Everything; anything. The strangest things – a complete hotchpotch. College business, whether the car needs servicing, how d'you convert a magnetic bearing to true – do you add or subtract the variation – something you've said.'

Jackie was quiet for a moment, but any fool could have followed her train of thought.

'And what if . . .' She paused and started again. 'And does your mood affect your operating? Do you operate better if you're in a good mood?'

David turned his head, a discussion on America's involvement in the Middle East suddenly of no consequence to him. He smiled.

'I've seen you disappear in a foul temper with a manuscript under your arm more than once when I haven't given the poor sod of an author much chance. There've been times when I reckon Graham Greene would have been hard put to get anything past you.'

That, normally, would have been sufficient to bring her out fighting. She bit her lip, flushing slightly.

'Of course it does, Jackie. Operating always seems easier if you're in a good mood.' He couldn't get used to the soft voices, the intimacy, the warmth, the concern. 'Everything seems to go better when you're relaxed. When you're angry, muscles are tense, movements jerky; you pull that bit harder, sharper. You tell yourself the end result is just the same. If it isn't, then you put it down to technical difficulties, the patient's fault. You can always blame the poor bloody patient.'

'So – some mornings, when I've been a real bitch and you've gone straight from here into theatre . . .'

She watched as he picked up the remote control. The zap as he cut off the President of the United States in midsentence stopped her too.

'What you mean is, have you indirectly caused widespread death and destruction over the years?' He laughed, wondering at the affection in his voice. 'No, Jackie, you haven't. You needn't worry about that.'

She frowned at the electronic ember at the centre of the TV screen, all that was left of the most powerful man in the world.

'Do you ever regret not having married a nurse?' she asked softly. 'Or another doctor?'

'Of course not.' David laughed as he turned his head. 'Whatever made you ask that?'

'I just wondered. I'm not much use to you, am I – talking about your job, I mean? I don't even know the language.'

'About as much use as I am to you. I haven't a clue about what really goes on in publishing.'

'But I've never made an effort to find out. I've never really stopped at some time in the day and wondered what you are doing. I've been too busy.' Her hand moved to stroke his hair gently. 'I'm going to try from now on, David. I promise you that. Why do we both work so hard? Why? God knows we don't need the money. Is it selfishness, d'you think? Is it just to fill very empty lives? And it's not just me.' David heard some of the old Jackie return. 'You're just as bad. You put ambition above everything. You've got to change too.'

She took a deep breath as if she were turning a page.

'There's nothing in this case tomorrow that's going to stop your coming skiing? Now – you're quite sure of that?' She paused long enough to feel the head shake beneath her hand. 'You've been looking tired lately, David. You need a holiday.'

'In ten days time, either His Royal Highness is going to be

fine or he's going to be dead – well, perhaps that's putting it a bit dramatically, but it's more or less true. You can usually tell within four or five days whether they are going to do well or not. So, you can look out for me in ten days' time, a fortnight at the most. I'm so glad you've decided to go for three weeks this year. You need a break too. And you're not taking any manuscripts, now are you?'

She did not answer, simply laughing as she leaned down to kiss him.

'Now I really am going to bed,' she said.

At the door, she turned.

'It's been a good Christmas, David.'

He swivelled round in his chair to smile at her. 'Can't remember a better one, Jackie.'

'I suppose we ought to make the most of them. I don't know how many more we'll have Debbie home with us. It'll be just the two of us then.'

'Thank God we've got a daughter, not a son. They tend to come home to mum for Christmas, don't they – until they have kids of their own, anyway. Take care now. Don't go breaking any bones. Don't you think you're getting a bit old for skiing?'

'You speak for yourself,' she grinned.

'But I don't have this osteoporosis problem.'

'Pig.' She stuck out her tongue. 'I'm not *that* old.'

Half an hour later, on his way to bed, David saw a light under Debbie's bedroom door. He knocked gently, opened it and put his head into the room. She sat on her bed, cross-legged in her pyjamas, her elbows on her knees, her head in her hands. She looked up and smiled.

'Why aren't you asleep?' he asked, walking in. He peered into her lap. 'Why is it that the two women in my life have always got their head in a book? What are you reading?'

Sitting down on the edge of the bed, he took the paperback from her, carefully keeping the page as he did so. He turned the cover face up.

Papillon. He raised an eyebrow.

But why? What had he expected? A physics textbook? Barbara Cartland? It dawned on him he had never stopped to wonder what his daughter read. If he had, he would have guessed it would have been something with good red meat in it. He could sense beneath the thin pyjamas the pent-up energy of a compact body packed with an explosive teenage passion. A hurler of javelins rather than a pounder of tracks. She even spoke that way, her sentences surging bursts of words, a challenge in every phrase. God help her husband.

'Well?' She fixed her father with a glare that demanded the truth.

'Hardly a bedtime story.'

'What's bedtime got to do with it?'

David lifted one hand as if in apology for such a stupid remark and, as a gesture of forgiveness, Debbie moved over, patting the bed beside her. He swung his legs up and lay back in the freshness of clean linen, holding the book up in front of his face. He flicked from page to page.

'Man's inhumanity to man,' he muttered.

'Exactly what I was thinking, Daddy. Aren't men horrible?'

'No, they're not; not all of them.' He gave her back the book and watched her throw it on the floor beside her. 'Gandhi, Albert Schweitzer, Isaac Newton, Pasteur – they were all men if my memory serves me correctly.'

'And what about those men – with Mum?'

She looked at her father, frowning furiously.

'I know, darling. I just thank God you were not here as well that night. A couple of nights later and you would have been.'

He had not allowed himself to think about that one. Somehow he had managed to keep that horror at bay. Now, lying on her bed, his defences crumbled. He looked round the room, saw for a fleeting moment two men in crotch-bulging jeans, their filthy T-shirts stretched over beer bellies. He closed his eyes as they lunged towards the bed. He smelled their lust.

'Dear God.' He shuddered.

'Did you *have* to go away without her, Daddy? Couldn't Mum have gone with you?' The frown deepened. 'Did you *have* to go at all?'

'I've got to go where my job takes me, Debbie. Thousands of

men have to do it much more often than I do: reps, seamen, long-distance lorry drivers.'

'But they *can't* take their wives with them – you could.'

'Come on, Debbie. It's not *all* my fault.' He smiled. '*I* never get asked to New York on one of Mum's trips.'

'Would you go?'

He thought about it. 'Maybe,' he said. 'From now on.'

'I don't believe it. You two'll never change. I give you three months. I know things are all lovey-dovey at the moment, but – three months – you'll be back where you were.' The first flicker of doubt crossed her face. 'Maybe Mum – perhaps she *has* changed. I don't know. I'll wait and see. But you?' Her tone was dismissive, almost derisory, but her look was of tolerant, affectionate forgiveness. 'You, you old devil, you'll *never* change. But then, it wasn't you who was bound to a chair for hours waiting to be raped and murdered, *was* it? But then *again*, I can't imagine anything – or any*one* – changing *you*.'

Out of the mouths of babes and sucklings. She went on as if laying a man's soul bare was as nothing.

'I realise those ghastly Middle East places don't welcome women, but what would have happened if you had refused to go without her?'

'Then they would have asked someone else and probably never asked me again. That's how the system works. It gets you by the tail.'

'But Daddy, what with you and Mum *and* Grandpa Lee, we've got more money than we will ever know what to do with. What's the point?'

'Because . . .' He hesitated. 'Because,' he said slowly, 'money is not the only spur. I suppose that's the answer. It might be much simpler if it was. Perhaps then one could bring it down to the beauty of simple mathematics. You could set yourself a target and give up once you reached it. But it's more than that. What is it?' He thought for a moment. 'Fame? Is that it – "the last infirmity of noble minds"?'

'Daddy.' Debbie sat upright, her eyes wide. 'I *am* impressed.'

He went on with a small, offhand wave. He'd picked up one of Jackie's manuscripts a few days before and been struck by the quotation. No point in dulling the impression of hidden literary depths.

'No, it's not just fame. It's . . . vanity. Yes, vanity; that's nearer the mark. It's not just *being* famous, you must be *seen* to be famous. No one wants to be famous after they're dead. You don't make enough money to buy a BMW and then drive it around in the dark. You want people to *see* you driving a BMW. You don't work hard for years to become a Member of the Council of the College of . . .'

'Yes?' His voice had died away but was flogged back to life with one whiplash word.

'I must admit, just between you and me, I rather enjoy parading round in my robes in front of mere Fellows and Members.'

'I'd love to see you, Daddy.' For a moment, Debbie shed ten years. 'Can I, one day?'

'I expect that can be arranged.'

'But . . .' The young probing mind took over again. 'Where now?'

David shrugged his shoulders as if he hadn't the faintest idea what she meant. He struggled to keep a smile at bay.

'What d'you mean?' he said.

'Where d'you go from here? What are you . . .' She stopped, thought and, in one explosive movement, turned on her stomach, rearing above him by leaning one elbow on his shoulder. 'You want to be *President*, don't you? You're not going to be happy until you're *President, are* you?'

Each *President* was pressed home with a thrust of her elbow that drove David into the bedsprings.

'You do, don't you? Be honest.'

She took to thumping his chest with her fist and David allowed the smile to burgeon.

'It would be rather nice, wouldn't it?'

'You old devil.' The prospect obviously did not displease her either.

'It must be every surgeon's dream, Debbie. I'm no different from anyone else.'

'And from there?'

'One or two *have* gone on to the House of Lords.' Something never before even whispered in his mind.

'And after that?' Her voice was now a high-pitched, tight-throated shriek.

Her father laughed. 'There *is* nothing after that. There *is* no life after the House of Lords. Everyone knows that.'

Debbie dropped prone, her shoulder on her father's, her face close to his on the pillow.

'Would that mean a knighthood, Daddy – the presidency, I mean?'

'Well, yes; usually.' He tried to make it sound as if he had never thought of it that way before.

'You would be Sir David Royall?'

'Yes. But you mustn't say that to anyone else. It's far from certain. There's a long way to go yet.'

'And Mum would be Lady Jacqueline Royall?'

'No, she'd be Lady Royall.'

Debbie rolled on her back, savouring the words. 'Sir David and Lady Royall.'

Laughing, David turned on his elbow towards her. 'Stop dreaming your life away, young lady. Much more to the point – have you decided yet what you're going to do?'

'Yes. I have.' Immediately, there was a defensive note in her voice.

'You have? What?'

'I know what you are going to say. I know what you think of these people. You haven't got a good word to say for them.'

'Try me.'

'I want to go into politics.'

'Politics?' David's body jerked in his surprise as he blurted out the word. 'Did you say *politics*?'

'There you are,' Debbie pouted. 'I *knew* that would be your reaction. But I'm going to do it anyway. I don't *care* what you think. But I'm going to do law first – I must get a good law degree first. I want to go to Oxford. I . . .'

She stopped as she saw the look on her father's face.

'I love you very much, Debbie. Come here.' He stretched towards her. 'Give your father a kiss.'

As they settled back, there were a few moments of silence before Debbie murmured softly, 'You don't really.'

'What?'

'Love me.'

'I do.'

'No, you don't. If you did, you'd be coming skiing with us tomorrow, not operating on your old crown prince. And don't tell me you couldn't get the time off. If Mum can suddenly decide to take three weeks off, so can you.'

'As long as one of us is there to keep an eye on you, young lady. I don't altogether like the way Jean-Louis's beginning to look at you.'

'Did Mum tell you he's promised to take us off piste this year, maybe stay away one or two nights? And there seems to be masses of snow this year. Now, you *are* coming out, aren't you, Daddy?' She raised herself on her elbow once more to watch his face. 'You've promised. Ten days, you said.'

'Well.' She watched his face squirm. 'It might be a fortnight before I can be sure he's all right.'

'And if he isn't then?'

'Look.' David sat up. 'I've got to get to bed, otherwise I won't be in very good shape tomorrow morning. But I'll promise you this, whatever happens. You know how you've always wanted to go sailing in the Greek islands?'

She nodded, her eyes lighting up.

'Well, next summer, come hell or high water, I promise you we'll take a boat and go cruising down there. Who knows, perhaps your mother and I could put up with each other in a small boat for two weeks now. We could go in a flotilla or bare boat, whichever you prefer.'

Debbie, now kneeling beside him, bounced with excitement. 'Flotilla,' she said. 'More company in the evenings. And it's got to be Yugoslavia. They say there's more wind there, more fun.'

'The only problem is, I don't see Mum in too small a boat, do you? Do you think the three of us could cope with, say, a thirty-five, forty-footer?'

'I'm sure we could, Daddy. But couldn't we ask someone else

along? Couldn't we . . . Perhaps . . . There's . . . Do you . . . ? Do you think we could ask Richard?'

'Oh, yes? And who's Richard?'

'He's the boy I told you about. He's crewed on Admiral's Cup boats. He's awfully good. He's . . .'

'Tell him to put his application in in triplicate,' David grinned. 'Tell him . . .'

He got no further as arms were wrapped around his neck and a face pressed to his. She gave an extra squeeze. 'Isn't life just *too* blissful?'

David was turning the corner into the ward as Drew was coming out. They almost collided. They both took a step back.

'Morning, Digger. How is he?' David smiled with the confidence of someone talking of a case that has gone brilliantly well. There had been no sign of secondary deposits in chest or abdomen. The primary tumour had almost fallen into his hand. A crime to take the money. The smile faded when he saw the look on Drew's face.

'Oh, no,' he groaned.

'Nothing terrible, David. His chest is fine and he's taking his fluids by mouth with no problem.'

'But?'

'But he's got one fat leg this morning.'

'Oh, no.' David closed his eyes as he threw his head back. 'Shit.' The word exploded as he jerked his head back again.

'It wasn't there when I saw him last night – I checked. But there's no doubt about it this morning, I'm afraid.'

'We'd better organise some anticoagulants then.'

'I've just given him his first dose.'

The hint of a frown crossed David's face. Who was in charge?

'I'd better have a look myself,' he said, adding stiffly, 'Though I'm sure you're right.'

Together they walked past the bodyguards at the ward entrance and again at the door to His Royal Highness's room. A few minutes later and David was examining the swollen leg of a whining ingrate. He was in no mood to heed the yelps as he pressed gently into the fleshy part of a royal calf.

David straightened up, smiling reassuringly, wondering what His Royal Highness would say if he knew just how close to sudden death he was at that moment. In his mind's eye, David saw the soft, friable blood clots in the deep veins of the leg. He saw their smooth, slithery surface, no more adherent to the walls of the veins than toothpaste to a tube. One squeeze out into the big veins and all his technical skill of days before would be wiped out in a few seconds of terrifying respiratory collapse and cardiac arrest.

Five minutes of reassuring explanation did nothing to improve His Royal Highness's mood. He did not look convinced that the trouble with his leg was sheer bad luck. The fact that a highly technical and complicated operation had gone without a hitch until then did not seem to impress him at all. In fact, the longer David talked, the more suspicious his patient became, and David was glad to find himself out in the corridor once more with Drew.

'That's a damn nuisance, Digger,' he said.

'I wouldn't worry, David,' Drew smiled. 'Not your fault. An act of God or, in this case, the will of Allah. I suppose if you are going to make a habit of operating on crown princes, you had better get used to it. I imagine you'll find Sod's Law written somewhere in Arabic. But he'll be all right. We've spotted it pretty early. Fill him up with anticoagulants and he shouldn't come to any harm. Would you like me to write them up for you?'

'Would you? That would be very kind of you. Actually,' – a slight grin spread slowly over David's face – 'I have to admit, I wasn't thinking solely of the patient when I said that.'

'Oh?'

'No. I was just wondering what Jackie's going to say. I rang her last night and told her to expect me in the next day or so. Now I'll have to ring her again tonight. She will not be pleased. It's getting to look as if I won't get out there at all now.'

David tried his best not to feel relieved at the thought. One whole week away – damn nuisance really. Private practice was a fickle thing. A GP might be impressed to hear you were away consulting in the Middle East – he'd keep his patient until you came back. But skiing – off enjoying yourself – that was different. There were other Masters of Surgery around, even Members of Council, who didn't spend their time gadding about on the slopes.

'I still don't see why you can't go,' Drew argued. 'He's essentially a medical problem now. There's nothing that can go wrong with his swallowing. As soon as his blood levels are right, he's not going to come to any harm. He's not going to have a pulmonary embolism. Even if he did, what could you do about it? So, why not go? You could at least have the last week out there with them.'

Why was he looking for reasons not to go? 'And have him bleed from somewhere due to his anticoagulants? Can you imagine what His Royal Highness would say if he found his dressings full of blood one morning and his surgeon is off skiing somewhere?'

'Very unlikely, David. I'd watch him like a hawk. And, if that did happen' – Drew hesitated, pulling a face before going on, realising fully what he was saying – 'if the worst came to the worst, I could always call someone else in if I couldn't cope with it myself.'

That settled it. David's expression hardened as he finally made up his mind. 'I'll ring Jackie tonight, tell her I can't make it.' He paused before muttering, 'And I'll double the miserable old sod's fee to make up for it.'

'Is that you, Jackie?'

'Yes; I'm here. Isn't this an awful line?'

'Dreadful, isn't it? Are you all right?'

'Yes, I'm fine. I . . .' – a moment's hesitation – 'I'm missing you.'

'What's the skiing like?'

'Not too bad. Plenty of snow, but it's very icy in the mornings. It's so warm during the day that it gets quite slushy at times, and then it freezes again overnight. Still, it's snowing hard at the moment, so perhaps things will improve.'

'And Debbie?'

'She's fine. Getting a bit impatient waiting for you to come out. She's talking all the time about this overnight trip she wants to make, nagging poor Jean-Louis to death. There are two other men who want to go with them, but I'm not leaving her alone for a night with someone like Jean-Louis and two strange men. So, I'm depending on you, David. You know how I like my creature comforts; I don't fancy staying overnight in some moutain hut when there's a five-star hotel about. Apart from that, you were right; I am getting a bit old for this off-piste skiing.'

'That's really what I'm ringing about.'

'Oh, no.' He heard the sadness and winced. 'You're not coming.'

'Well – I'm not sure now. He's had a deep vein thrombosis. I'll have to stay for another couple of days at least. I'm sorry, Jackie.'

'Another couple of days? It will hardly be worth coming then. You're not coming at all, are you? That's what you're trying to say, isn't it?'

'Well . . .'

'Oh, David.'

There had been a time, not many weeks before, when David could have predicted Jackie's reaction to the last bitter syllable. He would have weathered it, walked away from it, dismissed it from his mind. Lacerating remarks would have left no marks. Now soft vulnerability cut deeply.

'I'm sorry, Jackie; I really am. I'll ring you again in a day or so, as soon as I know he's out of danger.'

'All right, David.' He had never heard her cry before; he had not thought it possible. 'I love you, David.'

'I love you too, Jackie.'

He had said it before – when he'd felt obliged to. Suddenly, meaning it gave him a whole new sensation.

12

It was the first time David had seen His Royal Highness smile. The very mention of Claridge's and his face lit up. When David told him he thought a mimimum of three to four weeks' treatment there would be necessary, and that he would call in to see him every day, the Crown Prince positively beamed. Out of the room, His Royal Highness's private secretary looked equally pleased.

'It would be foolish of me not to admit, Mr Royall, that I too will be quite glad to return to Claridge's. I must thank you for the great diligence both you and Dr Drew have shown.'

'It's been my pleasure,' David replied. 'I'm only sorry things were held up by that thrombosis in his leg.'

'It was the will of Allah.'

David smiled condescendingly to himself, then wondered why.

'His Royal Highness is not a demonstrative man, Mr Royall, but I know he is grateful for all that has been done for him. I understand that you have forgone a skiing holiday in order to give him your personal attention.'

David shrugged his shoulders philosophically. 'In this business, one learns to take the rough with the smooth.'

'His Highness also knows of this and has told me how much he has appreciated your sacrifice. I have no doubt that he will attempt to show his gratitude in some more material form in due course.'

'Perhaps you would inform His Royal Highness what an honour he has done me by putting his trust in me.'

The secretary paid David the compliment of allowing him the last word, bowed and turned away, leaving David busily preening his ego. Elegant communication between two cultured, wordly men. It felt good. This was what it was all about. And, with the reputation this case would bring in its wake, it could be just the beginning.

His head jerked as he gave a little grunt. He had decided. Those sessions at the Merton; they had to go. They didn't really fit any more.

'Telephone, Mr Royall.' Not even such a mundane interruption could spoil his mood. Inside the office, he was handed the receiver. 'Your consulting rooms.'

There was something of a flourish to the way he put the phone to his ear.

'Martha – good morning to you. What have you got for me?'

A chair creaked as he slumped into it, pushing it backwards to stretch out one leg and rest it on a desk top.

'If it's anything less than a crown prince, I'm not interested.'

'Mr Royall . . .'

The foot was removed from the desk during the silence that followed. Frowning, he sat up straighter.

'Martha?'

The sob he heard had David rising slowly to his feet, his forehead now deeply furrowed.

'Martha – what's the trouble?'

'The police, Mr Royall. There's an Inspector McGovern here. He . . .'

David stood almost to attention, closing his eyes as he felt a leaden ache begin deep in his chest.

'He wants to speak to you.'

Slowly, silently, he stood back, as if striving to disembody himself, fighting to distance himself from what he knew would be nothing but pain. He heard himself tell Martha to put the Inspector on the phone.

'He says he wants to speak to you personally, Mr Royall.'

'Tell him I'll be there as soon as I can.'

He heard voices discussing him in his own house.

'No, Mr Royall. He says for you to stay there. He'll be with you in ten minutes.' He heard her sobbing. 'Oh, Mr Royall, I'm so sorry.'

He hung up.

He walked out on to the landing with its windows overlooking the busy street. The commuter rush was over, the traffic settling down to its steady midmorning pace. He should have been in Queen's by now, starting his first case. He found he couldn't remember what operation it was. He listened to the swish and zip as car wheels sped busily through the rain. He watched an elderly couple pick their way between the puddles, huddled together beneath one umbrella. Had anyone ever stopped in London to offer a lift to two old people caught in the rain?

In spotless grey raincoat, its collar turned down, and with trouser creases like razors above gleaming shoes, who else could it be but a police inspector walking towards him? And why did they always have to come in twos? To bear witness that the bad news had been broken with all possible tact?

'Mr Royall?'

'Yes.'

'Mr David Royall?'

'Yes.' How many other Mr Royalls were there whose wife and daughter had just died?

'My name's McGovern, sir. Inspector Mc——'

'They're dead, aren't they, Inspector?'

'I . . .'

'Oh, come, Inspector. We're both intelligent men. Why else would you be here? If one of them had been injured, the other one would have rung me. If they were both injured, the hospital would have rung me. You don't need to be the richest surgeon in London to work that out.'

'Sir?'

'If one was dead . . . What happened, Inspector? D'you know?'

It was the one job McGovern loathed. He cursed his reputation for being so good at it.

'An avalanche, I understand, sir. They were out skiing and were swept away in it. Three are missing altogether and I'm afraid your wife and daughter were two of them, sir.'

'They haven't found them yet then?'

'Apparently not, sir, but they say they will. May I say, sir, just how . . .'

David stood at the top of a slope that stretched away to

infinity, white, unsullied and inviting. To one side of him stood Jackie, to the other his daughter. They had stood there many times, three individuals thrown together briefly by a mutual love of skiing. Sweating in the warm air, he was shaking his head, looking up at the wet, cottonwool clouds that besmirched the mountaintops. But his daughter would not listen, tossing her hair as she plunged down the slope. His wife raced after her, looking back at him as she did so, her expression appealing. He made feeble attempts to follow them, but snow around his ankles had set like concrete, and he began to cry as they disappeared beneath a silent avalanche that spread over the mountainside below him like a grubby fan.

'. . . And if we can be of assistance in any way, Mr Royall . . .'

'Thank you, Inspector. You've been very kind.' David smiled at him. 'It's a lousy job, breaking news like that, isn't it? I know; I've done quite a bit of it myself over the years. I never thought I'd ever be on the receiving end.'

McGovern had seen all the usual reactions to tragic news. He had known people behave as David Royall had – clear-eyed, unemotional, taut as a drum – but never quite to that degree. Perhaps it was only to be expected from someone at the very top of a discipline trained to react to sudden emergencies with ice-cold control. He could imagine what his sergeant would say on the way back to the station. 'Cold bloody fish' might be the most complimentary description he would find. What his sergeant would not realise was that these were the ones who took it the hardest. Not for them the luxury of the safety net of howling grief into which they could hurl themselves, drawing around them, like a protective cloak, all the sympathy they could muster. The David Royalls of this world were the kind of men who turned inwards on themselves.

'I can't say how sorry I am, Mr Royall. Is there anything we can do? Anyone we can . . . ?' He looked round at the empty corridor. 'Perhaps someone . . . ? A friend?'

David shook his head and smiled. 'As I said, Inspector, you have been very kind. Thank you. I shall be all right.'

The lift doors took an embarrassingly long time to close on parting smiles, frozen in professional compassion.

David waited until he saw the police car pass below the window. Taking his car keys out and bouncing them in his hand – an old habit Debbie had laughed at so often – he walked slowly down the stairs and out to his car. Clipping on his seatbelt and starting the engine was automatic. He drove away with robot-like efficiency.

Along Marylebone Road, every traffic light turned red as he approached. He sat patiently waiting where normally he would have fumed. A car cut across in front of him and he braked, smiling courteously where normally he would have cursed. He turned to drive down Harley Street, looking to neither right nor left, as if the place had never been of any consequence to him. It was only when he reached its lower end that a frown began to spread over his face as if he was not quite sure where he was being taken.

He recognised Oxford Street and, before long, he found himself turning in to Southampton Row and Kingsway, then in to Lincoln's Inn Fields. As if of its own volition, the car stopped, double-parked, at a spot where, through the windscreen, he had a clear view of the Royal College of Surgeons. The frown deepened to that anxious look of someone who begins to suspect he might be seriously ill. With the distaste he always struggled to hide when examining someone with a generalised seeping skin rash, he looked down at himself, seeing the expensive cloth of his suit, fingering the heavy gold cufflinks and watch strap as if they were signs of some hideous disease he had only just found. His gaze swept the car's dashboard, his face screwing up at the banks of switches and dials, the on-board computer, the radio telephone. He gazed out at the venerable pillars of the Royal College. Lights shone from the imposing old building in the gloom of a winter's morning. He could see the window of the President's office. A movement caught his eye as a man hurried past the car, his pin-striped trousers and gleaming black shoes bustling beneath his Crombie overcoat. His black briefcase bulged. David watched the man – he watched himself – run up the steps and get sucked through the revolving doors like a piece of fluff up a Hoover.

He put the car in gear. Slowly and deliberately, he drove on, swinging across the road and into the arc of the College's driveway. At its exact midpoint, immediately below the steps that led up to the main entrance, he stopped, pulling viciously on the hand brake. His watch slid off easily and he tossed it on to the passenger seat. He tore at his cufflinks, ripping his shirt sleeve as he did so, before they followed his watch.

Leaving the engine running, David Royall, Master of Surgery, youngest Member of Council, past Hunterian Professor and member of the Court of Examiners of the Royal College of Surgeons of England, consultant surgeon to Queen's College Hospital, Fellow of the Royal Society of Medicine, Harley Street specialist, surgeon to crown princes, got out, slammed the car door and walked away.

A sudden heavy squall of rain that sent shoppers scurrying for doorways had no effect on his stride. He walked, hands deep in his trouser pockets, shoulders hunched. He muttered to himself, loud enough to turn a few heads. Half-closed eyes were raised for a moment to scan ahead, searching for something, someone. Suddenly he veered across a wide pavement and a burly man of about his own age cursed as David barged into his shoulder, knocking him off balance. Time ceased to exist as David trudged on through a steady drizzle, not knowing where. Sounds of voices came from inside an open door set below Tudor timbers. Confident voices. The sound he knew so well, that of self-assured men, successful men. He walked in and the noise level dropped for a moment – it is not often one sees a Savile Row suit soaking wet. David shouldered his way to the bar.

'Whisky. Large.'

He stood at the bar, facing it, being quietly cursed as the lunchtime drinkers began to flood in. Several whiskies later, he turned round, leaning back against the bar, supporting himself on jutting elbows. The corners of his mouth turned down as he surveyed the groups of loud-mouthed, toffee-nosed bastards.

'Bloody lawyers.'

The young man alongside him laughed softly, looked at David's face, and the smile drained away. He saw the wildness in the eyes of a man looking for a fight.

'You don't like lawyers?' he asked.

'Who the hell does? You buggers don't even like each other. Leeches on the back of society. Almost as bad as the fucking doctors.'

The young man suddenly saw someone he knew the other side of the room and left David to curse his receding back.

'Ill-mannered sod.'

Swinging round to get another drink, he sent a glass flying. It fell and shattered behind the bar. The barmaid in black skirt, white shirt and black bow tie looked appealingly at the manager standing at the end of the bar. He took her place in front of David.

'Another whisky. Large.'

'I'm sorry, sir, but don't you think perhaps you've had enough?'

'Whisky, I said.'

'I'm afraid I'll have to ask you to leave, sir.'

The landlord's voice was easily heard as heads were turned in David's direction. He glared back balefully. 'Aaaaaach. Sod off, the lot of you,' he snarled as he stumbled towards the door.

Another hour's aimless wandering and the whisky began to lose its effect. He began to feel the terror of what he knew clearmindedness would bring. Finding a bar where a mute, pokerfaced barman was happy to give him all the whisky he could pay for, he sat for an hour, his eyes angrily searching in vain for someone to argue with. The sight and sound of the metal grille descending on the bar like a guillotine added to his frustration, and a voice, screaming inside him, drove him on with increasing urgency deeper and deeper into the backstreets. Halfway down a deserted, cobblestoned alleyway he stopped.

Licensed bar, the sign said. The words 'Regina Snooker and Pool Club', painted in letters twice as large, hardly registered. The breeze block walls of the shack oozed a slime on which grew fungi he had not seen since his Cory Street days. Rainwater dripped at his feet off a corrugated iron roof that rattled in the wind. The doors, painted a lurid purple, were covered in spraycan graffiti. He watched a dog cock its leg against the wall. With a short grunt of satisfaction, David pushed open the door and walked into a smoky atmosphere through which he heard the click of snooker balls against the background of crude repartee, chopped up and spat out in short, foul-mouthed gobbets.

The lissom black youth behind the bar scanned David from head to toe.

'An' what could I possibly do for you, sir?' he asked.

'I could do with a drink.'

'Couldn't we all, darlin', in these tryin' times?' A sharp brain was rapidly analysing all the data eyes and ears could provide. 'But you must understand my predicament, friend. I am legally bound to serve only those who are bona fide members of the Regina Snooker and Pool Club. Now I just don't remember no member of mine' – an arm stretched out across the bar and long black fingers and a thumb caressed David's lapel – 'wearin' no threads like that. No, sir.'

David heard a snigger behind him. He turned to see a pink scalp shining through close-cropped hair as broad shoulders in black leather leaned over one of the tables to play a shot. A smouldering cigarette burned into the wood alongside him. Hidden in the shadows beyond the light that hung over the table, David sensed more of the same animal species. The barman saw the strange change in the face that turned back to him. To him, David, coming through the door, had been no more than some well-heeled wino who had drifted off course, maybe looking for a bit of rough on the side, but mainly booze – like oblivion. Now he was not so sure. The look of a man who would give his soul for a drink had gone, replaced by a calmness that was reflected in a cultured voice.

'And how exactly does one become a member?'

'Annual subscription is thirty pounds, darlin'.'

He realised he had pitched it too low when he saw the readiness with which David reached for his wallet.

'Plus ten, joinin' fee.'

'And does that entitle me to a large Scotch?'

The barman looked sadly at the wad of notes remaining in David's wallet after taking his share.

'Man, with that sort of foldin' money you c'n buy me too, body an' soul.'

Conscious of the silence that had descended behind him,

David pulled a wooden stool up to the bar. He paid for his drink with a twenty-pound note, leaving the change where it lay. With his wallet halfway back to his hip pocket, he changed his mind, laying that also on the bar beside the change. The barman slid it in front of him.

'Might be better to put that away, my friend. You don't need to go *lookin*' fur trouble roun' here. *It* just comes right on lookin' fur *you*.'

David took no notice, draining his glass and pushing it to be refilled. He had to be careful. He must not drink to the point of anaesthesia.

'Must have a pee. Where do I go?'

'Outside, darlin'. Round the back. Just follow your nose.' The barman watched as David got up unsteadily.

'An' take this with you.' He thrust the wallet into David's hand.

'Of course.' David nodded gratefully. 'How stupid of me.'

As he relieved himself, he leaned his head against the wall as if to get as close as possible to the foul stench around him. He turned, smiling, as he saw them crowding to get through the narrow entrance. His forehead crinkled with disappointment at how little the first toecap hurt as it was driven into his crotch. He did not resist as his arms were pinioned. Hurled back against the wall, his scalp split on the filthy brick. He saw the colours of the spider's web tattooed on someone's neck, the gold studs in his ear as a Stanley knife criss-crossed his chest. Try as he might not to block them, instinctive reflexes tightened his belly muscles against the blows that rained down, but there was no defence against the sickening pain as another boot smashed his kneecap. They let him slide to the floor before driving in with their boots once more. The sound of ribs cracking was no different from that he had laughed at when racking up the spreader in His Royal Highness's chest. Standing back, they looked down, curiously intrigued at the total lack of response.

'Hang abart.' The wallet did not come out of David's pocket without a struggle. 'This fuckin' geezer's givin' me the creeps. Look at 'is face. He's bleedin' well enjoyin' it.'

'P'raps this'll take the grin off 'is face 'en. Try this fur size.'

His eyes no more than inches above the reeking filth, David smelled once again the degradation of being brought down to the level of animal excrement. This time, he made no attempt to fight his way up from the depths of his humiliation, welcoming the boot that thudded into his cheek as if accepting a priceless, bejewelled gift from some Arab prince.

Even in the madhouse atmosphere of a Casualty Department, there can be traced, through the mosaic of human misfortune, a vague diurnal pattern that imprints itself subconsciously into the mind of anyone who has worked there for any length of time. Frosty early mornings bring in the old ladies who have broken their wrists while tottering to the supermarket. Late nights produce the slashed face, the broken jaw. The ennui of the long afternoon, combined with the drugging repetition of the production line, provides everything from the sliced fingertip to an entire limb avulsed by some remorseless machine. Early evenings are deceptively quiet periods when the staff prepare for the scalded child and the distraught mother whose concentration after a long day has lapsed at bathtime. As a result, it is not unknown for even full-time casualty officers, worldly men, difficult to surprise, occasionally to raise an eyebrow simply on account of the type of injury and the time of day.

John Coles, one of St Bartholomew's casualty consultants, sighed as he heard the knock on his door. He did not bother to hide his displeasure as one of his registrars poked his head into the room.

'Well?'

'Sorry to trouble you, Mr Coles, but would you come and have a look at this one?'

'Why? What is it?' He had other things on his mind – a request for a solicitor's report on the desk before him and school fees to be paid.

'Mugging, sir. The Nightrunners again, judging by the signature – except I thought they'd all be in each other's beds this time of day.'

'So they've taken to working an afternoon shift. Times are

hard. What's so special? I've seen a slashed chest before. What else has he got?'

'First glance – facial injury, few ribs, maybe pneumothorax, possibly spleen. But it's not just that.' The registrar hesitated, searching for words to define the indefinable. 'I don't know – there's something odd about him. I think you ought to see him.'

'Police?'

'No sign of them at the moment. He was just brought in by ambulance.'

'Where did they find him?'

'Lying on the floor in the outside bog of a backstreet snooker club.'

'Where else. How very stupid of me to ask.' He jerked his head. 'All right, I'll be there in a minute.'

When Coles pulled back the curtain and stepped into the cubicle, he carried out the instantaneous, head-to-toe scan that had become second nature. In seconds he had drawn a base line upon which to pile detail. The quality of the clothes, evident even through the bloodstains and the reek of urine, did not altogether surprise him. He had seen that often enough. The big wheel from the City – one too many drinks after clinching the important deal – gets to feel a bit randy – goes cruising for that bit of rough that alone would bring peace, his wallet bulging with enough money to buy him the most expensive hooker in town, only to fall into the wrong company. It happened. It was the man's attitude that struck him as odd, the disinterested calm where there was usually fear and pain, remorse and humiliation. Except for the shallow, jerky respiration, he might as well have been lying on some Mediterranean beach, soaking up the sun.

'Good afternoon,' Coles smiled. 'First things first: what's your name?'

The man might have been stone deaf for all the reaction that provoked. Coles looked at the sister who was cutting away the sodden shirt sleeves. She simply shrugged her shoulders – she had her own problems. Coles tried again.

'Your name, please?'

The eyes that stared back were not entirely blank. But they evinced none of the usual fear of white coats and the power wielded by those who wore them, the terrified glances at monitors and drip stands, the searching out of nurses for compassion and comfort. In their place was the calm of someone happy in a normally hostile environment. The registrar had been right – it was bloody odd.

'You must help us. You've obviously been beaten up. We *must* find out just how badly you've been injured. To do that, we need your help. Now tell me, where exactly have you got pain?'

Total detachment. Hell – the hint of a smile? Coles turned his back, frowning in irritation.

'Get him stripped off, Sister.' He stretched out his hand. 'Let me have his jacket and trousers. I imagine his wallet's gone?'

'It has.' The registrar looked up, needle poised over a distended vein. 'I looked.'

'And have you been through all his pockets?'

'No.'

With the look reserved for juniors who had missed some critical physical sign, Coles thrust a hand deep into an inside pocket to produce a sealed envelope. The name of the embassy to which the letter was addressed had him pursing his lips. He hesitated, holding it in front of the patient's eyes, waiting for some reaction. There was none. His movements slow and deliberate, allowing the man every chance to stop him if he wished, Coles inserted a thumb under the flap and tore the envelope open.

'Bloody hell,' he muttered as he read for the second time the letterhead, heavily embossed into the parchment-like paper. He held the sheet in front of his registrar's face long enough for him also to read the name. Quick enough to realise it was an account, ready to be posted, the registrar held Cole's wrist with his free hand, unfolding the sheet sufficiently to see the bottom line. He whistled softly, working out how many months of hard graft he would have to put in to earn that much. Both men took a sudden renewed interest in their patient, lying there so still, naked, lacerated and battered. Without another word, Coles started at the top, working his way down with as much care and concentration as if he were back examining his long case in his Fellowship finals.

A scalp wound that would need suturing – a depressed fracture of upper jaw that would probably need elevating – the noughts-and-crosses pattern, now so instantly recognisable, slashed into his chest – some ribs gone on the left side with possibly air in his pleura – a rigid belly that might mean a ruptured spleen, one testicle four times the size of the other – and a smashed knee.

Could be worse.

Now it was a question of priorities, not all of them surgical. He turned to the sister and registrar who watched him with more than the usual interest.

'He needs an X-ray of skull and upper jaw, chest, abdo and right knee. If he's got a pneumothorax, put an intercostal tube in it with an underwater seal. I'll get the general surgeons to see his belly. Put a back splint on that knee for now and we'll get the orthopods to see that later also. The lacerations can wait until we know whether the general surgeons or the orthopods want to do anything under GA. All right then – any queries?'

They shook their heads.

'Right then – move.'

He turned to smile at his patient once more.

'Hopefully, nothing too bad, Mr Royall. But you're going to need a few things patched up. I think you probably have a pneumothorax, so the first priority is to . . .'

His voice sank, tailing away altogether as he was ignored. The total indifference on David's face slowly doused the brisk professionalism, leaving Coles staring back, dumbfounded. Coles could smell the whisky, but there was none of the stupor of booze about the eyes, rather the reverse, shining as they did with the intensity of someone seeing things only too clearly.

'We need to get in touch with your family, Mr Royall,' Coles began. 'Will Mrs Royall be at home?'

Again he stopped as, for the first time, he saw in David's face the agony that he had expected from his physical injuries. One eye was closing rapidly as a result of the jaw fracture, but nothing could hide the tortured look as David became agitated.

'Don't worry, Mr Royall. I'll speak to her myself. I'll be very careful not to worry her unduly. I'll tell her you're going to be fine.' Coles turned his back on the grunting, meaningless noises David made. 'I'll be back shortly.'

'He's in Bart's, Dr Drew.'

It was the second time Martha had rung. The first time had been as the search for its youngest Member of Council had started when the College had found the BMW, abandoned on its steps like some treasured sacrifice on the altar of ambition.

'All right, Martha, I'll go and see how he is. What did they say about him?'

'They wouldn't tell me much, Dr Drew. Such a nice young man. So upset when he heard about Mrs Royall and Debbie – he didn't know. He just said Mr Royall had one or two injuries – nothing more. He said he'd been mugged. Mugged, Dr Drew.' Martha began to cry again. 'As if he didn't have enough troubles, poor man.'

'Don't worry, Martha. He couldn't be in better hands. I'll ring you back and let you know how he is.'

'I'm so sorry to have involved you, Dr Drew, but I didn't know where to turn. And when they found his car like that, with the engine still running, I didn't know what to think. I thought he'd . . .'

'I know, Martha.'

'You were the only one I could think of, Dr Drew. There was no one. He has nobody now. Only Sir Marcus, I suppose – and he's on his way back from Singapore.'

'I'm glad you rang me, Martha. I would have been very cross with you if you hadn't. Don't worry, I'll look after him. What was the name of the doctor at Bart's?'

'A Dr Coles. Such a kind man.'

Twenty minutes later, John Coles's face lit up as Drew introduced himself.

'Christ, am I bloody glad to see you!' He ignored the flicker of pain that crossed Drew's face. 'Here I am with a badly mauled Member of Council on my hands and I can't find anyone to take any bloody notice.'

'You've heard about his wife and only daughter?' Drew asked.

'Yes.' Coles pulled a face. 'Poor sod.'

Men at the cutting edge of the profession need to harden their hearts. They see human tragedy acted out on a stage where the blood is real, where death is real, happening to different people each night, not a sham performance by the same man night after night. Was the play any more real if the central character was a Harley Street man? No cause for a standing ovation.

'What's he got altogether?' Drew asked.

'Lacerations of scalp and chest. A local fraternity, well known for their suppressed artistic inclinations, got at him with a Stanley knife. No great problem there really. Fractured zygoma that needs elevating. Fractured ribs and a pneumothorax – we've put a tube in that. The general surgeons are seeing him now but I don't think he's got a ruptured spleen. His urine is loaded with blood so he's having an IVP. That's about it. Oh' – Coles raised a hand as if he had just remembered something trivial – 'and a comminuted fracture of patella. The orthopods will want to do something about that.'

'Can I see him?'

'Of course. And the best of luck to you.'

Drew raised an eyebrow. 'What d'you mean?'

'I mean no one's been able to get a word out of him yet. Strange bastard. If that's what it takes to become a Member of Council, I think I'll stick to my golf. Just lies there as if in a coma. Didn't flinch when we put the intercostal tube in. For one moment I got the impression he smiled. Any sort of anaesthesia at the moment seems to be a complete waste of time.'

Drew waited patiently outside the cubicle until the general surgical team emerged. He stood in the path of an anxious-looking senior registrar and introduced himself once more.

'What d'you think? Anything in his belly?'

'No, I don't think so.' He spoke to the anaesthetist from a district general hospital with the friendliness of someone sure in his own mind that he, too, was not going to get a teaching hospital appointment. 'I think the rigidity is reflex from his ribs and kidney damage. But I'm not carrying the can for this one. I'm just off to ring my boss.' He put on a look of nervous determination. 'This is one he's going to come in for, wherever he is. I'm not having the last word on a guy like this; they just don't pay me enough. Anyway, I could be up for a job in front of him in six months' time.'

Drew laughed sympathetically. 'But you don't think you'll have to do anything?'

'No. He's obviously not bleeding to death from his kidney so they'll probably treat that conservatively. Just a patching up job all round, really. Three months' time and he'll be as good as new. What I can't understand is' – the voice hushed conspiratorially, the face twitching to the scent of a petty scandal – 'what the hell was he doing in a place like that?'

'You haven't heard?'

The SR shook his head, his eyes shining as the mystery deepened, while Drew took a sudden dislike to the young man, seeing no reason to spare his feelings.

'His wife and only daughter were killed in a skiing accident yesterday.'

It had the desired result. The SR closed his eyes as if rendering up a plea for forgiveness.

'God, I'm sorry. That probably explains the . . .'

He never got to tell what it explained, for at that point he saw Drew's back disappear between the curtains.

With one eye now completely closed, David watched Drew as he worked his way around the couch amongst the drip stands and drainage bottles. He said nothing, but there was a questioning appeal in the one eye that now seemed to clamp its attention on Drew and follow his every movement. Drew reached for the hand free from the intravenous drip, but David pulled it away as if he had come close to contaminating something sterile. It took ten minutes of gentle but sturdy compassion to bring the hand within range once more. Once he had clasped it, Drew felt the grip of a drowning man.

13

Mary Drew pulled back the curtains to gaze through the patio doors out on to the garden. The sight of the snowdrops and crocuses brought a look of pleasure to a serene face. Behind her, grinning from ear to ear, stood her son, holding a loaded breakfast tray as if bearing gifts to a king.

'Breakfast for Mr Royall. Mr Royall is a nice man.'

'Good morning, David.' Mary Drew turned towards the bed. 'Did you sleep well? It's a beautiful day. Just like the first day of spring. I can't believe it's still only February. You must wrap up warm and get out into the garden today, now you've had your plaster off. And John's got a new joke for you.'

Smiling, Mary Drew nodded to her son. His face beaming across the toast and coffee, John Drew asked, 'Where was King Henry VIII crowned?'

'I don't know, John. Where was King Henry VIII crowned?'

'On his head.'

John's peal of laughter died away as he saw little or no reaction on David's face. A quick glance at his mother and he tried again.

'Where was the Magna Carta signed then?'

David gave a faint, polite smile as he shook his head.

'On the bottom.'

'Very good, John.'

There was a sadness in David's voice that had John looking questioningly at his mother, crestfallen that he had failed to cheer Mr Royall up with jokes they had rehearsed together so many times. David saw the disappointment and struggled to smile.

'You should go on the stage, John; you tell your jokes so well. You'd make a fortune, making people laugh.'

Reassured, John's radiant smile returned. He put the tray

down in front of David. 'I made the toast.' He put his head back to roar with laughter. 'Three pieces – big fire.'

Mary Drew saw David's attempt at a laugh. 'Go along now, John,' she said. 'Let Mr Royall have his breakfast in peace. Don't forget you promised me you'd help me with the potatoes this morning.'

John Drew's face instantly became serious. 'Mr Royall likes potatoes. And carrots.'

For a moment, they listened to his voice as he headed for the kitchen, repeating the words over and over to himself as if committing an important message to memory.

'He's such a lovely boy,' Mary Drew said wistfully. 'Such good company. I really don't know how we're going to manage when he goes to Clavely Court.'

'You're still going to send him?' David looked at Mary Drew's unlined skin. He wondered why anyone bothered to wear makeup.

'Yes. Michael and I have made up our minds. We've decided we mustn't be selfish and keep him. We must think of John's future – that's all that matters. And, of course,' she smiled, 'yours.'

'You must be the two most generous people . . . I don't deserve . . .'

Mary Drew saw the crumpling face and moved quickly to pour the coffee.

'Now don't start that again. It was the least we could do.'

'I can never repay . . .'

David looked down dejectedly at shaking fingers that toyed with a blackened piece of toast.

'There's no question of repayment, you silly man. I know Michael will be only to happy to help you get settled again as soon as you're fit. If there's any question of repayment, it's we who owe you; all that private work you've put Michael's way.'

'Which, of course, has now come to a halt. I don't imagine for a moment anyone else has given him any private work. Someone else I've let down.'

'David Royall, I shall be very cross with you if you go on talking like that.' She gave emphasis to her words by jerking the bedclothes straight. 'We have more than enough to live on quite comfortably. I know Michael misses working with you – he's told me so – but frankly I'm not too sorry. As you know, Michael's not one to shirk his NHS work for the private side, and he used to come home looking very tired at times. It wouldn't worry me if he never did another private case in his life. However' – she took the tray away, leaving the coffee – 'no doubt, knowing what you men are, you'll both be back there, working yourselves to death again very shortly.'

She watched the slow shake of his hand.

'Yes you will.' She smiled encouragingly, looking around the room. 'And, in some ways, the sooner you get out of here the better. At least then I can have my dining room back.'

They had all come and gone. Sir Marcus Lee, a thrusting tycoon transformed overnight into a dazed, shrivelled old man, had offered all the help money could buy. The President of the Royal College of Surgeons had arrived at the bedside at Bart's, modestly unannounced, to offer his condolences and ask if there was anything he could do. Colleagues and senior administrators had shown their faces, only to go away embarrassed and discomforted by something in David's baleful stare. The only person to have appeared regularly, following faithfully from hospital bed to converted dining room, undeterred by the silence, had been Mal. Never staying long enough to sit, he had stood at the foot of the bed, awkward and inarticulate, flowers or chocolates clamped in one hand. The longest sentence he had managed, exploded through suppressed Celtic passion, was, 'Wish I'd been there with ew, boyo. We'd 'ave shown 'em a thing or two.'

Even Mal had not understood.

It was the first day on which the weather was warm enough to work with one of the large steel doors rolled back. Still limping slightly, David crossed the floor to where Drew had piled the bags of cement. Grunting with the effort, he tried to lift one and failed. On the other side of the building, John Drew put down his trowel and started out to help. He looked puzzled as his father put out a hand to stop him.

'John's strong. John'll lift it for Mr Royall.'

'No, John.' Drew shook his head. 'Let Mr Royall do it for himself.'

They both watched as David struggled. The bag split and his feet disappeared under a mound of grey powder. They saw him sink to his knees, the picture of dejection, trying to scoop the cement back into the broken bag with his hands. This time, Drew did not stop his son from helping.

The derelict brick-built garage had been a godsend to Drew and his son. Between them, they had put on a new roof, Drew taking pride in his son's great physical strength. They were now lining the solid brick wall with another wall of breeze blocks, John laying each block with a concentration that was painful to watch. His father, never failing to praise, had learned to resist the temptation to correct so long as the wall remained safe. The result was enough to make the most amateur of bricklayers shudder. To Drew, Wren could have done no better.

John chuckled as he picked up the broken bag, carrying it to where David had been mixing the cement. He bent to pick up the shovel.

'No, John,' Drew called. 'That's Mr Royall's job. Mr Royall's mixing the cement today.'

Laughing, John held the shovel out to David. 'John's laying the bricks today. Mr Royall's mixing the cement. We must make Mr Royall strong again. John's strong already.'

He returned to the block he was laying, squinting along it with intense concentration, leaving his father to watch David mix the sand and cement. Drew walked over, bending to pour some water from a bucket.

'You couldn't have done this a month ago, David. Feeling stronger?'

The only answer was a morose grimace in the direction of the split cement.

'Happens to everyone. Picking up these bags is more a knack than a question of strength. Except for that bit of a limp, you look back to normal to me. You've got to be feeling better.'

David paused just long enough to shrug his shoulders.

Drew took his time before saying gently, 'It's time you got back to work, cobber.'

'Trying to tell me something?' David's smile was not entirely convincing.

'Of course not.' For the first time, Drew showed signs of losing patience with the self-pitying monotone. 'I just hate to see skill such as yours going to waste, that's all.'

'Balls. I shan't work again.'

The derision was not aimed at Drew and Drew knew it. As the weeks passed he had come to accept the reaction as inevitable whenever anything was mentioned in which David had previously taken any pride. But he smiled as he saw what might be the first ray of hope – David glancing down at his hands, the skin thickened and coarse from weeks of shovelling concrete.

'Nothing scrubbing up a few times wouldn't get rid of,' Drew murmured.

David looked up suddenly, in time to catch the smile.

'I'm serious, Digger. At the moment I just don't see myself going back at all. And I can't stay here for ever.' His forehead creased. 'What I'm going to do when you and Mary finally get fed up with me, I just don't know.'

'There's no hurry, David; you know that. But . . .'

They both looked up as a small red BMW convertible scurried past the open door. There was hardly time for the spasm of pain to pass over David's face before they heard it stop and a door slam loudly. They heard voices and brisk, purposeful footsteps before someone stood framed in the doorway, the sun at her back, someone tall, confident. She took her time, coolly looking up and down and from side to side before striding towards them, her hard leather shoes kicking up the dust. She stood in front of David, upright and slim in a tight-fitting cashmere jumper and slacks, hands on hips, her face expressionless, as if unaware of anyone else's presence.

His face equally mask-like, his eyes half closed, David waved a hand towards her. 'Digger – Faye Grainger.' He did not take his eyes from her face as he introduced them. 'This is Michael Drew, a friend of mine.'

'How d'you do, Miss Grainger,' Drew smiled. He spread his palms, looking down at his clothes apologetically. 'I won't shake hands.'

A hand was thrust his way. He shook it and smiled as she made no attempt to brush it clean before replacing it on her hip. He looked down to see the dust already showing on her shoes and slacks. For some reason, he found no offence in the way he was otherwise ignored as this woman from another world stood silently waiting.

'John,' he called. 'It's time we took a break. John,' he repeated, more sternly, as his son showed reluctance to leave what he was doing.

'And this is Michael's son, John,' David said, calling John over. 'Come and meet Miss Grainger, John.'

'I'm Mr Royall's friend too. Mr Royall is a nice man.'

Faye Grainger, treated to the full impact of a beaming smile, suddenly looked disconcerted as if, for the first time, dealing with something she did not know how to handle. It was obvious that people like John did not feature largely in her world, and it took her a moment to sum things up, looking John up and down and then glancing over his shoulder.

'How d'you do, John? What are you building?'

'I'm building a wall.'

'It's a very good wall, John. Are you building it all by yourself?'

'Mr Royall is helping me. We're making Mr Royall strong again.'

'John.' Drew called his son gently, and moments later David and Faye were alone, free to stare at each other, tight-faced, the one challenging the other to show the weakness of speaking first.

'You took your time,' David said at last.

'Did I *have* to come?'

Faye searched his face, her own still emotionless.

'I'm sorry to have disappointed you, David, if you've been waiting for me to come and wipe away your tears. But I was never much good at the compassion bit. I can't say I enjoy the fact, but fact it is. I can't just turn it on like some women can.

That doesn't mean I wasn't sorry to hear about your wife and daughter – I was. That must have been a sod to take. I liked your wife. We could have got along.'

'You knew Jackie?' It was the first time he had spoken her name aloud, jerked from him in the first emotion he had felt for weeks other than self-hatred.

'We met once. I seem to remember telling you I was over here looking for a book to serialise.' A small smile played around her mouth. 'To be honest, I'd chosen a book already, but I thought it would be a good opportunity to see what sort of woman you'd married. I thought she was great. I was impressed – and surprised. But then, you never can tell, can you?'

'What d'you mean?'

'I always thought you'd marry someone rich, but I figured you'd go for someone who'd warm your golden slippers for you. I never saw you marrying a career woman.'

She stood back, surveying him from Mary Drew's haircut to his filthy boots.

'You look pretty fit to me. Filthy – but fit.' She glanced round, her lip curling. 'What the hell are you doing in this godforsaken dump?'

David looked round him also, smiling affectionately.

'Dusty, yes. Draughty, yes. But godforsaken?' He shook his head. 'That it most certainly is not.'

'Still looks a dump to me. How long are you going to stay in a place like this?' Her eyes focused more sharply. 'Dear God, look at you. You look pathetic, you *really* do.'

She waited with intense interest for his reaction. She had hoped for anger and pride; instead she saw abject submission. His eyes asked for pity, not for help. She stamped her foot, sending up a cloud of dust. 'I'm a bloody fool. I shouldn't have bothered,' she snapped, turning to leave.

'I'm so sorry if you flew over specially for such a short interview.' There was sufficient spark of human reaction to make her turn round. 'But there I go again, vanity of vanities, imagining for one moment you came all this way just to see me. That wouldn't be your style, would it. Not the successful business woman. I've no doubt I've been fitted in between more important appointments.'

'Got it in one, Davy boy. Though I must admit, while I've had a hell of a lot on my plate back in LA recently, something inside kept telling me I should come over. Well, thank God I didn't waste my time. I've got better things to do than wetnurse some spineless misery who caves in the first time he really gets kicked in the teeth.'

Her face twisted in fury, she took a step nearer to him.

'I wouldn't be so goddamned mad with you, David Royall, if I hadn't always had a soft spot for you. There was always something about you, ever since you were a kid. But now you disappoint me, David; you bloody well do. The first real hardship you run into and you throw your hand in.'

She saw him move, raising one hand.

'Yes; don't kid yourself. You've never known *real* hardship before. You might think you have, but you haven't. So you were born poor – where's the hardship in that if you've got a doting mother and enough brains to kick yourself out of the place? Try having a drunken slut for a mother and a father who rapes you, night after night, at the age of eight. Then you can talk about hardship.'

Faye stood quivering, the nearest to tears he had ever seen her. Slowly she calmed down, though her face remained pale.

'I'm sorry, David – about Jackie, I mean. And – what was your daughter's name? Debbie?'

'Yes. Debbie.'

He nearly choked on the name.

'But . . .' Faye wrinkled her nose as she looked down at her dusty trousers – 'grovelling in the dirt is not going to bring them back, David.'

'Maybe not. But I can't go back to that life again, Faye. It was so . . . so sham.'

'What's so goddamn wicked about achieving what you set out to do?' She paused, waiting for an answer. 'Tell me.' Still no sign. 'There's nothing wrong with success, David.'

He shrugged his shoulders, happy to slip back into the warm

cocoon of self-protection. Faye saw him fold in on himself once more.

'David,' she said, softly. 'Come back to LA with me for a couple of weeks. Let me help you straighten yourself out.' She looked around the old garage. 'You've done your penance.' She shifted her gaze to the calluses on his hands. 'Haven't you felt enough pain yet? Where's the sense in self-destruction? Your wife and daughter would not have wished it. It's not called for.'

She saw him shake his head.

He walked with her to the car, careful to keep a gap between her elegance and his grime. Faye turned to him after opening the car door.

'Goodbye, David.' Her child-of-eight eyes held his for a moment before she stretched up to kiss him lightly. 'You always were a stubborn bastard.'

The sound of the BMW's vicious acceleration brought Mary Drew to the front door.

'Oh,' she said, genuine disappointment on her face. 'She's gone – and I had the coffee all ready. Never mind. Perhaps she'll call again.'

'No,' David said, slowly. 'Somehow, I don't think that's very likely.'

'David.'

Drew got little reaction from a man who had found salvation in physical exhaustion. He shook his shoulder once more.

'David.'

He turned on the light and David rolled over on to his back, blinking as he struggled to shield his eyes from the glare. He grunted something unintelligible.

'Wake up, David.'

He closed one hand to rub the sleep from his eyes. 'What's the matter?' he growled. 'What time is it?'

'Just after six. It's John. I've been up all night with him. Come and have a look at him – *please*, David.'

A load of breeze blocks had been delivered the day before – a chance for John to show his strength. But the powerful young man had ignored them, a sure sign something was amiss. He had sat staring into the fire, rocking gently with his arms folded across his stomach. With Drew at work, it had been left to David to grab the chance of unremitting, mind-numbing toil, heaving the rough blocks until his hands bled. An evening had been spent in silent tension as they had pretended to watch TV, listening as they did so to John's quiet groaning.

John was vomiting into a bowl held by his mother as David walked into his bedroom, the colour and the smell of the vomit instantly triggering responses that had lain dormant for months.

'Have you got a pain, John?' David asked and saw mute appeal in the eyes that looked at him questioningly.

'John's strong. John's going to help Mr Royall get better.'

'And you have, John; you have. Now it's my turn to help make you better. Did you go to the toilet yesterday?' he asked and saw the confusion in John's eyes. 'Did you pass . . . ?'

'Did you make any rude noises yesterday, John?' his father broke in, helping out with a family patois developed over long, loving years.

John Drew blushed that his father should ask him such an embarrassing question in front of Mr Royall. He shook his head. Gently, David felt his noisy, distended abdomen, John pushing his hand away whenever he pressed on one particular spot. With Mary hovering in the background, two men who had seen it all before looked at each other across the bed. Drew saved David the task of putting it into words.

'Obstructed, isn't he?'

A simple nod.

'We'd better get him into hospital then, hadn't we?'

Again David nodded, anxious to do and say no more than would allow him to retreat once more behind the emotional wall the Drews were so lovingly breaching.

'Ryles tube and a drip for a few days; he should be all right.'

Drew's words were half question, half statement, his eyes not leaving David's. This time, David did not respond, his mind in agonised conflict as he felt himself slowly being dragged by love and affection where he did not want to go, back into a world on which he had turned his back.

'No?' Digger's eyes narrowed.

'Not this one, no, Digger.'

Pain and tenderness – not to be confused one with the other. It was possible to have one without the other; unusual to have tenderness without pain, but far from rare to have someone, rolling round with colic, who would allow you to knead his abdomen without complaint. The facts were dragging at David with their inevitability. He could see where they were taking him. Tenderness meant irritation of the peritoneum that lined the inside of John's powerful abdominal muscles, a glistening membrane as sensitive as the eye's conjunctiva. That meant a roughened, engorged loop of his gut rubbing against it. With John's obvious obstruction, that spelled one thing and one thing only – gangrene.

'I wouldn't treat this conservatively, Digger, not if it was left to me. If it was pure obstruction, then yes, I think you'd be right. But he's got quite definite localised tenderness. That means, almost certainly, a strangulated loop in there. And, if I'm right, then the sooner he's operated on the better.'

'All right,' Drew said, quietly. 'We'd better get going then, hadn't we? And you *will* do it for us, David?'

His mind as blank as if time were standing still, David slowly shook his head.

'I couldn't, Digger,' he whispered.

'Yes you could,' Drew replied. 'And you *will*.'

'Please don't ask me.' David found difficulty in controlling a tremor in his voice. 'I couldn't.' He held out his hands. 'Look.'

'Nothing that a bit of soap and water won't fix,' Drew smiled. 'Good honest grime, that is. Never did anyone any harm. That's cement you've got under your fingernails, not staphylococci. At the moment, you're probably the most sterile surgeon in London.'

'That's not what I mean, Digger.'

'I know. But you will do it, won't you?'

David suddenly realised just how much he owed the man the other side of the bed.

'You'd risk your only son like that?' he asked.

'Nnnnoooo.' Drew's face frowned as he thought about it. He

spoke with the deliberation of a man weighing every word. 'No, I wouldn't risk my son's life for you. It's just that I think you are made of sterner stuff than the man who has been shuffling around this house for the past month or so. Deep down, you may not be the same *man* you were, but you're still the *surgeon* you were. There was nothing false about your surgery, David. Nothing will change that. You need never feel any guilt about that, whatever else you did. You're still the best surgeon I ever worked with. It wasn't *all* froth, that life you were leading.'

John's attention had swung back and forth between the two men as they spoke. It settled on David.

'Mr Royall make John better again? John helped Mr Royall get strong again.'

David felt the tender thrust go home. He smiled at Digger. 'What can I say to that?' he asked. 'I suppose I'd better go and get dressed.'

Two hours later, he stood naked and vulnerable beneath flimsy theatre garb. The brilliance of theatre lighting seemed to penetrate every guilty corner of his mind. He felt everyone's eyes on him, heard the whispers above the rattle of instruments. He took an age scrubbing up, his mouth as dry as that of a house surgeon about to do his first appendicectomy. As he pulled on his gloves, he tried to conceal his tremor from the nurse standing behind him tying up his gown. The registrar, gowned and ready to assist him, was new to him. They said nothing as they waited for the trolley to be wheeled in.

As he painted John's abdomen, the long swab holder exaggerated his tremor. It must have been obvious to Drew, though he affected to take little interest in what David was doing. David picked up the scalpel, his shoulders hunched, his head down, his hand trembling. He made one or two tentative attempts at incising the skin, drawing back each time at the last moment.

He put the scalpel down. With one hand leaning on John's chest, the other on his hip, he bent forward for the last time, staring at the floor like a high jumper balancing mind and body for the supreme effort. Taking a deep breath, he straightened to his full height, picked up the scalpel once more and, with a silent inward scream of pain, as if feeling the cut himself, made a firm, precise paramedian incision.

Once inside the abdomen, sheer professional pride drove out all thought of self. His mind slotted into a routine as if he had never been away. Ignoring the distended, obstructed gut that fought to spill from the wound, he searched for and found some collapsed bowel, tracing it back to the cause of the obstruction, a length of adhesion, the thickness of strong twine, a result of John's previous appendicectomy, under which a loop of small bowel, black and engorged, had become trapped. The accuracy of his diagnosis brought a quiet grunt of satisfaction.

He asked for scissors and snipped at the taut adhesion. It sprang back, freeing the loop of small bowel some six inches long. The theatre sister had the warm, moist towels ready and David gently enveloped the bowel in them. He stood back, waiting patiently, shutting his mind to any stimuli that might bring the outside world crashing in on him once more. Drew joined him to peer anxiously as David removed the towels.

The colour had improved, the arteries dancing to the heart's beat. David nipped the bowel between finger and thumb, and both men sighed their relief as they saw the muscle contract. The two constriction rings, however, the narrow, transverse strips of bowel that had lain immediately under the adhesion, remained deadly white.

'Could be worse, Digger,' David murmured, the first words he had spoken. 'The loop is viable but I will have to oversew these constriction rings. No great problem.'

He took the straight needle he usually used for such a procedure and found his tremor returning as the skin of his fingertips, as thick as any bricklayer's, dulled his sensitivity. He changed it for a needle holder and small curved needle, and the concentration he put into the two rows of sutures drained him as much as if he had just finished a punishing three-hour operation. By the time he had closed the abdomen he was too inwardly weary to acknowledge Drew's quiet 'Thank you, David.'

It took another half an hour for Drew to see his son safely on his way back to the ward. He found David in the surgeon's sitting room, still in his theatre clothes, his back towards him, gazing out of the window. When David turned, there was a look on his face that made Drew catch his breath. There was a rough, loving awkwardness about the way his arms fell on Drew's shoulders – rather as his son John's might when physically hurt – and Drew felt the racking sobs. He glared furiously over David's shoulder at the registrar who turned and fled. Drew kicked the door shut before clasping David's shuddering chest to him. Patiently, he waited for the emotional storm, brewed in months of guilt, to blow itself out.

'I've been so bloody selfish, Digger. I feel so guilty. I . . . I couldn't even wait to find them and bring them home to bury them.'

'Stop tormenting yourself, David,' Drew said quietly. 'You've been through a dreadful time. No one can be sure how they'd react under conditions like that. But it's over now.'

They sprang apart, David turning quickly towards the window again as an unmistakable voice was heard trumpeting down the corridor. Drew stood back as Brian Pullman strode through the room on his way to the changing room.

'Some people can be very inconsiderate,' Pullman growled at the floor as he marched between them. 'Why is it I'm always the one to be held up whenever someone wants to fiddle some minor case in? Being senior surgeon means nothing these days. It should be enough that I carry the brunt of the major surgery in this hospital. No damned respect, that's the trouble . . .'

David waited until he heard the door to the changing room slam before daring to turn and face Drew once more. The smile on his face deepened to short grunting laughs as he swept the back of one hand across his cheeks. Drew began to grin, giving out snorting sounds, and soon both were doubled up with laughter.

Drew was the first to control his splutterings.

'*Plus ça change, plus c'est la même chose*,' he grinned. 'Welcome back, David.'

14

It had to start somewhere. But did the rebirth process have to be so noisy, so emotionless, his choice of birth canal so grubby, so loveless?

David smiled inwardly. The train clattered to a halt, faces gliding past the windows as expressionless as targets in a shooting gallery. Tooting Bec. Mute zombies climbed aboard. With empty seats to spare, many chose to stand to judder and sway like aristos in their tumbrils. David smiled outwardly at the row of fellow human beings sitting opposite him. He shifted in his seat, looking round for human contact; but eyes which, in other surroundings, could register love, anger, hate, stared back stonily. The only reaction came from a teenager, someone about Debbie's age, her eyes as hard as the gold studs in her ears, her lips as tight as the jeans in her crotch. With a dimissive jerk of her head that sent a ripple through her green cockscomb, she looked away, her message loud and clear – dirty old bastard. Having made her position clear, the girl turned her head once more to find David still smiling her way. She stopped chewing gum for a moment to stare back brazenly. Slowly, arrogantly, she scanned him from head to toe and back again. The look on his face had not changed. It had not done the trick. Look 'em up an' darn as if you'd just eaten 'em an' then spat 'em art. That usually worked. But not with this one.

'Am I botherin' you or sump'n?'

The voice, brave and worldly, cut the gap between them, drawing towards him robot stares as he became the centre of her neighbours' patient apathy.

'Not a bit.' His smile only intensified.

''Ad a good look, 'ave yer?' The wad of gum appeared for a moment at the corner of a mouth drawn back in scorn.

Mentally David wiped away the glistening brown lipstick,

pinched out the gold studs. He lifted thick dark tresses as he pulled a sailing jacket round her shoulders.

'I'm sorry. You reminded me of someone I knew once.'

'Piss orf, won'tcha?'

There was a snigger from further down the compartment and David swung his head in the direction of this tiny fragment of human response. But he was too late. Eyes front. Wipe that smile off your face.

Dirty old man – was that how he looked? Was that all that was left to him – the porno mags, the flasher's mac? He looked down at himself and gave a little laugh that brought a nod of confirmation from the girl. He could not remember how much his plain fawn raincoat had cost – two hundred pounds? three hundred pounds? – but it would do nicely for a flasher – single-breasted, not too long. A rich flasher maybe – but then, were all flashers poor? He thrust his hands deep into the pockets, trying to pull it out of shape, make it look less noticeable, as his head bent in contemplation. The supple brown leather of his hand-made shoes gleamed below the fine check of his trousers. He drew his feet back, but there was no space beneath his seat, no hiding place for what still helped separate 'him' from 'them'. The compartment filled the nearer they got to the spawning ground of the West End. Clapham Common. Stockwell. By the time they reached the Oval, the girl came and went in glimpses between swaying bodies. David looked up at the roof. Somewhere up there – they must have passed it by now – was Queen's. Queen's College Hospital. Centre of excellence. Centre of his universe. He saw white coats and heard voices, fast-talking, competitive voices. He heard hurrying feet and voices, more fast-talking, competitive voices. He saw a clinic – and talk; a surgeon's room – and talk; a clinical meeting – and talk. Talk. Talk. If you didn't talk, you were dead. It did not matter how good you were – or how bad – you must talk or go under. To ask questions without a view of your own, even on something outside your own speciality, revealed a fatal flaw. To concede a point in an argument was to show an inherent weakness. Statements – categorical statements – they were the building blocks of professional success. Confidence. Self-assurance. Head up. Steely-eyed. Silver-tongued. Brass-necked. Feet of . . .

And that wasn't strictly true either. David wriggled guiltily in his seat, his mind running ahead of a wave of envious paranoia. He would have to watch out for that in this new life he had planned. There were a lot of very able, articulate men and women up there too.

Leicester Square. He must change trains. The girl stood up also. David let others get between himself and her as they squeezed out of the doors – no point in pushing his luck. He followed at a safe distance, his eyes glued to where the seam of her jeans disappeared between the rhythmic buttocks. He sighed. He felt – nothing. Three months before and it would have excited him, a reminder of the sex that was all about him, pressing in on him, there for the taking. Now, he felt – nothing. Was he sad – or glad? Would it come back? Did he want it to come back? He felt a strange sense of loss at the parting of their ways, she of the tight jeans towards the exit, he of the new life towards the Piccadilly Line.

High Holborn tube station meant but one thing to David – examinations. To the north, up Southampton Row, was Queen's Square and the forbidding Examination Hall, to the south Lincoln's Inn Fields and the awesome façade of the Royal College of Surgeons, both within easy walking distance. He felt again the tense expectancy as he trundled up the long escalators. It brought back what had been for him a time of quietly competent professional achievement. Not for him the neurotic discussions in the corridors, the last-minute searching through text books, the endless shuffling queues to the basement urinals. He had warmed himself in the instinctive nods of approval from old men in dark suits and gold-rimmed glasses and had walked away with no doubt about the outcome. He had needed no one at that stage, his ambition then a private matter, churning away inside him. Only in later years had his ruthless drive broken the surface to become obvious to all.

Turning in to Lincoln's Inn Fields, he looked at his watch. He was early. He walked across the spot where he had sat in his car after hearing of their deaths, taking a deep breath as if afraid, at the last moment, his courage might fail him. He had to convince himself he was over all that. There would still be no-go areas – he had accepted that – but they would be of his own choosing, not created out of fear or remorse. He used up another ten minutes walking round the square. Another look at his watch and he straightened his shoulders, turned and pushed his way through the revolving doors.

Sir Berkeley Reynolds, President of the Royal College of Surgeons, was a kindly man. He was also a very large man. He extended towards David a hand of which any lumberjack would have been proud. (The myth of the surgeon's hands – the long, slender, sensitive fingers beloved of romantic novelists. Had they not seen the ham-sized fists of some concert pianists?) David shook it with respect.

'Good of you to see me, Berkeley.'

'Rubbish. Sit down.' Sir Berkeley waved vaguely beside his desk as if there should be a chair there somewhere. 'Always pleased to see you, you know that, David. What's this appointment business?' He tried to point as he wedged a Cambridge rowing blue's frame into a standard-size chair. 'Door's always open.'

'I . . .'

'Not more trouble, I hope?'

For you or me? David was no different from anyone else and the immediate reaction passed through his mind, but another look at the craggy face reassured him.

'No. No trouble.'

'Appointment,' Sir Berkely rumbled on. 'Member of Council making an appointment like a rep in outpatients. Not gone to work for some bloody drug company, have you? Not trying to sell me anything, are you?' he grinned.

'I wouldn't dare,' David grinned back, more at ease with the most powerful man in surgery than he had ever imagined possible. On previous occasions, personal ambition had always stood in the wings, censoring every word, analysing every reply. If he could not impress, at least he must not offend. Now – it was different. Now, he did not have to think over every word before uttering it. 'I just thought it would be courtesy to come and let you know my plans – officially,' he added, smiling. 'Hence the appointment.'

'Kind of you, David, but not really necessary. If I can help in any way . . . Goes without saying. But first things first – how are you? You're looking really well.'

David laughed to himself. It seemed even presidents of Royal Colleges used the oldest of medical tricks – ask someone how they are and then cut the ground from under their feet by telling them how well they look.

'I'm fine.' He wondered whether any patient of Sir Berkeley's had ever had the courage to say otherwise.

'Better than the last time I saw you, sitting up in bed. And I don't just mean physically.' Sir Berkeley lowered his head like a bull about to charge. He stared at an immaculate blotting pad, embarrassed as he always was when it came to dealing with emotions. 'Awful business, David. I don't feel we helped very much. Not much good at that sort of thing, we surgeons, are we?' He picked up a paper knife, drawing a long curving groove in the soft paper. He threw the knife across the desk as if it displeased him suddenly. 'Always feel so bloody inept.' He looked up. 'How did you manage? I heard you went to stay with someone from the Merton – is that right?'

'That's right. Two – no, three,' David corrected himself, smiling, 'very wonderful people.'

'It's a time when you find out who your real friends are, that's for sure.' Sir Berkeley cleared his throat, a noisy process, before going on with a fresh voice as if starting a new paragraph. 'So . . . What now? As you can imagine, there have been all sorts of rumours.'

'I'm sure there have.'

'We're all the same, David,' the President grinned. 'I'm sure you're as bad as the rest of us. Show me the surgeon who doesn't like a bit of a gossip.'

'What have you heard?'

'Mainly that your apartment in Harley Street is on the market? Is that true?'

'Yes.'

Theoretical implications had already been pencilled in on hearing the rumour. Time now for black and white.

'But you're keeping your rooms there.' A statement, not a question.

'No, they're going too,' David said quietly, firmly, watching genuine concern spread across honest features.

'David.' Sir Berkeley drawled the name like someone trying to slow things down. A mind that had difficulty in finding the right words of comfort in time of bereavement knew exactly what he was talking about now. 'I hope you are not doing anything bloody stupid. That doesn't mean . . . ?'

'Yes – that means I'm giving up private work.'

'I'm sorry to hear that, David, I really am. No doubt there'll be joy in quite a few places south of the Bayswater Road when that news gets out' – he had to swing his chair through a right angle so as to cross one massive thigh over the other – 'but it makes me sad.' He waved a hand in the air. 'I know people think of this place as responsible for training and research and standards of NHS appointments and all that – all the things that are good and wholesome and proper. But I would like to see the College as at least the guardian of our conscience about the private sector too – even if we have damn-all control over it. So, as I say, it saddens me. There are enough sharp customers out there – we can ill afford to lose men of integrity like yourself.'

'Integrity?'

Sir Berkeley heard the bitter edge to the one short word. One look at David's face confirmed it. He saw the conversation going down a road he had no intention of following. In one swift movement, he held up a broad palm.

'Now hang on. I'm here to help, David, but one thing I do not do – I do not take confessions. I'm a surgeon, not a priest. Yes, integrity – integrity in your surgery, which is the only thing I understand. Outside the theatre and the ward . . . in the home . . .' He shrugged his shoulders. Had he too seen the photographs; the dripping, naked girls? 'But between you and the patient, private or NHS, no; I've never heard a word against you.' A grin wiped away some of the gravity. 'Which is unusual in our racket, isn't it? Still . . .' He slid one hand up under his jacket collar to enjoy a good scratch. It was an unconscious habit to be seen in his lectures and committee meetings. He had even done it in the middle of a TV interview, driving his wife wild – making him look as if he needed a bath, she had fumed. 'Harley Street's loss will be Queen's gain. More time for research. The students will be glad.'

'I've resigned my sessions at Queen's.'

'You've *what?*' Sir Berkeley stopped in mid scratch, his lower jaw sagging.

'I've resigned from Queen's.'

'David, you can't.' The big man swung back towards his desk, agitated, his arms now extended, his hands outstretched as if trying to stem some invisible torrent. 'You must be mad. Have you thought . . . Let me ring . . . You can't leave Queen's.'

'My letter of resignation has already gone in.'

'But . . .' Sir Berkeley stopped, reluctantly accepting the inevitable as he saw the look on David's face. What was it he saw there, true peace or just a masochistic calm? Whichever it was, it did not go with the person he had known, the able, energetic, thrusting man. He could not reconcile the two. They just did not fit. Could it last? 'Are you sure you're not making a terrible mistake, David? What are you going to do?'

'I've applied to increase the number of my sessions at the Merton, up to full time if possible.'

'Hm.' Someone who had never held a session outside a teaching hospital was not impressed. Bloody waste. 'How many sessions do you have now?' he growled.

'Three.'

'Will there be any problems?'

'I don't know. There's plenty of work there, enough for four surgeons really. I've told them it is not my intention to do any private work, so that might help.'

'I'll make a few calls – if you're absolutely determined, that is?' He saw David nod. 'Let me think. Who's senior surgeon down . . .'

'Pullman. Brian Pullman.'

'Oh, God – him. Of course; I'd forgotten.' The President's eyes narrowed. Memories of a strained interview after the

Council elections soured the moment. 'Hmmmmm.' Regret at an earlier promise was obvious. 'I'm not sure I'd be doing you any favours by ringing *him*, David. Could well have the opposite effect. Strikes me as an awk'ard beggar – not an easy man to work with, I imagine, David. It won't be like a teaching hospital, you know. You're so much more in each other's pockets in a DGH.'

'I'll manage.'

'Where will you live?'

'I've bought a small terraced house in Wimbledon – ten minutes from the Merton.'

'A small terraced house in Wimbledon,' the President repeated quietly, frowning as if trying to imagine such a place.

'It's not as bad as it sounds,' David said, smiling. 'Quite attractive actually.'

They fell silent. It was a time for surveying the wreckage, picking up the pieces. Sir Berkeley started the process.

'At least some good will come of it. If you're going full time, with no private work, we can get our pound of flesh out of you here. I'll see to it you're on every subcommittee and working party we've got. I'll . . .' He stopped, his words slowing to synchronise with the shaking of David's head. 'You're not . . . ?' he began again, his face the picture of disbelief.

'No, Berkeley,' David reassured him. 'I'm not resigning from the Council – the last thing I would want to do is cause *you* any embarrassment. But I will not be standing for re-election next time.'

It would have been nice, sitting there, Sir David Royall. But maybe it had never been on the cards, right from the start. Without the slightest tinge of envy, he looked across the desk at Sir Berkeley. He felt nothing but admiration, an emotion he had been too busy, too competitive to experience very often before. Sir Berkeley Reynolds, KBE, PRCS, Winchester, Cambridge and Bart's. An Olympic oarsman from a patrician family, one brother an appeal court judge, the other a rear admiral. A surgeon's surgeon, someone you sent your wife to see, yet with the academic ability to write half a standard textbook of surgery. A shrewd medical politician with the common touch, equally at ease with royalty and registrar. *That* was the way to become President of the Royal College of Surgeons. His own beginnings had been too lowly, his upward path too steep, too frenetic, certain to go through the roof sooner or later. It would be different at the Merton, his sights lowered. Time to watch the grass grow. Reflect. Think of others.

'That, I am sure,' Sir Berkeley growled, 'would be a great mistake. You realise what you might be giving up?'

David shrugged his shoulders. There was a smugness of the converted about his look that began to get under the big man's skin, bringing sudden anger to his face.

'You're being a bloody fool, David. Why? What are you trying to do to yourself?' A hand closed into a fist. 'Now look – you've got at least three years to think about it. Don't go doing anything stupid. You are *not* resigning from anything in this place – I'll see to that. If anything comes in here in writing, I will personally see that it is torn up.' Sir Berkeley leaned his elbows on the desk, directing his fist at David as if in invitation to Indian wrestling. He squinted over the top of it. 'I don't think people change. To my way of thinking, you are what you are – what you are from the moment you are born.' The fist began to pump up and down. 'You're a survivor, David; a competitor. There's nothing you can do about it and there's no shame in it. But sooner or later it will show through again whether you're in the Merton or Harley Street.'

'In that case, we'll have to see, won't we?'

'Yes, we will.'

Self-righteous bastard, Sir Berkeley Reynolds thought.

15

They sat in the ward sister's office, waiting for Pullman to finish his ward round. Harry O'Connor looked down ruefully at his plastered wrist and thumb, then apologetically up at David.

'Jeez, David, but I'm sorry. Bloody stupid thing to do.'

His flat round face creased in disgust around a snub freckled nose. His frown pulled bushy black eyebrows together, furrowing his forehead beneath tight black curls that covered his head like an astrakhan cap. The colour of his cheeks labelled him a boozer, which he was not – he was far too healthy an animal for that. Bright blue eyes shone from a ruddy complexion, heightened by his second visit of the year to the slopes above Cortina. He squinted over his injured right hand now raised in front of him.

David smiled sympathetically. 'What exactly have you done to yourself?'

'Bennett's fracture. Fracture dislocation of the thumb.'

'I know what a Bennett's is. There's no need to explain.'

O'Connor looked across at him sharply, saw his face and grinned back.

'How did you do it?' David asked.

'Sex.'

'Sex?' Confused pictures of naked interlocked limbs flashed through David's mind.

'Yeah – sex. I was coming down this slope, minding my own business, when this little Italian girl with a bottom like a peach went past me, doing a ton, and I went after her with my tongue hanging out. I think I must have skied over my stick – anyway I went arse over tip, that's for sure. When I picked myself up about a hundred feet below, this thumb looked as if it had been stuck on the wrong way round. Bloody dangerous this skiing. That's the first inj——'

His voice died away. His head fell back for a moment, eyes closed. Slowly he reopened them and levelled an honest gaze at David.

'I'm a stupid bastard sometimes, David. Please forgive me. But it's very difficult, watching every word. Can I just say how sorry, sorry, sorry I am – and then treat you as normal? If we're going to work together, I can't go pussyfooting around for ever. I'm not the type.'

'And thank God for it. Don't worry about it, Harry. I'm over it now.' David nodded at the plaster cast. 'Must make things awkward.'

'You've no idea.' O'Connor's face broke into a relieved grin. 'Have you ever tried wiping your arse left-handed?'

O'Connor sank further into his chair, his trouser legs rising to reveal powerful hairy ankles above garish socks. He paused as David, still shaking with laughter, signed a form his house surgeon had pushed in front of him. O'Connor's suit was as close to professional conformity as his essentially sporting nature allowed, the cut and cloth the best that could be obtained with what was left out of an income into which two sons at prep school, two skiing holidays a year and membership of Sunningdale made considerable inroads. He waited until the housesurgeon had left the room.

'It means more work for you, I'm afraid, David. I'm sorry. I reckon I can do outpatients and ward rounds as long as I dictate everything but, obviously, operating is out of the question. Would you rather I went sick so they can get you a locum?'

David shook his head. If O'Connor went sick, then, legally, he was not fit to do any private work either. If you were sick for one, you should be sick for all – legally. But there were the consultations, the legal reports, the domiciliary visits, good moneyspinners that could be managed even with a hand in plaster. 'No need,' he smiled. 'In some strange way, I'm glad. No doubt my bone-idle nature is bound to surface again sooner or later, but at the moment I just feel I want to work myself into oblivion. Have you ever felt like that?'

O'Connor managed to laugh and look horrified at the same time. 'God forbid.'

'How long do you expect to be in plaster?' David asked.

'Dunno. Cagey bastards, these orthopods. Six weeks at least, I imagine. About my intake . . .'

'No problem,' David broke in.

'But Brian's going to play hell, you wait and see.'

'No problem,' David repeated. 'I'll do your intake. No need to bother our beloved leader.'

'That's good of you, David, but there's no reason why the bastard shouldn't do his share. He'll walk all over you, you know, if you give him half a chance. He's just the type. And I'm not sure you realise what it means, doing two out of three weekends' emergencies in a DGH. Teaching hospital staff don't know they're born. It can . . .'

David let O'Connor ramble on. Sod Pullman. Puzzled, he listened to his own thoughts. Why didn't that sound genuine any more? He tried again, and again it lacked conviction. There was no bite to it. Sod him, sod him, sod him. Nothing. It meant nothing. It roused about as much emotion as he felt now at the sight of a beautiful woman – zero; blank; zilch. Empty. Even the sensuous satisfaction of hatred had gone. How could O'Connor possibly understand how much he needed the work to fill the hollowness?

'. . . Not to mention the private side.'

David once again became conscious of O'Connor talking. 'How are you going to manage about that, Harry?' he asked.

O'Connor shrugged his shoulders. 'I'm not – that's the simple answer to that. I'll still have the odd consultation, of course, but you know as well as anyone, it's very difficult to carry on seeing patients if you're not able to operate. It soon gets around amongst the GPs. I had a gall bag and a mastectomy booked for the BUPA hospital next week.' He grinned ruefully. 'I'd ask you to do them for me if I didn't think it might give you a taste for private practice again.'

'No fear of that, Harry. What will you do about them?'

'The gall bladder I think I can keep on ice until this is off.' He waved his plaster.

'And the mastectomy?'

'That, I'm afraid, will have to go to one of those vultures in Queen's. Can't keep her waiting.'

'You wouldn't ask Brian?'

'Brian?' O'Connor became agitated. 'Not bloody likely – money-grabbing old bastard.'

David's eyebrows shot up. 'Money gra——?'

'You didn't see it?'

'See what?'

'The programme.'

'What programme?'

'About six weeks ago. I think it was BBC – one of their documentaries.'

David shook his head. 'I haven't exactly been in the mood for TV recently.'

'You *have* been out of touch, haven't you? Didn't Digger tell you?' O'Connor's voice dropped. 'It was . . .' He got up, walked to the door and closed it, sat once more and leaned towards David. 'It was a documentary about investigative journalism. It was . . .'

The cameras had been there, all the way from the initial editorial conference to the final ambush. A predatory, hard-nosed reporter, making a handsome living from moral rectitude, had hovered over his prey, the Wimbledon ticket tout. The trap had been baited, the word put about – the wealthy American, a pair of Centre Court seats, the men's final. The meet had been arranged, the hush of the thickly carpeted hotel lounge, the background music, the bargaining, the repeat of the price in case the microphones had not picked it up the first time – followed by the hardening of the voice, the close-ups, the kill.

But then had come the sudden change of tack, the hope of bigger prey. They had got the dealer. Now they wanted the supplier. The deal had been spelled out – an even wealthier American wanting a block of six Centre Court tickets – name the price, money no object, but the deal must be direct, no middle man. Set up a meeting with his supplier, and the tout could crawl back into the woodwork. No meeting, and his face and name would be plastered over every tabloid the next morning – take it or leave it. He had taken it. Dishonour amongst thieves.

The reporter had sat at the wheel of his car in the darkness of a high-hedged Surrey lane. Disjointed sentences had checked his wire for sound levels. They had waited. The car drawing up behind had flashed its headlights before dousing them. The infrared cameras had picked out the shadowy figure climbing in beside the reporter. Millions of righteously indignant, tax-dodging viewers had gasped at the asking price, had revelled in the man's torment as the lights had been turned on. The cameras had not shown the man's face as he had struggled to justify his greed. Anyone switching off as the credits rolled would have missed the baldly stated epilogue.

THE IDENTITY OF THE SUPPLIER, A SENIOR CONSULTANT EMPLOYED AT A HOSPITAL IN SOUTH-WEST LONDON, HAS BEEN WITHHELD ON THE UNDERSTANDING THAT HE TENDERS FORTHWITH HIS RESIGNATION AS AN UMPIRE AT THE ALL ENGLAND TENNIS CLUB.

'Brian?' David seemed to be trying to push the word out of the top of his head. 'You mean Brian?'

'D'you know any other consultant who's a Wimbledon umpire?'

'Good God. Poor Brian.'

'Poor Brian, be buggered. I warn you, David, he's a mean bastard.'

'But can you be sure – that he was the man, I mean?'

'Easy way to find out,' O'Connor grinned. 'Ask him if he can get you a couple of tickets for Wimbledon this year.'

They should have heard him coming. Perhaps it was now so much in character that Pullman's venom no longer registered above a ward round's ambient sounds. Pullman's tirade at his house surgeon, stripping away a young man's loyalty along with his dignity, had been loud enough. Only the patients, who had no previous experience to reassure them, sat, mute and upright, their thoughts their own. The door to the office opened and his juniors and ward sister, sullen and hangdog, followed him into the room. Pullman turned on them.

'Leave us,' he snapped.

He shepherded them out, closing the door behind them. He could no longer contain his fury, words spitting out uncontrollably even before he had turned to face his two colleagues. The sight of their half smiles, half grins of astonishment only fuelled his anger. Though he was anxious not to spare O'Connor, there was no doubting the real target of his wrath.

'Everybody knows all the beds down the right-hand side of that ward are mine, always have been, ever since we moved in. So – what the hell's going on?' He did not bother to look at O'Connor any more. 'What do I find on my ward round? Half of your patients in my beds.' His voice rose to an near-scream. 'They've actually cancelled two of my admissions for tomorrow.'

'I'm sorry, Brian. I meant to have a word with you about that. We had a particularly heavy intake last night. I should have come to see you to make some arrangements about the beds. Obviously we'll need to make some changes, now there are three of us.'

'*We*? Let's get something straight, shall we? You may be on the Council, but I'm still senior surgeon here – is that clear?'

'Brian – for Christ's sake.'

O'Connor's quiet interjection drew Pullman's fire. 'These things have got to be said, Harry. It's all right for everybody to fall over backwards, bending every rule in the book to change his contract for him – you can imagine the phone calls from the College, can't you? A couple of buzzes through the old boy network and everything falls into place. To him who hath . . . But where was he while we were taking all the flak down here these last few years? Up there, making money. Money, money, money. Let's not forget that. Well, he can find out what the other side of the coin looks like now.' He swung back to David. '*I'll* say who has which beds, d'you understand? And I'll be grateful if you'll keep your patients in your own beds in future. I'm not having you . . .'

Sod you. Go on, say it – sod you. They're not *your* sodding beds. Go on – say it. Feel. React. You're smiling, actually smiling, as you let him treat you like a third-year medical student. Tell him to sod off.

'I'm sure we can work something out quite amicably, Brian.'

'There are plenty of beds,' O'Connor said soothingly, 'scattered over three wards. I'm quite sure, with a bit of goodwill, we could make three separate wards. That way we could stay out of each other's hair. If there's any real problem,' he grinned, 'you can have all my lot, David, just so long as they keep sending me my cheque every month.'

The sniggers of the two younger men seemed to quieten Pullman, who suppressed his anger as he withdrew within himself. 'And that, if I might say so,' he hissed, 'is the sort of irresponsible remark that's typical of someone who takes part in a dangerous sport without thought for the possible consequences to his family and colleagues. If you two don't have work to do, I most certainly have.'

Pullman made an exit that left the two friends grinning.

*

Ennui. Five-thirty on a Saturday evening. His weekend not on emergency call. The hospital visited, coffee drunk. Empty offices. Deserted corridors. Duty nurses and house surgeons too harassed to talk to a lonely consultant. A drive back to Wimbledon, dawdling amongst the thrusters. A beer and a microwaved pie swallowed in a local bar, alone in the midst of other people's chatter. A walk on the Common. Frowning concentration in a supermarket, trying in vain to remember what Jackie had given him to eat on a weekend. The trudge home, his plastic bag dangling from one hand, threading his way between soccer mad fathers and sons in their matching mufflers, their faces flushed, ready for their tea.

He closed the front door behind him. A whole evening stretched ahead of him. Tomorrow was Sunday.

The phone rang.

'David?'

Someone wanted him.

'Yes.'

'Mal.'

'Yes, Mal.'

'Ew busy tomorrow?'

'No.'

'Do me a favour 'en.'

'Of course.'

'Drive me down Basin'stoke way.'

'I'd be glad to, Mal. I don't think I've ever been to Basingstoke. But what's happened to Danny?'

''E's got the flu. 'Leven o'clock do ew?'

Telephones magnify accents.

'That would suit me fine, Mal. Which one of your massage parlours is . . .'

But the line had died in his hand. Mal had sounded . . . How had Mal sounded? Devious. Yes, that was it – devious. Mal devious?

David was ten minutes early as he swung into the driveway through open gates. Mal had been ready even earlier. He stood in the porch, neat in a dark grey suit and silk tie, a folded raincoat draped over one arm, a brown parcel under the other.

David, in sports coat and slacks, suddenly felt ill at ease. He leaned across to open the door. He waited until Mal had settled in his seat, bolt upright, his coat now across his knees, the parcel on the floor between his feet.

David cocked his head on one side as he surveyed him. He remembered the days when *he* had dressed like that. 'Where the hell are we going, Mal – Buckingham Palace?'

'I told ew. Basin'stoke.'

'Yes, I know – but . . .' He took one look at Mal's face, staring ahead through the windscreen. 'All right,' he said, relenting. 'How d'you get to Basingstoke from here?'

'Down the M3. We want a little village just this side of Basin'stoke. Place called Clavely Court. Get off at exit 5 an' I'll direct ew from there.'

Clavely Court. He'd heard that name before.

'Put your strap on then,' David smiled. 'Unless you're afraid of creasing that suit.'

One motorway looks like any other. It could have been the M4. He could have been barrelling up the fast lane in his BMW instead of watching the Ford's speedometer. Marlborough wasn't *that* far from Basingstoke. He could have been going to see Debbie, taking her out for the day. Looking back – he found he was able to now – he could have done it far more often than he had. He only remembered her in snatches. That night she had croup, her appendix, strained conversation in school car parks with the rain beating on the roof. He could have kept her at home, talked to her, listened for the sound of her coming through the door after school, got to know her. He could have sent her to the local school, but does Harley Street have a local school? He could not remember seeing many young girls on the pavement of Harley Street, school bags over their shoulders, waiting for the bus to the local comp. She would have looked up from where she stood, would have waved to him, smiling, would . . .

'I gotta go an' see my son.'

It was safer to drive like hell in the fast lane. Then you kept your wits about you. Adrenaline kept you awake. A droning engine lulled the senses. Daydreams were often the prelude to sleep. He mustn't nod off. The danger came when sequential thought, however vaguely directed, gave way to shapes, colours, strange, dreamlike voices . . . It was possible to hear the strangest things.

''E's a Mongol.'

'He's a . . .'

The car lurched and a few seconds of concentration were needed to balance it once more. David pulled over into the slow lane.

'He's a what? Who is?'

'Tommy. My son. 'E's a Mongol.'

David had to brake to adjust to the speed of the car ahead. He had not realised just how slowly some people drive on a motorway on a Sunday. It gave him the chance to catch his breath.

'You have a *son*?' He snatched a glance at his passenger.

'Yes. 'E's a Mongol.' Mal twitched at the coat still neatly folded over his knees. 'Poor little bastard.'

'You mean a Down's. Down's syndrome.' Now David knew where he'd heard of Clavely Court before – from Digger Drew.

'Mongols they were in Cory Street. Remember?'

'Yes, but . . . You've got a *son*. I never knew that.'

'Not many people do.'

'Obviously. Faye – what about . . . ? She *must* know. But she's never mentioned it.'

'She wouldn', would she?'

'Good God.' David stared ahead for a moment. 'How old is he, Mal?'

''E's nineteen – today.'

'Nineteen. And how long has he been at this place?'

Mal seemed disinclined to answer that one.

'Ew should've seen 'im, the day 'e was born, the size on 'im. Shoulders on 'im like an ox, 'e 'ad.'

Mal was silent for a moment of proud memory.

'I go an' see 'im reg'lar.' For the first time, Mal turned to face David, leading with his jaw. ''E doesn't want fur nothin'; I see to that. It's a smashin' place.'

'I'm sure it is, Mal. I've heard of it before. Digger Drew, the one who anaesthetised you, he's got a handicapped son, a bit older than your boy. He's seriously thinking of sending his son there too.'

Mal grunted, as if that put everything right, and they drove a few miles in silence.

The boy's mother must have been Mal's second wife, David reflected. What was her name? Rachel? She must have been quite old when she had the baby – it would fit. At that age, surely she must have had all the tests? But were they always reliable; were they always positive? And – of course, she *had* committed suicide.

'D'you ever have him at home?' he asked.

If he had helped Mal feel some sense of justification, the question stripped it away again. Mal spoke defensively.

'No.'

'Why not? That's not like you, Mal.' He took his eyes off the road long enough to turn and smile. 'You're one of the most generous-hearted men I know. Why don't you?'

'I might get to love 'im, might'n' I?' Mal mumbled.

'What did you say?'

'I said I might get to like 'im.' Mal paused. ''E's a helluva nice kid.'

'So – where's the problem? Why don't you bring him home?'

'An' what would I do with 'im, 'en? I'm no bloody use at that sort o' thin'. Ew need a woman about the place for that. A man's no bloody use. An' anyway,' – he shook his head as if he'd been through all this before – 'what would 'e do with 'imself in that big ol' 'ouse, all on 'is own all day? No – 'e's better off where 'e is, amongst 'is mates. 'E always looks very 'appy when I see 'im.'

'They always do.'

'Who?'

'Down's.'

'Well 'en.' Mal pointed into the distance. 'Next exit an' turn left.'

Clavely Court was a square, upright, honest-faced Queen Anne house set back from the road. There were no gates, no fences. A wide gravel drive led up to the house, past stately beeches towering above well-mown lawns. A noisy, disorganised game of football came to a halt at the sight of the car coming up the drive. Abandoning the ball where it came to rest, a dozen pairs of arms and legs, smiling faces, jostling bodies milled around them amid shouts and laughter as David brought the car to a halt in front of open, solid oak black-hinged doors. He had difficulty opening the car door against the crush. The youngsters escorted them into the hall, squeezing through the doors in a noisy, slowly moving swarm. Which one was Tommy? It was not difficult to pick out at least three Down's, one of them unmistakable, but Mal made no sign of singling out any one in particular.

''Ullo, Mrs Berry,' Mal called over their heads.

A pleasant-looking woman of about fifty smiled back. What had David expected? He had tried to imagine, over those last few silent miles. A smell. There would be a smell. All long-stay institutions had a smell. A cold, dank atmosphere from all the fresh air pouring through the open windows in the vain but eternal struggle to rid the place of the tang of Dettol and urine and unwashed skin. A sound also. Ringing footsteps on bare boards and stone corridors, slamming doors, echoing voices. An aura. Eton crops and long black skirts, heavy bunches of keys chained around pinched waists. Mrs Darnley. Suffragettes and Holloway wardresses.

'Good morning, Mr Evans.'

Two or three of the youngsters detached themselves to go to the handsome woman who stood, smiling, in front of the vast stone fireplace. One placed his head against her shoulder as she put her arm round him. Her free right hand she extended towards Mal.

'Nice to see you again.'

'Nice to see ew too, Mrs Berry.' Mal pointed to his right. 'This is Mr Royall – friend o' mine.'

'How d'you do, Mr Royall. Welcome to Clavely Court.'

'How d'you do. Thank you.'

He found himself shaking a warm dry hand, looking into eyes that teased, as if she had been reading his thoughts.

She turned back to Mal.

'He's all ready – has been since early this morning. He was up at six, all washed and shaved by seven.'

Shaved. Did Down's shave? David had never thought about it. Did they *need* to shave? Of course they did. Nothing wrong with their hormones. Not a hormonal thing. Chromosomes. Something wrong with their chromosomes. Women having babies in their thirties and early forties. Down's always looked clean-shaven. He'd never seen one with a beard. But could they shave themselves, or did they have to be shaved, patiently, gently, day in, day out, all their adult lives? He'd never thought.

'We had the greatest difficulty making him wait until after his breakfast to open his cards.'

'Cards?' Mal asked.

'Oh, yes. We all send each other cards on our birthdays, don't we?' She beamed around at the chorus of agreement while the sickly grin on Mal's face told of the one card Tommy had *not* received. 'He's all ready for you. He's been waiting in the dining room, looking out of the window, since about nine o'clock. I'll take you in. Just let me get this lot out in the fresh air once more; they say it's going to rain again later.'

She returned to lead Mal through the dining room door. David followed. Inside, they stood line abreast.

Tommy Evans stood with his back to the window, his head bowed, his face in shadow. Grey open-necked shirt, grey V-necked jumper, grey flannel trousers, black sturdy shoes, all spotless. His left arm hung vertically, his right arm doubled up behind his back to grasp the left around its elbow. Broad of shoulder, scant of waist, the outline of his trunk against the light was almost square. The contours of his trousers suggested stocky, powerful thighs.

'There now, Tommy.' Mrs Berry walked over to him to straighten his collar. 'I told you your father wouldn't be late, didn't I?'

Tommy managed to nod without raising his head.

''Appy birthday, boyo. Got a present in the car f'r ew.'

'Thanks, Dad.'

'An' this is Mr Royall. An ol' friend – known each other since we were kids together, 'alf ewr age. Say 'ullo to Mr Royall.'

The head did not move.

'Tommy. Say . . .'

'Mal, please, don't.' David put a hand on his sleeve. 'Plenty of time for that.'

'What's that, toothpaste?' Mrs Berry broke in to turn Tommy, her hands on his shoulders. 'Give me your hankie. Put out your tongue.'

A young face was lifted to the light as a fleck of white was wiped from the corner of his mouth, giving David a chance to study it for the first time. Was that what she'd said? 'Put out your tongue.' To a Down's? David's mental picture had been of narrow, oblique eyes with the characteristic epicanthic folds that gave the appearance of high cheekbones, a flat bridge to the nose, jug ears, a receding chin, perhaps a squint. But the tongue – above all the tongue. He had visualised the wet, drooling, furrowed mass, wedged between open lips.

Tommy was a Down's all right – but some people might need a second look to be quite certain. There was no doubting the eyes. And the ears – which looked straight forward like a bat's. But the nose, the chin, the shape of the skull – David had seen worse in many a lecture theatre. And before Tommy turned his face to the shadows once more the tongue had disappeared behind lips firm enough to suggest a stubborn streak.

'I'm sorry, Tommy,' David said. 'I didn't know it was your birthday. Otherwise I'd have brought you a present too.'

The face was raised just long enough for him to see the flicker of forgiveness.

'Come on 'en, boyo. Let's go. Where's it to be 'en, the *Master Brewer* again? Steak an' kidney pie again, is it?'

'That'll be nice, won't it, Tommy?' Mrs Berry gave him a gentle push in the direction of his father. 'Only don't eat so much you can't enjoy your birthday cake when you come back.' She turned towards Mal. 'I take it he'll be back in time for his tea?'

'Oh, yes.' The reply was a mite too prompt. 'Wouldn't want to miss ewr cake, now would ew, Tommy bach? Come on 'en.'

David followed Mal and Mrs Berry through the hall and out to the car. Tommy, his right hand still clasping his left elbow behind his back, walked a pace behind. Each time David stopped and turned, Tommy stopped too, head down, his eyes never rising above David's waist. He stood back and waited politely for David to open the rear door for him. Slamming his own door behind him, David wriggled behind the wheel. Pulling his seatbelt across his chest, he half turned to clip it in place, feeling as he did so the coarse grating of thick hair against his forehead, the animal warmth of youth on his face. Tommy was sitting on the edge of the seat, leaning forward with his shoulders wedged in the gap between the front seats, his head almost in line with theirs, close enough for them to smell the soap and the earthy good health. No reeking aftershave. No nauseating deodorant. Just a vast grin.

As David accelerated away, he snatched sideways glances at a face inches from his own. Mal saw his surprise at the transformation.

'Like the car, don' ew, Tom?' Mal waited for the violence of the nods to subside before turning to David. 'Always did like the car, ever since 'e was a nipper. Seemed to love lookin' out the window; always wavin' at people in the street. Amazin' it was, how many of 'em waved back.'

He bent forward to reach between his knees.

'S'pose ew wan' ewr present now, d'ew?'

'Yes, please, Dad.'

David tried to watch Tommy's expression in the mirror as Mal teased, pretending for a moment to have lost it. Smiling as he relented, Mal handed the package to his son, and the head and shoulders disappeared from between them. There was the sound of snapping string and tearing paper, a pause – and an explosion of joy as an uninhibited belly laugh filled the car. The space around their heads still vibrated as Tommy took breath and roared again.

David looked sideways, grinning.

'What the hell have you given him, Mal – the Crown Jewels?'

As if in answer, an open cardboard box was thrust between the seats. In it lay a pair of trainers, virgin white with red and blue patches, their thick white laces extending all the way up padded ankle extensions.

'Can I put them on, Dad?'

'Didn' buy 'em f'r ew to look at, Tommy bach.'

They heard the thuds as heavy shoes dropped to the floor.

'How marvellous,' David murmured, and Mal heard him.

'What d'ew mean?' he asked.

'To be able to give such happiness so easily. Blissful happiness for the price of a pair of shoes. How much did those cost you?'

Mal looked sheepish. 'I got a sports shop up in 'Ighbury. I get 'em 'olesale.'

Three burly, laughing men tumbled out of the car outside the *Master Brewer*. Heads turned as they made their way to the bar. Cautious, hostile looks, searching for any threat posed by noisy newcomers, turned to smiles at the sight of Tommy. Everyone smiled at Tommy. Husbands and wives, silently eating in gentle, bored hostility, looked up, smiled and began talking. The local lush, one buttock on his stool, one elbow on the bar, his glass half empty, his cigarette half smoked, winked. A sweating barman found time at midday on a Sunday to crane his neck to see the new shoes Tommy was so anxious to point out.

'What will Tommy have to drink?' David asked.

''Alf of shandy. I'll 'ave a Coke. Ew get 'em in an' Tommy an' I'll find a table. What d'ew wanna eat?'

'Whatever Tommy's having.'

Steak and kidney pie. How did a Down's eat a steak and kidney pie? David had visions of a fully grown man, wearing a bib, being fed with a spoon, everyone sniggering, their heads turned away. Half an hour later, he sat next to an upright, almost prim young man whose eyes darted watchfully as he did everything Mrs Berry had taught him. David laughed to himself as he looked at the slouching, shovelling table manners all around them. He marvelled at how crude they looked compared with the way Tommy ate his double portion of apple tart and cream while he and Mal sipped their coffee. How did they manage to put food in their mouths without taking their elbows off the table?

'Is Clavely Court a nice place, Tommy?'

'Smashin' place, innit, Tommy?'

'It's a very nice place, thank you.'

'What do you find to do with yourself all day?' David asked.

'You 'ave teachers come in every day, don' ew?' Mal answered for him.

'Yes, but . . .' David tried once more.

'An ew 'ave discos in the evenin'.'

'Yes, but what I mean is . . .'

'An' ew've got a big kitchen garden, 'aven' ew? Grow nearly all ewr own veg, don' ew?'

David half turned, trying to put one shoulder between Mal and his son.

'But do you ever go anywhere out of the place?'

'We go to the beach sometimes,' Tommy said proudly.

'Got a smashin' minibus, 'aven' ew?'

David showed his irritation as Tommy nodded.

'D'you like the sea?'

Tommy's nods increased in amplitude, his eyes shining. Clear blue eyes. David had built up a theory over the years that patients with clear blue eyes like that didn't feel pain as much as the browns and the greens, the greys and hazels.

'Can you swim?'

'I swam twenty lengths one day last week.'

'Twenty lengths? You've got . . . ?'

'. . . a 'eated pool. Yeah. Cost us a bomb, I tell ew.'

'And what about football? Do you take after your father?'

''E's not 'alf bad, though I say it m'self. Ew should see 'im . . .'

It had begun to rain as they ran to the car. Mal hunched his shoulders against a sudden squall as he waited for David to unlock the doors. Tommy stood erect.

'Where now?' David asked as he started the engine.

'Tha's the problem,' Mal growled. 'What the 'ell d'ew do now?'

David crawled aimlessly. Headlights flashed in his mirror as he dragged out to their limits the few short miles back to Clavely Court.

'Is there nowhere we can go?'

'Ew try an' think of somewhere round 'ere we can go to on a wet Sunday afternoon.'

The beech leaves glistened, the branches dragged low by the

weight of cascading water. Tyres hissed in wet gravel and rain drummed on the roof as David switched off the engine outside the front door.

Silence beneath a steady drum roll.

'Better be gettin' back in 'en, 'adn' ew, Tommy bach?'

'All right, Dad.'

'Mustn't miss that cake, must ew?'

'No, Dad. I've seen it.'

'Ew've seen it? Nice one, is it?'

'Mrs Berry made it.'

'Come on 'en. Say goodbye to Mr Royall.'

'Goodbye, Mr Royall. Thank you for my beer.'

'It was a pleasure, Tommy. I've . . .'

Tommy waited, a smile on his face, but David found nothing to say. He wanted suddenly to touch this gentle young man but did not, simply swivelling in his seat to watch him follow his father obediently into the house and out of sight. He sat, alone in a still-warm empty car.

They were climbing Wimbledon Hill before either spoke.

'Thanks fur comin', David.'

'My pleasure, Mal. I mean it.'

'Ew workin' late tomorrow night?'

David shrugged. 'No idea. I take it as it comes these days. The later the better as far as I'm concerned. Why?'

'Faye's on TV, seven o'clock.'

'Oh? I didn't know she was in this country. What's she doing on TV?'

'She's on *Strait Talkin'*.'

'Good God. How did she manage that? But then, of course,' David smirked, 'he's a neighbour of yours, isn't he? Didn't you say he lived next door to you?'

'No. Fair play to the gel – nothin' to do with that. She's won some business 'ooman's prize or other.'

The smirk faded rapidly, revealing once more the preoccupied look that had been there throughout the return journey.

'Mal.' David hesitated long enough for Mal to turn towards him, raising one eyebrow. 'Mal, would it be . . . Would you mind if *I* were to take Tommy out sometime?'

'Course I wouldn't. Why should I? As I say, 'e's a lovely kid really. But what would ew do?'

'I don't know. I expect we'd think of something.'

16

Two slices of bread, uniform slabs of speckled brown, a slick of polyunsaturated fatty acids, a sliver of ham, a few microns thick, picked out of its plastic cover – his evening meal stood before him. David looked at the jar of chutney and decided he couldn't be bothered. He'd survive without such luxury. He was pouring boiling water on his instant, decaffeinated, unsweetened coffee when he heard the first strident chords of a signature tune that rallied more souls in a night than church bells in a month. He splashed milk from the bottle into the mug and hurried through into the living room, sandwich in one hand, mug and spoon in the other. He didn't want to miss her entrance.

David enjoyed Strait's programme. He even admitted it in public. A professional himself, just as he could appreciate a fellow surgeon's technical expertise, so he enjoyed the sheer professionalism of the man. He saw in an interview, in the opening, the development, the closing, similarities with many an operation. He sensed that an interview, skilfully conducted as a rounded whole, might give the interviewer the same satisfaction, leave him on the same high as an operation that had gone like silk from first cut to last stitch. And he'd seen the converse. Not all operations, after all, went like silk. Strait was no simpering crowd-pleaser. That he was a warm, compassionate man was obvious from the way he subdued his personality when talking to a crippled child or a dying man. But he was a vain man – it was *his* show – and the crinkles round his eyes deepened and set the moment he felt threatened by a competitor. He was also an irascible man. With pebble-glass spectacles, an untidy bushy moustache and a florid complexion that would have gone well with a monocle, he was a man capable of losing patience, leaving his incisions open if he found, deep inside someone, sham pomposity. He had been known to run verbally amok, oblivious to frantic floor managers waving their cue cards, and one of the reasons people watched the show was to see whether there would be blood on the floor that night.

'Good evening.'

Not for Strait the warm-up, the contrived introduction designed to squeeze enough squeals and laughs and claps to convince the viewer of the live audience. He sat four-square to the camera. No flowers.

'This evening, I would like you to meet two remarkable ladies who have both reached the very top of their chosen vocations, having started their climb to fame from very different backgrounds. One, born and bred in one of the most affluent parts of Pasadena, California, a distinguished member of an honoured profession where taking part in a chat show, while not strictly illegal, is perhaps frowned upon, is appearing for the very first time on TV on this programme. She is on a private visit to this country, so I consider it both an honour and a privilege that she has chosen my show on which to break with tradition. But more of her later. First, a lady who was born in a Rhondda Valley backstreet and now lives in Beverly Hills – someone who makes a habit of breaking every rule and getting away with it. Recently she hit the headlines in the United States by going to the Supreme Court to obtain membership of one of the most elite of all male clubs in Los Angeles, only to resign after paying her dues, saying she wouldn't be seen dead in such a stuffy place. And what does she do in Los Angeles? There has been a trend in recent years for some of America's glitziest magazines to be edited by women from this country. This lady has gone one better. Having made a fortune in this country, she got bored, sold up and now *owns* one of the most successful women's magazines in America. Had she gone in for politics, there is only one place in London this lady could possibly live. Please welcome – Faye Grainger.'

Strait stood and turned. The camera swung and Faye appeared from the wings. Head up, unhurried, slim and tall in her Karl

Lagerfeld tweeds, she walked over to shake hands with Strait. She sat, crossing her long legs. She shook her shoulder-length hair, smiled, and waited.

'Faye Grainger, you . . .'

'Why did you call me a lady?'

Clearly that had not been in the script. Strait had not had the chance to meet her beforehand. Faye had arrived at the studio only minutes before the show, as cool as an autumn morning. A nod and a smile in makeup and they were on. Not that that was so unusual – many liked to give the impression of being so busy that even Godfrey Strait had to be fitted in. It hadn't worried him – he had done his homework on her earlier that afternoon. He had then been briefed by his researchers in the usual way. But nothing had prepared him for her question. The sudden lift of the head said it all – *he* was supposed to ask the questions. Strait's eyes narrowed though he still smiled.

'Does that bother you?' he asked.

'Not if it's deserved, no. But what evidence have you that I'm a lady?' The question was asked through the broadest of smiles. 'For all you know, I could be the biggest bitch since Salome. If I'd been male, how would you have introduced me, as a man or as a gentleman?'

Strait was honest enough not to reply.

'Well then, why not say "woman"?'

'And are you?'

'What?'

'A bitch.'

She threw her head back and the open-mouthed laugh was no contrived act rehearsed in front of the mirror, but the relaxed, spontaneous response of someone who was enjoying herself, someone who felt she had every right to be where she was, the focus of millions of pairs of eyes.

'I'm a woman – ' she looked down at herself – 'as you may have noticed. But I'm no lady, that's for certain. As to whether I'm a bitch, that's what you're here to find out, isn't it? So, perhaps we'd better get on with the interview. What d'you want to know?'

Grinning, totally in command of the situation, she settled back in her chair.

A long curving thigh. David frowned as something tightened deep in his gut. Her face was rounder than he remembered. There was none of the bone-hugging skin tautness.

'You like a fight.' A half question, half statement from Strait, the bit now firmly between his teeth, oblivious to prompts and all attempts at stage manipulation.

'You bet. There wasn't a girl in my class in school I couldn't lick – and I could lick most of the boys too. Nowadays, of course, I've got to be a bit more subtle – but not much.'

'And d'you always win?'

Faye took her time to think about that.

'Yes,' she drawled, 'I think I do. I may lose a battle here and there along the way, but I usually win the war.'

'So – would you call yourself a crusader?'

'No way.' The grin broadened and her eyes shone. 'To me, a crusader is a man who goes off enjoying himself, hunting Saracens, with the key to his wife's chastity belt in his saddlebag.'

David had never seen her looking so happy – or so beautiful. Did success do that to all women, as it had to Jackie? But Faye Evans – beautiful? Outwardly they were still there, the athletic body, the sharp mind. So where was the change? In the eye of the beholder perhaps?

Strait joined in the laughter, real respect and admiration beginning to mould his features. To add to his pleasure, anyone who could make his audience laugh was always welcome.

'Let's start from the beginning, shall we?' He leaned forward, trying to lessen the gap between them. 'You were born in very humble circumstances . . .'

For a while, Faye behaved herself impeccably, answering Strait's questions as he traced her upward path.

'. . . culminating, of course, in your being voted this year's Veuve Clicquot Businesswoman of the Year. That *is* true, is it not?'

'That's correct.' Faye gave as modest a nod as she could muster.

'And *Mr* Grainger?'

'He's long gone.'

'You were divorced?'

'Let's say we both found we'd made a mistake and I haven't dared repeat it.'

'So – who do you share all this success with?'

'Does one have to?'

'Most people like to share.'

Strait played the pause to perfection, gathering the silence of the audience around him as they pressed in on her.

'I have a brother. We are very close.'

David saw her hands grasp the edge of the cushions beside her knees.

'Of course.' The surprise was genuine. He *had* forgotten. 'I should know that better than most – he is, after all, my nextdoor neighbour. Mal Evans, the legendary footballer – Arsenal, Juventus, Wales – *he* is your brother.'

'No.'

'No?'

'No. *I* am Mal Evans's sister.'

In the silence that followed, David sensed the audience's sympathy swing from Strait exposing a flint-hearted loner to a basically vulnerable woman facing a tough world alone.

'Clever bitch,' David muttered. But he wondered. Was she *that* good an actress? Or could it be that was exactly what she was – alone in a man's world, her only protection the no-go area with which she surrounded herself?

'My brother has been just as successful in business as I have and, as I've told you, it was his backing in the early days that set me off. He shared everything he had with me then. It's just that he doesn't seek the limelight as much as I perhaps do. But it *is* possible to be successful without being famous, you know.'

'And what of this new venture of yours, this magazine? *Soigné*?' Strait used one index finger to push his glasses up his nose, lowering bristling eyebrows over them as if clamping them in place. 'How's that going?'

'Very well.' Faye stretched like a cat. She now looked so relaxed David almost expected her to kick her shoes off and tuck her feet up under her.

'Is it true,' Strait asked, 'that you tried to get a job on the magazine, failed, so bought it and sacked the woman who turned you down?'

'Absolutely.'

As the laughter died down, David wondered how he had come by that story.

'Bit vindictive that, wasn't it?'

'Not at all. She was obviously incompetent. I didn't want anyone working for me who couldn't recognise talent when she saw it.'

'And is that all it takes to be successful, the ability to recognise talent?'

'It helps, especially if, like me, you don't have any talent of your own.'

'Oh, come now,' Strait began. But Faye waved him down.

'It's true. I've no talent. I work extremely hard and I am eternally optimistic – never for one moment do I entertain the idea of failure. That's why I never listen to accountants – they are all born pessimists. But I've no God-given talent. What I've got out of this world, I've screwed out of it. I admire talent, I envy it – but it's not enough on its own. You've got to have determination as well. The most talented people come a cropper from time to time, so it's no use employing someone who goes and cries her eyes out in the john the first time anything goes wrong.'

'And men? D'you employ men on your magazine?'

'Of course.' One corner of her lips was pulled downwards. 'I'm a great believer in equal rights for men.'

'And do you enjoy employing men?' He did not give her a chance to answer. 'Because, be honest now, isn't that what this magazine of yours is all about, convincing women of their superiority over men?'

Faye turned her face away so that she could look at Strait out of the corners of her eyes. It was obvious to David that this had not been in the script either and that Strait was now getting his own back for her initial attack on him.

'Let's face it,' Strait went on, 'the women who read your

magazine are more likely to achieve a satisfying orgasm than bake a cake.'

The laughter was short-lived in the anxiety not to miss one iota of Faye's reaction. Her face filled the screen.

'And how long did it take you to come up with that one, Godfrey?' The cameras backed away. 'I'll accept that as one of your famous provocative remarks. I can't believe you are so stupid as to really believe that.' This time she did not give him time to come back at her. 'You make it sound as if the two functions are mutually exclusive. I have news for you – they are *not*. You make it sound as if you're an old Blimp who believes the wife should lie back and think of England – and, somehow, I don't think you are, Godfrey. Do you really want to know what my magazine is trying to say?'

Lissom and animated, she betrayed no anxiety in either her manner or her face that she might be boring anyone or overrunning her time. Strait nodded encouragingly, settling back in his seat as a born businesswoman grasped the heaven-sent opportunity for some free prime-time publicity. He let her run and run until passion began to break through the poise.

'. . . That's why we're so militant on the question of child care for working mothers.' She began to hear the passion herself. She looked up, hesitating. 'That's why . . .'

Flushed, suddenly knocked off balance by the silence, she looked over her shoulder at the quiet, shadowy figures beyond the lights. She turned her head back to find a delighted Strait grinning broadly at his audience.

'I don't know about you out there, but I could go on listening to, and looking at, this *lady* all night. Perhaps now you will understand what I meant in my introduction. Ladies and gentlemen – ' he stretched out his arm, palm up – 'Faye Grainger.'

David watched Faye's suprised reaction to the sudden explosion of applause. He saw the excitement in her eyes as she sucked it in, momentarily oblivious of Strait. He smiled as he saw Strait stretch to put a hand on her knee and then think better of it, waiting instead for her to turn towards him before taking her hand in both of his. 'Remarkable,' he heard Strait say as the clapping persisted. 'I think we must have a few frustrated housewives in tonight.'

Strait was no mauler, but he seemed reluctant to release the hand before making his next announcement. 'And now, before my second guest tonight, some music from a group that's just returned from . . .'

'Hell, no.' David hit the sound button on his remote control. For a while he sat, pondering on what a beautiful woman success and money had made out of a backstreet alley cat, while five ill-clad young men jerked and gyrated in blessed silence. Abstractedly, he bit into his sandwich, which was now dry. He sipped his coffee, which was now tepid. Did he have time to make a fresh cup? When he returned to his chair, Strait was already walking across the stage to greet his new guest, escorting her back to sit next to Faye, who had now moved over on the sofa to make room for her.

'Welcome,' he heard Strait say as he pressed the button once more.

'Thank you.'

Two words and David laughed. Poise. Poise, poise, poise. *This* one had poise.

Strait nodded across at Faye.

'I understand you two have already met?'

The woman turned and smiled at Faye, who sat sideways, her back to the audience. One leg doubled up beneath her, her elbow on the back of the sofa, Faye rested her head on her hand, her face the picture of rapt devotion.

'We most certainly have,' the woman smiled as they touched hands. 'Hullo, Faye.'

'And I understand this is your first visit to this country?'

'I regret to say it is, yes. I've always wanted so much to come to England, but somehow' – she shrugged her shoulders – 'there never seemed to be time. One is so busy.'

'And this is also is your first time ever on TV, I believe?'

'That's right. While it's not, as you say, strictly speaking, illegal for us to appear on chat shows back home, it is not exactly encouraged either. Retired judges appear now and then. Is that not so in this country also?'

Strait laughed. 'We have managed to coax one or two of our more controversial judges to appear now and again – one in particular who seems to need to appear on TV to explain some of his gaffes in court – but, by and large, yes, they tend to keep out of sight. I trust that your appearance here tonight doesn't mean you are retiring prematurely?'

She did not answer, merely smiled and shook her head.

A judge. An American judge. A female American judge. David leaned forward in his chair. It had to be the one Faye had talked about that night in her apartment. What was her name? Logan. That was it. Jo Logan. He listened intently as Strait probed her reasons for being in London, but while he listened to what Strait and Jo Logan were saying he found himself fascinated by Faye's face as she too took in every word.

The look of adoration remained undiminished as Faye listened to Jo Logan claiming it was just as difficult to break free from the bonds of being born into a wealthy family as it was from backstreet poverty. However, as Strait went on to discuss Jo Logan's nomination as only the second woman to sit on the Supreme Court, David saw doubt cloud the adoration in Faye's eyes as she detected hesitation in some of her idol's replies.

By the time Strait was pushing his guest to say what difficulties might arise if a Supreme Court judge's husband decided to run for President, Faye had abandoned the languorous pose of someone bathed in admiration for the more tense, forward crouch of someone anxious to put some questions of her own.

'If you had the choice, Judge Logan,' Strait asked, the twinkle in his eyes seemingly magnified by the pebble lenses, 'which would you rather be, a Supreme Court judge or President of the United States?'

'I make it a rule, Mr Strait, never to answer hypothetical questions.'

'We in this country have had our first woman Prime Minister.' Strait grinned broadly. 'Be honest now. Wouldn't you like to be the first woman President of the United States?'

There it was again, the infinitesimal hesitation that had nothing to do with modesty.

'I'm sure it will come, a woman President, just as, sooner or later, there must be a black President of the United States. Or a Jewish one. But – ' her eyes seemed to lose their focus – 'not just yet, I don't think.'

'Why not?'

Faye's question, crisp and staccato, had the camera swerving. David saw her, stiff and erect, her face drawn by sudden doubt.

'These things have to be brought about gradually.' Jo Logan knew she was not being altogether convincing and her face showed it. 'It takes time. But it will come.'

She turned to Strait.

'Mr Strait, I am not going to answer any more questions along this line. We're getting into the realms of fantasy.'

'Are we?' Once again Faye's voice came, sharp and incisive, from off camera.

'All right,' Strait grinned. 'But you wouldn't deny your husband intends running for President?'

'Gort is his own man, Mr Strait. If you want an answer to that, you'd better ask him.'

'I might just do that. Meanwhile . . .' Well pleased, Strait's tone signalled the interview had ended. 'I can only thank you again, Judge Logan, for doing me the honour of making your first TV appearance on my show. It has been a pleasure talking to you. Perhaps, next time, you'll bring your husband with you.' He turned to the audience. 'Ladies and gentlemen – Judge Logan.'

The applause was probably as loud as that given for Faye, but of a totally different texture – polite and respectful, rather than warm and enthusiastic. Strait and Jo Logan faced outwards, smiling at where the applause came from behind the cameras. Faye Grainger kept her back to the audience, ignoring everyone else as, from a few feet away, she stared intently at Jo Logan's face.

Strait was signing off when David zapped him. He sank into his chair, staring at what he imagined was going on behind the grey, faint reflection of himself on the blank screen. Faye would not stay long. No drinks at a bar afterwards for her – not her scene. She might leave with the Logan woman, but somehow, after the way the interview had ended, he doubted that. He sensed a barrier between the two. He couldn't really see them in harmony: Faye, like Jackie in the old days, assertive, as subtle as a Chieftain tank, and Jo Logan, intellectually aloof, as impenetrable as Fort Knox. No – Faye might well be on her way out already, calling a cab. Back in her apartment in half an hour. Alone. Still on a high. Restless. He had her number. He looked at the phone, trying not to believe the sudden ache. His reflection in the TV screen brought him back to earth – the sloppy corduroy slacks, the shapeless jumper, the slippers. He remembered her apartment. Two different worlds now. There *was* another possibility. Faye and Strait, a table for two in some discreet Mayfair restaurant favoured by the famous. Mental pictures of Faye's tigerish nakedness and what must lie beneath Strait's flabby bulk made all thoughts of carnality ludicrous. But conversation, late into the night, fizzing like sparks between two bare high-tension wires.

Ach – sod it. Sod it all to hell. That was all over.

17

Mrs Berry looked from David to Tommy and back again. Suppressed anxiety manifested itself by jerky, purposeless movements as she convinced herself for the second time that Tommy had a handkerchief deep in one trouser pocket.

'He's got no money on him, Mr Royall. All he's got is that pair of trainers in that plastic bag. Are you sure he doesn't need any money?'

'Yes, Mrs Berry.'

'He had quite a nasty cold last week. You won't let him get wet?'

'No, Mrs Berry.'

'And you're quite sure there's nothing else he needs?'

'Yes, Mrs Berry.'

She wasn't finished yet, standing her ground between the two men.

'Mr Evans didn't say anything about you keeping him out overnight. Perhaps I should ring him first.'

'Please do so if it will put your mind at rest, but I did mention it to him, I give you my word. It's not certain we will be away overnight; it depends on how we get on with each other. But if we're not back here before eight this evening, then I'll bring him back sometime after lunch tomorrow.'

'But pyjamas. He must have pyjamas if he's going to stay away overnight.'

'No need, really, Mrs Berry.'

'He's *got* to have pyjamas. What about cleaning his teeth? I can't let him go like that.' She snatched at a moment's hesitation on David's part. 'Stay there,' she commanded. 'I'll go and get them.'

She hurried away, leaving David and Tommy alone together for the first time.

Tommy was standing in the posture that David had already come to associate with him, his right arm bent across the small of his back to grasp the left elbow. The plastic bag hung from his left hand. His lowered eyes were raised to David's from time to time as they waited, each glance wreathed in a beaming smile.

'It's going to be a nice day, Tommy,' David said, smiling back.

'Yes.' There was excitement in what was no more than a whisper.

'There you are.' Tommy disengaged his right hand to take the second plastic bag Mrs Berry pushed against him. 'And I've put your razor in. I know you worry if you can't shave in the morning.' She zipped up the lower half of his blue and grey anorak. 'Now you do everything Mr Royall tells you, d'you hear?' Tommy blushed as she stretched to kiss his cheek, turning his head away from David until it had subsided.

Outside, Mrs Berry looked up at the blue sky and scudding clouds. 'Where exactly are you taking him?' she asked.

'I don't know,' David lied. 'But don't worry; he's perfectly safe. As I say, if we're not back by eight this evening, then we'll be back tomorrow sometime.'

'Mmmmmmmmm.'

For David, the excitement, the joy of it, had started the evening before. For the first time in months, he had been in as much of a hurry to get out of the Merton as he had been in the old days. The difference had been that, this time, his one intent to *spend* money, not *make* it, had given a spring to his step as he had crossed the staff car park. The supermarket had seemed so much less crowded, people so much more friendly, with everyone smiling at him. Or had it been that *he* had been smiling at *them*?

Gripping the trolley with a new determination, he had stopped and thought, deciding he must be methodical. Tea and coffee – obviously. Breakfast – cereal, bacon, sausages, butter and marmalade. What kind of cereal? He should have rung Mrs Berry to ask. And milk and sugar. Those cartons of long-life milk. Lunch – some rolls (he'd already thought of butter) and some ham or cold beef. But they would need some hot food too. Some cans of hash or steak and kidney. And potatoes. Jackie had always managed to produce some potatoes. Potatoes in cans? Did they make potatoes in cans? Where would they keep potatoes in cans? And fruit. And biscuits. And chocolate. Everyone liked chocolate.

And drinks, plenty of soft drinks. And beer? Did a Down's drink beer? His father had given him a shandy.

Through the checkout and then there had been the search for an empty cardboard box into which to stuff the goodies, the satisfying grunt as he had lifted it into the boot of the car. Had he forgotten anything?

Now David looked sideways at Tommy, who strained forward against his seatbelt, his profile eager and excited.

'Where are we going, Mr Royall?' he asked breathlessly.

'We're going on a boat, Tommy. Will you enjoy that?'

'Yes, Mr Royall.'

'Have you been on a boat before?'

'No, Mr Royall.'

'And we can't have you calling me Mr Royall all the time.'

'No, Mr Royall.'

They turned to laugh at each other – not quite a roar maybe, but it was a start.

Why did the very sight of this young man's face make him smile, bring with it a tightening in his chest? Would he feel the same way if Tommy's face had been dull and brutish, his eyes sluggish and watering, his tongue dry and coated? Would he be taking him away for the night if he had been warned of embarrassing incontinence or bursts of uncontrollable hyperactivity, screaming attacks or foul-mouthed obscenities? The answer was – no. He was in the company of someone who was only on the fringes of abnormality, a gentle, powerful young man who radiated the very joy of living. There was no cause for smug self-satisfaction. Of the two of them, there was no doubt who was doing the favour.

'I can't stand being called uncle so it will have to be David. Is that all right with you?'

'Yes.'

That problem solved, Tommy could give his full attention once more to the road ahead. Dog, telephone box, lorry tailboard, shop window – one after another they were given his total attention, his head and shoulders swinging round until they slipped out of sight. David swore gently, braking hard as someone stepped on to a pedestrian crossing. Tommy waved.

'Where is the boat?' he asked.

'Southampton.' David snatched a glance as he accelerated away once more. 'D'you know where Southampton is?'

Tommy shook his head. 'Is it far away?' he asked.

'Not far. Less than an hour from here.'

It was difficult to tell whether Tommy was pleased or disappointed. Perhaps both.

'Is it a big boat?'

'Quite big.' Tommy's smile faded, to be replaced by a frown. David misinterpreted it. 'Don't worry,' he said. 'Nothing we can't handle between us. It's got a *big* engine.'

The frown remained. 'Will I get wet? Mrs Berry said I mustn't get wet.'

'No, you won't get wet, Tommy; I'll see to that.'

The smile returned.

The sway of the pontoon beneath their feet, the smell of rope and diesel fuel, the boat's welcoming bob as David climbed over the side, his sailing bag in one hand, the loaded box under his other arm. He gritted his teeth against the memories. It took a while to turn the key in the padlock. Stale air welled out as he pushed back the sliding roof. He took his stuff below before sticking his head back out of the companionway. Tommy stood, a plastic bag hanging from each hand, waiting politely.

'Come on, Tommy. Jump aboard.'

Upright, with no reassuring grab for shroud or guardrail, Tommy climbed aboard. His shoes grated on the deck.

'First thing, Tommy – get those shoes off and put your trainers on. Can you tie your own laces?'

'Yes.' He was still smiling proudly when David started the engine. Pride mingled with excitement as Tommy heard it settle into a steady throb.

'Wasn't too sure it would start,' David explained. 'I thought the batteries might be flat.'

Tommy nodded.

How did one talk to a Down's? Tommy had nodded, but that might be nothing more than inherent politeness. Did he know what a battery was? Time would tell. It would be fun teaching him.

Tommy climbed down into the cabin. The Moody was a spacious boat, but suddenly it felt smaller. Jackie and Debbie had been lean, compact people, but Tommy seemed twice their combined sizes. David felt his weight as they barged shoulders. He surveyed Tommy up and down.

'Is that all you've got to wear?' he asked.

Tommy glanced down at himself anxiously, looked up and nodded.

David rummaged in his bag and brought out an old blue polo-necked cable-stitched sweater.

'Take that anorak off and put this on. It's always cold out on the sea. Keep your anorak in case it comes on to rain.'

A tousle-haired, grinning face emerged, bursting from the sweater. Joy that could no longer be contained in silence came to the surface as a bubbling, groaning, grumbling sound from somewhere deep in Tommy's chest.

'Right.' David pulled the sweater down around a nonexistent

waistline. The garment was a little too tight and made Tommy look a little more pot-bellied than he really was. 'Now – do you think you're strong enough to hold the boat while I undo the warps – the ropes?'

'Yes.' No hesitation.

Back out on the pontoon, David showed Tommy what he wanted done. Tommy's face set in grim concentration. Holding the guardrail as if his life depended on it, he watched as David untied the mooring warps and threw them on board. If he felt any anxiety as David stepped back on board, leaving him alone on the pontoon, he did not show it. David took the tiller in one hand. A small thrill of panic ran through him. Was he asking too much? He had visions of Tommy falling between pontoon and boat, being crushed. Legs got broken that way.

'Right,' he called. 'Give it a push and then jump on.'

A powerful pair of shoulders were bent to the task and the boat began to gather speed.

'Gently. Not so hard,' he laughed. 'All right, jump on.'

Moments later, Tommy stood in the cockpit, watching the gap widen, the pontoon slowly recede. He stuck out his chest, his jaw jutting. *He'd* done that. The power in his back and shoulders had produced something of beauty, moments of pure magic – the gentle glide of a boat on the first few yards of a journey.

The Hamble was crowded. It might only be April, but there was enough traffic for David to have to concentrate. Once out into Southampton Water, he turned to Tommy.

'Come and stand here. Now – hold this.'

He took Tommy's hand in his and placed it on the tiller. As he held it there, gently moving the tiller beneath their hands to give Tommy the feel of the boat, he sensed the dry, wholesome warmth of human contact. He was actually *touching* someone, someone who did not have a pain in his belly or a lump in her breast. Skin to skin, but not the sweaty, frenetic gropings of some transient lust. This was a happy, healthy young man who asked for nothing. He looked at their hands. Tommy's was broader, stronger than his. In its palm and on its fingertips would be some of the stigmata of Down's syndrome. Criminals and Down's children had their fingerprints taken. And the 'simian' crease in the palm – how the medical profession loved that name, handed down from generation to generation in lecture theatre and at bedsides. How many thousands of minds had been conditioned to link the Down's and the ape?

'We'll motor back and forth here for a while until you've got the hang of it,' David said.

He swung the boat in a wide arc to port, a sigmoid wake streaming from the stern, then the same to starboard. He repeated the process time and again, the arcs getting shallower until they held a straight course. Reluctantly he took his hand away, resisting the temptation to replace it as the boat began to lurch. Each sudden correction brought an anxious glance from Tommy, a reassuring smile from David. Slowly his smile was reflected in Tommy's features.

'Very good, Tommy. That was excellent. My daughter, Debbie, took much longer than that to get the feel of it.'

David stood back, the words still echoing in his brain. It had seemed so natural, so open.

'Is she coming today?'

'No, Tommy. Debbie's dead.' He straightened up, looking around. He pointed. 'See that buoy over there?'

Tommy's eyes swept vaguely through a wide arc and David clucked at his own stupidity. How could you expect a Down's to know what a buoy was? It was not only Tommy who had a lot to learn.

'That tall thing floating on the water over there, the one with two spikes on top that look like two black icecream cones. That's called a buoy.'

The eyes still made no sign of focusing on where David pointed and he felt his first twinge of disappointment. So he had just bumped up against the first boundary fence of the young man's intellect. What had he been expecting, four 'A's and an open scholarship to Cambridge? He smiled forgivingly at Tommy's anxious look of apology.

'I'm sorry . . .' Tommy said with difficulty.

'That's all right,' David murmured. 'Don't worry. It's not important.'

'I'm sorry . . .' Tommy tried again. 'I'm sorry Debbie's dead.'

David felt his throat constrict and his eyes fill, but there was a new strength, a new determination in the words he ground out.

'So am I, Tommy. So am I. Now – ' he took a deep breath, bracing his shoulders back ' – let's get this boat moving in a straight line, shall we?' He pointed once more. 'See that great big black thing over there, sticking up out of the water?'

Tommy nodded.

'Well – see if you can *hit* the bloody thing.'

It did not take long for it to become obvious that Tommy, once he had stopped laughing, could steer a boat, at least in a straight line. Grim determination produced a look of such intense concentration on his face that David laughed.

'All right. Let's head out into the Solent, shall we?' He put his hand on Tommy's once more as they turned round. 'There – d'you see where we want to go? Just keep going in that direction. Are you hungry?'

'Yes.'

'Ham rolls and coffee – all right?'

Tommy's eyes flickered away from the horizon for a moment. 'Yes, please.'

'Right. I'll go below and brew up. Call me if another boat comes anywhere near.'

Jackie had always done this sort of thing, neatly, tidily, appetisingly. For some reason the ham, curled into shiny, springy coils, refused to stay in the bread rolls that had crumbled to a shambles around solid lumps of butter. He should have brought a lettuce. At least he could hardly make a mess of the coffee. Was there enough . . . ?'

'David.'

The first gentle use of his name. He climbed out into the cockpit and saw the anxious frown, the arm outstretched. He looked where the finger pointed. The other boat was heeled, carving its way towards them on starboard tack, all sign of its crew hidden behind a vast quivering genoa.

'We must give way to them,' David said.

Panic began to show in Tommy's face. He took his hand from the tiller and backed away.

'No, Tommy,' David said quietly. 'You do it. Turn the boat to the right.' Did he know right from left? 'Over *that* way. Let them pass down our left side. That's the way.'

Someone waved from the other boat as they passed, and Tommy waved violently back, relief and a sense of achievement competing on his face.

'Right,' David laughed. 'Now point us back the way we were going before those show-offs messed us about. Shall we try and sail like that later on?'

The answer spread all over Tommy's face.

'They were going very fast,' he said. 'Can we go as fast as that?'

'We can try, Tommy. We can try.'

Tommy did not seem to notice the travesty of a lunch that David produced. The sight of the food was the only thing that induced him to relinquish his post at the helm. David watched in amazement as the food disappeared, leaving Tommy obviously appreciative but, equally obviously, far from replete.

'More?' David asked.

Tommy nodded.

'Same again?' There was a note of panic now as he wondered whether he had brought enough.

'Yes, please, David. Have you got any apples? I like apples.'

'No, Tommy – no apples. But I'll remember next time.'

He let Tommy clear the crockery away and watched him take it below. Strong, sure-footed, his centre of gravity close to the ground, he looked a natural. Out into the Solent, they headed for a relatively clear patch of sea. David slipped the diesel engine into neutral.

'Now then, Tommy. We're going to put the mainsail up – that's the one that goes up the mast. First of all, we've got to take the sail cover off.'

He could never get Debbie to fold the cover – she used simply to throw it into the open cabin. Tommy watched intently as David showed him how it was done before giving the engine a short burst to turn the bows to the wind. David wound the main halyard around a self-tailing winch and gave the handle to

Tommy. 'When I say "wind", turn that as hard as you can and I'll guide the sail up the mast. Don't start until I tell you.'

His arms around the mast, David called 'Wind'. Within seconds, he was shouting 'Whoa' as Tommy's full strength was applied in the service of this man who had opened a completely new world to him.

'Take it easy,' David yelled. 'Don't go mad.'

He closed his eyes. What a bloody stupid thing to say. To a Down's. 'You stupid bastard, Royall,' he whispered to himself. He opened his eyes again, an apology on his lips, only to see a face grinning from ear to ear. Stupid bastard indeed. He looked at Tommy again. He had, in a strong, fit body, a mind that Providence, in its malevolence, had decreed should be kept in a straitjacket, secured with bonds no one could undo. But he was not mad. He had not gone crazy like some genius whose overburdened trolley had come off its rails. He did not have a brain that had been scrambled by emotional trauma or the effect of strange enzymes. Inside that skull there was no dead brain tissue that had been starved of oxygen or pickled in alcohol somewhere along the way. What brain Tommy had was probably more normal than his, devoid as it was of the avarice and jealousy that would inevitably pour in to fill the vacant space if anyone were to find some way of suddenly enlarging its mental capacity.

With the mainsail hoisted, they stood in the cockpit looking up to where it rippled and slapped above them. David switched the engine off and, in the silence it left, the sound of slapping sail and rattling rigging took a quantum leap in the stiff breeze. It was the moment of truth for many a first-time sailor – the moment when the comforting sound of the engine dies and they are left at the mercy of the elements. He looked anxiously at Tommy and saw nothing but excitement.

The boat payed off and David let it go until it began to run before the wind.

'Just let him get the feel of a boat under sail,' he muttered. Tommy raised his eyebrows as if he had not quite heard. But David was talking to himself. 'And just the mainsail today, I think.'

'Come on,' he said out loud. 'Come and take the tiller again. It's just the same as before only *that*' – he pointed up to the sail – 'is your engine now.'

Slowly, over the next hour or so, David turned the boat across the wind, watching Tommy's face as the cockpit floor beneath his feet began to heel more and more. He saw, to his delight, that the steeper the boat heeled, the broader the grin was that split Tommy's face.

'And *now* look what happens.'

David took the tiller from him and turned the boat into the wind, bringing it to a flapping, rattling halt once more.

'What you *can't* do is to sail *straight* into the wind. This is the nearest you can go to the wind.'

He sheeted in hard, and the boat heeled once more as he got it sailing to windward.

'Now,' he said. 'Try and keep it just there.'

He had come to expect too much. Disappointment spread over an earnest face as Tommy failed to find the slot and the boat, time and again, shuddered to a halt or fell away to leeward. What had he expected? Many normal youngsters took weeks to acquire the skill.

'Time to go back now, Tommy. I'm hungry, aren't you? Steak and kidney and potatoes – will that do you?'

The memory of the ham rolls still fresh in his mind, he looked for enthusiasm and saw only anxiety on features normally only too ready to explode into a smile.

'What's the matter?'

The anxiety only deepened as Tommy hung his head. What was going on inside that mind? The only clue he had was a troubled glance down at the tiller that was now clutched under one arm like some treasured possession with which he would never part.

'Is it because you found it hard to steer going against the wind? Is that what's the matter?'

Tommy said nothing.

'Tommy, it took me *months* to learn how to do that. It took me a long time to learn how to steer a boat at all. I think you've been marvellous. You've only been in a boat five minutes and it takes years' – there was the nanosecond gap from which 'for a *normal* person' had been mentally censored – 'to become a really good sailor.'

The anxiety cleared, though not completely.

'Would you like to try again tomorrow?' What was he saying? 'The weather forecast is not so good for tomorrow, but would you like to try again?' He wanted to *give*. 'With *both* sails up this time?'

The smile was back.

An hour later, Tommy held the boat against the pontoon as David tied up.

'That's all right, Tommy, you can let go now.'

Tommy stood back, head high, his arms across his chest. He walked up and down, surveying the boat from bow to stern, masthead to water line. *He* had steered that. *He* had pushed it out into the water to set it on its way. That great big boat had done what *he'd* wanted. *He* had done all that. He and David. He turned to an elderly woman, watching from the boat moored on the other side of the pontoon.

'*I've* been sailing today,' he told her proudly.

'Have you?' The woman closed the book she had been reading. 'Did you enjoy it?'

'*I* steered.'

'Did you?' She turned to David as a grey-haired man stuck his head out of the companionway. 'It's nice to see *Sally* being used again. She's looked so sad.'

They had never spoken before, though they had been moored alongside for two years. Just the polite smile, the mandatory wave as they had left for sea.

'It's nice to be back, except' – David pulled a face – 'I've now got to cook a meal, something at which I am *not* very good.'

'If you're in real trouble, give me a shout.' A gentle face turned back to Tommy. 'Would you like to have a look at *our* boat?'

A beseeching glance at David, a nod, and Tommy was clambering over their guardrail.

'D'you like Coca-Cola?' David heard as he watched them disappear below.

The meal, a mush of gravy and a mush of custard, the one conveying dices of meat, the other slices of banana, was devoured in a silent, steamy enclosure. They cleared away and sat. It was eight o'clock. What do you talk about with a Down's? What time did Tommy go to bed? What governed his life, his nineteen-year-old body or his (David tried to pick a figure) nine-, ten-, eleven-year-old mind? Not that Tommy looked worried about it, sitting quietly, upright, his hands in his lap. It was he, David, who was on edge.

'Let's go and have a beer. I know of a nice little pub over near Warsash. Put your anorak on; it's chilly outside.'

It was only after they had settled, David with his beer, Tommy with a Coke, that they found out why the only vacant seats they could find had been against the far wall. No one with any sense chooses to sit where the competitors in a local darts league match tread on one's feet and spill their beer in one's lap. Similarly, locals do not appreciate strangers who intrude in their ritualistic antics and smile condescendingly at their hackneyed jokes. David would have expected, at best, cold indifference; at worst, enough trampling of toes and spilling of beer to make him move on. But he had never sat in a pub with a Down's before. He had no previous experience on which to draw, but he should have guessed. He'd seen it often enough now – the way everyone who looked at Tommy smiled.

The match was a close one, the excitement infectious. Tommy contributed to the bawdy, beer-fuelled fever with peals of laughter, dispensed with an even-handed generosity that had everyone staring at him, laughing back. The match was won and lost, the frenzy subsided. Most of the players drifted away to the bar, leaving a few to throw their darts in a fitful attempt to show what *might* have been. One, dismayed by his failure, thrust his darts in Tommy's direction.

'Go on, son,' he grinned. 'Have a go. You can't do any worse than me.'

A moment later, Tommy, red-faced and breathless, stood where they told him to stand. His first three darts clattered against the wall, two falling to the floor. Willing hands picked them up and returned them. Cheers went up as two of the next three thudded into the board, causing the crowd to drift back from the bar, their glasses in their hands. Now each throw brought its reward, a cheer of triumph for a hit, a shout of encouragement for a miss. The sounds of good-natured disapproval met David as he forced his way through to put a hand on Tommy's arm.

'Come on, Tommy. It's time we were going.'

With touching obedience, Tommy handed back the darts and followed him to the door.

'Aaaaaaaah. Good night, Tommy.'

'All the best, Tommy.'

''Night, Tommy.'

Tommy Evans, Down's syndrome, centre of attention, made his exit. David Royall, Master of Surgery, Member of Council, followed facelessly, anonymously behind.

Body sweat and toothpaste, soap and cold water, and the embarrassment of a young man who had not undressed so close to another human being before. The first attempt at inserting a bulky frame into a sleeping bag. The first feel of tough, wiry hair under David's hand.

'Good night, Tommy. Sleep well.'

There was no reply. It seemed there had to be something more. David leaned towards the muffled words.

'What . . . ?'

His arms enfolded within the sleeping bag, Tommy raised his head and shoulders. His kiss was dry, gentle and warm.

Sea air, physical exertion, food and beer – enough normally to ensure oblivion. But David lay awake, one cheek burning away all hope of sleep. He stared up into the darkness, listening to every breath, snort, snuffle, snore, every movement, every muttered sound. He had done that the first night Debbie had slept in her cot beside their bed. He had scarcely closed his eyes that night either. One of the halyards had begun its rhythmic slap against the mast. The wind the Met Office had promised was freshening. He heard a spatter of rain and did not relish the thought of a trip on deck in his pyjamas to secure the halyard. But if it was going to wake Tommy . . . He wriggled his way out of his sleeping bag and crossed to where a vague, warm, shadowy mass lay, innocently trusting.

Breakfast over, they stood on deck. David looked up and around. 'Are you sure you want to go out again today?' he asked.

Tommy nodded, smiling.

'I know I promised, but it looks as if it's going to blow.'

With Jackie, he would have chickened out and driven home, feeling inadequate alongside Jackie's critical silence. But now there was to be no escape. He was going to have to keep his promise. He'd have to be more careful with what he promised in future.

'We might get a bit wet.'

For the first time, Tommy looked concerned. It could blow as hard as it liked. Getting wet was a different matter altogether. David saw disappointment as well as the fear of angering Mrs Berry.

'Right,' he said, briskly. 'Come on, follow me.'

Would the chandlers be open on an April Sunday morning? It was. A proud, grinning Tommy walked out, clad from head to toe, from smart peaked cap to yellow wellies, in spanking new foul weather clothing.

The woman in the next boat saw them. 'You're going out?' she asked, frowning.

'I've got a new suit,' Tommy said. 'David bought it for me.'

'I can see.' She looked up at the sky before turning to David. 'Take care, won't you? We're going home.'

Just out of the river, David put a reef in the mainsail and, gingerly, unfurled some of the foresail to teach Tommy how to tack. Tommy bent to the winches with a will, until the rigging vibrated in response to his strength. Between tacks, he cast covetous glances at the tiller.

'Can I do that, David?' he asked.

'Not today, Tommy. It's really blowing a bit too hard. Let's just see what it's like out in the Solent. If it's too rough, we'll turn round and come back.'

A short, irregular sea made it difficult to meet each wave, and soon the spray began to fly across the deck. With a slate-coloured sea beneath a louring sky, David searched for a reason to turn back. The last thing he must do was frighten Tommy.

'Tommy,' he shouted, 'we'll tack just once and then make for home. Are you ready?'

Tommy let the one sheet go as David had shown him. As he turned to haul in on the other side, the foresail, flapping wildly, snagged on a fitting on the front of the mast. Taken aback, the boat lurched, heeling violently, sending David grabbing for any handhold. By the time he had regained his balance, Tommy was already up on the sloping deck, freeing the sail to thrash away to leeward.

'Come down,' David yelled, but Tommy, his back to him, took no notice.

'Tommy, come down,' he yelled again, but still Tommy, his arms spread wide as he braced himself between mast and shrouds, did not turn.

David let the tiller go long enough to winch in the foresail. With the boat under way once more, it quietened as it steadied, butting once more into the waves as David headed back towards the Hamble. Anger, born of fear, welled up at the thought of what would have happened if Tommy had gone overboard.

'Tommy,' he bellowed, 'don't ever do a thing like that again. Come back here, Tommy, d'you hear me?'

Tommy half turned, his dripping face and chest still proud to the swingeing spray. David could only see him in profile, but there was no mistaking the elation as Tommy lifted his head in a joyous roar.

'Hmmmmmmmmmmmm. You look as if you've enjoyed yourself, I'll say that much.' Mrs Berry brushed the front of Tommy's anorak. 'You didn't get wet, did you?'

Both Tommy and David grinned and she sensed a secret.

'Off you go then. You're late for your tea but I've saved some for you. What d'you say to Mr Royall?'

'Thank you.'

This time David was not taken by surprise. He leaned his head sideways as Tommy stretched to kiss him.

236

'Goodbye, Tommy. See you soon.'

'Hmmmmph.' Mrs Berry did not seem impressed. She gave Tommy a push. 'Go on now. Off with you and have your tea. I'll just see Mr Royall out.'

They watched Tommy's receding back before walking towards the door. David smiled.

'Something's bothering you, Mrs Berry.'

'Hmph. Where did you take him?'

'I took him sailing down at Southampton.'

She bent her head to look out through the open door. 'In *this* weather?'

'It wasn't quite as bad as this early on,' David said defensively.

'Sailing.' She made it sound a deadly sin that could only result in inevitable retribution. 'Tommy sailing.'

'He was excellent – an absolute natural.'

'Huh. Surprised, were you?'

David turned to face her. 'You don't approve, obviously.'

'It's not for me to approve or disapprove, Mr Royall.' She'd met a few consultants in her days as a ward sister. They didn't frighten her. 'I'm just the matron here. I just have to bring them down to earth again on a Monday morning. And where will you be tomorrow morning, Mr Royall, when I'm explaining that kind men like you don't come and take him sailing every day of the week, in fact, may never come and take him again?'

'You needn't worry on that score, Mrs Berry. I intend . . .'

'When?'

'When? Well . . .'

'When *you* feel the need. When *you* want some company. You're all the same.' Her face softened for a moment. 'I don't mean the parents. There are times when my heart bleeds for them – the torment they go through wondering whether they're doing the right thing. But some of the do-gooders. The regular ones, they're great – the ones that turn up like clockwork every week with their minibuses and their trips to the seaside. But the other ones – here today and gone tomorrow, a smug, sanctimonious smile on their faces, appearing every now and then when they want to salve their consciences and chalk up a few credits towards an everlasting life.'

David had had some experience of handling ward sisters too. He laughed. 'And what the hell's got into you today?'

'Shuh.' She gave a short laugh and the suggestion of a smile pulled at her mouth. 'I'm sorry, Mr Royall, but I worry about them and – I try not to have them – but Tommy is something of a favourite of mine. And Mr Evans is such a kind, generous man.' She pulled her eyebrows together in a frown of mock fury. 'And I didn't really know where he was and I don't really know you. And I can't stand these people who come and take a child out just as if they're taking a horse for a ride and then come back here and stick him back in the stable when they've finished.' She turned the full force of a formidable personality on him. 'You're not going to be one of those, are you, Mr Royall? Because if you are, I'd rather you didn't come at all.'

She lifted and then dropped her shoulders as if a weight had suddenly been removed.

'I'm sorry to speak so bluntly, Mr Royall, but it's better we know where we stand, don't you think?'

David stretched both arms in front of him like a sleepwalker to rest a hand on each of her shoulders. He flexed his head so that he had to raise his eyelids to look her straight in the eyes.

'There's nothing you've said, Mrs Berry, that I have not said to myself in some way or other over and over again this weekend. I *know* who was doing the favour, and the last thing I want to do is to upset Tommy. So don't worry. I won't use Tommy, I promise you.'

'Hmmph.'

It was obvious it would take more than a little soft soap, skilfully administered by a good-looking consultant, to convince *her*.

18

Ward rounds on adult and on paediatric units are spheres of medical activity as disparate as it is possible to conceive, despite the fact that both are evolved around the study of identical human organs – heart, lungs, brain, kidney. The reason is simple.

Adults can be impressed; children see right through you.

Of the adult units, there is probably more playacting on the surgical wards than in any of the others – understandably, perhaps, since the dramas can be as real as the blood that is spilt. To the cynics, the healthy ones, the ones not in fear of an imminent operation, the strutting, pompous surgeon is the principal character in what they see as a charade, a farce. In the case of the Brian Pullmans of this world, they would be correct. But then, an actor may sometimes be taken over by the character he is playing.

David, a traditionalist, always made two formal ward rounds a week, something to which he had stuck religiously at Queen's even in the most frenzied days of his private practice. Each of his patients knew that, at least twice a week, he would be answerable personally to them. This basic commitment to the NHS had, in some ways, been a saving grace, putting him into the category of 'a bit of a bastard', which was acceptable, rather than 'a complete bastard', which was not. Now, without the demands of a private practice, he visited the wards at the Merton every day, though the two formal rounds still remained the twin buttresses of his clinical routine. Twice a week, he put on the mantle of infallibility he knew his patients expected of someone who would wield the power of life and death over them. Unlike Pullman, David gladly shed that mantle at the first opportunity. Many times it weighted him down like a yoke, but while he wore it he saw nothing wrong in reinforcing its effects with all the trappings of enforced silence and the classic entourage of registrars, house surgeons, ward sister, staff nurses, secretaries and students.

He shook his head in disbelief as he pushed open the doors into the paediatric ward. Bedlam. Roderick Beavan's ward round was in full swing.

A nine-year-old Kojak, fighting every inch of the way the sapping effects of a bloodstream full of cytotoxic drugs, charged at David, trying to take his legs from under him with the small trolley he pushed. In one corner the sound of the TV was drowned by the chatter of the jostling, wrestling semicircle of children in front of it. In another corner, a rudimentary school class held sway. A four-year-old bruiser stood, his pyjamas around his ankles, trying to wrench apart the sides of his cot, while kneeling at the next bed, her arms resting on it as if in prayer, a wide-eyed mother looked at David, silently beseeching him to tell her that her daughter was not about to slide back into status epilepticus again.

Roderick Beavan and his team were clustered round a bed halfway down the ward. Beavan, the sleeves of a brightly coloured shirt rolled up, sat on the bed, a child's head in his lap, as his registrar struggled to insert a cannula into the last available vein. His house physician hovered with a blood drip. Struggling to see just another patient and not a pale, dying child, the students tried to whisper amongst themselves. The sister left them for a moment as she heard the sound of vomiting further down the ward. David joined the back of the group.

Beavan smiled. 'Be with you in a moment, David.'

'No hurry.'

'Trying to get a bit of colour into these cheeks, aren't we?' Gently, he pinched a wan face and was rewarded with a smile. He turned back to David. 'Anything urgent?'

'Not really.'

David joined the others willing the registrar on to success. Five minutes later, he sighed with the rest as they watched the longed for rhythm in the drip chamber.

'What can I do for you, David?' Beavan enquired.

'I've come to pick your brains.'

'God help you then.' Beavan gave the child's face a last caress before standing up. 'We'd better go in my office out of this noise.'

Between bedside and office, Beavan was waylaid by another anxious parent and David had to wait. Finally they sat behind closed doors.

'Well?' Beavan asked.

'Down's syndrome, Roddy. What d'you know about Down's syndrome.'

'Not a lot,' Beavan laughed. 'There isn't much to know. It's all been worked out many years ago. Good God, a surgeon with an interest in Down's. Don't tell me you've found another cause for duodenal obstruction, because that's been known for a long time.'

'No,' David snorted. He made vague movements with his hands. 'What . . . What I want to know . . . How bad are they? What happens to them usually?'

'It's all there in the library. Why don't you go and read it up?'

'Because it's easier to come and ask you.'

'Typical bloody surgeon. It's a big subject, David. It might help if I were to know why you're so interested. Am I allowed to know?'

Paediatricians are frequently good listeners. Beavan was a good paediatrician. It took David five minutes and more to tell what he knew of Tommy.

'He's got to be a mosaic,' Beavan said with a nod.

'A what?'

'A mosaic.' Beavan looked at the blank stare. He grinned. 'God, but you surgeons are bloody thick. You don't know what a mosaic is?'

David said nothing, simply grinning back sheepishly.

'There are three kinds of Down's.'

'*Are* there?'

'Yes. By far the majority, perhaps ninety-five per cent, are the so-called 21 Trisomy cases. They are the ones with the extra 21 chromosome. They are the really classical ones – the tongue, the eyes, the hands, the pot belly. It's in this group you usually find the really severe ones – there are all degrees, as you know

– with mental retardation, possibly congenital heart lesions as well, occasionally imperforate anus.'

'And intelligence?'

Beavan shrugged. 'Varies,' he said, 'from very low in the bad cases to – what? – seventy-five or possibly more in the milder ones. A Down's *has* passed his driving test, you know.'

'Has he, be damned?'

'Yes.' Beavan tilted his chair and clasped his arms behind his head. 'But they're such nice, happy kids, even the bad ones. The occasional tantrum, and sometimes they get a bit too keen to find out what girls keep up their skirts. But, great kids to have around.' He let his hands drop as the chair came crashing back on all four legs. 'Any heart trouble, this lad of yours?'

'Not that one can tell. He looks as strong as an ox.'

'The boys often are.'

'But these – mosaics? You *did* say "mosaic"?'

Beavan nodded. 'There is another kind, the so-called translocation group, where bits of one chromosome get stuck on to another. They're rare, but not so rare as the mosaics. Now *they're* the fascinating ones.'

'Why?'

Beavan's eyes narrowed. 'D'you know what mosaicism is?' he asked.

'Not really, no.'

'Good God.' Beavan shook his head. 'And you're on the bloody Council. But you know about chromosomes, that they come in pairs and that a Down's has one set of three instead of a pair?'

'Yes, Roddy.'

'Thank goodness for that. Well – in a case of mosaicism, not all the cells in the body have the chromosomal abnormality in their nuclei. Some of the cell lines have the normal set-up, and just how bad a Down's a patient *is* depends on the proportion of normal to abnormal cell lines he *has*.' Beavan spread his hands, his fingers splayed out on the desk in front of him. 'There's a grey area – you must have seen it. I'm sure everyone has seen the person who looks like a Down's – just. You wonder whether he is one until you speak to him. Then you find he's perfectly normal and you sense that, by the grace of God, he's fallen just the right side of the fence. And then again, there's the Down's – an obvious Down's, no doubt about it, but who behaves so well, has all the manners, that you feel – also by the grace of God? – he's come down just the *wrong* side.'

David nodded. 'Like Tommy.'

'If you say so. Now *they're* usually mosaics.'

For a while there was silence as Beavan, a skilled observer, watched David's face.

'Would you like me to see this Tommy of yours?' he asked quietly.

The corners of David's mouth dropped. 'Difficult, Roddy. For one thing, he's not *my* Tommy. He's someone else's. For another, he's nineteen; hardly a paediatric problem.'

'I wouldn't let that worry you,' Beavan grinned. 'No reason why the physicians should find out. Anyway, they're as bad as the surgeons: they know bugger all about Down's too.'

He waited for David to stop laughing. 'What d'you say, David? Let me have a look at him.'

'How d'you find out whether he's a mosaic?'

'There *are* tests. You do chromosomal studies on some of his cells, skin fibroblasts, peripheral lymphocytes. If they *are* normal, then that is definite evidence. But even if they're abnormal, it doesn't completely rule out mosaicism. It takes a bit of chasing sometimes.'

'And if you find it?'

A shrug. 'At least you know.'

'But there's nothing you can do about it?'

'Nnno.'

David heard the tone, saw the honest eyes lowered. 'No?' he asked.

'No.' It was more decisive the second time, as if Beavan were anxious to correct any false impressions.

'But?' David insisted.

Beavan squirmed in his seat. 'There is *nothing* anyone can do about it.' He looked hard at David as he drove the point home. '*Nothing*. But . . .' Again the body movement. 'It is pretty well documented that the proportion of abnormal to normal cell lines can vary over the years in an individual case, with, if anything, an increase in the proportion of the normal. But,' he added quickly, 'that usually occurs in the early years of life, and Tommy, you say, is now nineteen.'

Beavan's voice did not fall away as if that was the end of the subject. He reached for a pen and picked it up, only to throw it down again. He looked at David's face and knew he was not going to let him off the hook.

'All right, you bastard. There *has* been the very, very rare case reported where there was some evidence that an abnormal cell line might have almost burnt itself out completely and, of course, if there were very few abnormal lines to start with . . .'

He shook his head regretfully.

'I shouldn't have said that. That's real rocking-horse stuff. And, if it happens at all, it happens in the first few years of life. There is no *way* it could happen to Tommy.' He leaned towards David and thumped the desk. 'David – what this lad Tommy is, he *is*. There's *nothing* you can do to change him.'

Lever – a name David was not likely to forget. But that had been back in Queen's. The poor devil Pullman had made such a balls of. He *must* be dead by now. It was a common enough name. Anyway – he picked up the notes and read the name once again – this was a woman. He turned to the nurse.

'Ask Mrs Lever to come in, would you?'

There was no mistaking that hangdog face, blind faith seeping from every pore. It was yet another in a long line of faces that still haunted him.

'Mrs Lever. But . . .' – he picked up her notes, making great play of looking at her address – 'don't you live just down the road from Queen's Hospital?'

'I used to, Mr Royall. But after John died I came to live down here with my sister.'

'Aaaah, he's dead, is he? I was afraid that might be so. He was a very nice man, Mrs Lever; a very brave man.'

'He had a terrible death, Mr Royall. He lingered for months, poor man. But, as you say, he was very brave; never complained, though it was obvious he was in terrible pain.'

Go ahead: turn the knife. You've earned the right.

'And he was so grateful for all you and Mr Pullman did for him, right to the end, he was.'

And thrust and turn again.

'And now you're the patient.' Why hadn't she gone back to Pullman if he'd been so bloody marvellous? 'Let's see what the trouble is.'

He turned to the GP's letter, scanning the essential words like a bar code. Sweet – lady – lump – breast – don't think – able – do much – thank – seeing.

'Your doctor says you've got a lump in one breast, Mrs Lever.'

'Yes.'

'Which one?'

'Right.'

'How long have . . . ?'

How many times now had he entoned the dreadful catechism?

He watched through an aura of defeat as her back disappeared into a cubicle. Two in the same family. Husband and wife. How often that seemed to happen. The diagnosis was written in the face of the nurse who came to tell him Mrs Lever was ready.

The fixed mass, the glands in her armpit and neck, the big liver.

'Any pain anywhere, Mrs Lever?'

'Bit of backache.'

'Uh-huh.' The gentle, kindly look that, to someone of intelligence, would have been a sentence of death. 'You've had that a lot longer than a few weeks, Mrs Lever.'

A knowing smile.

'He was so ill, Mr Royall. He had troubles enough, poor man, without worrying about me.'

'But when you knew he was dying, when you went to see Mr Pullman, why didn't you tell Mr Pullman about it then?'

Glenys Lever said nothing. She looked away, pulling the sheet up higher over one shoulder.

'Why didn't you?' David persisted gently.

'We didn't see Mr Pullman again.'

'You didn't?'

'He's a very busy man, Mr Royall. And after a while it was as obvious to John as to everybody else that he was dying and that Mr Pullman could do no more for him. We were just so grateful to know that everything possible had been done, and we were so grateful to *you* for sending him to see Mr Pullman in the first place. But you can't expect miracles, can you? I know Mr Pullman did his best.'

'But – did you see *anyone*, anyone at all, after you saw me in Queen's Hospital that day?'

'No, Mr Royall. Just my own doctor at home. He was very kind.'

'Mrs Spencer, please.'

'Speaking.'

'Good morning. David Royall.'

'Mr Royall.' Obvious genuine pleasure. 'It's good to hear your voice again. You've rung up to say you're coming back.'

He was in no mood for pleasantries.

'Lever. John Lever. One of the last cases I saw at Queen's. Carcinomatosis. D'you remember him?'

'I do, Mr Royall.' A sudden change of tone to cold, stony defensiveness.

'I referred him back to Mr Pullman.'

'I know you did.'

'Then why the hell . . . ?'

'Don't shout at *me*, Mr Royall.'

'I seem to remember I wanted to make the arrangements, but you said I couldn't be trusted and that *you* would see to it.'

'*You* were going to see Mr Pullman, but decided you were too busy and asked me to arrange it instead.'

Memories stirred up guilt. Guilt blunted righteous indignation.

'And did you?'

'Yes and no, Mr Royall.'

'What the hell does that mean?'

'Mixing with that rough lot down at the Merton hasn't done

your language any good, Mr Royall. Yes – I made the arrangements. No – he was not seen by Mr Pullman.'

'Why not?'

'Because Mr Pullman refused to see him, Mr Royall.'

It took a while for Royall to absorb her reply, analyse it and respond.

'He *what*?' he hissed.

'I tried, Mr Royall; I really did. I made an appointment and thought no more about it. It was weeks later, after Christmas, when you were – ill – that Mrs Lever came to say her husband was much worse and ask when Mr Pullman was going to see him. You know what they were like, poor things. They hadn't been sent an appointment. I rang Mr Pullman's secretary the same day, and she said she'd have a word with him and ring me back. Nothing came of that, so I rang Mr Pullman himself.'

'And?'

'I won't tell you what he said.'

'But he didn't see Lever?'

'No.' She spoke now with the weariness of the long-serving, corridor-wise NHS secretary. 'So I fell back on the last resort. I rang Lever's GP and suggested he ask Pullman to do a domiciliary visit, and the GP agreed.'

David waited in silence.

'But he refused.'

'Pullman? Pullman refused a *domi*? I *don't* believe it.'

'That's right, Mr Royall. He just – turned his back.'

The bastard. The sodding bastard. The pompous, sanctimonious, hypocritical, penny-pinching, sodding bastard.

19

Tranquil excitement – was there such a state? David laughed to himself as he twisted his trunk sideways, leaning his head back against the driver's window to stare at Tommy. Three whole weeks. Three whole weeks away from that bastard Pullman. Only now would he be able to put the two-faced creep completely out of his mind. Tommy sensed David's scrutiny and turned to smile before resuming his lively vigil through the windscreen with no hint of embarrassment. Tranquillity and excitement; contradictions in terms – but David could come up with no better description of Tommy's mood. They had been stationary, nose to tail in a queue, surrounded by other cars, for nearly an hour, but Tommy still sat, his seat belt pulled taut as he leaned forward, eagerly watching the comings and goings around him. There was no doubting his excitement, but it was not the neurotic, mercurial restlessness of someone who tired quickly of one novelty only to look for another. His face shone with the joy of someone glad to be alive, happy to live for the moment with no fear of the future, while there was also an urgency about him that spoke of things to see, places to go. But, beneath it all, there was a peace that was perhaps Providence's apology for its cruelty. Tranquil excitement, yes, that would have to do.

'Mal – would you let me take Tommy on one of these flotilla holidays around the Greek islands?'

That was how it had started. He had been surprised how easy it had been to say. A mental vision of Debbie had hung before him, but she had simply smiled and nodded her approval. His voice had been strong, his words positive. Memories of what might have been no longer clutched him by the throat.

'Why not? F'r 'ow long?'

'Two weeks, maybe three.'

'If ew think ew can put up with 'im fur that long.'

'I don't see any reason why not. He's a born sailor.'

'Does it *'ave* to be the Greek islands?'

'No, there's Yugoslavia. But . . .'

'Why don' ew go down Grimaud? There's a boat down there doin' nothin'. An' it'd save ew a coupla bob. I'll fix ew a flight to Nice. An' a car.'

'Hang on a minute.' Mal had been halfway to the phone before David had stopped him. 'Where exactly is Port Grimaud?'

'Near St Tropez – just across the bay. Tidy place.'

'You've got a house down there. Now I remember. Faye told me.'

Mal had headed for the phone once more. 'I'll get 'em to clean the place up f'r ew – get some food in, make sure the boat's OK.'

'Whoa,' David had cried. 'Not so fast.' He had held his hand up, taking his time to think while Mal had stood, hovering over him. 'All right. That's very kind of you, Mal. But we'll drive down; we'll take a couple of days over it. Tommy would like that.'

It had been as easy as that.

Tommy had been waiting at the door, hopping from one foot to the other. David had felt an arm around his shoulders as Tommy had kissed him while Mrs Berry had fussed over the suitcase.

'Are you sure you've got all those clothes Mr Royall bought you?'

'Did he sleep last night?' David had asked her.

'Never known him miss a night yet,' she had laughed. 'It'll take more than a trip to the South of France to keep *that* young man awake.'

Tranquil excitement.

David made the jerky movements of mock panic as the car in front suddenly moved off. Tommy laughed. The laughter gave way to gaping wonder as David drove up the ramp and manoeuvred the car through the side of the boat, squeezing it between the ranks of those already aboard before them.

It was half-term. The Portsmouth ferry teemed with the children that convoys of buses had disgorged. Harassed teachers strove to induce some vestige of stability into a hyperactive mass of humanity. Tommy saw, milling around the decks and lounges, a life that had been denied to him and, for the first time, fell prey to divided loyalties.

David turned. No Tommy. No instant smile, no genial presence, no stocky frame, one arm straight, one arm crooked behind his back. Anxiously, David fought his way up stairs, along corridors, through lounges.

Tommy stood at the back of a group of children who were

pushing and shoving to get to a list pinned to a board. David drew him away guiltily, ready to apologise, as if retrieving his ball from someone else's garden.

In the dining room, he chose a table in the far corner, maintaining the cordon sanitaire expected to surround a Down's. Later, in the heads, David hovered protectively.

'I've got to do big jobs, David.'

'All right. Just close the door and I'll stand outside.'

He stood guard, eyeing suspiciously everyone that came and went. He had not appreciated before that the world was populated with homosexual prowlers who spent their lives going on boat trips with the sole purpose of seducing the mentally handicapped.

Tommy slept the sleep of the innocent. David dozed fitfully in the steel cell that reverberated to Tommy's snoring. Tommy was awake and bright-eyed within seconds of being shaken by a bleary-eyed David. Breakfast, accumulated in a shuffling queue, saw David lose patience for the first time. Tommy was obviously not to be hurried when it came to food and did not appreciate that ferries operated to rigid deadlines.

'Buck up, Tommy,' he snapped – and regretted it. Let the bastards wait.

The roaring engines and choking fumes. The open road and the Tancarville Bridge. Tommy's gasping delight at the sight of the river. The frenzy of Paris with Tommy's roars of laughter at David's curses. Lunch in Beaune. *Feuillette d'escargot* and *cuisse de canard*. Jackie always used to order. He had not dared order fish and chips, Tommy's favourite. A walk amongst the mottled tree trunks and shuttered windows, and then it was the hurtling madness of the road south once more, with Tommy proudly working the tolls by throwing the coins or pressing the buttons.

A hot evening sun through the windscreen dried their mouths and sapped their concentration. David looked sideways. Although he smiled back bravely, Tommy had slumped in his seat, the telltale folds around his eyes deepened with fatigue.

Narrow roads and quiet villages. A stop amongst the white acacia to consult a guide book with no one to argue. Vacqueyras.

Yes, they had a room – a double bed, would that be agreeable? Dinner would be at eight.

A superb meal and an excellent wine. The innocent warmth of another human body in a double bed. Breakfast with coffee and fresh bread on bare wooden tables set on cool stone floors. Out into the peace of whispering trees.

'Come on, Tommy, let's go for a walk. I can't face the car again just yet.'

They set off, Tommy, one pace behind, his arms slotted into place.

The house, a quarter of a mile away, was set back from the road. Raised on a small mound, its formal, immaculate terraced gardens fell away in front, embraced by long twin curving drives that descended to closed wrought-iron gates. White walls could be glimpsed in the gaps between the hedges that surrounded fountains and stone carvings. Money and position and power. Both Tommy and David had their heads pressed against the bars of the gates when, without warning, they suddenly swung away from them, and they stepped back as they heard the crunch of tyres on gravel. The woman driving the big Renault stopped the car before pulling out into the road. She spoke, animated and beautiful, to a teenage girl alongside her. Tommy and David she ignored with that true arrogance of someone who *really* had not noticed them, looking as if the poor were always sticking their noses through her gate.

David grinned to himself. A tiger in bed, that one. There had been a time . . . He sighed.

'Time we got on, Tommy. We've still a fair distance to go.'

As they made their way back to the hotel, David wondered what he would have to do to get Tommy to walk alongside him.

Few surgeons are linguists. David's French got him nowhere in their search for the house amongst the attractive terraces that snake their way along the waterfronts of Port Grimaud. Hot and tired, he tried to hide his disappointment when ultimately they found the tiny gate. It was locked and he shook it angrily. Mal had said it would be open. David stamped up and down, cursing to himself while Tommy looked on anxiously. Where the hell would he find a key?

'I am sorry, monsieur.' The woman appeared the other side of the gate as if from nowhere. Elderly, grey-haired and slim, she smiled as she turned the lock. 'We were not expecting you until tomorrow.'

She led them along a short, secluded path amongst the shrubs and out on to a patio surrounding a swimming pool. At the end of but separate from a long terrace of multicoloured apartments, the house stood, white, alone and surrounded on three sides by water. Balconies on the upstairs windows looked down on cool lawns that sloped to the water's edge. From where they stood they could see endless rows of ocean-going yachts squeezed into every available inch of mooring space in front of the terraces. Tied up in splendid isolation at the apex of the promontory on which the house was built was a motorboat of monstrous proportions.

They followed the woman dutifully as she showed them the house. She looked at David in total disbelief when he told her they would do their own cooking, and it seemed to him an age before she left with one last motherly look at Tommy and the promise that she would be back promptly at nine o'clock the next morning.

David stood in the middle of the lounge, looking out through open patio doors over green lawns and smooth water. He felt – what did he feel? A homecoming? No, it was not his home. He had abandoned what little of his home had not been torn from him. He had no home. He lived somewhere, that was all. A sort of peace? No. He had had enough peace. One might say he'd had a bellyful of peace. What, then? What did he feel? Liberty? Almost. Liberation, perhaps? Yes, that was it: liberation. His house in Wimbledon was small, looking nowhere, backing on to nothing, crushed between two other houses shrouded in stultifying mediocrity.

In these opulent surroundings, amidst the spacious privacy that only money can buy, he took a deep breath of air heavy with the scent of wealth that came from the Clarence House leather upholstery, the Stark carpets. He tried to conjure up a picture of Mal against this background and failed. Mal, whose money had bought all this, shut away alone in a house he had dreamed of as a snotty-nosed urchin.

David raised his arms above his head, arching his back to stretch on tiptoe as if snapping the last strand that bound him. He blew out a long whistling breath as he relaxed.

'I don't know about you, Tommy,' he grinned, 'but I think *I'm* going to enjoy myself here.'

'Yes, David. It's a very nice swimming pool.'

'All right,' David laughed. 'I can take a hint. You go and have your swim while I rustle up some supper. I'll keep an eye on you. But no swimming in the sea now, d'you hear?'

Peals of laughter greeted the very idea.

The time had come to look over the boat. Tommy, still in swimming trunks, a towel round his neck, watched David's face intently, uncertain at the doubt to be seen on the face of someone so omnipotent, so omniscient. They walked its length, wondering at the inflatable dinghy hanging from the davits over the stern, the sailboard lashed to the deck, the vast fenders hanging over the side. It did not move as they climbed over the rail. A key in a door, and there was white leather, drinks cabinets and TV. David sat in a deep armchair at a wheel the size of a Grand Prix racing car's. In front of him was an instrument panel that would have graced a jet, while two phallic symbols, readily to hand, would command the power of enormous twin diesels. Tucked discreetly out of sight, as if in danger of making the place look like a boat, was the chartroom. The bows housed a huge double bed with dressing table and bathroom suite. Lesser berths were aft of a galley that would have fed a banquet. They climbed high to the secondary steering deck that looked down on a deck flat and bare for the sunworshippers.

'What d'you think, Tommy?'

Tommy stared hard, keeping his options open, trying to glean some clue from David's face.

'It's very big,' he said.

'I think it's horrible.'

Relieved, Tommy's face took on a look of haughty disdain.

'It's *not* a nice boat,' he said decisively. Slowly, uncertainty returned. 'Why isn't it a nice boat, David?'

'I don't trust engines, Tommy. Engines stop. We like boats with sails, don't we?'

'Yes. Sails are much better.' He paused as his forehead puckered. Something worried him. '*Sally*'s got an engine.'

David laughed. 'You're quite right, Tommy, but that's only for when there's no wind or for coming into the mooring.'

The skin furrows only deepened as Tommy looked around the deck anxiously.

'Where can we put the sails then, David?'

'We can't.' David kept a straight face, shaking his head sadly.

'This boat is no good then. David and Tommy can't go sailing.'

'Yes, they can.'

Mouth, cheeks, eyes and forehead – all screwed up in perplexity as simple, uncomplicated thought processes struggled to cope.

'If there aren't any sails, how can Tommy and David go sailing?'

'Because tomorrow' – David put out a hand, palm down on the boy's dripping hair, and shook Tommy's head gently – 'we are going out to hire a nice big sailing boat like *Sally*. Not too big; one that we can handle easily ourselves. And then we'll go sailing on that lovely blue sea out there. We'll go and have a look at St Tropez. And we'll go up the coast and stay the night somewhere. I think there are some islands not too far away we could go to. Would you like that?'

It took a moment for Tommy to analyse what David had said. When he was sure there were no snags to be found in what filtered down, the beaming smile returned. He took two strides and David rocked back on his heels as he found himself encircled in powerful arms and felt a head pressed to his chest.

'Cut it out, Tommy,' he laughed. 'You're soaking me.'

20

It had taken longer than David had expected. There had been so many agents' offices to visit, so many boats on offer. They had sat sipping coffee under a blazing sun, amidst a confusion of glossy photographs. A decision had been made, an inventory checked and money paid. The *Anna Marie*, a beautifully balanced thirty-six-foot Gibsea, had been brought round and moored next to the powerboat – and a day had gone. The next day had brought rain, slanting and warm and incessant, and David, tense and impatient, had fretted away the hours while Tommy had contentedly turned the pages of *Vogue* and a year-old *Architectural Digest*.

The next day had been fine with a gentle breeze. They had criss-crossed the bay, sticking their noses into St Tropez, chasing other boats, overtaking them to Tommy's huge delight. They had practised reefing. Time and again, they had gone through the routine until Tommy could do it all himself. Again and again, David had expected Tommy to rebel – 'It's so *boring*, Daddy,' Debbie had always complained, 'I *know* how to do it' – but Tommy seemed to relish the chance to use his strength, glowing with pride the more expert he became.

Their evenings had settled into a pattern. An evening meal that Tommy called tea, and a walk to the dusty square with its bars and pool tables. A beer and a Pepsi sitting out in the last of the sun – and smiles of welcome for Tommy from all and sundry. He had become an instant favourite with the boule players as they had allowed him to move amongst them, one arm behind his back, standing back politely at the merest touch. *Pointeurs* and *tireurs, la pétanque* and *la longue* had meant nothing to him, but he had hopped and roared in sympathy as tempers had flared. A disputed result had come to the point of clenched fists, when they had heard his peals of laughter, soaring above their fury. Slowly, he had subdued them with his joy until, one by one, players and onlookers had found themselves laughing with him.

They had made a stop-over trip to St Raphael, prizing open a berth on the crowded visitors' quay. Another to Le Lavandou and Iles d'Hyères, where it had blown hard and they had been double reefed. A week had flown.

It was Tommy, standing on deck, the bow warp in his hand, who saw her first. They had been across to St Topez to watch the start of a Maxi race and were still some three hundred yards from their own moorings when Tommy pointed.

'David. There's somebody there.'

David squinted into the sun. Someone lay on one of the beds alongside the pool.

'It's Auntie Faye.' Tommy began to jump up and down and wave his free hand. 'It's Auntie Faye.'

Although she had appeared asleep, she must have seen Tommy waving, for she rose slowly and walked across the grass. She stood, hands on hips, making no attempt to help as they made fast.

'This is a pleasant surprise,' David called.

'What's the matter with our boat? Isn't it good enough for you?'

David laughed as he jumped ashore. 'And I'm so pleased to see you too,' he grinned. 'Don't you ever say anything nice to anybody?'

A smile suggested for a moment that there was another Faye, but it was short-lived, quickly replaced by a look of suppressed anger. They stood side by side as David shouted instructions to Tommy to tidy up.

'Can he do all that?' Faye asked.

'And check how much diesel is left,' David shouted, as if in answer to Faye's question, before turning and starting to walk up the slight slope towards the house. 'Come on, grumpy,' he said. 'You sound as if you need a drink.'

She took no notice, and he was forced to stop and turn back to look at her. He had never seen her in a swimsuit before. She neither flaunted it nor struck any prissy pose to mask it, but, standing tall, lean and hungry, she simply radiated arrogant physical attraction. The muscular delineation was perhaps more that of the student's model than the Rubens subject but, with hands on hips, brown forearms led David's eye to a flat belly and on down to long legs set slightly apart. He thought he had finished with all that. But it was still there, that silent grunt deep down, that herald of days of exquisite tension that could only be resolved one way. He felt it, there, once more, deep and intense.

She stood, waiting until Tommy reappeared to busy himself on deck, seeming to know exactly what he was doing.

'Tuk.'

Faye jerked her head sideways as she made a sucking noise between her tongue and palate. 'Quite the little sailor.' She turned and strode past David. As she did so he sensed, for the first time ever, that for some reason she could not look him in the eye. Inside the house, she picked up a silk embroidered kimono and slid into it as if, like some smooth-skinned chameleon, she felt the instinctive need to blend with her surroundings.

'And what the hell brings you down here?' he asked as he handed her her glass. 'This is where people *spend* money, not make it.'

'I decided I needed a holiday,' she said defiantly.

'Rubbish. You've never needed a holiday in your life.'

For a split second, hellcat and teacher's pet faced each other in a school yard once again. But this time Faye backed off, scanning him coolly from head to toe. His hair was long, the skin of his face engrained with sun and salt. The wide-striped rugby jersey made him look broader than he was, and he wore it loosely outside his well-fitting navy shorts, a sign of an enlarging waistline, but his legs looked strong, muscular and weatherbeaten. His feet were bare but for simple leather sandals.

'You look better,' she said. 'You sound better.'

'I *am* better.' David strove to keep his eyes on her face, persuading himself it meant nothing to him that the kimono had slithered off one thigh.

She saw where he looked, snatched at a hem and the thigh disappeared.

David grinned broadly, enjoying himself. 'I seem to remember your telling me,' he said, 'how you couldn't stand women who locked themselves in the loo whenever something went wrong. Is that what you're doing – only on a grand scale? What's happened?'

'Where do you eat in the evening?' she hissed, anxious to change the subject.

'Here.'

'Oh, God. How domestic of you. And afterwards?'

'A beer or two, over in the square, watching them play boule. Tommy's in bed usually not long after nine.'

'And what do you do for excitement?'

'Is that what you've come for, excitement?'

Faye cooked their evening meal, eating little herself, her silence challenging them to utter one word of criticism. She drank Perrier, watching David dispatch the greater part of a bottle of claret. Beer, he had said; but later, watching the boule, she saw the large whiskies he bought himself at the bar. There was more than the usual warmth in the greetings Tommy had come to expect, greater passion in the argument, more of the action played out in their corner of the square, due perhaps to the presence of the tall English woman in cashmere jumper and slacks with the titillating challenge in her look of disdain – only the English.

Faye went to bed at the same time as Tommy. She did not look it, and she made it sound as if she was admitting to someone else's crime, but she claimed she was tired. David poured himself a half-tumbler of neat whisky and went out into the twilight. It was the first time he'd drunk spirits since . . .

He paced the lawns, his head buzzing, feeling the thump of his carotids. He ached. He walked down to the *Anna Marie*, lying at rest. With exaggerated care, he switched his glass to his left hand, running his right along her rail, up and down her shrouds. He looked up. Tommy's room was in darkness. Faye's light was still on, her curtains drawn back.

He peered into his glass, suddenly dead sober, the smell of

whisky distorting his face. Angrily, he threw the dregs into the grass.

He lay in bed, brilliantly awake, curling and straightening in snake-like agony, listening to Faye's rustling sounds in the next room. It was getting light when he finally fell asleep.

'We'll go to St Tropez today,' Faye announced at breakfast. 'It's not the place it used to be, but I'd still like to see what they're selling.'

Tommy looked anxiously across the table at David.

'Please yourself,' David said. 'Tommy and I are going sailing. We haven't many days left.'

'But you've sailed every day, and I don't want to go on my own.'

'Tough titty. That, if I remember correctly, is the phrase you reserve for situations like this?'

There ended the breakfast-time conversation.

Tommy had cast off and was holding the *Anna Marie* while David went below to start the engine. With his back to the house, he neither heard nor saw Faye as she came down the lawn behind him. He jerked erect, startled, as she jumped aboard alongside him. Nonplussed, he waited to see David's reaction before deciding on his own. The grin on David's face as he climbed out of the cabin reassured him. He grinned too, though he was not quite sure why.

'If either of you says one word,' Faye growled, 'I'll hit you with something. Now then, do I have to pull anything?'

'All you have to do is sit there and look beautiful,' David said, smiling. 'Tommy will do all the rest, won't you, Tommy?'

Tommy jumped aboard. 'I can reef,' he said, '*and* tie a bowline. And David is going to teach me to splice ropes.'

'Always was the clever beggar, our David Royall.' She managed a smile for Tommy but switched the scowl back on for David. 'Where are we going?' she asked.

'Just round the corner towards Le Lavandou. A couple of hours. Nothing special.' For the first time her clothes looked out of place. 'Have you sailed before?'

'Yes, but never in anything smaller than that.' She jerked her thumb in the direction of the receding motorboat. 'That's more my style.'

'D'you get seasick?' David asked.

'Certainly not.'

The coastline towards Le Lavandou was not without its risks from offlying rocks, but it was Tommy's favourite. David kept inshore. They were about two miles off Rayol when, out of a clear blue sky, the wind hit them like someone slamming a door. In a trice, they were laid flat. Seconds later, the *Anna Marie* came up, bow to wind, frenzied sails and strident rigging dancing in the wind that had hurtled at them from out of the north. With little in the lee of the land to warn them, they had been caught totally unawares. Picking himself up, David hurriedly released both sails and took stock. A large weal was already visible on one of Faye's cheeks. Her eyes showed fear, but controlled fear. The Faye Graingers of this world do not scream. Tommy was already on his feet, looking for instructions.

'Faye – are you all right?' David yelled.

'Just get me home,' she yelled back.

He grinned, feeling the first drops of rain on his face. He looked up at a rapidly blackening sky and shouted something unintelligible at it. He had a sudden feeling that he could do anything. Not only was he a Master of Surgery. 'Quick as you can then, Tommy. Get the sails down.'

'Reef?'

'No. Take the mainsail right down and then roll up the foresail. I'll go and start the engine.'

'Thank God for that,' he heard Faye mutter as he climbed through the companionway – but it was not to be. 'Engine's dead, I'm afraid,' he said as he climbed out again. 'Something must have come loose when we were knocked down. I can't possibly look for it now in these conditions; I'd be as sick as a dog in no time.' He turned to yell at Tommy a few feet away. 'Put all three reefs in, Tommy, and we'll have a tiny foresail just to keep her balanced. Then get your waterproofs on and give my jacket to Aunty Faye.'

As the *Anna Marie* began to sail, the noise from the rigging lessened, only to give way to the howl of the wind. It was not long before they were overpowered once more, and David heard the crack as Faye tumbled across the cockpit. She got up, rubbing her knee furiously, cursing their stupid macho grins. He taught Tommy how to play the mainsheet whenever he called, and Tommy was soon roaring his delight at the strength it needed to pull the sail back in. Around the headland and into the bay and they were dead to windward. The tacks became too hairy for Tommy to handle efficiently on his own, and David, soaked to the skin, roaring his exhilaration, cursed a rebellious, bruised and battered Faye into giving a hand. It was with something close to regret that he felt the power go out of the boat as they made the lee of the entrance to Port Grimaud. He rolled up the foresail before handing the tiller to Tommy.

'Take this, Tommy. Sail up and down here while I see if I can get the engine started.'

Ten minutes later – ten minutes during which Faye, in torn slacks and a shapeless sailing jacket several sizes too big for her, had sat in the driving rain, cursing her stupidity, her weakness in placing herself in a macho environment where she could not compete, where, but for the strength and knowledge of two men, she might well have died, where they had given her something she could not return with interest and she had ended up *in debt to a man* – an exultant face appeared in the companionway, followed almost immediately by the throb of the diesel.

'One of the connections had come loose behind the switch panel,' David explained as if it happened to him every day. 'You can take the sail in now, Tommy, and we'll motor in.'

As soon as they touched land, Faye stepped ashore with neither a word nor a backward glance, leaving David and Tommy to tie up.

'What did you think of that, Tommy?' David asked.

'The wind was very strong – and the sea . . .' Tommy made expansive wave-like movements with his arms. 'But I was strong too.'

'You were indeed, Tommy. I couldn't have managed without you.'

'I don't think Aunty Faye likes sailing,' Tommy said.

'I'm not so sure,' David laughed and saw Tommy's simple

logic fail him. To Tommy, someone who had not wanted to go in the first place, had got wet and cold, been bumped and battered and cursed at, had cursed and sworn back, obviously did not enjoy sailing. 'I have a feeling, Tommy, that if your aunt would only let me teach her, the way I've taught you, she too would get to enjoy it. In fact, I think she'd love it. She's a fighter, your aunt. There's nothing she enjoys more than a good scrap. What she did not like today was that she did not know what to do. She was dependent on us to get her home, and she must have hated that.'

There was silence as Tommy studied the rope in his hands. He looked up, concerned.

'Are you going to bathe the cut on Aunty Faye's face?'

'No, I don't think so,' David laughed.

'You bathed the one on mine when *I* bumped it. You made it better for me.'

'Yes, I know, Tommy. But I think we'll find that Aunty Faye bathes her own cuts. She likes to be a big girl and look after herself.'

The evening meal Faye served was superb, Tommy and David benefiting from the burst of smouldering energy Faye emitted on the rebound from her feeling of helplessness earlier in the day. She spoke little, flashing warning signs at any approach, a glass ever close at hand. She was not a drinker, resenting the loss the dull-witted hours brought with them, but David had watched her constant sipping, too wary to comment. She paced the floor as the two men played draughts until it was Tommy's bedtime. David waited until he heard the bedroom door close before he turned.

'Now then, what the *hell* has got into you?'

'Nothing.'

She stopped for a moment, her arms folded across her chest, to kick at patio doors that streamed with rain.

'And you're drinking too much. I've never seen you drink like that. What's the matter with you?' He sat down opposite her, leaning towards her. 'Tell your Uncle David all about it.'

'Bitch.' She spat the word into her glass, halfway to her lips.

'I beg your pardon?'

He had to wait a gulp.

'The bitch.'

'Who?'

For a moment, David thought she was about to withdraw into mumbling introversion, but suddenly it all exploded to the surface.

'Jo Logan. The two-faced, devious bitch.'

David put his head back and roared. 'So *that's* it. That's what's got under your skin. That's why you've come down here. That's why you've run away.'

'That is not the reason,' she said quickly, and then appeared to hesitate, just long enough for David to wonder suddenly. Surely not – not for him? Faye hurried on as if regretting revealing a weakness. 'And I haven't run away. You know me better than that. But when I think of how I used to idolise that bitch.'

'You've changed your tune, haven't you?' he laughed. 'You were all starry-eyed that night you were together on TV. What's happened to make you change your mind? What's Superwoman done to upset you so much?'

'She's resigned.'

'From what?'

'Don't be so stupid, David. As a judge. From the Court of Appeal. She's thrown it all in.'

David listened as Faye gave vent to her anger at what she obviously considered a personal betrayal. Jo Logan had withdrawn the nomination for the Supreme Court and resigned from the judiciary – in order to bolster the ambition of a man with half her intellectual ability. Faye's fury drove her to pace the floor once more, her arms across her chest as if in pain, her glass still clutched in one hand.

'The cow.'

She looked across suddenly and saw the grin.

'Why do you always laugh at me?' she hissed.

'I don't,' he said but also wondered why. 'Or if I do, I think it's because you frighten me. Lots of people laugh when they're frightened; it's like whistling in the dark.' He stopped to think. 'And women have always frightened me. Looking back, I think Jackie frightened me.'

'Rubbish,' Faye growled.

'She did. I always felt I had to be on my best behaviour. There were times when I felt I should go outside every time I wanted to break wind.'

There was a pause in her pacing and the flicker of a smile at that, but it did not last long.

'Do *I* frighten you?' she asked the next time she faced him.

'You terrify me,' he laughed. 'You're so intense. And unpredictable. I never know what's coming next.'

That seemed to please her. Her manner relaxed for a moment, but it was not long before she became angry again, describing how she saw Jo Logan's role from then on – always at a man's shoulder, writing his speeches for him, suppressing her personality for fear of overshadowing him, endlessly visiting schools and hospitals. 'I still can't believe she's handed herself over to be manipulated like that.'

'Perhaps she hasn't.'

'What d'you mean?'

'There's got to be a good reason why she should give up so much power. Nobody gives up all that without expecting something in return.'

'Some women are stupid enough,' Faye growled.

'Perhaps she wants to be the power behind the throne.'

'Your *éminence grise*,' she smiled, her eyes narrowing.

'You don't forget much, do you?' he laughed. 'Perhaps she feels she can exert more power from the White House. After all, a Supreme Court judge's jurisdiction is confined to the USA. Perhaps she's beginning to feel the States is too small a stage for her. Perhaps she wants the Kremlin, and the Palace of Westminster, Buckingham Palace. Perhaps she . . .'

'. . . wants to be Vice President. Now *that's* a possibility.' She set her glass down, looking as if she now regretted her dulled senses. The anger remained but was tempered by a new excitement. 'A husband and wife haven't run for office together before – at least, not to my knowledge. But there is a precedent in recent years for having a woman running-mate – a pretty disastrous one, admittedly – but having a woman as Vice Presidential candidate would command a lot of support. Now that . . .'

"You wouldn't mind that? That would be acceptable, would it?'

Faye considered for a moment. 'Yes,' she said.

'And who knows?' David grinned, trying to ignore the ache that was burgeoning inside him once more. Caught between anger and a new train of thought, flushed with the excitement of both, Faye looked as near to vulnerable as it was possible for her to do. 'Perhaps she knows something we don't. Perhaps her husband gets a pain in his chest every time he makes love. Perhaps she's got her eye on the presidency and can see a way of becoming the first woman President of the USA. As soon as she's safely ensconced in the White House, she'll slip a teenage bimbo between his sheets and – bingo.'

'Don't be stupid,' she muttered.

But David could tell she was visualising the scene, and it suddenly riled him. Where he had taken enjoyment from her disillusionment, he now found anger surging at the intensity of her newborn interest. He had triggered a new enthusiasm that would help her keep everyone at bay once more. He felt the corners of his mouth droop.

'And just think,' he said, 'you would then be on Christian name terms with the most powerful woman on earth. Just imagine what that would do for your magazine's circulation. So perhaps you'd better still be careful what you print about her.'

Faye was way ahead of him, obviously already considering that with an intensity that had blotted out all else. David might have begun the train of thought, but now she no longer needed him. She turned her back, as if he had become an irritating diversion. Stung to anger, he stood up and took hold of one shoulder, swinging her round to face him, driven suddenly by something inside him that wanted to confront her, probe, get through to her, hurt her.

'Given you new hope, that, hasn't it?' he sneered. 'No doubt you'll be on the next plane back to LA now. That's all that matters to you, isn't it – your blasted magazine's circulation.

That's why you came down here, running away from what she's done to your sales.'

'That had nothing to do with it,' she growled, standing her ground as David came nearer.

He sensed his own arousal. She had a body that was lean and fit – but a mind honed to a fine edge, about as soft and yielding as a stoat's. So where was the attraction? Was it nothing more than a challenge to find that other Faye he was convinced must lie beneath?

'Yes, it did. You don't give a damn now about Jo Logan, not really. All you were worried about was the effect on your precious magazine. Failure is the only thing that really hurts you, isn't it?'

A small naevus, nestling in the smooth-skinned valley, difficult to keep in focus, suggested more beneath the coolness of the shirt. That flat belly. A hand through her hair.

'And I can imagine what your Superwoman's defection to the other side has done for you. You must be the laughing stock of the magazine world with everybody watching the flagship of your fleet sink without trace.'

'You bastard.' Faye raised both arms as if she were going to bring them down on his head, but he seized her by the wrists.

'But now I've given you new hope, haven't I? I've been of *some* use to you. All is not necessarily lost.' He held her arms high. Their sudden compliance failed to register through the blur of emotions as he closed in on her. 'She could still be of use to you. You could still have the last laugh over your competitors.' Now all he could see was an eight-year-old's fearless blue eyes. 'Think of the publicity . . .'

He tore at the buttons of her shirt with the lust-driven uncoordination of the rapist. She was a fit, strong woman, but no gouging fingers, no thudding knees or swinging fists were going to deny him now. He fought with hands that tangled with his until he found that they were trying to help. He held back for a moment while she struggled in her haste to bare herself, feeling her breasts brush his fingers as she dropped the shirt from her shoulders. He held her head in both his hands, grinding his lips against hers, as she stooped to hook her thumbs in skirt and briefs and thrust them down. When she pressed against him, he felt the nakedness that sent his hands exploring while Faye began to tear at his clothes. In a gasping, wordless frenzy, with enough of his skin exposed for Faye's clutching fingers to prey on, they fell to the floor in a writhing, wrestling, ineffectual heap.

Hungrily, David indulged himself in a body unhampered by clothing while Faye began to grunt her frustration as one layer or another barred her way. All reason now beyond recall, reality no more than an uncontrollable urge to thrust, and thrust, and thrust, David freed himself enough to rear over her. For one fleeting moment, Faye was still, her eyes closed, her arms outstretched. But even as she opened her eyes, she twisted violently, throwing him on his side. He felt her hands search up his back and he gasped at the searing pain as her nails furrowed their way down again. He pulled her hands away as they moved upwards once more, but she rolled him on his back and he felt the clawing hands converge. Suddenly he longed for the agonising crescendo that would bring at least some sort of peace, but the look of triumph on Faye's face as she moved to straddle him killed all hope of that. He was beginning to writhe in the torment of black defeat even as he shrivelled beneath her hand. An outstretched left arm, pressed against her left shoulder and swung in a violent arc, sent her sprawling across the carpet in a confusion of arms and legs. He crawled to a chair, burying his face in the cool, dry cushion as he struggled to stifle the humiliation of his racking sobs.

Had it been sleep or some kind of protective narcolepsy? David lifted his head from the chair. His mouth was dry, his tongue felt twice its normal size. His only measure of time was the stiffness in his neck as he turned to look round for Faye. He tried to hitch his trousers up and button his shirt but couldn't. He stood to do so, feeling crumpled and unclean. He opened the patio doors and walked out into the night, hoping it was still raining. It must have only just stopped, for the *Anna Marie*'s rigging was still wet and glistening, clean and pure and honest.

Indoors again, he climbed the stairs and, without knocking, opened Faye's bedroom door. He walked through the gentle, feminine, shadowy room – what had he expected? – and out on to the balcony, where she sat, silk-clad from neck to ankle, her head leaning back against the chairback as she stared out across the water. Her eyes did not move as David crossed to stand, his back to her, his arms folded, his elbows on the balustrade.

Silence but for the small sounds that travel over water.

It was several minutes before Faye spoke in a flat, empty voice.

'What the hell's the matter with me, David?' she murmured.

'Nothing.' He twisted his head round to show he was smiling, then turned and peered over the balcony. 'Nothing I can't match,' he said, laughing grimly, as if talking to someone on the grass below. 'I'm sorry about that fiasco back there.'

Faye made no sign that she had heard him.

'Will it ever stop?' she asked.

David shrugged hunched shoulders, too preoccupied with his own emotions to wonder what she meant.

'Is it always going to be like this? What about when I'm sixty-five? Will it be the same? Seventy-five? Who's going to die first, I or this demon that flays the inside of me? Eighty-five? Surely it's got to have burnt itself out by then?' She moved for the first time, subtle muscular adjustments as if trying to feel what it would be like. 'Make me a promise, Davy boy,' she asked in a voice he had never heard before.

'What's that?'

'Meet me here, on this balcony, when I'm eighty-five and you're eighty-four and we've been everywhere, seen everything, done everything and are too feeble to want and too tired to hate.'

'All passion spent,' he murmured.

'What a lovely way of putting it.' Faye smiled gently as if to show she could.

'Someone already did.'

They both heard in the stillness the humping, thumping sound of Tommy rolling over in bed. 'No such worries there,' David smiled, turning to face Faye.

'No. I have often thought that if you put Tommy and me together, he with that quiet, loving nature of his, and I with my anger and my hatred, if you mixed us both up and then divided us down the middle, you'd have two normal people. Of the two of us, he's the lucky one. I envy him.'

'You don't really. I can't believe you'd change places with him.'

'There are times when I would – like an hour ago, for instance. Do you realise' – her forehead creased – 'we didn't say a word to each other? Not *one* word of tenderness, not *one* gentle touch.' She stopped, then went on gently. 'And that was *my* fault. I could see you were aching your guts out last night. I could hear you in bed. A few soft words from me, a touch. But I couldn't. I couldn't lift a finger. *You* had to make the first move and, when you did . . .'

'Next time,' David smiled.

Faye was quiet for a moment, her eyes narrowing to dark slits.

'It's at times like this,' she murmured, 'that I wish my father was still alive.'

'You what?' David yelped in astonishment.

'Because,' Faye said slowly, drawing out every word, 'then I could take a length of nice, thin, strong piano wire, creep up behind him and slowly, ever so slowly, garrotte him and watch his tongue and his eyes bulge out.'

'Faye!'

'Or stick a long knife in his guts and twist it and twist it and watch his face as he died.'

'Faye!' Appalled, David tried to soothe the hatred on her face. 'You mustn't speak like that. Whatever the man did, he's dead.'

'And took part of me with him.'

He waited silently.

'I've often wondered,' Faye said, so softly that David had to lean towards her, 'what it would be like to be totally, completely and utterly besotted with a man. Just once. I imagine such a state of bliss can't last, but while it does it must be a wonderful feeling. Painful in a way, I'm sure, but a nice kind of pain. I said it can't possibly last, because it must be such an intense feeling – and yet hatred lasts, doesn't it? And if hatred can last . . . That's what my beloved father took from me, the ability to feel like that about any man. For that, I hate every rotting bone in his grave. Because if I have the power to hate like this, I have often wondered if I could only love . . .'

She turned her head towards him to give a small, wry grin.

'It'll be small consolation to you, I know, David, after what I did to you in there, but there's no doubt in my mind who'd have been number one on my list to be besotted with. I think it would have been quite beautiful to have loved you. As it is,' she said in the whisper of the confessional, 'I get scared.'

'Scared?' he laughed quietly. 'Faye Evans scared? I don't believe it.'

She said nothing.

In the morning, when Tommy shook him awake, she was gone. And David wondered at the aching void she had left within him.

21

'Mal.'

'Yes, David.'

'It's David.'

'I know.'

David had to wait a moment as Mal Evans lowered the phone to talk to someone nearby.

'Mal, would you, by any chance, have such a thing as a full-size snooker table?'

'I've got – let me see . . .' Mal's mental arithmetic was quite a noisy process. '. . . About a hundred and thirty.'

'I don't mean that sort. I mean one of your own – at home.'

'Yes, as a matter of fact I 'ave. 'Aven't ew seen it?'

'No, but I had an idea you had one.'

''Asn't been played on for years. The ol' boy I bought the 'ouse from was a first-class billiards player, but I'm no bloody use. I thought of sellin' it, but I wouldn't know wot to do with the room an' it goes with the panellin'. Lovely 'and-carved one, it is. None of ewr modern rubbish. Why d'ew wanner know?'

'Is it in good nick?'

'Perfec'. A bit dusty under the covers like. 'Ave ew decided to take up snooker or wot?'

'Can I come round and see you?'

'Wot, now?' Not Mal's usual response.

'Yes.'

'Don' be long 'en. I go to bed early these nights.'

Mal met him at the door and led him into his living room. 'Sit down. I suppose ew wan' a whisky as usual,' he said, heading for the decanter.

'Er . . .' David hesitated, taken aback by the cool indifference of the woman sitting on the floor, one elbow crooked on the cushion of Mal's chair, flicking idly through the pages of *Vogue*, so relaxed that he expected her at any moment to lick a paw and wash her face. 'Er . . . No thank you, Mal. Not this evening.'

'Ew feelin' all right?'

He saw where David's eyes were fixed.

'Oh – this is Dariella. Dariella, this is David Royall. Old mucker o' mine. I told ew about 'im, 'aven' I?'

She smiled, nodded but said nothing, turning her attention back to what Mal was going to have to buy for her for two weeks of her time.

'Dariella's come to look after me while Mrs Parker's down 'er sister's in Tredegar for a cupla weeks, 'aven' ew, love?'

'That's right, Mal,' she murmured, and David marvelled at the true professional's ability to simulate affection.

'How d'you do?' David smiled, wondering what he'd have done if he'd found Gemma Ainsleigh sitting there.

'Ew off the booze or somethin'? Is that why ew're takin' up snooker – take ewr mind off the bottle?' Dariella lifted her arm to allow Mal to sit, replacing it on his knee. 'Bit old to learn new tricks, i'n' ew?'

'I haven't come about myself. I'm a bit concerned about Tommy.'

'Tommy? Wot's wrong with Tommy?' Mal sat up, pushing the arm from his knee as if clearing the decks for action.

'Nothing. Tommy's fine.'

Mal studied David's face for a moment before settling back in his seat. 'What, then?' he asked.

'It was very strange. In some ways I still can't believe it. That's why I rang.'

'Wot's strange?' Mal's voice rose in frustration, and even Dariella put her magazine down and frowned at David.

'It was our last night in Port Grimaud . . .'

'Did Faye turn up afterwards? She came through 'ere, lookin' f'r ew, in a 'ell of a mood.'

'Yes, Faye turned up – but Tommy's much more important than your sister at the moment. Faye can look after herself.'

He started again.

'As I was saying, it was our last night in Port Grimaud. Tommy had become a great favourite amongst the men who play boule in one of the squares they've created there. D'you know the one I mean?'

'No. I 'ate the place.'

'Well, when they heard it was his last night, they took us both into their local bar for a drink and made a great fuss of him. In the bar there was one of those pool tables – you know the ones, you put a coin in the slot?'

Mal nodded.

'Well, it got a bit noisy and there was a crowd around the table. And you know the way Tommy loves to stand just behind people?'

'Always done it, ever since 'e were a kid.'

'Well – when they finally walked away, someone had left three or four balls on the table. So Tommy picked up a cue and potted them – bang, bang, bang – just like that.'

'So?'

'So, someone saw him and – as I say, he was a great favourite down there – put another coin in for him. And he promptly potted all of those too. He had no idea of the rules, of course, and he was potting his opponent's balls as well as his own, but he cleared the table.'

'Anyone gets 'em down eventually.'

'You don't understand what I'm saying, Mal. He potted them all first time. *He did not miss one shot.*'

'Good God.'

'Exactly. I took him back to the house then as quite a few were pretty drunk by this time and they were crawling all over him. But I couldn't get it out of my mind. I couldn't sleep, thinking about it.' David shifted his position as if tossing in bed. 'So the next morning, before we left, I took him to the same bar – it was empty then, of course – put my money in and scattered the balls all over the table.'

'And?'

'He missed *one*, hard up against the top cushion. Nobody could have potted it, not even Steve Davis. And when I questioned Tommy about it on the way home, it turns out they've got a full-sized table at Clavely Court.'

'I know. I gave it 'em.'

'Then I had a word with Mrs Berry when I took him back. It seems Tommy spends hours at the table every day – six, eight hours a day, seven days a week in the winter. She says it seems to calm him, that he gets a bit agitated if, for some reason or other, he can't play. And he watches every minute of snooker on television, knows all the players by name.'

'So?' There was a wary look on Mal's face as if he had already worked out the next few stages of what David had in mind.

'Who's Tommy?' Dariella asked.

'My son,' Mal replied, half proudly, half defensively.

'Your son?' She sat up to turn and look at him. 'I didn't know you had a son.'

''E's a Mongol, love. 'E's away in a 'ome.' Mal turned to David. 'So?' he repeated.

'So – what if Tommy is one of these prodigies you hear about and has a real talent? It's not unknown, you know, for someone . . .' The words 'these people' loomed in his mind and he had to concentrate not to use them. '. . . with a mental handicap to have a quite bizarre gift for something like mental arithmetic or line drawing. What if he could be a real *class* snooker player? Don't you think we ought to find out? How would one go about it?'

'Wouldn't be difficult,' Mal muttered. 'Why were ew on about the table 'ere 'en? Where does that come into it?'

'I thought if you were to have Tommy home for a few days and see for yourself . . .'

Mal shook his head. 'I've told ew, David. I don' wan' 'im 'ome.'

'Mal.' Dariella squirmed round, surprise and disappointment in her voice. 'That's not like you.'

'Ew don' understand, love.' He put a hand gently on her head. 'Ew don' understand. An' I don' think David does, neither.'

'Just for a few days, Mal.'

'No.'

David had seen that stubborn look before, on an eight-year-old's face. He knew there was no gainsaying Mal.

'But,' Mal went on slowly, 'what I *will* do is sen' ol' Benny Boston down the Court to 'ave a look at 'im. 'E'll know, straight away.'

'Who's Benny Boston?'

'Benny Boston? 'E's a snooker coach in one of my clubs. Never quite made the big time, but a marv'lous teacher. 'E's a carpenter and joiner by trade, an' a bloody good one, but 'e loves teachin' the kids. 'E'd 'ave been a WPBSA coach only 'e didn' agree with 'alf they taught at Lilles'all. Not only that, but 'e's a sort of guru to one or two of the top-class professionals. They go to 'im and 'e watches 'em if they're not 'appy about their play. 'E's got the knack of seein' wot somebody's doin' wrong – you know, like some golfers 'ave somebody they go an' see when they think there's somethin' wrong with their swing.'

'And if he agrees that Tommy's got talent?'

''Ang on. The fact that 'e can pot a few balls doesn' make 'im another Steve Davis, ew know. Pottin' the bloody things is the easy bit.'

'I realise that. But you'll get this Benny Boston to go and see him?'

'I'll give 'im a ring tomorrow.'

Stress and the general surgeon. Everyone has seen it from their armchair. The heat, the sweat running into steely blue eyes above the green mask, those glances so tellingly exchanged with the adoring nurse who reaches over to mop his brow. The snapping demands for instruments, the calls for more blood, the anxious enquiries of the anaesthetist, the ultimate victory.

Balls. David laughed to himself. What could one find more relaxing, more therapeutic to one's blood pressure, than a morning in theatre if . . .

His house surgeon looked across enquiringly, intrigued by one of those pauses in operating for which there is no apparent cause.

If. David conceded that there was always a big 'if'. *If* everything was going well. *If* there was nothing on the list you had not done a hundred, perhaps a thousand times before. *If* the patients were all thin, not the first-born babies of elderly parents, not on anticoagulants for heart disease, or insulin for diabetes. *If* there was no frozen section of breast to be done on a colleague's wife. *If* your registrar was on leave, not watching and analysing every move you made. *If* your assistant was not your house surgeon whose mind was too full of the nurse in Casualty to want to be taught. *If* the theatre sister was happily married. *If* Digger Drew was giving the anaesthetic.

Then – under those circumstances – there was nothing like the peace of mind which gave the blissful opportunity to exercise a God-given talent. Where had the talent come from in the son of a collier and a nurse? Had he had this talent inside him back in Cory Street? Had it been there all the time, just waiting to express itself? Had it been inevitable? Would he have become a surgeon if he had not had a patient, strong, ambitious mother behind him at every turn, goading him, praising him, encouraging him? Could he just as easily have become an architect, or lawyer? Had it been a talent purely for surgery on which he had been fortunate enough to capitalise? Did everyone have just one gift, and lucky the man who finds it? Had he and Mal and Faye just been fortunate? And what of Tommy?

David shifted his weight from one foot to the other, unsettled by a stimulus as yet not powerful enough to overcome his interest in a small stone at the lower end of a common bile duct. The noise increased and he raised his head.

'What the hell's going on?' he asked Drew – and found it wasn't Drew but Drew's registrar who smiled back. He looked round, bewildered for the moment.

'Dr Drew's gone next door, sir,' the registrar explained.

'Why? What's happened?'

'Don't know, sir. Some sort of flap on.'

David turned his attention back to his gall stone, but it wasn't the same. He knew Drew would not have left him without somebody perfectly competent to carry on, but now he had to be slightly more vigilant and could not think of other things. Tommy would have to wait.

The case finished, he paced the theatre floor, waiting for the next, listening to the sounds from the adjoining theatre – Pullman's theatre. If it had been Harry O'Connor's theatre, David would have been in there, asking what the hell all the noise was about. But Pullman's theatre? – let the bastard get on with it.

He turned to his theatre sister. 'What's all the flap, sister, d'you know?'

'Stab wound of abdomen, I believe, Mr Royall.'

'So?'

The shrug of the shoulders, the line of the mouth and the silent sniff said it all. David got the message and relished it, rolling it round his mind like good brandy round a glass. It was Mr Pullman's list. As far as she was concerned, anything could happen.

The next case was going to be difficult: the removal of a piece of colon matted down by diverticulitis. Positioning the patient would be important, abdominal relaxation essential. Try as he might, David failed to find cause to complain to the registrar at the absence of his consultant, and nearly an hour later he was engrossed in the operation when he became aware of Drew at the head of the table once more.

'Welcome back,' he growled. 'I thought the anaesthetic had suddenly got a bit rough. Where've you been?'

Drew said nothing. It was unlike him not to respond – he was, after all, an Australian – and his silence made its impact. David put his instruments down and turned his head towards the top of the table, his eyebrows raised enquiringly.

'We've got a problem next door, David.'

'What sort of problem?'

Drew glanced round rapidly at the house surgeon, the nurses, the orderlies. He could not ask them all to leave, and he couldn't ask David to leave the table.

'Difficult to explain,' he said.

'An Australian lost for words? I don't believe it. Is Brian there?'

'Yes.'

'So. Where's the problem?'

'There is something of a difference of opinion going on.'

'That's happened before now.' David nodded approval as the sister, sensing delay, put warm towels over the wound. 'Who's arguing with whom?'

'Brian with the registrar.'

'Which registrar – Shah?'

'Yes. At least, they *were* arguing. Shah has now shut up like a clam. There were a few remarks made about emerging nations that didn't go down too well.'

'Oh, Gawd.'

'Precisely.' Drew shuffled his feet uneasily. 'I know I shouldn't think this way, but I wouldn't be quite so concerned if the patient wasn't who he is.'

'And who is he?'

'That man Strait – the chap with the chat show.'

'Godfrey Strait? Is that what all the flap was about? From here, it sounded as if they'd brought the Queen Mum in.' Without realising it, David patted the towels lying over the wound as if reassuring the patient he would be with him in a moment. 'What's happened to him? Sister here thought it was a stab wound.'

'Too right. He was woken in the night by intruders and was crazy enough to take them on.'

'That figures,' David muttered.

'Anyway, they knifed him in the belly – twice. Then they left him on the floor, tore out his telephone and locked the doors on him. He lives alone apparently. His cleaning woman found him about ten o'clock this morning.'

'Much damage?'

'Mostly bowel. Nothing much else.'

'Oh.' David began to lift the towels as if that was the end of the matter. 'No great problem then. What was the argument about?'

'It's over what Brian's doing with the hole in his colon. He had lacerations of both his small and large bowels, and everything was sweetness and light when he was resecting the small bowel. It was when he came to the colon that the argument began.'

'As I said – no great problem. Exteriorise the bit of colon with the hole in it; come back in a couple of months and close it; end of story.'

'Which is exactly what Shah said.'

Everyone in David's theatre heard every word and appreciated the intonation. In deathly silence, they stood looking at him.

'Oh, Ch——' David checked himself just in time. He had seen the pain on Drew's face at the sound of blasphemy. He dropped the towels back on the wound as if that would now have to wait. 'So what's Brian doing?'

'Sewing it up and dropping it back. Ranting on about all the outmoded surgery that's still practised. Reminding Shah of the paper he's due to read at the RSM soon. Should make some of the old fuddy-duddies sit up, he reckons.' Drew paused to look at David under raised eyebrows. 'Might be all right, I suppose? Fill him to the gunwales with antibiotics? Put a drain in? Nothing by mouth?'

'Anything's possible,' David growled, 'but why take the chance? Perhaps it was just a small puncture wound.'

Drew shook his head. 'A long ragged laceration. By the look of the wound in the skin, it was one of those knives with one serrated edge. D'you know the ones I mean?'

For a moment there was silence as David could find no more to say. His mind was full of pictures, like a succession of gory lecture slides, beginning with a scuba diver's knife and the thrust of its saw-toothed edge, through to the filth and stench of what he saw as the inevitable results of Pullman's decision. Quietly, across the silence, came the words he had been dreading.

'Do you think you could just go in and look over his shoulder, David? There's nothing more Shah can do. The lad did his best.'

Royall stood dumstruck.

'Brian would probably enjoy having you watch him operate on a TV star,' Drew wheedled. 'And then, perhaps a word from you . . .'

'Impossible.'

Was it? Or was it that he couldn't bring himself to crawl to Pullman? So – the great man was making another balls of a case. So tell him something new.

'Please, David.'

'Look, Digger, you know Brian. You know that if he thinks he's right nothing on God's earth will make him change his mind. And the way Brian loathes my guts' – the conversation would have spread throughout the hospital by lunchtime – 'Shah would be more likely to have some influence over him than I would – and you say he's tried. No, Digger. There's no way I can interfere.'

'Even if someone is likely to die as a result?'

'Digger.' The two men stared at each other, oblivious now of those around them. 'You know as well as I do that Brian is not going to change his mind for me. I am the very last person he would do that for. So – the only way I can influence the management of that patient in there is to go in and physically remove the surgeon and take his place. To do that, I've got to have pretty positive reasons. I can't do that simply because I don't agree with what he's doing. Now – is he drunk? Is he certifiably mad or high on drugs? Has he had a stroke?'

Drew said nothing.

'So.' David spoke slowly and deliberately. 'Let me get on with my own job. There's *nothing* I can do.'

'David. Mal 'ere. 'Ave ew got a minute? I've got Benny 'ere.'
  'Benny?'

'Benny Boston. 'E's been over to see Tommy.'

'I'll be right over.'

This time, Dariella sat in one of the window seats, looking very much at home. She smiled before turning back to gaze wistfully down over the gardens and paddock.

David had already formed a mental picture of Benny Boston. A carpenter and joiner and a snooker coach. A big-boned, coarse-skinned, thick-wristed, thick-skulled, flashily dressed heavy smoker with gold chains around a hairy neck.

'David, this is Benny.'

Short and portly, with a round, bald head made to look rounder by Brylcreemed hair cut close, he wore a made-to-measure pin-striped suit with white shirt and plain dark tie. His face was permanently creased as if life was one long joke being told simply for his benefit. The hand David shook could have been a woman's.

'Well, Mr Boston – what d'you think of Tommy?' he asked.

'Benny, *please*.'

'All right – Benny. Thank you. Now, what about Tommy?'

'Give 'im a chance,' Mal laughed.

David had to wait until they were all seated. 'I'm sorry, Benny, but I've been dying to know what you thought. Did you see him play?'

'Yes.'

'And?'

Boston obviously enjoyed teasing. He laughed at David's impatience as he delayed his reply.

'Remarkable, Mr Royall. Quite remarkable. I don't think I've ever seen anything quite like it.'

David sighed as he sank back into the cushions, relieved that his embryonic hopes and dreams had not just been aborted. It was a while before he became conscious that the other two men were looking at him, saying nothing. He sat forward once more.

'So?' he asked.

'So?' Boston mimicked, looking sideways at Mal.

'Don' ew look at me,' Mal said briskly, getting up to walk over to where Dariella sat. 'It's got nothin' to do with me.'

Puzzled, Boston looked to David for help.

'Just how good is Tommy, Benny? Just how good a snooker player do you think he could become?'

'Aaaaaah.'

'You've got doubts.'

'Not doubts exactly, Mr Royall. How can I put it?' He ran a fingernail along his hair above one ear like a stylus in its groove. 'Tommy pots balls like a professional – and I don't mean any old professional, I mean a *world-class* professional. I'm prepared to go further than that. I think he's the best I've ever seen at his age. He seems to have the ability to see the correct angle immediately with never a moment of doubt in his mind. He lines up, bang, and it's down. He's . . .' He looked round, smiling at Mal, fearful of giving offence. 'He has the advantage of not being as neurotic as you or I might be.'

He held his hand up as he saw David's excitement.

'Now steady on. That's only part of it – the easy part, as I think Mal has told you. There are three main aspects to snooker, potting being only one. The other two are positional play and safety play. His ability to pot the ball means nothing if he hasn't got those skills too. At the moment, he simply pots the balls as they lie, in any old order.'

'But, to do that, surely he must have some sense of position. He couldn't possibly pot so many if he wasn't positioning the cue ball to some extent?'

'You're beginning to talk like an expert,' Boston laughed, and rocked his head from side to side. 'All right,' he conceded. 'So there was some sort of positional sense there one could work on. He's bound to have learned something from watching so much on TV; he's obviously a good mimic because I can't fault his stance. But safety play – no.' A pair of very expressive hands, fingers extended, fanned out horizontally. 'There's no way he could become world-class at that even if he had the mental ability.' He stopped to grin. 'And yet, when you come to think of it, I suppose he might even have that. There are one or two amongst the world-class professionals who are hardly likely to end up sitting on the Woolsack. But Tommy just hasn't the temperament.'

'So where do we go from here?'

Boston did not answer. He swung his head round to look at Mal again, his eyes simply transferring the question. Mal stood, his face in shadow from the window behind him, scowling at the floor. He lifted his head enough to answer, his voice gruff and reluctant.

''Oo said we 'ave to go anywhere? 'Ave ew considered the possibility that Tommy might be perfectly 'appy where 'e is?'

'Yes, Mal, I have,' David said quietly. 'But what if he's got a huge talent bottled up inside him that's trying to express itself?'

''E looks 'appy enough to me. P'raps 'e's better off left as 'e is. Ew don' miss wot ew've never 'ad.'

'That's not true, Mal. What about you? What if you'd never been given the chance to exploit your talent as a player?'

'Two thin's wrong with that argument, David. One, I'm not a Mongol, am I? All right, I'm no bloody genius, but I'm not *that* daft. An' *I* always *knew* I was good, right from a kid; Tommy doesn't. Second, nobody *gave* me the chance. I made my own chances.'

'I'm sorry, Mal. I shouldn't have said that. But Tommy's so full of *living*. You should see him on a boat.'

'Aye. Sailin's one thin'.' Mal shook his head as if he'd found another basic flaw in David's case. 'Good 'ealthy stuff. I'm all fur that just as long as it's not given one day an' taken away the next. But snooker's another thin' altogether. It's not all like ew see on TV, ew know – thick pile carpets an' frilly shirts. It's 'amburgers an' cold coffee from plastic cups in empty 'oliday camps in the middle of freezin' winter, takin' ewr turn at the table with a stream of 'ungry youngsters.'

'But with your clubs . . .'

'Ew can see 'im as bloody world champion, can't ew?' Mal glared but found David was not going to back down. 'Ew want 'im to start competin', don' ew? Why else would ew be naggin' for 'im to come 'ere? 'Cos that's wot it would mean. Benny's told me 'e can't get to Basin'stoke reg'lar, so it 'ud mean Tommy comin' 'ome 'ere. An' I don' like it.'

He stood, grim and determined, and felt a hand slide into his. He looked down to see the gentle smile on Dariella's face as three individual silences combined to work on a generous spirit.

'All right, ew bastards,' he growled, his stony expression crumbling. ''Ow long would ew wan' 'im for, Benny?'

'Couple of months. If he can't pick it up in that time, he's not going to do it at all. If he *has* picked up the principles of positional play, then it's nothing but experience from then on.'

'An' the snooker season is roughly – what? – four months each side of Christmas?'

Boston nodded.

'Right 'en. We'll 'ave 'im 'ome sometime in July. But the moment I feel 'e's un'appy, back 'e goes, d'ew 'ear?'

'Good morning, Brian.'

'Good morning.'

There had been no way they could avoid each other, meeting head on in a narrow, otherwise deserted corridor.

'And how's your VIP patient?'

'Strait, d'you mean?'

How many VIP patients have you got, you oily sod? 'Yes.'

'He's fine.' Pullman had made no effort to conceal what he thought of such a stupid question.

Yes, he's fine at the moment. But how is he going to be in a week's time? – if he's still here at all. But then, knowing your luck, you bastard, you'll probably get away with it. Didn't get away with your fancy ideas with that poor sod Lever, though, did you? 'Nasty business. Quite the TV star yourself now, Brian. I watched your interview. Very impressive.'

'Yes,' Pullman had drawled. 'It's always safer to give these interviews oneself, don't you think? These administrators sound so stilted, reading from a grubby piece of paper as if they can't remember their lines. They can so easily give the wrong impression – don't you find that?'

Pompous prig.

That had been five days ago. Five days during which David's ear had been tuned constantly to the hospital gossip circuit. Harry O'Connor was on leave and David had been covering for him, running two units with twice the normal scandal input – and he had heard nothing. It was simply not done to go asking specific questions. That smacked of overt clinical jealousy, an emotion proscribed by tribal custom. Nothing would induce him to find some excuse to enter Pullman's ward – imagine the disappointment at finding Strait sitting up in bed, looking like a million dollars. So he must wait, patiently. But time was passing. He should have heard something by now. It was very irritating.

The first inkling came from his ward sister.

'I hear that man Godfrey Strait is not so well, Mr Royall.'

Aaaaaah – tell me more. 'Is that so, Sister? I'm sorry to hear that. What's the problem?'

'I don't know, Mr Royall. I just heard he was not so well.'

David went hunting, finding reasons to visit almost every department in the hospital. It did not take him long to cross Pullman's path. 'Hullo, Brian . . .' But Pullman went past without stopping.

If Pullman would not talk, Shah was only too ready to do so. Time now to make discreet, oblique enquiries.

'How's Strait?' David asked.

'He's not well, sir.'

'So I gathered. What's wrong exactly?'

'He is having a pyrexia, sir. Then he is vomiting and he isn't having any bowel sounds. Now his belly is very rigid and *I* think he's having a mass now.'

'But Mr Pullman doesn't?'

Shah said nothing, but his face took on the look of a dog that has been whipped for no good reason.

'So what are you doing for him?'

'We are putting the Ryles tube back down and he is back on his drip. And he is on antibiotics . . .' Shah's voice tailed away as if there was more to tell.

'But you're certain you can feel a mass.'

'Yes. I was telling Mr Pullman at the time that it was not a good thing he was doing. And now the patient is leaking, and I think he is lucky at the moment that he is localising into an abscess, but if that is rupturing into his peritoneum . . .' Thin brown fingers imitated a grenade exploding. 'If we are not doing something . . .'

'And Mr Pullman? What does he think?'

'Mr Pullman is looking at the patient like a blind man, laughing. He is making jokes, Mr Royall. The last time he is in the ward, he is not looking at the abdomen. He is not even pulling the bedclothes back. I am trying to speak to him but he is not listening; he is looking somewhere over the top of my head. He is giving me a lecture in front of the patient and the nurses as if I am a student who is ignorant, Mr Royall.' Shah's voice rose in righteous indignation. 'And I am Fellow of the College of England, Mr Royall, and have Mastership of Madras.'

For three more days, no more news came from Pullman's ward while the surgical side of the Merton held its breath. David was halfway through a long outpatient clinic when the call came.

'David – it's Digger here. Come up straight away, would you?'

'Up where?'

'Pullman's ward.'

'Pullman's ward? But I'm in the middle of outpatients.'

'Quick as you can, David. This guy's crook.'

The last time this had happened . . .

Drew was waiting outside the ward door.

'Where's the fire?' David asked.

'It's this guy Strait. He looks like he's jacking it in.'

'I guessed that. But what's that got to do with me?'

'We couldn't find Brian so we rang his home. It seems he's on leave.'

'He bloody well isn't,' David spat. 'He can't be. He was here yesterday, and with Harry away he wouldn't go off like that and leave me on my own without saying anything to me, not with this guy so ill. Get the bastard in. I'm not picking up his fag ends. He's got to be at home.'

David turned to walk away, but Drew caught his sleeve.

'Of course he's at home. I spoke to Iris. She was in tears, trying to find some excuse. God alone knows what that poor woman has had to put up with. Look, David.' He pulled on his sleeve to turn him round to face him again. 'The time's rapidly approaching when we'll have to seriously consider doing something about poor Brian. The man's in trouble.'

'You could have fooled me,' David growled. 'If you were to

ask me, I'd say he's simply keeping his head down now the proverbial's hit the fan.'

'Maybe,' Drew smiled, 'but don't you think that's perhaps a reason for pitying him rather than anything else? And that certainly doesn't solve the problem of one very sick man in there.' Drew's smile faded as he slammed the door on any hope of escape David might have had. 'You may decide he's too far gone to do anything – that's up to you – but I'm prepared to anaesthetise him if you want me to.'

Splat. Get out from under that one if you can. Don't look over your shoulder. You *are* the super specialist. Even if the man had been fit enough to move, there was *no one* better qualified.

And it was someone else's cockup he was being made to tackle, one he had seen coming for days, one that could have been avoided, one that any young registrar from Madras would have avoided, one that was due to the vanity of a man who could not bring himself to accept that he was just a run-of-the-mill surgeon – as if there was some disgrace in that.

David was on a hiding to nothing. If he did something and Strait died – he could just see the newspapers. If he did nothing and Strait died – he could still see the newspapers. In either case, Pullman would come roaring back. He could see his face.

'All right – let's get it over.'

The shaggy eyebrows did not look the same without the thick glasses Strait usually wore, but the bushy moustache was instantly recognisable despite the matted furrow where the Ryles tube disappeared up one nostril. The rest of the face could have been that of anyone with a belly full of faeces and pus, the dry skin and sunken eyes of the Hippocratic facies with all its loneliness, its fear, its supplication and – in this case – its anger.

'My name's David Royall, Mr Strait. I've been asked to see you as Mr Pullman is not available at the moment. How are you feeling?'

A bloody stupid question, and a defiant flash in Strait's eyes told him so.

'Let's have a look at your stomach then, shall we?'

There was an aura around Strait that made David hear the

words anew. What bloody stupid things surgeons said. He waited courteously in the best Harley Street manner for the staff nurse to turn back the bedclothes. One look was enough – the tense, shiny skin stretched over the distension – but clinical justice must also seen to be done. He felt the mass with the gentleness of a bomb disposal officer searching for a time fuse. He waved away Drew's stethoscope – there was little point in listening to deathly silence.

When he looked up, he found his decision had been made for him. The muscles at the corners of Strait's jaw were clenched. His eyes said – get me out of here.

'You need another operation, Mr Strait. You have an abcess in there that needs draining.'

'Get on with it then.' Feeble but defiant.

'There's one thing that I *must* explain to you. You also need what is known as a colostomy. I must bring a bit of your bowel out on to the surface for a while. It will *not* be a permanent one, d'you understand that?' Why was it necessary to shout at someone lying at death's door? 'But it's the only way that abscess is going to heal.' Something you should have had done in the first place. 'You are in for several weeks of filthy smells and messes that you are going to loathe.' And which could have been avoided. 'But you're damn well going to have to put up with it because, if you don't have it done, you are going to die.'

David smiled gently as he said it, feeling instinctively that that was the sort of language Strait would understand. Strait nodded, his eyes, too small for their grey-black orbits, burning.

'But,' David said, straightening up, 'in three to six months, you will be back to normal, I promise you. D'you believe me?'

Hang on, you bastard, and I'll get you out of there.

Strait nodded once more.

Twenty minutes later, David and Shah stood, gowned and gloved, one each side of a bare table.

'Problem, isn't it, Shah.' His arms folded, David kicked gently at the base of the table. 'The abscess is obviously leaking into the peritoneum but, as yet, hasn't completely ruptured – otherwise he would already be dead. So – open the belly to do the the colostomy first and we relieve the intra-abdominal pressure, probably the only thing that's keeping the abscess more or less intact, and whoosh . . . I've known of patients dying on the table when that has happened. There are even stories of it happening simply as a result of the relaxation of the anaesthetic. However, if I drain the abscess first, we are going to have pus all over the place when I do the colostomy. What would you do, Shah?'

Purring like a cat, Shah smiled beneath his mask.

'I think I would be draining the abscess first, sir. It is too big a risk to be taking. We can always be covering it up and changing our gloves. If we are very careful, I think this will be the best way.'

'I quite agree, Shah.'

And the Master of Surgery, Madras, beamed.

The doors opened and Drew headed the knot of people wheeling Strait in.

'How is he?' David asked as Drew passed him.

'Dodgy. The least you can, the quickest you can.'

Ten minutes later and the theatre was filled with a stench that would linger in the sinuses for days, the stench of the Victorian surgical ward, the Flanders field hospital. The muttered curses and the exclamations of disgust. They cleaned up as best they could, changing gowns and drapes and gloves and, through a small area of bare skin, David fished out the bit of colon and opened it. He turned to Drew.

'That's the best I can do for him. How is he?'

A shrug. 'Which ward to you want him to go back to? Yours?'

David thought for a moment. 'No,' he said. 'Send him back to Brian's.'

'D'you think that's wise, David? Couldn't you keep a better eye on him in your own?'

'No.' Who the hell cared? Let the theatre staff hear. The whole hospital must know by now how they felt about each other. 'If our glorious surgical leader suddenly comes back from leave tomorrow, I want him to see exactly what a mess this guy's in. I'll take great pleasure in calling in to see him twice a day, and I don't want Brian stamping all over my ward. Still – ' David pulled a face – 'it might all be a bit academic, mightn't it? The guy's got to survive first.'

22

Parts of David's life that had died with Jackie and Debbie, left for months inert and numb, were gradually being revitalised. Some, dead beyond recall, he felt had sloughed away, the raw, tender wounds now healed and painless – his private practice, the titled patients, the breakneck chase after gold. Perhaps the first part to return to life, revascularised in a sudden flood of young blood, had been when Tommy had taken him to sea again. Another, the Council, had been forcibly, painfully reopened; the President had seen to that. Now, slowly, one by one, the no-go areas were being reoccupied. Was another about to fall?

In the six months since Jackie had died, David had avoided one area of London as if it glowed with radioactivity. Marylebone Road, Portland Place, Wigmore Street, Baker Street formed the sides of a square that might have been a black hole in outer space, somewhere not to approach too closely for fear of being sucked into its crushing gravity. Now it was there, challenging him to take it on once more.

He was early. The earlier he arrived, the longer he would have to stand and talk, become part of that life on which he had turned his back. He saw a space at the kerbside but ignored it. It was difficult to find a parking place even at seven in the evening, but he must drive around a while longer. He took a deep sighing breath as he turned a corner. The first time he drove up Harley Street, he did so as if up a tube, the houses blurred in the periphery of tunnel vision. The next time, he slowed, turning his head and staring, proving to himself he could do so, seeing clearly the steps, the door, the windows. As if to confirm his little victory, he toured the rich acres of medicine's Promised Land, where brass plates and Bentleys shone in abundance, where ambitious mediocrity and furtive charlatanism flourished cheek by jowl with the sheer professional excellence of the best in the world, and where, once . . .

As he parked, he found his mouth dry, his hand shaking as he locked the car door.

The Royal Society of Medicine, 1 Wimpole Street, was a building Royall knew well. For a time, he had been the secretary of its surgical section, a position much sought after by those with any real ambition. The RSM is the highest point of academic medicine where all disciplines meet under the same roof, a place where the physicians and the surgeons, the obstetricians and the pathologists, divorced from the arcane cloisters of their own Royal Colleges, permit themselves to rub shoulders with lesser mortals. To some, the introverts, it can be a frightening, forbidding place; to others, the pacesetters, it is a friendly, open-doored London club. The hallway bustles before any meeting of one of the major sections, and surgeons make a lot of noise when herded together into animated groups of dark suits and black shoes, the discreet club ties their symbols of belonging. David took a deep breath before walking in. Warily, he began to circulate.

'Evening, Royall. How nice to see you again. Keeping well?' A silver-haired old doyen who hadn't missed a meeting in thirty years.

'David.' A nod. 'How are you?' The terse greeting of a competitor disappointed at David's decision not to resign from the Council along with Queen's.

'David, you old bastard. Good to see you again.' A contemporary who had come to terms with the fact that he was going no higher.

'Good evening, Mr Royall. Urquart, SR on the vascular unit at Queen's. Perhaps you remember me. I came to watch you do that hydatid last year . . .' A senior registrar, coming to the end of his term, with a wife already happily secure in a permanent consultant post in the big city.

'Hullo, David. I wondered whether you'd come too.' Harry O'Connor.

'Harry. Thank God.' David led O'Connor into a corner. 'Don't leave me,' he grinned. 'It's my first time back amongst the ravening hordes.' He looked around him. 'Just look at them, Harry. I can't believe I used to be in there with the best of them, competing like that.'

'Never found the need myself,' O'Connor drawled. 'When are *you* going to be President of the section then, David? It's some time now since you were Secretary.'

David made vague, dismissive movements with his hands while striving to deny the twinge of pleasure the thought produced.

'There was a time, Harry, but' – he shook his head – 'not any longer. As far as I'm concerned, Brian is welcome to it.'

'You should be in line before Brian. Mind you, if you were to get it, it would rule out poor Brian ever being appointed. They're not likely to appoint two Presidents from the same DGH within a few years of each other, are they? And Brian can't have long to go now. This has got to be his last chance.'

'As I say, Harry – he's welcome to it.'

Or was he?

'He's not going to be the most popular President we've ever had, that's for sure.' O'Connor looked down at his hands, interlocked in a golf grip. He waggled an imaginary club. He'd been hooking badly recently. 'All his creeping and crawling hasn't endeared him and, of course, he's got that chap whatshisname, from the Northern – nice fella – breathing down his neck. He's only got to make one slip.' He swung broad shoulders back and forth. 'And I hope Brian gets there.' Perhaps he wasn't finishing with his hands high enough on the follow through. 'The poor old sod seems to have missed out on everything else. I was only saying . . .'

'Well, look who's here, rallying around their beloved *Obergruppenführer* like the good little stormtroopers they are. So – who's looking after the sick and dying in the Merton tonight then? Sending them all to some decent hospital, I've no doubt.'

Ricky Forsythe, a fine surgeon with a memory that sucked in facts like a sponge, a fast, highly competent operator with boundless energy, a non-smoking, teetotal fitness fanatic with no shred of time-wasting political ambition; all personal attributes he cheerfully admitted dedicating to screwing the last penny out of the system. Even the gravel tattoo, proudly worn like a Prussian sabre scar on one cheek of an otherwise too perfect face – a mangled car in a motorway pile-up had sunk inches lower as a gutsy young casualty officer had crawled beneath it, syringe in hand – he reckoned was worth thirty grand a year from adoring dowagers.

'Ricky.' David held out his hand to the likeable rogue who always looked over your shoulder in search of someone more interesting. 'You're putting on weight.'

'Comes of living off the fat of the land since you gave up private work, David. It's an ill wind. Seriously, though' – roving eyes held David's for a moment – 'we were sorry to hear of your troubles.'

A shrug, a smile and a nod – for a death, a death and a guilt. It was incredible how easy it was becoming.

'But tell me – ' Forsythe looked quickly around before taking a step nearer, his face so close to theirs now that he had to turn it sideways and speak from the corner of his mouth, which gave a furtive hissing sound to the words – 'what's all this bullshit Brian's on about? Crap, isn't it? Literally. Hey?' He turned his head to face them again, his eyes squinting. 'Bullshit, isn't it? What d'you think?'

'Unlikely to find universal favour, I agree,' David said carefully. 'It's open to argument.'

O'Connor said nothing.

'Open to argument,' Forsythe mimicked. 'Bloody nonsense, if you ask me. We've both been on the Court of Examiners, David.' He began to prod David's lapel with a forefinger. 'How would you have reacted if a candidate in the final Fellowship had said he'd do what Brian's doing?' He waited long enough for David's silence to be his answer. 'Exactly. You'd have kicked his arse from here to Sunday, wouldn't you?'

'What's this?' O'Connor laughed. 'Ricky Forsythe one of the Establishment now? I don't believe it. You must be getting old, Ricky. Of all the surgeons in town, I'd have said you were the one most likely to take on some new operation.'

'So long as I reckoned it was an advance, Harry, yes – I'd have a go. But this is no advance and you know it. I respect your loyalty, boys, but this is bloody nonsense, you've got to admit it. It's wrong in concept, and it isn't even as if there isn't a perfectly good, well-proven operation available as an alternative. Do you go along with it?' Forsythe asked O'Connor. 'Have *you* done the operation?'

O'Connor shook his head.

'And *you*, David?'

'I've sent him one case,' David answered quietly.

'And?'

David saw the groups drifting slowly towards the door of the lecture theatre. 'It's time we went in,' he said, pushing his way between O'Connor and Forsythe.

'And?' Forsythe demanded, following him, but he got no reply.

The room was too small to offer any place to hide. The President of the Surgical Section, Reggie Bevington, already sat at his table, raised on a dais, scanning everyone who came through the door. The front rows were occupied by the old and the rich, the famous and the titled, retired and honoured, out for an evening basking in their fame. Behind them sat the younger, thrusting consultants, already working on how they could catch old Reggie's eye so that, for that all-important few moments, they could get on their feet, head and shoulders above all others, and say something, anything. To join them, David and O'Connor passed through the rear flanks of young registrars who would not want to offend by being seen to push themselves ahead of their elders and betters.

At the end of one of the front rows, his head buried in a sheaf of papers, sat Pullman.

As David sat down, he saw Bevington raise his fingers from the desk in front of him in silent salute. He smiled back, wondering what Bevington was thinking, his own mind a mosaic of pale breasts in cold floodlights, dripping water from young thighs, blinding flashbulbs. A summer's night. And Gemma.

'Good evening, gentlemen.' To Reggie Bevington, there was no such thing as a female surgeon. 'A lot to get through tonight, so – if I could have your attention, please. The main topic for discussion is, as you know, recent advances in the management of carcinoma of colon. Not all of it operative, as you will see from your programme, but still centred around Mr Pullman's paper, in which he will give details of his operation, and to which, I am sure, we all look forward with considerable anticipation. But, as hors-d'oeuvre, Mr Lithgow, from Sheffield, has some film to show us on the use of . . .' Reggie made a play of having difficulty with pronunciation as he riffled his papers – 'something called a choledochoscope in the removal of stones from the common bile duct.' He leaned forward and towards the venerable pates below him. 'Didn't have much trouble finding them in your day with just a Desjardins, did you Charlie?'

It set the heads nodding and bobbing happily until the room was plunged into darkness. For a while they watched the magic of fibre optics turn a long, narrow bile duct and its gravel into an underground railway station full of boulders. The next paper, a ten-year follow-up of the results of surgery for carcinoma of the caecum, was given in the tremulous voice of a registrar whose chief was presenting the identical paper in Mexico City. There followed a discourse on the futility of chemotherapeutic agents in the management of inoperable colonic cancer, and then it was Pullman's turn.

From the sudden hush, there was little doubt which paper most had come to hear.

'Here we go,' David heard O'Connor murmur.

Pullman's walk to the lectern had the slow deliberation, not of the condemned man fighting for self-control on his way to the scaffold, but of someone enjoying every stride. He held his head high, not with the dignity of someone facing the rope, but with the pride of personal achievement. David felt his own face contort as a wave of angry nausea overcame him. He fought to control his cheeks and eyes and mouth as he looked round, catching, in furtive glances directed his way, the smirks of those who were wondering what he must be thinking. The shooting star of the London surgical galaxy, now a burnt-out ember, junior to a pompous old windbag in a DGH, sitting back to be told how to do it by a man he would have pissed on six months before.

Sod 'em. Sit where he was, say nothing – that's what he'd

sworn to do. If he got up and said anything it would make the bastards' evening for them, watching Pullman and himself tearing each other to pieces in public.

'Gentlemen.' Pullman had started. 'The surgery of the colon has not progressed, in my opinion, since the basic principles were hammered out, mostly in the light of hard clinical practice, in the first half of this century. Results *have* improved in more recent years, but mainly as a result of better anaesthesia and intensive post-operative care. As far as surgical technique is concerned, I feel we have all been guilty of dragging our feet, and I decided some time ago to give some thought to the matter, particularly in regard to the very early growth where the size of the operation commonly used is out of all proportion to the size of the tumour. With this in mind . . .'

No one dozed as the lights dimmed and slides were pulled into focus on the screen. There was the occasional terse whisper, plainly not some joke being cracked but hostile comment germane to some figure or diagram or graph. A few growled words were followed by a snigger. There was at least one sudden movement with the sort of audible snort that suggests an encounter with something visually offensive. The lights came on again and Pullman drew his conclusions, oblivious in his ecstasy to the stony faces below him. He stood waiting for the inevitable questions from the floor, gazing out over the shuffling feet and suppressed coughs like some lofty conductor between movements in a symphony.

Reggie Bevington's elbows were spread wide across his table, his shoulders hunched, his head down as if peering cautiously over a parapet. 'I'm sure Mr Pullman would be happy to answer any questions you might have, gentlemen,' he said.

Shoes were examined, fingernails cleaned, features of interest on the ceiling noticed for the first time.

'Perhaps I can start the ball rolling then.' Bevington scowled at his audience, bravely finding a smile for Pullman as he turned towards him. 'A stupid question, in view of the results you have described this evening, Mr Pullman, but have you any reservations, any doubts *at all*, about what is, after all, a pretty controversial procedure?'

Pullman replied instantly. 'None, Mr President. Absolutely *none at all*. I would suggest that that is the only reasonable conclusion to be drawn in the light of my follow-up statistics.'

'Hmmmmph.' Bevington tried to think of *one* procedure he'd practised for thirty years about which he had absolutely *no* reservations *at all*. 'You'd do it on the wife of one of your colleagues?'

'Mr President, I treat *all* my patients as if they were my colleagues' wives.'

'Holy shit.' O'Connor was doubled up as if he had colic, his forearms wrapped round his waist. He hissed the words at the floor.

Reggie Bevington stared bleakly out at the audience. His broad, kindly features had hardened into an open invitation to someone in the audience to do something protocol, if not simple good manners, forbad him to do himself. His gaze honed in on David.

David turned his head away from the big, generous man who had done him a big favour, only to look straight into another face. Ricky Forsythe, one eyebrow raised mockingly, tilted his head in invitation. There was an almost discernible movement of his hand as if to indicate it was David's entry. David saw the dawning disappointment, the dulling of the eyes as respect drained away.

Forsythe got to his feet almost wearily. 'If I may, Mr President?' he asked, his face still four-square to David's.

'Please do,' Bevington growled.

Forsythe turned towards the lectern, his upper lip drawn back as if wincing at what he was being forced to do. 'You say you have had no regrets after your operation, Mr Pullman?'

'None.'

'Nothing that might make you question what would be, to most surgeons, a questionable procedure and is replacing an existing operation which, while not perfect, satisfies most surgeons' demands.'

'Nothing.'

'I envy you,' Forsythe murmured, quietly enough to allow some sniggers to be heard. 'Because, let's face it, your operation literally cuts across the accepted theories of tumour spread.

Tumours of the colon spread primarily by the lymphatics, do they not? As far as I can tell, your operation takes no account of that, and therefore, as happens with operations that *do* allow for the lymphatic spread, it must sooner or later run into trouble. Do you mean to tell me that you have had *no* early recurrence?'

'I don't think, Mr Forsythe, that you have altogether grasped . . .'

Forsythe felt sure the operation was wrong and was doing his utmost to say so. Bevington was convinced the operation was wrong but was not allowed to say so. In the experience of the venerable gentlemen in the front rows, the operation was wrong, but they feared being considered out of date if they said so. Almost to a man, the rest of the audience felt it was a bad operation but doubted their ability to put it any better than Forsythe was doing.

Only David *knew* it was a bad operation. He sat and watched as Forsythe's questioning, without the backing of solid evidence, broke against the stone wall of Pullman's conceit. Forsythe was a rogue – but an honest rogue, and a fine surgeon – and he was being publicly talked down to by a condescending prince amongst bullshitters. And David was going to sit by and watch it happen? He looked across the heads to where Pullman and Forsythe confronted each other.

A bag of wind and a man with balls.

There was a dream-like aura around him as David slowly got to his feet. In the buzz of excitement, he heard Harry O'Connor say something as from a long way away. Bevington he ignored as he saw the two men, Pullman and Forsythe, turn towards him – one the epitome of smug surgical self-righteousness, the other the David Royall of yesteryear. The grin that spread over Forsythe's face as he gave way to David seemed to be welcoming him back.

'Mr Lever. Mr John Lever.'

The audience hushed as if afraid Pullman might miss a word.

'What?' Pullman asked sharply.

'Not what – *who*, Mr Pullman. Mr Lever was a man, a patient – you know, one of those people you always treat like a colleague's wife?'

'I can't say I recognise the name.'

'John Lever, 36 Clevedon Close, Kennington. Any clearer now?' He took a deep breath as he saw Pullman shake his head, the sort of breath he might take with Tommy beside him, battling to windward. He smelt again the close, second-hand air of the stuffy room as his adrenaline began to flow. 'A case I referred to you back in June of last year, a case perfect for your series you remarked, as any one of a dozen students who were at the Merton at the time will testify.'

'The name does ring a bell.' Pullman began to look uneasy as Forsythe quietly took his seat once more. 'However – I'm not too sure it turned out to be colon.'

'Oh, I assure you, it was colon. And you performed your operation on him. And, within some nine or ten months, he was dead from a pelvis full of recurrent tumour. Surely you must remember him now.'

'That can't be true.' Pullman was now white and shaking uncontrollably. 'My figures . . .'

'. . . are false.'

'It is simply not possible.' There was a tremor now as if Pullman was near to tears.

'No? I have the patient's notes in my car outside. With the President's permission . . .'

'I don't think there is any need for that, Mr Royall.' Bevington looked sadly at the two men. 'I have no doubt what you say can be borne out. Equally, I have no doubt that Mr Pullman has overlooked some point in his follow-up records. It's easily done. We've all done it at one time or another.'

'This patient never got on any follow-up records, Mr President. He never was followed up despite the efforts of my secretary at Queen's, as she would be only too pleased to confirm. No.'

David turned towards Reggie Bevington, who was taking no joy in watching two surgeons savaging one another.

'If this operation was a valid one, proved by Mr Pullman's work, then I would be the first to compliment him on it.' Would he? 'But frankly' – got the sod – 'I have every reason to doubt his figures, and so, with so many young minds present here this evening, Mr President, unpleasant as it has been to air my doubts publicly' – you're enjoying it, you bastard – 'I felt it would hardly be in the tradition of the RSM to propagate ideas that could result in some tragic mistakes.'

As David sat down, he heard Bevington trying to pick up the pieces. 'Stimulating discussion. Grateful to Mr Pullman. Not often a paper keeps all the two front rows awake throughout. Next month, something a little less controversial . . .'

'That took a bit of courage,' O'Connor smiled sadly as they shuffled towards the door. 'It means, of course, after what you said, that Brian can kiss the Presidency goodbye. You realise that, don't you?'

'Couldn't have happened to a nicer guy.' The adrenaline still coursing, David felt he could lick any two of them with one hand tied behind his back.

'Maybe . . .' O'Connor shrugged his shoulders.

'Come on, Harry. I couldn't let him get away with that.'

'P'raps you're right.'

'David – I'm proud of you.' There were no such doubts in Forsythe's mind. 'I miss you, you old bastard. When are you coming back into private practice, give me a bit of competition?'

'No chance of that, Ricky. It's all yours.'

'Really? Somehow I can't bring myself to believe that. There was a bit of the old David Royall in there tonight. I reckon you'll be back. And it's a bloody awful waste, you stuck down there in the Merton.' His face lit up. 'I tell you what – I've had an idea.'

His wife reckoned he had a hundred new ideas a day.

'What now, Ricky?' David laughed. They had been one of a kind.

'Let me bring the Surgical Sixty Club down to the Merton this autumn. Would you put something on for them – let them watch some *real* surgery? They'd love that. Harry does a nifty selective vagotomy, I know and' – he put his head back to give a full-bellied laugh – 'perhaps Brian will do one of his operations for them.'

'No, Ricky. I'm finished with all that.'

'Oh, come on, David. Give 'em a treat.'

'I'll think about it.'

'Attaboy. I'll give you a ring to fix the dates.'

David gave the heavy door a shove and walked in. Except for the fact that the hallway now rang to a cultured 'hullo' rather than a lilting 'cooee', it was Cory Street all over again. No locked door. No knock. No wait on a cold doorstep. He put his head around more open doors: no one – until he came to the kitchen. Dariella looked up. He wondered what he would have to do to surprise her.

'Hullo,' she said. 'I'm just making them some sandwiches and a cup of coffee. Would you like some?'

'Sandwich – no; coffee – yes, please.'

'Hang on then. You can help me carry them in.'

She moved around the kitchen like someone accustomed to men watching her. She had her back to him when next she spoke.

'Yes, I *am* still here.'

'I beg your pardon?' he gasped, taken aback.

She did not bother to turn to repeat herself. 'I said, yes, I *am* still here.' Now she turned and, for the first time, held his gaze. No fear. No embarrassment. It was almost as if she were saying 'I haven't looked at you like this before. Not because I'm scared of you; you just haven't been worth it.'

'I still don't understand.'

'Don't you? Every time you walk into this house, you look at me and your face says "What – are you still here?"'

David was honest enough to apologise. He watched as she reached for the coffee jar.

'But I never thought I'd see the day when another woman looked so at home in Mary Parker's kitchen.'

'She's got a touch of phlebitis,' Dariella explained. 'I told her to go and put her feet up for a couple of hours.'

Someone telling Mary Parker to go and put her feet up?

'And what about you?' he grinned. 'If you ever showed any emotion on that beautiful face of yours, what would it say when *I* came in? "What – you here again?"'

Dariella's chest and shoulders made all the movements of a small laugh, though she gave no sound. 'Something like that,' she admitted.

'I rather suspect you don't like me,' David said, switching on a smile of patronising forgiveness even before he had heard the answer.

She leaned back against the unit, her ankles crossed, one hand supporting the opposite elbow as she nibbled at a piece of meat. She considered for a moment.

'Can't say I've given it much thought,' she said.

If she had set out to make him feel small, she was certainly succeeding. Someone who sold her favours, not giving a Member of Council a second thought; someone who had probably left school at sixteen, with no time for a Master of Surgery. If she was not capable of appreciating his intellectual powers, perhaps he should tell her of some of his physical conquests. But she hadn't finished with him.

'We're very alike in many ways,' she said coolly.

A hooker and a consultant surgeon – with something in common?

'I suppose you might say we both operate on people to make them better. Who knows?' This time she gave a short chuckle. 'Perhaps my cure rate is better than yours. One thing's for certain. Apart from our professions – where, I suspect, we can both take 'em or leave 'em – we both need other people. At the moment I'm living off Mal, I admit it – but so are you off Mal and Tommy. There is, however, one difference between us.' She took her hand from her mouth so that he could see her whole face. 'The moment I feel that Mal is tired of me, I'll go. Will you?'

'Dear God,' David muttered. 'Who needs a conscience with someone like you around? You may not believe me, but I *have* thought about it.'

'That's all right then.' She uncrossed her legs, brushing non-existent crumbs from her cashmere jumper. 'I've known . . . I'd hate to tell you how many men like you I've known, just too damn clever by half but good enough at heart. Half the brains and you'd have been OK – someone more like Mal. Now he's a *real* man.' She turned and picked up two cups. She held them towards him. 'Here.' She smiled, obviously pleased with herself. 'Cop hold of these and take them in. I'll bring the rest.'

'Where *is* Mal?' David asked over his shoulder as they walked along the creaking, echoing passageway.

'Manchester. He's gone mad since he's been allowed to drive again.'

'Why didn't you go with him?'

'I've *been* to Manchester. Anyway – I told him – I'm staying to keep an eye on Tommy.'

'How *is* Tommy?'

'All right.'

All right. Not 'great' or 'fine' or 'very well'; not even 'miserable' or 'brassed off' or plain 'rotten'. All right – and in that tone of voice. But David was to have no chance of finding out what exactly 'all right' meant, for two beaming faces greeted them as they entered the room.

He had known that Benny Boston was there – he'd seen his Saab parked outside. He put the coffee cups down as he saw the little man hurry round the table, cue in hand, his cheeks and temples ravined with pleasure. Tommy stood back, smiling also as he watched the two men shake hands.

'Hullo, Benny.'

'Mr Royall.'

'How's he doing?'

Boston turned so that his back was to Tommy. He looked up at the ceiling, his eyes almost disappearing under the upper lids while his lips pursed into a silent whistle.

'Really?' Royall said.

Boston returned his features to the neutral, radiant mode and nodded. His lips conveyed one silent word: 'Fantastic.'

Delighted, David turned to Tommy, but before he could say anything he was enveloped in a bear hug and felt on his cheek once more the full force of one of Tommy's kisses. As Tommy released him, David saw the look. It was the same each time they met. Will you come again tomorrow?

'Hullo, Tommy.'

'Hullo, David.'

'You're getting fat, Tommy. You're eating too much. Just look at that stomach.'

Tommy did as he was told, looking down to clap hands to his waist and roar with laughter like an adolescent Falstaff. 'Dariella's a good cook,' he said. He was serious for a moment, his forehead creasing as he pronounced judgment. 'Not as good as Mrs Berry.'

'Thank *you*,' came languorously from a shadowy corner of the room.

The generous smile returned. 'But her rice pudding is good.'

'And how's the snooker going?'

'Benny says I'm very good. Dariella says I'm very good.' There was that serious look again. '*I* think I'm very good.'

He looked perplexed at the laughter that caused and Boston went over to put his arm around the young man's shoulders.

'Tommy's got a new trick, haven't you, Tommy?'

Tommy nodded vigorously. 'Benny's taught me a new trick. And he's bought me a new cue.'

'Come and show Mr Royall your new trick then, Tommy.'

David stood back as Boston placed several red balls in a line obliquely across one corner. At one end of the line he placed the black. 'All right, Tommy,' Boston said quietly. 'Off you go.'

Tommy picked up his cue, settled into his stance, and there was silence as he steadied himself. Setting the black off slowly towards the far corner pocket, he potted the row of reds into the same pocket ahead of the black, the balls hitting the back of the pocket with cracks like pistol shots. He turned, smiling, looking to David for praise.

'Fantastic, Tommy. And can you do that every time?'

Tommy nodded. 'That's easy,' he said contemptuously.

'Let's show Mr Royall how you can *really* play,' Boston said, bending to lift the balls out of the pockets. 'You have one of Dariella's sandwiches while I set 'em up for you.'

Boston took his time, squinting down the table as he centred the triangle of reds. Chalking his cue, he broke off, purposely disturbing all the reds and leaving the cue ball at the top of the table. He walked across to stand shoulder to shoulder with Royall. 'Now watch this,' he whispered.

Tommy looked at the remaining sandwiches regretfully before coming back to the table. He wiped his mouth with the back of his hand as he walked round the top end, chalking his cue as his features set in stony concentration. He set about potting reds and blacks as Boston dodged back and forth replacing the blacks, and David stood open-mouthed. The break stood at forty-nine when he heard Tommy catch his breath, his face a picture of apology as he looked up to search for Boston's reaction. With a flicker of hooded eyes, he included David in his apology.

'Don't worry, Tommy.' Boston hurried to his side. 'Steve Davis doesn't make a century break *every* time, you know. Now – do you know what you did wrong?'

Tommy nodded. He pointed. 'I didn't leave the white ball there.'

'Absolutely right, Tommy. And can you remember how I taught you to get the ball just there?'

'Yes. I didn't hit it on the side so that it would come off the cushion like that.' He turned his cue to show the angle he meant.

'So – ' Boston said, taking the red from the pocket and replacing it where it had lain, 'do it again.'

The break went on.

'Good. Very good, Tommy.' A few minutes later and Boston seemed to David to be about to jump up and down. 'You were quite right. You couldn't possibly have got the black from there and now you're the right side of the blue. Remember – you've got to be below the blue to get back to the reds. Excellent, Tommy.'

An unfortunate bounce off the corner of a pocket and Boston had to take a shot himself to set Tommy up once more. With only the colours left, Boston came to stand beside David. 'Don't forget to take them in the right order now, Tommy,' he called. They stood watching silently. 'What d'you think of that?' he whispered out of the corner of his mouth as the black rattled down.

'Speechless,' David whispered back. He stood watching Tommy survey the empty table as if puzzled where all the balls had gone. Tommy caught sight of him and the beaming smile returned.

'Was I good?' he asked.

'Very good, Tommy. Very good indeed.'

Tommy looked pleased. 'Can I have another sandwich now?' he asked.

'Yes, of course, Tommy. Benny and I are just going to have a word together. You have your sandwich and I'll come back and see you after I've spoken to Benny here.'

'Mrs Berry used to make nice sandwiches,' Tommy said wistfully, 'but Dariella makes nice sandwiches too.'

David led Boston back along the passage to the kitchen. Inside, he turned. 'Well?' he asked.

'Well what?' Boston countered, laughing.

'What d'you think? Just how good *is* he?'

'Depends.'

'For God's sake, Benny – depends on what?'

'What you want him to do.'

That made David stop and think. 'What I would like to know is . . .' He had to step back suddenly as Dariella, tray in hand, with room to spare on either side, marched between them. '. . . what would his chances be in a competition?' He winced at the sound of cups and plates being thrown into the sink. 'How would he get on?'

'Again, that obviously depends on the level of competition, but in his age group, in some aspects of his game, he is in a class of his own.'

David was excited. 'You really mean that?' he asked.

'Look, Mr Royall. There are not many Oxford dons amongst professional snooker players. In fact, take away their God-given talent and some of them would have difficulty finding a job. So – the fact that it does not take an Einstein to become a world-class snooker player doesn't mean that you can get away without a certain level of intelligence – because you can't – particularly when it comes to safety play. Now, the problem is, has Tommy that level of intelligence?'

Dariella leaned forward, listening, her head bowed, her arms wrist-deep in washing-up water.

'And has he?' David asked quietly.

'There was nothing I could teach him about potting a ball.

He's on a par with anyone in the world on that. I'd back him against anyone. I was surprised, too, just how good he was at positional play – he must have watched a great deal of TV – and I've been able to teach him stun and screw, side and topspin, that sort of thing, mainly because he will happily practise for hours at a time and has unlimited access to a table – which many youngsters would give their eye teeth for. And,' Boston added, as if throwing it in for good measure, 'I've managed to teach him the colours, how to go for the others if the black is not on, what order to take the final colours in. He still makes the occasional mistake on that, but not very often. But . . .' He shook his head.

'But?' David echoed.

'Safety play. I've tried, and by God, *he*'s tried, but we're up against a brick wall there, I'm afraid. Perhaps it's because I'm a lousy teacher. Perhaps someone else . . .'

'I don't think so, somehow, Benny,' David smiled. 'But what does all that add up to?'

'Well – there are some world-class players for whom safety play has not been the strongest part of their play and who have got by on the strength of the rest of their game. It would remain to be seen whether this would go for Tommy too. Although – ' he paused to grin – 'something tells me that Tommy wouldn't use safety-first tactics even if he could. He can be a stubborn young beggar when he gets the bit between his teeth. But to counter that he has, of course, one enormous advantage going for him.'

'What's that?'

'His temperament. I've never seen such concentration and patience. I've left him practising that shot you saw him miss. If I didn't go back for another two hours, he would still be there, quite happily doing the same thing over and over again. And, in competititon, I don't think the pressure would get to him like other people. I think the only thing that would upset him would be the thought that he had let you or me down.'

'So – where do we go from here?'

'As I said, Mr Royall – it depends. Where do you *want* to go?'

'How difficult would it be to arrange a game against someone his own age, someone you know is good?'

'No problem. I know a nice young lad who's won a few local amateur competitions but hasn't got the money to go any farther afield. Some of the lads are a bit rough, might be inclined to take the piss out of Tommy given half the chance, but this lad won't.' Boston raised his eyebrows. It was the first time David had seen him without a smile. 'D'you want me to fix it?'

'Yes.'

Behind them, Dariella turned slowly. 'I don't suppose it has occurred to you to ask Tommy what *he*'d like to do? And Mal? Don't you think he should have a say in it too?'

23

An Englishman's home is his castle. Home to the on-duty junior staff at the Merton was an enclave of rooms into which a consultant was as likely to enter uninvited as royalty into the humblest commoner's shelter from the injustices of a rich man's world. Within those rooms at least, safe amongst their peers, registrars and housemen could, should they so desire, revile their chiefs to their hearts' content, secure in the knowledge that they could not be overheard by those who had the power to snuff out their ambitions at the stroke of a pen. At the bedside, they had to play bit parts, feeding the stars in front of an adoring audience. But in their sitting room, sprawled in chairs, underpaid, overworked, frustrated, with the impatience of youth, they could always find a sympathetic ear as they mimicked their chief's voice, imitated his mannerisms, ridiculed his methods. The consultants knew this; it was nothing new – they'd done it themselves. David remembered the camaraderie of the junior staff common room with great affection, and had often wondered where it disappeared to as soon as anyone was appointed to the consultant ranks.

It was with a mixture of unease and nostalgia, therefore, that he followed Shah into his sanctum sanctorum. He smiled apologetically at two young men who sat more upright in their chairs at the sight of him. A young woman, her white coat thrown over the back of her chair, stuffed her knitting out of sight as if career girls of high intelligence were not supposed to indulge in anything so domestic.

'I'm sorry to barge in,' David said, 'but we're waiting to get into theatre and Shah here is very anxious to watch the Strait programme. D'you mind?'

As if they'd dare.

Shah waited politely for David to sit down before he did, too diplomatic to mention the fact that it had been his chief who had put the case back half an hour and had reminded him about the programme. 'It is Mr Strait's first time back after we are operating on him,' he explained proudly. 'We are wondering what he is going to say. Perhaps he will be mentioning our names.'

'God forbid, Shah,' David laughed – and the rest laughed with him, just for safety's sake. 'If he does, we might find ourselves up in front of the GMC. Now you wouldn't want that, would you, Shah?'

'Indeed, no, sir,' Shah simpered.

Conversation hung fire as the flickering screen moved on agonisingly slowly. In the awkward pauses, David wondered where Pullman would be watching.

There was to be no compromise, no sham make-up, no avoidance of close-ups. The opening shot was to be as usual, head and shoulders, full face. Strait had left his producer and director in no doubt about that. He was back, warts, colostomy and all.

David laughed quietly to himself as he saw the impatience on Strait's face as he waited for his signature tune to fade. He saw also the impatience change to emotion as Strait had to wait even longer as, without prompting, wave after wave of applause overwhelmed him. Eventually the last handclap tailed away and they waited in silence.

'Thank you. I'm back.'

The smile, as the applause exploded once more, showed Strait's relief at getting the first words out.

'First . . .' Strait put his hand up until he could be heard. 'First, let me thank all of you who sent so many cards and flowers and good wishes. I had no idea that a bad-tempered, ill-mannered old curmudgeon like myself could have so many friends out there.'

As the old pro got back into his stride, milking his audience of every last drop of sentiment, David fought off his disappointment as minutes went by with no mention made of Members of Council or Masters of Surgery. He imagined the millions glued to their TVs. And not a word.

'. . . and devoted nursing. That I can never repay. But, to me, the most irritating aspect of the whole affair is that I cannot thank, by name, in public, the man who undoubtedly saved my life.'

'Hsssss.' Shah sat forward excitedly and David felt the others glance his way.

'There is nothing I would like more than to have that surgeon on this programme, to show him my gratitude, to show you all my gratitude, but stupid convention forbids it. Isn't it crazy? A man gives me ten, maybe twenty, who knows, perhaps thirty more years of life – if I don't have a stroke on this programme before that – and I can't even tell you who he was. Well, I *could*.' He made a enfeebled attempt at his old bulldog face. 'But that would only cause him considerable embarrassment, and I have no desire to do that. So, I wondered' – Strait timed the pause to perfection – 'what else could I do to repay him in some small way?'.

David leaned forward, hoping Pullman was watching.

'And so, I decided that the first person I would present to you on my return would be – myself. Ladies and gentlemen – ' Strait, thin and gaunt, looked full into the camera – 'I have a colostomy.'

In the silence that followed, the cameras backed away as Strait turned towards the studio audience.

'Strange, isn't it' – he smiled tolerantly at the rank upon rank of deadpan faces – 'how embarrassed that makes you? I'll say it again. Ladies and gentlemen – I have a colostomy.'

The cameras cut to a brief, distant shot of an audience hanging its collective head.

'If it is any consolation to you,' Strait went on, 'six months ago my reaction would have been exactly the same as yours. It's odd, isn't it, that we can interview brave men with faces destroyed by fire, thalidomide children with no limbs, women jerking and stuttering their way through the terminal stages of some dreadful nervous disease, and we are more than happy to show our compassion and respect. We have even applauded someone who has had the courage to tell the world on this programme he has Aids. But a colostomy? Oh no.'

'Hell's teeth, what's he going to do next?' a voice behind David asked. 'Pull up his shirt and show it to everybody?'

'Yes, I have a colostomy – but I'm one of the lucky ones. Mine is only a temporary one. The noises you may hear my microphone pick up, the smells the microphone cannot pick up – isn't that fortunate for you? – I have to endure for only a short while longer. In a month or so, I'm going to have it all put back. But there are many who have to come to terms with the fact that they are going to live the rest of their days with a colostomy or an ileostomy – a stoma, as they call it. And that only came home to me when, as I was getting better and was able to walk around a little, I overheard a sensitive man the other side of a curtain breaking the news to a beautiful twenty-year-old girl with colitis that she must either have a permanent ileostomy or die.' Strait waited for the murmer he expected. 'I listened. Yes, ladies and gentlemen, I eavesdropped on that conversation – and it made me feel very humble. It made me realise what a contrived, superficial ego trip this show of mine so often is. If you want to hear a *real* chat show, ladies and gentlemen, *that*'s the one to listen to, not mine.'

Sweat began to show on a sick man's face as Strait held the silent attention of millions.

'That's why, tonight, I have with me three out of many, many people around this country: a famous West End actress, a well-known member of the House of Lords, and an Elephant and

Castle barrow boy.' The skin, glistening beneath the thick glases, crinkled. 'Please don't ask me how I found out their names. All three have had a permanent stoma of one kind or another performed by this particular surgeon, and all three have agreed to appear tonight to testify gladly that they would not be around to talk about it if it had not been for, one, the skill of that surgeon and, perhaps more importantly, two, the strength and compassion he brought to bear to help them face the outside world once more. And if, by speaking about their handicap, they will make that surgeon's task that little bit easier the next time he has to pull those curtains around him, then that will, in some small way, repay something of what I owe him.'

The barrow boy David could not remember. The other two faces brought back memories.

Shah was dumb until they stood, half an hour later, side by side, scrubbing up. 'My friends will be very jealous, Mr Royall, sir, that I am working for such a famous man.' He looked down, frowning into the palms of lean, brown hands. 'I am wondering what Mr Pullman is thinking.'

They missed it the first time they walked up the High Street. Mulligan's Snooker Club – Licensed Bar – Members Only. There it was. They had been looking too low, at eye level, whereas the sign was screwed to the wall between two murky, diesel-streaked windows on the first floor, partly hidden by the canvas roll-up shade of the greengrocer's shop below. The entrance, squeezed between the shop and a black-walled pub, was partially blocked by a box of oranges at which a dog sniffed with obvious intent. They had to step over both to get to the foot of the bare wooden stairs that led up from the narrow alleyway. At the top of the stairs there was a locked door; to the side of the door a small microphone and a button. David pressed the button.

'Yes?'

'My name's Royall. We're not mem——'

There was a click and the door sprung ajar. David pulled a face at Tommy, pushed the door and led the way into a world of varnished wood and matt green baize, deep shadows around islands of bright lights through which vague shapes came and went, a constant murmur of voices punctuated by the irregular clicks that sound like nothing else. As David approached the bar, Tommy following, his cue case upright in his hand like some ceremonial rod, there was a deepening of the hush as strangers were spied.

'Good afternoon. I've . . .'

'Table eighteen. Benny's expectin' you.'

'Table eighteen. Thank you. Which . . .'

'Over in the corner.'

Which corner was indicated with a jerk of the head that did not distract attention from the beer being drawn at the same time. David eased his way between the tables, pausing here and there as a shot was taken, accepting apologetically the guilt for breaking the concentration of a postman, still in uniform, as he missed an easy pot. In the corner, a young man moved around the table with confident, almost arrogant flourishes. Without raising his head, he carried on practising as Benny Boston emerged from the shadows.

Waving a hand as David apologised for being late, Boston introduced the young man at the table.

'This is Wayne. Wayne is our club champion – one of the best amateurs around these parts.'

'Wotcha mean, Benny?' Wayne looked up between shots, his face split in a broad, white-toothed grin. '*One* of the best? *The* best, i'n' I. An' not just round 'ere neither. Wot you tryin' to do then, Benny, break my confidence or somethin'?'

David looked at the youngster who was going to be Tommy's first yardstick. Jet-black hair, plastered into shape, hung like sticky stalactites down the back of his bare, pock-marked neck. Skinny arms, shoulders and chest were revealed by a thin, grubby, sleeveless vest, all he wore above the waist on a chilly October evening. On the back of one forearm was tattooed a crude dagger, on the other the Prince of Wales feathers. Ragged jeans and trainers completed the ensemble. David wondered what his underpants looked like.

'It's kind of you to give Tommy a game like this, Wayne. I'm sure he appreciates it very much.'

'No sweat, Mr Royall.' He turned his grin on Tommy. 'Pretty hot stuff, are you, Tommy?'

'Yes. I'm very good. *Benny* says so.'

'Oh, 'e does, does 'e?' It was obvious Wayne had known all about Tommy before they had arrived. He had made no sign on seeing Tommy's face for the first time. 'But then Benny says that to all the boys, don' chew, Benny boy?' He turned his attention back to Tommy, a streetwise sharpness wiping out the grin. 'How you wanna play, then? You got a handicap?'

'No – you'll play all square,' Boston said as David nodded, trying to look knowledgeable. 'Best of five, like I said. Call.'

He spun a coin, caught it and placed it under his hand on the edge of the table.

''eads.'

Boston lifted his hand. 'You to break then, Tommy.'

David took Tommy's jacket and cue case, his hand trembling, as Boston and Wayne set up the balls. He smiled, anxious not to transmit his nervous excitement, only to see Tommy chalking his cue as if still alone in his father's house. He took a seat in the corner as Boston hovered over the table, ready to replace the colours.

One mistake from Wayne and that was the last shot he played in that frame. A break of thirty-five had Wayne smiling again until a bad kick let Tommy in to clear the table. By now a ring of onlookers pressed in on Boston as he dug the balls out of the pockets, making him squeeze behind Wayne as he rounded one end of the table.

'You shit, Benny.' Wayne's lips were the only part of him to move.

Tommy turned to Boston with a broad smile as he brought the cue ball snugly under the baulk cushion after breaking off. Boston did not smile back, so Tommy switched to David. David nodded, sticking out his jaw, clenching his fist and shaking it in front of him. Wayne, now bent in a curve as tense as a drawn bow, miscued, sending the reds in all directions. It was the last shot he played, for Tommy, to cries of 'Yeah' and 'Get in there' and 'Give it the 'ammer' from the shadows around, cleared the table once more with a century break.

Through and above the acclaim, as Tommy sank the black, came the spitting reaction of a threatened street fighter.

'Bleedin' 'ell, Benny, wotcha tryin' to do to me? You set me up, you bastard. This geezer's no beginner. You tryin' to make a monkey outa me or somethin'?' The voice, as thin and as tense as the body, rose to a shriek. 'You bring your poncy bloody friends in 'ere, takin' the piss . . .'

'Don't take it that way.' Boston tried to put a hand on his arm, but Wayne drew back as if Boston had the plague. The applause had subsided and Boston could see that some of the crowd were beginning to see things Wayne's way.

'You're a fuckin' bastard,' Wayne screamed as he heard small movements of support behind him. 'Wot's 'e payin' you then?' He pointed to David.

Boston leaned towards David, a man in a grey suit amongst the jeans, sweatshirts and anoraks. 'I think it's time we got out,' he muttered. 'How did you get here?'

'Taxi.'

'I've got a car round the corner. Let's go.' He beckoned to Tommy. 'Come on, Tommy. Time to go now.'

'Isn't Wayne my friend any more, Benny?'

'You weren't here to make friends,' Boston muttered to himself as he pushed Tommy gently towards the door.

An hour later, with Tommy delivered safely into the hands of Dariella, Boston pulled up outside the terraced, freehold, executive-style, centrally heated townhouse with integral garage, balcony and small patio garden in the much-sought-after area of Wimbledon that was now David's home.

'Care for a drink?' David asked.

Boston switched the engine off. 'Perhaps I should,' he said.

But inside he shook his head as David waved at the bottles, explaining as he sat down that he never touched the stuff. He spread both hands, putting his fingertips together as if connecting a five-pronged electric circuit before quietly and succinctly explaining to David the unseen effects of what his ambition for Tommy had done that evening. He painted the picture of a young man living in a squat with an epileptic girl, six months pregnant, who brought in a few bob a week working part time in a burger bar; a young man who had that evening been shown the limits of his only asset – and that in front of his peers by a Down's.

David offered the money that would put everything right, but Boston smiled as he watched David's reaction to his suggestion of how such money might best be spent – by sponsoring Wayne for a couple of years, by buying him some clothes, by paying his expenses to enter some pro-am tournaments. Some of the top amateurs, Boston explained, made more money these days than the botton half-dozen professionals. Boston's smile broadened as David's face revealed his gradual realisation of the implications for Tommy.

'Backed like that,' Boston said, 'Wayne will certainly improve. He might even become real opposition for Tommy if you harbour any hopes for him in that direction.'

David felt as if he were standing stark naked in front of Boston – and Boston was obviously not too impressed with what he could see. There was a weariness now about the smile that said it all.

'Well?' he said – and saw David's mouth harden. 'So where do we go from here with Tommy?'

David said nothing.

'Yyyyyy-es. Poor little runts like Wayne always seem to end up on the hind tit, don't they?'

'All right – so I'm a bastard,' David growled. 'So where *do* we go from here with Tommy?'

He listened intently as Boston outlined what might be possible – winning sufficient local competitions to get him into the Rothman's UK. Then the English Amateur.

'April in Bradford,' Boston smiled. 'Can be quite nice up there that time of the year, provided, of course, it's stopped snowing by then.'

They laughed together and David felt at least partially forgiven. 'Can things happen that fast, a matter of a few months?' he asked.

'Terry Griffiths went from insurance salesman to world *professional* champion in less than a year.'

'Good God.' David's mind raced ahead into realms taboo

315

even to himself. He dragged himself back from fantasy. One step at a time. 'Only one thing worries me,' he said.

'What's that?'

'I'm not going to be able to take all that time off to go round with Tommy, and obviously he can't go on his own.'

'Already arranged. Mal's thought of that. So long as this business with Tommy's snooker goes on' – David could hear Mal saying it – 'I'm to look after him, every step of the way. We might even have to employ a minder. But don't worry,' he added quickly as he saw David draw breath. 'He's paying me handsomely for doing so. And anyway, he's not the sort of man you can say no to, is he?'

'But he doesn't altogether approve.'

'No. But that's the kind of man he is, isn't it?'

Mal Evans. Snotty-nosed illiterate. In the wings, watching. The world of medicine apart, anywhere David went, Mal seemed to have been there before him.

Boston stood up and turned to leave. 'And you're sure this is the best thing for Tommy? This is what you want?'

'Yes.'

'*All* the way?'

'*All* the way.'

'Is the great man in?' David asked.

'In the single room.'

'Behaving himself?'

'He's just had his first washout. He had a few things to say about falling into the hands of some cowboy plumber's mate. But I can handle him. He's as soft as putty really.'

David looked at his ward sister. Perhaps Strait *had* met his match. 'I'll take your word for it, Sister,' he said.

'But he must have forgiven us. He's given us four tickets for a show.' David saw her put her hand to her waist. 'A change from the usual chocolates. When d'you want to do him?'

'As soon as you tell me his washouts are clean. Day after tomorrow if we can. I'll go and see him. You're busy – no need to come with me.'

Someone in a crisp white coat, standing tall with all the legal authority to inflict almost unlimited physical pain, is in a position of considerable advantage over someone, even someone like Strait, in fear of that pain, sitting in a low chair, feeling slovenly in pyjamas and dressing gown. Having shaken hands, David half sat on the edge of the bed, bending his knees to help bridge the gulf.

'I'm not sure I want to talk to you,' he smiled.

'Why not?'

'Not after the way you treated me in that first show of yours. You've no idea the amount of stick I've had to take from my colleagues since then.'

'Not sure I want to talk to you either, not after the amount of stick your damned ward sister has just given me.'

David grinned. 'Gave you a hard time, did she?'

'I told her – as a nurse, she'd make a damn fine fireman with that bloody great hosepipe of hers. And then she threatened me. Yes, threatened me. She said that if I didn't stop my yelping she'd do the next washout with turps. Florence Nightingale be damned. Bloody Boadicea more like.'

Strait gave a chuckle as he looked up to watch David laugh. 'And how are *you*?' he asked.

'I'm fine.'

'And how's my friend Tommy?'

'Tommy?' David's jaw dropped. 'How do you know about Tommy?'

'You forget – we're neighbours. Well, as near to neighbours as anyone gets in a place like that. I found him wandering around my garden last week, and as you know I've never been too keen on prowlers. So I asked him what the hell he was up to.'

'And?'

'And,' Strait laughed, 'the happy soul asked me if I'd had my tea yet. I rang next door to say I'd found him, and a very anxious but quite beautiful lady called Dariella came over and stayed to tea as well. I haven't had such charming company for years.'

David pictured the scene.

'He tells me he's going to be world snooker champion.'

'Oh, I don't know about that,' David replied hurriedly. 'He's

317

telling everybody that at the moment. He's very, very good – but world champion . . . I don't know where he got that idea from.'

'Somebody must have put the idea into his head.' Strait shot David a shrewd look. 'Unlikely to have thought of it himself, is he?'

'Possibly not. But what about this colostomy of yours now?'

A professional observer of human reactions, the significance of the sudden change in body position and the equally abrupt change of subject was not lost on Strait.

'I imagine you still want to have it closed. I had a patient once who was most reluctant to have it closed as he said it had done wonders for his golf swing.'

'You can get attached to the strangest things. Do you know I find myself talking to it at times?' He laughed. 'And getting the rudest replies.'

Grinning, David stood up, jerking his head behind him.

'Up on the bed then. Let's have a look at it.'

Minutes later, two pairs of eyes scanned the obscene orifice, one with ill-concealed disgust, the other with professional satisfaction – small stoma, thinnish abdominal wall, well-healed scars, no herniation. Should be a sitter.

'No problem there,' David said. 'As soon as . . .'

Strait was buttoning his pyjama jacket when the door was flung open. Brian Pullman was already talking as he came through it. Prevented from standing at the usual side of the bed, he crossed to the other, confronting David over Strait's recumbent form.

'Good morning, Strait. Glad to see you looking so well. Good to see you back at work. So many people just give in to these colostomies, you know. Fit, are you? All set for tomorrow?'

'Tomorrow?' Strait, his glasses seeming to be embedded between cheeks and eyebrows, glanced at David.

'Yes.' Pullman gave the impression they were the only two in the room. 'All fixed. I'm afraid I won't be able to do you until towards the end of the list as yours is what we call a "dirty" operation. I've got a couple of major abdominals first, and I'm afraid I can't bend the rules even for a famous man like you.'

He put his head back and roared with laughter.

'Brian . . .' David felt Strait's eyes on him.

'Can be quite tricky little operations, closing colostomies.' Pullman was in full spate. 'Nothing as bad as you've gone through already, of course, but it needs a bit of experience to make sure they don't leak afterwards. Done properly, you should be out in a week.'

'Brian,' David said again, his anger roused by the man's tactless arrogance. 'It's all fixed. I've arranged to do this the day after tomorrow.'

Pullman looked across as if seeing him for the first time, as if he had just been interrupted by some cocky young registrar.

'But that's impossible. We operate tomorrow. I'll do Mr Strait on the end of my list tomorrow morning. I'll . . .'

'It is all fixed.' David ground the words out. 'They've let me have a theatre, day after tomorrow.'

'Why not tomorrow?' To Pullman, the only man in the room now was David. 'No time? Started your games again, have you? I didn't think it would be long before you started chasing the money again. Can't give it up, can you? Too much of a hold on you, has it? Well, you're not going to do it on *my* back. I've had enough of carrying the can in this place. I warn you, Royall.' White-faced, Pullman leaned across the bed, one fist clenched. 'You put one foot wrong, you see one private case when you should be operating, and, by God, I'll be on the phone to Stockton before you know what's hit you.'

'Brian, this is not the time or place. I'll have a word with you later.'

'There's nothing to discuss. Now then.' Pullman made a sudden lunge with one hand for the tasselled end of the belt around Strait's dressing gown, pulling the bow knot loose. The other hand was opening the gown before either Strait or David could stop him. 'Let's have a look at what sort of a problem you've left me with.'

Before David could move, Strait had grasped Pullman's wrist, but he was not strong enough to fend him off. Stunned by disbelief at what he saw as a blur, David watched the struggle for a moment until Strait's voice cut through to sharpen up the picture.

'Are you going to just stand there? Get this raving maniac off me. What sort of place is this?'

David leaned across to grapple with Pullman, but Pullman just as suddenly snatched his hands away.

'But I must see it,' he screeched, his voice high-pitched, tight and thin. 'I never close a colostomy without seeing it first.'

'Let's get one thing quite clear, shall we?' Strait swung his legs off the bed to stand at David's side. 'Royall is doing this operation, and he does it whenever *he* says, no one else.'

'As senior surgeon in this hospital . . .'

'I don't give a damn what you are, Pullman – Royall does it, that's final. What's more, you can thank Royall here that I'm not taking the matter of your management of my case further. I'm not a complete idiot. They've closed ranks around you like they do in any hospital – and in some ways I respect them for that – but there's not much doubt in my mind that you made a balls of the original operation. I spend my life observing people. A glance, the raised eyebrows, whispers in the corridor – you'd be surprised how far voices carry in corridors.' His index finger replaced the errant glasses. 'It is only out of respect for Royall here and the rest of the hospital that I am not taking legal action. I would be more than interested in a totally independent surgical opinion on your management of my case. But to take you to court, which I would not hesitate to do, would mean inevitably dragging Royall through the courts too, and *that* I will not do. So . . .'

Strait and David stood for a moment, watching Pullman trembling.

'. . . That's something else you can thank Royall for.'

Sobbing, head bowed, Pullman made a rush for the door.

'Brian . . .' David instinctively put out his hand to stop him, then thought twice about it. What the hell. It was impossible to reason with someone like that. He turned to Strait. 'I'm sorry,' he said, waiting until the sounds of a crashing tray and Pullman's shouts had died away. 'I can only apologise about that. I can't imagine what came over him.'

'Can't you?'

David was beginning to wonder whether the trick with the

finger and the glasses was purely for effect. A new pair of glasses would cure the problem.

'He's crazy, isn't he,' Strait said.

Not a question; a simple statement.

'He's got to be, behaving like that. I wouldn't let him operate on my *cat*, certainly not on *me*. Be honest now, in the state he's in, would you let him operate on *you*?'

Strait laughed at the thin, tight lips.

'I know; I know. You boys stick together through thick and thin. Ask not for whom the bell tolls. But – think about it. If *I* wouldn't let him operate on *me*, and if *you* wouldn't let him operate on *you*, should he be operating on *anyone*?'

Again, Strait laughed at the stubborn silence.

'All right,' he smiled, 'but some bits of what he said made sense. What's the real reason why you aren't doing me tomorrow?'

'Your washouts won't be clean enough in time.'

'And even if they were, you still wouldn't be doing me tomorrow, would you?'

'You should have been a barrister,' David grinned.

'I was,' Strait grinned back. 'A failed one. Why wouldn't you operate on me tomorrow? Don't tell me after all that nonsense that Pullman got it right. *Are* you putting me off for some private patient?'

'No. I'm just making sure you're getting the best. I want Digger Drew to give your anaesthetic and he's away tomorrow. He has a handicapped son – I think I mentioned him to you – and he has arranged to take the boy into a home tomorrow, a place called Clavely Court.'

'In other words, this handicapped son of his is more important to him than anaesthetising some TV megastar?'

'I'm afraid so.'

'And quite right too.'

'He's a nice fella, this.'

Drew gave 'this' an almost affectionate rub. The head, lolling heavily on the thin black antistatic cushion, the razor-sharp intellect within its skull quelled temporarily by Drew's drugs, looked as grotesque as any other brought down to the vulgarity of the operating theatre. A high forehead was hidden behind an elasticated paper hat drawn down to the bushy eyebrows. His eyes, half open, half closed, glazed and sleepy like a drunk's, seemed sunken without the glasses. His upper lip was pulled up into his moustache by the endotracheal tube like a badly repaired hare lip. Drew rubbed his cheek again.

'Never look at their best, do they?' he laughed.

'If only his adoring public could see him now.' Scrubbed and gowned, David waited patiently as Shah painted Strait's abdomen. 'But I agree with you – a nice guy.'

'Must have done you a bit of good, all that free publicity.' Drew spoke to David, but his eyes were on his machine, his fingers instinctively adjusting taps and valves as he watched Strait settle. 'Have I detected a better class of patient coming through recently? Not seeing a few private cases on the side now, are you?'

'No,' David snorted. 'I've got more important things to do these days.'

'Why don't you?' Drew was not joking now. 'You were so good at it. It's an awful waste.'

'Get thee behind me.' David thought of joking about the fees at Clavely Court and decided there was no way he could make that sound right. He took the swab from Shah to clean out the stoma. 'How did John take to Mrs Berry yesterday?' he asked and saw the smile as Drew followed his train of thought.

'Fine. I'm sure he's going to be very happy there.'

There was a pause in the conversation as David and Shah put on the drapes. The clatter of a dropped instrument came from the next theatre.

'What's Brian doing next door, Digger?' David had dropped his voice as if Pullman might hear him, but it was Shah who answered.

'He is doing a gall bladder, sir. And he is upsetting the orthopaedic surgeons, saying it is an emergency and that it must be done this morning. They are very cross with Mr Pullman for breaking into their list.'

'A gall bladder? So urgent? What is it, biliary peritonitis?'
'No, sir. The patient is feeling very well.'
'When did he come in?'
'She has been on his ward for ten days, sir.'
'Ten days?'
'Yes, sir.' Shah stared stolidly at the skin forceps he was applying. 'And her cholecystogram is coming back normal.'

David and Drew exchanged glances. Consultants do not discuss other consultants in front of junior staff. Not in front of the children. David picked up his scalpel.

'Well,' he muttered, 'nothing to do with me.'

He had made his elliptical incision around the stoma and was deepening it when he heard Drew's sudden intake of breath followed by a long drawn-out 'Oh, nnnooo . . .' A small artery spurted and he reached for a forceps, unable for the moment to turn and look behind him. Caught off balance, he was forced to take a sudden staggering step sideways as Pullman shoulder-charged him. By the time he had regained his balance, Pullman had picked up a swab and was dabbing at the bleeder.

'Forceps, Sister,' Pullman snapped, snatching one from her hand, only to send it flying across the theatre. 'Not that rubbish. You know the kind I use.'

Recovering, hampered by having to maintain some semblance of sterility, David put his hip and shoulder to Pullman's and pushed, fully conscious of what a picture they must make. Two consultant surgeons fighting over a patient, physically in combat in front of witnesses while the patient bled. A description would be all over the Merton by lunchtime. Have you heard? Mr Royall and Mr Pullman, fighting in theatre over that TV chap, Strait.

'For God's sake, Brian.'

It had now come to the point of struggling over instruments as David tried to prise them from Pullman's grasp. Strait continued to bleed.

'He's *my* patient. He came in under *my* care.' Pullman's movements become more and more sluggish as he began to sob. For a moment, he broke into another flurry of activity as he felt David push him sideways. He struggled again, but only for a few steps, as Drew's arms locked round his chest and dragged him away from the table. Lapsing into silence, he let Drew lead him gently out of the theatre.

Dumbly, David surveyed the bloody disarray that, minutes before, had been a neat, controlled operation site. From the other side of the table, he heard Shah's quiet voice.

'I think there's blood on his gloves when he is coming in, Mr Royall.'

'I'm sure there was. Still –' David jerked upright as if he had to do *something* – 'I imagine the case next door is a reasonably clean one. However, we must take all this off and rescrub and start again from scratch. Just let me get this bleeder first.' He gave a short, fatalistic laugh. 'Thank God it's a closure of colostomy and not something like a craniotomy. If he gets any wound infection afterwards, we can always put it down to that.' He turned as he heard Drew's footsteps behind him. 'What's happening out there?'

Drew did not answer for a moment, walking over to his machine, checking first that Strait was still all right. He looked up, his face inscrutable.

'Brian's having a coffee.'

'And next door?'

'His registrar is sewing up.'

'Sewing up? If he can hang on until I've finished this, I'll give him a hand with whatever needs to be done.'

'No need. They didn't find anything.'

24

Dr Roderick Beavan; Dr William Alfred Drew; Mr David Royall.

One; two; three.

Chairman of the Medical Staff Committee; Secretary of the Medical Staff Committee; another surgeon.

Three wise men.

The consultant staff's way of washing their dirty linen in private, keeping it within the family. An internal inquiry. Outside those four walls, nothing more than nudge-nudge, wink-wink. Judgment by one's peers. All official – more or less. Stockton, the Authority's Medical Officer, had been informed. The meeting had his blessing. He would be more than interested to hear the outcome. But there would be no official record. Nothing in writing.

'Who are you going to get to sit with you?' he had asked Beavan when Beavan had gone to see him.

'I assumed I could sit as the usual physician as well as being Chairman of Medical Staff,' Beavan had replied.

'Quite so.'

'And I thought Digger Drew. Apart from being Secretary, he probably commands more respect than anyone else in the hospital.'

'Hmmmmmmm.'

'Not happy about that?' Beavan had asked.

'Over that little problem he had a few years back, is he?'

'Oh, absolutely. Solid as the Rock of Gibraltar now.'

'Poacher turned gamekeeper, eh? Useful, I suppose, to have somebody with some experience of these things even if it *is* from the other side of the table. All right, Roddy – Drew it is. What about your surgeon? You'll have to have a surgeon.'

'David. David Royall.'

'Now I'm not too happy about *that*. Hell, it's only a matter of months since the wheels came off *his* trolley. Why not O'Connor? I'd have thought he was the obvious one.'

'Because he has flatly refused to sit; says he hasn't got a clear enough conscience himself to sit in judgment on anyone else. Went off muttering something about "motes" and "eyes". I appreciate it's difficult, but we don't want to go outside the hospital for a surgeon if we can possibly avoid it, and when you think about it if the Royal College still consider David fit enough to sit as a Member of Council, who are we to say he's not fit enough to sit on this?'

'You need another surgeon down there, don't you – someone to keep the peace between those two bloody prima donnas, someone with a bit more balls than Harry,' Stockton had growled.

'I couldn't agree with you more. We've been telling you that in committee for months.'

'All right then, Roddy,' Stockton had said, standing up to show the interview was over. It had not been an interview he had enjoyed – and it had nothing to do with choosing three wise men. They had been students together and Beavan had won every prize in sight. 'Good luck to you. Let me know how it turns out. Do your best. I hope we don't have to take it further. Always very unpleasant when that happens.'

Blasted surgeons.

That had been the previous day.

Beavan now sat wondering what he should do if Pullman decided not to turn up. Pullman had no legal obligation to do so. Beavan conveyed his anxiety to his colleagues who sat, their faces equally hangdog, one on each side of him.

'I'm damned if I'd turn up to be treated like this.' David looked round the otherwise empty medical staff room. They sat at the top table on the other side of which stood a single empty chair. 'Why do we have to turn it into a court martial?'

'One – because it has to be semi-official. Two – this is hardly going to be a friendly chat. From what you say, it's going to be touch and go whether he punches one of us in the nose.'

'Somehow, I don't think so,' Drew murmured quietly. 'Poor man.'

Poor man or sodding bastard?

David gave an audible grunt which had his two colleagues looking at him.

Mentally sick or just a pain in the arse?

The mere thought that Pullman might be genuinely ill irritated him. That would call for sympathy and compassion, both of which he knew would be painfully insincere. Simple, straightforward hatred was so much less taxing.

'What are you going to say to him?' he asked Beavan.

'Yohhhh – hold on. We're all in this together. I just happen to be sitting in the middle. What are *you* going to say to him?'

David did not have to answer, for at that moment Pullman

strode through the door, closing it firmly behind him. He crossed the room towards them, chest out, shoulders back, but with a face that was grey and sweaty, its skin stretched bone-tight over cheek and temple. He sat down, looking anywhere but at the three men.

'Good morning, gentlemen. You wanted to see me?' he asked of the window behind their heads.

'Good morning, Brian,' Beavan smiled. 'It's good of you to come. A difficult business for all of us – we've known each other for so many years – but we *would* like to have a few words with you.'

'Quick as you can then, Roddy, there's a good chap.' Pullman looked at his watch. 'I'm due in theatre in half an hour. An oesophagus.'

David's head jerked up. An oesophagus? He hadn't heard of any oesophagus. *He* was king of the oesophageal world at the Merton, everyone knew that. The local GPs knew that. He'd made a point of lecturing to them on the subject to make sure they knew where to refer them. They wouldn't send an oesophagus to that creep.

'We won't keep you long, Brian.' Beavan leaned over the table towards Pullman, his hand searching for nonexistent papers to play with. 'It's just that everyone has been a bit concerned about you recently. You've been looking very tired. How are you feeling?'

'Fine. Never felt better.'

He wasn't going to make it any easier for himself.

'What can I say, Brian? You must know just how much we all appreciate the way you've carried the burden of the surgery at the Merton for so many years. It's always been a very busy hospital, and the number of staff has never really kept up with the increased volume of work going through. It's so insidious, isn't it, the way the work load builds up. And none of us is getting any younger. We all tend to feel the strain sooner or later, and surgery is probably the toughest of the disciplines, isn't it?'

'Nice to hear a physician admit it at last.' Pullman's head turned slowly as he watched a cloud drift across the window.

'You try running a department when you get absolutely no support from your junior colleagues. That's when you *really* find out what the loneliness of command is all about.'

'Precisely.'

David took a pen from his inside pocket and began to fidget with it. Come on, Roddy – hit the bastard. Get it over with.

'As I say, Brian, you're looking tired. You've obviously been working too hard. When did you last have a holiday?'

'Holiday? You must be joking. With one colleague off playing golf every weekend and the other sailing in the South of France for nearly three weeks at a time? Who do you think has been holding this place together? Even when they deign to do the odd night on call, I still have to be around. Somebody's got to be on hand if it's O'Connor's intake and he's off operating in some nursing home miles away. And my other colleague – well, he's had no *real* experience of emergency surgery, has he, working in a teaching hospital with all those senior registrars to wipe his arse for him? If you remember, I said so at the time, when he muscled his way into this hospital . . .'

David heard Drew interrupt. Let him run. He's digging his own grave without any help from us.

'Brian.' Drew saw Pullman's eyes flicker to his for a moment before settling somewhere over his right shoulder. 'When did you last have a break away from this place? You didn't even take your usual Wimbledon fortnight off this year.'

'And that was another thing. Someone must have set those hounds on to me. That couldn't have been just chance. Who, I've asked myself, hates me enough to have done that? Because *somebody* did. Why *me*? *Everybody* does it. Why pick on me? *All* the umpires sell their tickets for as much as they can get for them. And why not? They have to sit there, doing all the work, taking all the flak if they make the slightest mistake, while the stars make their millions. And then they pick on one man – one man – and ambush him on television as if they were hunting a murderer, just because he does something that isn't even against the law. A few lousy pounds – and others making millions out of the game. I've a good mind to name a few more who do it. Yes – that's what I should do. That would . . .'

Drew waited until Pullman's muttering died away. 'We don't really need to go into that. That's really none of our business.'

Pullman turned on him.

'And isn't that typical? It's *never* any of your business when a colleague is in trouble. No one leaps to your defence when you're being pilloried on TV. No one wants to know, do they? But you can be talked about on that man Strait's programme as if it was a commercial, advertising some sort of soap powder, and everyone is fawning all over you the next day. I'm amazed the GMC didn't have something to say about such blatant advertising. Absolutely nauseating. But then I suppose if you're one of the profession's blue-eyed boys, you can get away with anything.'

'Look, Brian.' Beavan sensed one of his colleagues was beginning to enjoy himself. The time had come to wrap it up. 'Without putting too fine a point on it, we all think you're in need of a break.'

'Oh, *do* you? How kind of you all. A break. Why?'

'You've been showing signs of strain, Brian. It's not just us.' Beavan was in obvious difficulty with his hands, not knowing what to do with them. 'Everybody's talking about it. We're just the poor suckers who've been given the job of talking to you about it.'

'And that's typical too,' Pullman mumbled.

'I beg your pardon, Brian?' Beavan was now obliged to lean forward, turning one ear, trying to catch what Pullman said.

'Everybody talking. They never come out and say it to your face. Oh, no. Too afraid to take you on, man to man. You do your best for everybody and what thanks do you get? You work until you drop and what . . .'

'Brian – we're here to help you. You must take a break from the hospital. It's no disgrace. It takes different people in different ways – a coronary – a stroke. It's just that other people can see it when perhaps you can't.' Beavan took a deep breath. 'You need professional help, Brian. A couple of months and you'll be back, fit and well, ruling the roost again.'

Pullman seemed not to hear him. He went back to gazing out of the window.

'I'm all right,' he said.

'Brian . . .'

It had to come. With Beavan and Drew drained of words, the silence condensed into the inevitable confrontation. Pullman turned to face David, his head high but beginning to tremble, his lip curled in a fragile defiance. The wounded man baring his chest for the *coup de grâce*.

'Brian, no one is enjoying this,' David said quietly.

'Are you *quite* sure about that?'

'You have *got* to stop work for a while and have some treatment.'

'And that would suit you, wouldn't it? You'd have the run of the place then, wouldn't you? O'Connor's no match for you. I'm the only one who can stand up to you. I'm the only one who knows what you're up to. Regretting resigning those sessions at Queen's, *aren't* you? Haven't a hope in hell of getting those back, *have* you? Worried your little tantrums last winter will have scuppered your chances of being made PRCS, *aren't* you?' The words now poured out as David sat back. 'That's why you're so desperate to be made President of the Surgical Section in the RSM instead, *isn't* it? A stepping stone. *That's* why you stuck your knife in my back that night. *That's* why you made up those lies about me.' His voice sank to a hiss. 'You enjoyed that, didn't you, sitting there, you and O'Connor, amongst all your cronies. You put Forsythe up to it, didn't you? I saw you talking to him before the meeting.'

'Brian – that has nothing to do with what we're discussing here this morning. The plain fact is your surgery has become unsafe and you have got to stop. It's as simple as that.'

'And that's the considered opinion of a Member of Council, is it?' Pullman attempted a snarl, but there was no real weight behind it.

'If you like, yes.'

'And what if I tell you to get stuffed?'

'Then . . .' David *was* enjoying it. If only the bastard had crumpled up and asked for help. As it was, he was inviting someone to put the boot in. 'Then we'll have done our best and there'll be nothing more we can do for you. We tell Stockton, who will then formally suspend you.'

'On *your* evidence?'

'On *my* evidence. His action will then come up before the next full Authority meeting for ratification. The ratification will be minuted. A nice juicy titbit for some local rookie journalist anxious to impress his editor. Can you see the headlines?'

'What evidence?'

Why couldn't he feel sorry for the poor bastard? He was helping to bring down a pile of shit on Pullman, destroying him just as surely as an avalanche of snow had destroyed himself, only a few months before. Then, though he had not looked for it, he had been treated with love and understanding that had given way to patience and tolerance as he had wallowed in self-pity. Could he not find just *one* kind word? How long had it taken for the bastard within him to rear his ugly head once more? Nine months? So quickly?

'It's virtually impossible to get a colleague suspended just on account of his being a right awkward bastard. We all know that, Brian. No doubt it's happened, but it's very difficult to explain to the general public what a problem that can be in a tight-knit DGH like the Merton, isn't it? It's easier in a vast teaching hospital, isn't it, to tuck some oddball out of harm's way.'

David found himself consciously relaxing as he got into his stride.

'And when someone develops a quirky method of treatment with which not one of his colleagues agrees, that gets bloody difficult then, doesn't it? You virtually have to wait for him to bump a few customers off before you can really come to grips with that. But, when you have colleagues with enough guts to get up and say that a patient's health, perhaps his life, has been put in jeopardy, then things get much easier.'

'You couldn't prove . . .'

'And again – two surgeons fighting in theatre over a patient who has specifically forbidden one of them to operate on him. If you don't agree to co-operate with us, Brian, I will have no hesitation in describing what went on in theatre when I was closing Strait's colostomy. I wouldn't be surprised if most of the lay members on the Authority knew about it already – unofficially.'

David's jaw clenched as, in a few short words, he ground out the pent-up venom of years.

'D'you want me to make it official? Just say if you do.'

'That was *my* operation.' Pullman now spoke to himself, his head bowed, his face frowning at fingers that seemed to be carrying out some indefinable surgical manoeuvre. 'Perhaps I *did* forget to change my gloves. Not that it mattered, a dirty operation like that.' He raised his head for one last feeble thrust. 'You *stole* that man Strait from me. He was *mine*.'

David threw the final shovelful on top. 'And that so-called emergency gall bladder?'

There was a pause broken by the scraping sound of Drew's chair being pushed back.

'Diagnostic laparotomy.' His chin on his chest, Pullman mumbled on as Drew stood up and walked round the table to him. 'Perfectly legitimate procedure.'

'Up you come, Brian,' Drew said quietly as he put an arm around Pullman's shoulders, helping him up from his chair. 'You've had enough.'

'Used to do a lot of them in my young days. Far too many investigations done these days. Waste of time, most of them.'

'I'm with you there, Brian,' Drew agreed. 'Come on. I'll see you home.'

As if out of respect for the dead, Beavan and David found themselves standing as they watched Drew guide Pullman towards the door.

'Digger,' David called after them, 'what about the oesophagus? Shall I go down and do it?'

Drew turned his head. Now the pity on his face was not entirely for Pullman.

'There *is* no oesophagus. I thought you'd have realised that.'

'Where's Tommy?'

Mal and Dariella looked up, Mal smiling as he took his eyes off the TV for a moment, Dariella scowling over the top of her paperback as David walked in as if he owned the place.

'Ew looked pleased with ewrself,' Mal remarked. 'Wot ew got to look so pleased about 'en?'

'I've just done something I've been wanting to do for years. Where's Tommy?'

'Gone up to 'is room. Poor little beggar looked bushed.' Mal's attention swung back to the TV. 'Come an' 'ave a look at this. Arrived today.'

'Didn't he do well?'

''Oo?'

'Tommy.'

'Oh, yes. 'E done fantastic.' Mal laughed at the screen. 'Met ewr match there, didn' ew?'

'What d'you mean?' David asked, looking puzzled.

'Faye.'

'Faye? What the hell's Faye got to do with it? I'm talking about Tommy and the Rothman's.'

'Yeah, sure. Benny told me – 'e did brilliant. Abs'lute walkover, 'parently. Benny reckons 'e'll walk the Amateur now.'

'You should've been there.' Dariella seemed to have the ability to talk and read at the same time – and put an inflection into her words that had David making excuses.

'I'm sorry, Dariella, but I just couldn't make it this time. This was something I just couldn't miss.'

'I understand,' Dariella said – but didn't specify exactly *what* she understood. 'No need to apologise. But *you'd* have *loved* the way the audience took to him, especially' – she cleared her throat – 'when he gave the man who made the presentation a great big kiss.'

'Did he really?' David grinned. 'Thanks for looking after him at the last moment.'

'No problem. I enjoy his company.'

Closing her book reluctantly, she stood up as if she had been in David's company long enough. 'I'll go up and see if he's in bed yet.'

David stood aside and let her pass before turning to Mal, who sat laughing at a flickering screen as he ran a tape back.

'What have you got there, Mal?'

'Video Faye sent; arrived this mornin'. 'Er in an interview.

Not often ew see our Faye bested,' Mal cackled. 'But I reckon she came off secon' best this time. Took a fair ol' 'ammerin', she did.'

'Who was interviewing her?'

'Nobody. *She* was interviewin'.'

'*She* was?'

'Yeah. An' 'oo was she interviewin', she an' a coupla others? Wives of the guys runnin' for President, that's 'oo she was interviewin'. Mixin' in 'igh society is our Faye, no doubt about it – real 'igh-flyer now. Ew've 'eard she's bought out two other magazines, 'ave ew?'

'You told me.'

'What a woman, that Logan woman. What a brain – an' 'er body aint 'alf bad neither.'

'Faye was interviewing Jo Logan?'

'That's 'er. The one she was on Strait's programme with. An' a coupla others, o' course. But this Logan woman an' our Faye topped the bill, no doubt about it.'

'And you say Faye didn't come out of it too well?'

'No. Made the mistake of lettin' 'er feelin's come across. She obviously 'ates that woman's guts an' it showed. Big mistake that. But I don' see our Faye leavin' it there. She's boun' to get back at 'er some'ow. Anyway, ew watch – see what ew think.'

Later, as he climbed the stairs, David still saw the looks on two faces, the quiet, assured triumph on Jo Logan's, the frozen hurt he knew so well on the other. He headed for the blaring sound of the latest Michael Jackson disc.

Tommy sat with his back to the pillows, his face pink and scrubbed above freshly ironed pyjamas. Sprawled across his feet, Dariella read her book. Tommy raised one arm as he saw David enter, and as David leaned down to kiss him Dariella got up and left. David took her place, the bedclothes warm beneath him, and in the pounding beat of drums and guitars allowed a smug peacefulness to envelop him.

25

The Town Hall clock struck, the booming chimes seeming to shiver in the cold. Bradford in April. A friendly, outgoing city driven in on itself by a bitter east wind that scoured its streets.

The Library Theatre was clearly visible from where they stood outside their hotel. But they were early – far too early. Cursing quietly to himself as the wind took his breath away, David set off to wander aimlessly around the streets. The sound of the traffic followed them everywhere as if taunting him that, sooner or later, he would have to turn and face the inevitable. Tommy, a step behind and to one side, followed without a word, smiling whenever David caught his eye, as if saying 'Don't worry; everything will be all right.' David tried to match the smile. Success hung by such a fine threat. One slip – a sprained wrist. He pulled Tommy's collar up around his neck. This cold wind – a sore throat, even a heavy cold. There were a lot of colds about.

'Sorry, Mr Royall,' Benny Boston had croaked over the phone, 'but I'm afraid you're on your own tomorrow. I'm in bed with flu.'

Tommy's first competition with no Svengali in the audience, and it had to be the Amateur.

'Not that there's going to be any problem, Mr Royall.' Benny had been huskily reassuring. 'Just try to keep him calm when he can't get to the table. That's all you have to do.' David had been obliged to wait as Boston's enthusiasm had brought on a fit of coughing. 'Take it from me, Mr Royall – barring accidents, Tommy's going to walk it. I'm sorry I won't be there to watch him.'

Barring accidents. Fame and fortune was assured – barring accidents – like thousands of tons of snow falling down a mountainside. David shuddered. He turned on his heel.

'Come on,' he said briskly. 'Let's go and win a National Championship, shall we?'

They stopped only once, for Tommy to gaze at the statue of J. B. Priestley.

'He's a *big* man,' Tommy said. 'Was he famous?'

'Yes, he was a famous writer.' David thought for a moment. 'Would you like to be famous, Tommy?'

Tommy tilted his head to one side and it was a while before he answered. 'Why don't statues smile?' he asked.

As they approached the Library Theatre David frowned. Something was not quite right. It was not as he had imagined it. Several times in the previous weeks he had wallowed in self-indulgent fantasies. He had seen the queues at the doors as he and Tommy had arrived, the nudges and whispers as snooker fanatics had seen the cue case in Tommy's hand, their reaction as they had seen his face for the first time. He had daydreamed of the crowded rows, heard the hush as the lights had gone down, the explosion of applause as Tommy had potted the final black in a whitewash. The presentation, the photo session. His imagination now unleashed, scenes had slipped through his mind: the Hexagon, the Crucible, thick pile carpets, dinner-jacketed referees, the world professional championship, a trophy held aloft.

But it was not like that. A trickle of people, snuffling and shivering, appeared more anxious to escape the cold than watch Tommy play. In the foyer, backs were turned as more interest was shown in forthcoming amateur dramatics than the next amateur snooker champion of England.

The officials, pleasantly avuncular, looked everywhere but at Tommy's smiling face – they had to be impartial – while the referee, sombrely dressed in a dark blue lounge suit, struggled against the full force of Tommy's loving personality. Gary Thorpe, the other contender, crisp and shining in white shirt and coloured waistcoat, three grim-faced men at his shoulder, smiled back broadly. There was a glint of gold rings as he shot out his hand.

'Let's give them a treat out there today, shall we, Tommy?'

'Yes, thank you,' Tommy answered vaguely, looking

perplexedly at David. To Tommy, a treat was Dariella taking him shopping, or his favourite icecream, or staying up late for some TV show.

David had expected reserved seats and found he had the choice of rows. The theatre was two-thirds empty.

Thorpe won the toss and Tommy broke off. Thorpe played safe, Tommy attempted the impossible and Thorpe stepped in to make a swashbuckling break of eighty-two. David had hardly settled in his seat and Tommy was one frame down.

David could only nod encouragingly. Was Tommy, after all the fantasy, going to cave in to one dazzling display by a cocky young extrovert? He had never entertained the idea that Tommy might lose. It was suddenly a bleak prospect – the long journey home, the empty days to come, his dreams once more in tatters, his motive power spent.

'Thank you, ladies and gentlemen. Frame two. Gary Thorpe leads by one frame to nil. Gary Thorpe to break.'

Thorpe strode to the table. There was a flourish even to the way he chalked his cue. He struck the triangle of reds just that little bit too hard and his lips curled in disappointment as he saw he'd left Tommy an easy pot. It was the last stroke he played in that frame, for Tommy, his face still strangely solemn, proceeded methodically, with neither neurotic indecision nor adrenaline-laced flamboyance, to clear the table with a break of a hundred and eighteen.

A break of forty-seven in the third frame brought the smile back to Thorpe's face – but not for long. Another clearance by Tommy gave him the frame and the corner of Thorpe's mouth began to twitch.

And so it went on, the skin of Thorpe's face now taut with the watchfulness of a threatened animal, his body tense as he struggled to control his facial tic.

David sensed the mutters and the shuffling feet behind him. He felt the first sweet thrills of success as someone whispered, 'Go on, Tommy,' and there were cries of 'Yeah' as Tommy thrashed a black home from long range to take another frame comfortably.

The first interval. Three discrete groups now: the officials, the

Thorpes, and Tommy, who looked on so dispassionately as to appear almost bored.

David looked severely at him, thrusting out his jaw.

'Come on,' he growled. 'You're going to win this.'

But the expression on Tommy's face remained unchanged, and an icy hand suddenly clutched at David's heart.

'You do *want* to win, don't you?' he asked.

The hand squeezed tighter as he saw Tommy shake his head. This was a conversation he should have had with Tommy before, not halfway through the English Amateur. 'You don't?'

'No.'

'But . . . But you don't want to lose, *surely*?'

'No.'

'Well then,' David said, relieved, as if there were no other possible option.

'I just want to make you happy. And Benny.'

'Aaaaaaaah. And your Dad, of course. And Dariella.'

'No.'

'No?'

'No. They don't want me to win like you do. They don't want me to be famous like you do. That's why Dad never comes to watch me play, only you and Benny.'

'But your Dad is very proud of you, you know that.'

'Yes, I know that. But I don't have to win for him to be proud of me.'

By the close of play on the first day, Thorpe, still with only the first frame to his credit, went away to ponder on how he could have played so badly. David, not happy to leave Tommy alone in a strange hotel room, found himself in bed by nine o'clock, brilliantly awake, with Tommy sleeping like a raucous baby in the bed alongside him.

The second day began where the first had left off. By the time they had got to the eleventh frame, Tommy had destroyed a man considered by the northern snooker cognoscenti to be within weeks of getting his pro ticket. The sheer power of Tommy's potting had driven Thorpe into a defensive game that had left him trailing 9–1 and lost him the support of everyone in the audience bar three. There was now a majesty about Tommy's play that had David gulping back tears.

Gary Thorpe scraped through one more frame to make it 10–2, but Tommy swept through the last three frames with such authority as to have half the audience on their feet as he potted the last colours, cheering uncontrollably as each ball hit the back of the pocket.

There was a blur of sight and sound – the applause – Thorpe's bravely smiling face – officials with their arms round Tommy's shoulders – 'never seen such potting since Jimmy White won it when he was only sixteen' – Tommy's pleasure at being the centre of so much happiness – 'can't wait to see how he gets on against the pros' – the flashlights making Tommy clap his hands and everyone laughing with him – 'you realise, don't you, Mr Royall, that Tommy now has automatic entry to the World Amateur Championship in Sydney next autumn'.

The triumphant return to the hotel for their luggage.

'It's a very *nice* hotel, David.'

'Yes, Tommy, it is.'

'It was the *best* one you could find.'

'It was.'

'Four-star.'

'Four-star, Tommy.'

'The shops are very nice too.'

'They are, Tommy.'

'They were very nice shops in Birmingham too.'

'Were they now?'

'Dariella bought me a new Michael Jackson disc when I won in Birmingham.'

Hours later, thundering south once more, David cradled his dreams of Sydney and the ranks of the pros while Tommy held in his lap his precious disc – would Dariella like it too?

26

By the time a nation's TV sets glowed with the picture of Strait's head and shoulders, Tommy had already produced a reaction from the audience no professional warm-up man could have hoped to achieve. Strait struggled to make his introduction against wave after wave of laughter off camera.

'As you can hear, ladies and gentlemen, this is going to be no ordinary interview. I have had the pleasure of this young man's friendship for some months now, and I can tell you, I'd rather interview the Crazy Gang, the Goons and Morecombe and Wise all at the same time. And who *is* it, alongside me here, who is in danger of wrecking my show with his good humour? Well – millions of you will have seen him on TV, some weeks ago, beating an ex world champion and doing it with such style and good manners as to have won the hearts of everyone, including, I hasten to add, the man he beat.'

Another wave of laughter overwhelmed him, forcing Strait to stop as a beaming Tommy stood up to wave at the audience. He waited, joining in the laughter as he stared into the camera.

'Tommy Evans, Down's syndrome, snooker player extraordinary, looks destined to become one of this country's sporting personalities and I would like you to meet him. However . . .'

The stubby finger prodded the glasses up the bridge of his nose as if he had turned a page.

'It is a double pleasure for me this evening, for the man behind Tommy's success, the man whose driving force has made the most of Tommy's innate talent, is *also* a friend of mine, though, unlike my first meeting with Tommy, my meeting with *this* man was very painful and distressing. I have tried many times previously to get him on my show and he has persistently refused, and if it was not for my principal guest tonight I'm sure he would not be here now.' Strait's shaggy moustache was pulled lopsided by a huge grin. 'I'm allowed to tell you his name. His name is David Royall. What I'm *not* allowed to tell you is that he is one of the most distinguished surgeons in this country today and that I owe him my life. If I were so stupid as to tell you that, he might be accused of advertising, which, again, would be stupid as this man no longer operates for money; he simply sits around, waiting to snatch from the jaws of death irascible old chat show hosts who are foolish enough to have knives stuck in their bellies. So – come and meet two fine people.'

The monitors flickered and, on a crescendo of clapping, Strait was seen to reach across and shake David's hand. As they drew back, it was also to be seen that Tommy, sitting, stocky and powerful, between them, had joined in the applause, clapping his hands as he threw back his head in laughter. The sound took a long time to subside, and as the applause finally died David could be heard speaking to Strait.

'. . . and, if I find out I've been struck off next week, I'm going to sue you.'

'You can always become Tommy's manager,' Strait could be heard replying, laughing, before raising his voice once more.

'As you know better than anybody, David, we have sitting between us someone who may prove to be one of the greatest snooker players this country has ever seen. Tell me now, how did you come to find Tommy's talent for snooker? Come to that, how did you come to find Tommy at all?'

'His father, Mal Evans . . .'

'The famous footballer,' Strait filled in.

'. . . was born in the same street as I was. We grew up together. By a strange coincidence . . .'

The story unfolded: Mal's car accident, the sailing, the holiday in Port Grimaud.

A wife's and a daughter's deaths took only a few words.

'Ending up with Tommy winning the English Amateur Championship last April,' Strait rounded it off for him.

'Yes. Though, of course, we're hoping that isn't the end,' David added hastily, 'as you saw on TV.'

'And what's the next step?' Strait asked. 'Turn professional, I imagine.'

'No. First – the World Amateur in Sydney later this year, then turn professional probably after that.'

'David,' Strait asked with no trace of emotion of any kind, 'do you ever feel you're exploiting Tommy?'

Bastard. David felt the blade's keen edge as millions waited for his answer.

'Do *you*?' David snapped back. 'After all, *you* invited us on your show. We didn't ask to appear.'

'*Touché*,' Strait grinned, delighted with the answer. 'Perhaps "exploit" was rather a harsh word. But you say Tommy was in a home when you met him first. Wasn't he happy there?'

'Yes, very happy, as far as one can tell.'

'So, why take him away? Isn't it true that one of your colleagues was putting his boy into the very same home just about the time you were taking Tommy out?'

'Quite true. But then that boy did not have this enormous talent that Tommy has. Don't you think it would have been unfair to Tommy not to have given him the chance to develop it to the full?'

'You don't miss what you've never had,' the arch provoker shot back, mischief magnified through thick lenses.

'Like the young people locked up in my valley before the war' – David had no thoughts for cameras now – 'who had ample ability to go to Oxford or Cambridge but not the money? Try telling *them* they haven't missed what they never had.'

The silence that Strait skilfully let fall on David's wrath made him feel transparent, as if the guilt within him that had sparked the fury was obvious to all. He heard Strait turn his questioning on Tommy.

'And how does it feel to be a television star, Tommy?'

His only answer was bellowing laughter as if the whole idea was ludicrous, and Strait saw his chance. Slowly and compassionately, he turned his guest inside out to the fascination of his audience. The young man they had seen as an obvious Down's, a lumbering mentally handicapped, one of nature's tainted, was transformed by a few skilful words, applied like an artist painting a portrait, into an affectionate young prodigy with an unbounded joy in living. But Strait also knew the cloying effect of prolonging unadulterated joy. He changed the mood to pathos as he got Tommy to explain how he had come to lose just the one tournament. Solemnly he listened to a serious-faced Tommy as he explained how he had had pneumonia due to bad germs inside his chest but that David had made him better – and Dr Beavan. Dr Beavan was a clever doctor too.

'But you're quite well again now?' Strait asked.

Tommy nodded emphatically.

'And you're off to Australia in the autumn for the World Championship, David tells me?'

'Yes.'

'But I believe you're going somewhere even more exciting before that. Is that true?'

A hirsute, bespectacled face looked kindly at a snub-nosed one and saw the faintest of nods.

'Where?' Strait almost whispered.

'Hollywood,' Tommy whispered back.

Strait thrust out his hand in irritation at the burst of laughter that produced and David's attempt to correct Tommy. But Tommy seemed not to have noticed either. To him, at that moment, the only person in the world was the kind Mr Strait.

'That's where all the film stars are,' he confided.

'And why are you going out there?'

'I'm going to stay with my Aunty Faye. David's coming too.'

'Your Aunty Faye, of course, being Faye Grainger, of *Soigné* who sat where you're sitting now a year or so ago. What with you *and* your father *and* your Aunty Faye, you're a very famous family now, aren't you?'

'Yes,' Tommy agreed with disarming modesty.

'And tell the audience why you're going out to America.'

'I'm going to play . . .' Tommy slowed to a halt, looking appealingly at David.

'He's going to play an exhibition match in Los Angeles against the American Pool Champion. It's to be the high spot in a convention for handicapped children.'

'To be televised, obviously.'

'Nationwide, apparently. It seems to have caught the

American people's imagination. You know what a generous nation they are.'

'And whose idea was all this?' Strait's researcher had been meticulous. 'Who's sponsoring it?'

'*Soigné*. Faye Grainger. It seems she has been running a series recently on the problem of families with handicapped children and thought it would help if she brought together a group of handicapped people who had managed somehow to make use of whatever talent they'd been given. Rather like the Handicapped Olympics, I suppose.'

'When do you go?'

'In three weeks or so. We hope to do some sailing out there beforehand' – he turned to Tommy – 'don't we?'

'It's very hot in America in August,' Tommy explained to Strait. 'I must remember to take my sun cream with me otherwise Dariella will be very cross with me.'

David had never been to Los Angeles before. He had anticipated a somewhat grander arrival at one of the biggest cities in the Western world. Funnelled into a bare corridor from the stark, unfriendly customs hall at LAX Airport, he and Tommy jostled their way to the exit, their emergence on to American soil being sudden and unexpectedly ordinary. Faye Grainger stood waiting, tall and cool, in the shimmering heat of late afternoon. Tommy dropped the heavy bags he was carrying to wrap his arms around her. She did not shrink from the embrace, closing her eyes and making a purring noise as if enjoying it. That surprised David. He had never thought of Faye as someone capable of feigning affection for anyone.

He and Faye exchanged wary nods – the last time they had been together had been on a balcony in Port Grimaud – and David lowered his luggage to the ground, prepared to touch, wanting to touch. But Faye led Tommy away, leaving David to pick up his cases and follow.

They waited to cross the roadway to the car park.

'Have a good flight?' Faye asked David.

'Very good,' he answered. 'Why is it,' he asked, smiling, 'that you can go on a trip on your own and you're treated like everybody else – but fly with Tommy and you have hostesses climbing all over you?'

Faye smiled at him for the first time. 'I suppose there have to be *some* compensations, David. Here . . .'

She made a grab for Tommy as he made to dash between the traffic.

'There was one called Angela,' Tommy explained. 'She had black hair – and one called Rosie, and an old one called Delia – Delia was the nicest.' All on one breath. 'Delia took me up to meet the pilot. He was called Ed and he plays pool. And there was another pilot there too. His name was Mr Ryan. He was there in case Ed fell out. And I saw Greenland and then miles and miles of nothing but ice.' Tommy frowned as if somehow he had let them down. 'I couldn't see any polar bears for them though.'

David followed Faye to her car with Tommy still chattering as he brought up the rear, his shoulders drooping under the weight of the cases.

A 6-Series BMW.

Faye saw the spasm of pain cross David's face. 'What's the matter?' she asked.

'Nothing. Nice car.'

'It is. You can use it while you're here if you like. I can take a cab. I can't say I enjoy driving in Los Angeles.'

'Thanks, but perhaps I'll hire one.'

'Please yourself.' She looked at Tommy, suddenly concerned. 'Tommy – what are you breathing like that for? I've never seen you gasping like that before.'

'He still hasn't completely got over his bout of chest infection,' David explained. 'He really had a rough time. He had us all worried for a while.'

Faye did not look entirely reassured. 'So Mal told me,' she muttered.

As Faye eased on to the freeway system, she and David had little need to talk, for Tommy, his head and broad shoulders thrust between them from the back seat, kept up a constant stream of chatter.

Faye had to lean forward to speak to David. 'Tired?' she asked.

'Not particularly.'

'Care to see some of LA?'

Tommy answered for him. 'Yes, please, Aunty Faye. Can we go to Hollywood and see the film stars?'

First there was the view from Baldwin Hills – to the outside world, a family on a sightseeing trip. Then downtown LA and the Dodger Stadium, feeling the body heat of Tommy's excitement across the car's air conditioning. Then the Hollywood Freeway and out into Hollywood, where Tommy was disappointed when he searched in vain for famous faces. Along Sunset Boulevard and out into the green and white sterility of Beverly Hills. Back on to Sunset and the sudden sweeping turn. The halt in front of the towering apartment block.

Faye got out, leaving the engine running as a man in uniform slid into the driving seat in her place.

David turned his head. 'I rather think we've arrived, Tommy.'

The apartment was a replica of Eaton Place, only twice its size. David was not surprised. Faye Grainger was Faye Grainger, Los Angeles or London.

'I thought you lived in Beverly Hills,' he said.

'I do, virtually. This is right on the edge. And, with my offices just down the road in Century City, it suits me very well.' She grinned. 'It's also a comfort to an innocent young girl like me to have the security a place like this provides. What did you think of Beverly Hills?'

'Awful. So lonely. Not exactly Cory Street, is it?'

'Everything's ready, Mrs Grainger. The Stroganoff is in the slow cooker and the sorbet's in the fridge. Do you need me any more tonight?'

David swung round. A dark-skinned, middle-aged woman stood in the doorway.

'No, thank you, Maria, but don't be late. Maria, this is Mr Royall and this is Tommy. They're staying with us for a few days.'

A 6-series BMW, an apartment and a live-in maid called Maria. Where were Jackie and Debbie?

Fed, washed and resplendent in new striped pyjamas, Tommy was asleep before Faye and David closed the bedroom door. David's body told him it was six o'clock the next morning. His mind told him it was only ten p.m. and that Faye had just poured him a whisky without asking. It was obvious she wanted to talk. She just did not say anything.

His thoughts sped back to the balcony overlooking the Mediterranean. Was she trying to pick up the threads of their last conversation?

'Everything laid on for the match?' he asked, wondering how he was to keep awake as he sank into deep cushions. 'Where exactly is it going to be?'

'The new Metropolitan – downtown at Temple and Figueroa.'

'Good?'

'The best.'

'Naturally,' David grinned.

'It wasn't easy. Over a hundred handicapped kids and their parents, teachers, nurses, wheelchairs. You try booking something like that on a day before a party convention opens.'

David screwed up his eyes. 'So why did you?' he asked. 'Why the day before? Why not the day after?'

'Because all the media will be in town, all the national networks. They'll be long gone the day after.'

'But you said the match was going out nationwide anyway.'

Faye stayed silent, watching David fight off his jet lag as he put the pieces together.

'The Republican Convention, isn't it? Logan's lot?'

She nodded.

'And Jo Logan. She's bound to be in town, kissing a few babies, stroking a few young heads – meeting a few handicapped children.'

Faye said nothing in denial and David now found himself wide awake.

'You mean you could fix something like that?'

'I've met Logan's campaign manager more than once.'

David gave a low whistle. 'You mean you'd use that woman Logan even after all the things you've said about her?'

'That's right, Davy boy.' She drew her lips back as if in pain. 'I don't change much. I'm still a bitch.'

But there was not the usual edge to her voice as she said it, and she could see that David was intrigued.

'I thought you were coming sooner,' she said. 'Why didn't you?'

'I've been busy,' he said. Tired, his voice sharpened with irritation. 'The College is . . .'

'Ah. Starting again, is it?'

She sounded like Pullman.

'Can't keep away from it, can you?' Her voice was sulky. She almost pouted. 'So – just how long can you stay after Tommy's match before you have to get back to your adoring public?'

'I'm afraid I've got some meetings I must – '

'No doubt you'll find the time to go to Australia with Tommy.'

'I wouldn't be surprised,' he grinned.

'But you can't stay on here even for a few days?'

'No.'

What was she trying to say? That she wanted him? That she didn't want him to go? He felt again the fingernails clawing down his back. He wasn't going to run the risk of that again. If she needed time, let her come to London. He could wait. He had Tommy. And the College. Thank God Berkeley had stopped him doing anything about that. There was that provincial meeting in Newcastle – the paper he had promised to read. Trying to break through the barbed-wire emotions of a dominant career woman now came well down his list of priorities. He was a busy man.

'Why not?' she demanded.

'Look.' David stood up, putting down his drink untouched. 'I wouldn't be here at all if you hadn't arranged this thing for Tommy. I have a life of my own, things to do, places to go. And – ' he held up his hands as if fending her off – 'if you've a mind to try again where we so miserably failed in Port Grimaud, forget it. At the moment, even if I had the inclination, I haven't the ability.'

'You don't understand . . .' The sudden appeal in her voice failed to penetrate his weariness. 'I . . . I . . .'

'Bed,' David snapped. 'All I need at the moment is bed. Where do I sleep?'

The next day was difficult. Tommy turned stubborn. David spent the day in a turmoil of jet lag and suppressed fury.

'Tommy – you haven't practised for days.'

'Don't care.'

'*Tommy*.'

The more anxious David became, the more Tommy's jaw stuck out.

'Let's go and find a snooker hall. There must be dozens out on Sunset Boulevard.'

'No.'

'Tommy, this isn't like you. You realise, don't you, that millions of people, all over America, will be watching you tomorrow? What's the matter with you?'

Tommy didn't answer.

'We can't sit about here doing nothing. If you won't practise, how about going to see if we can rent a boat for the day? A motorboat for a change.'

'No.'

David became exasperated. 'What *do* you want to do then?' he asked.

'Watch TV.'

Faye was no help to him. For the few hours she was at home, she sided with Tommy, only adding to David's fury by fussing over her nephew as if he was the only one that mattered.

She even took Tommy to bed early, staying with him, *talking* with him, leaving David to fume inwardly.

The morning of the match day was to David all the tension and ennui of the previous day condensed into a few hours. Stubborn and morose, Tommy sat glowering at the floor, raising his eyes from time to time as David paced round the room. At last it was over.

'Come on, Tommy, time to go,' David said.

'Go where?'

'Now, Tommy. You know perfectly well why we're here.'

'I want to go home. I want to see Dariella – and Dad.'

'Tommy, what's the matter with you? I hope you're not going to behave like this in Australia.'

Tommy did not answer that immediately. He hung his head, lifting it for one brief glance at David.

'Is Aunty Faye coming with us to Australia?'

It took a moment for David to overcome his surprise. 'No, Tommy, she isn't,' he said.

'She wants to.'

'How d'you know?'

'She told me.'

'When?'

'Last night.'

David hesitated, taken aback at the thought of sharing his prize possession.

'Oh, I don't know, Tommy,' he said. 'I'd have to think about that one.'

He hurried to change the subject – if they did not dwell on it too long, perhaps Tommy would forget.

'Come along. Get this match over and we'll go home tomorrow. We must find a present to take home for your Dad.'

'And Dariella.'

'And Dariella.'

At that, the smile returned to Tommy's face.

There were the usual wisecracks about Tommy's cue case as he protected it getting into the cab. The driver was the archetypal seen-it-all, heard-it-all philosopher who treated Tommy with the kindly condescension of an intellectual superior.

'What's your name, son?' he demanded as soon as he had slotted into the traffic.

'Tommy.'

'And what d'you reckon on doing with that?' He drove with one hand, leaving the other free to point.

'I'm going to play snooker.'

'Snooker. Ain't that what you British call pool? You are

British?' The driver turned round in his seat to ask. 'You sure as hell sound like it.'

'That's right,' David said, smiling at what he knew was to come.

'Nice pastime. I shoot pool myself now and again.'

For a while, they had to sit back and listen to a lecture on the finer points of the game. They were out into Wilshire Boulevard before he got round to Tommy again.

'The Metropolitan – ain't that an odd place to go shoot pool? You meetin' somebody there or somethin', goin' on someplace else?'

'No,' David answered ahead of Tommy. 'Tommy's booked to play an exhibition match at the hotel.' He paused, timing it to a nicety. 'Against someone called Joe Velucci.'

The cab swerved. It took the driver a moment to recover.

'You've got to be kidding.' He now looked round at Tommy long enough to appear to be driving from memory. '*You're* playing *Velucci? The* Velucci?'

Tommy looked at David for confirmation before nodding violently. 'We're going to be on TV all over America. I've been on TV before.'

By the time they had listened to the driver asking base to ring his wife so she could video the programme, they were into the manmade canyons downtown. A hundred yards from the Metropolitan, a police patrol car blocked their way. Nothing the driver said, even the mention of Velucci, had any effect.

'What's going on?' David asked, peering through the window. 'Why all these police?'

'I'll give you one guess. It's got to be Logan.'

'Logan? Gort Logan?'

The driver nodded. 'Got to be. Only he'd get this sort of protection in this town at the moment. Nobody's been able to get within a mile of him for weeks.'

'Don't worry,' David said, reaching for the door. 'We'll walk from here.'

He got out and paid the fare.

'Good luck, Tommy.' The driver put his hand through the

open window. 'Just make sure I've shaken the hand of someone who beat Joe Velucci.'

The hotel façade, twenty floors of glass and steel, reared above the entrance. Faye Grainger waited for them in the foyer.

'Logan's not coming' were her first words.

David smiled, struggling not to break into overt laughter.

'Ruined your whole day, has it?' he grinned.

'The bastard,' Faye growled. 'He promised.'

'Tough titty' was on the tip of David's tongue, but another look at Faye's face made him change his mind.

'You'd better come and meet Velucci,' she said, her voice now flat and fatalistic. 'He's been here for the last hour, practising.'

Her last remark went a long way towards wiping the grin off David's face. The remnant melted away as he was introduced to a man from the Bronx who, exhibition match or no exhibition match, was not going to let some Limey halfwit kid make a monkey out of him in front of his own people.

The match was a disaster. Even Velucci was visibly embarrassed. Played out against a background noise of uninhibited mayhem that was beyond any TV director's ability to control, it ended with Velucci blatantly setting up shots for Tommy in the hope of stimulating some response from a stubborn, downcast opponent who kept looking pleadingly over to where David sat.

Back at Faye's apartment, Tommy marched from hallway to bedroom to undress in sullen silence. Refusing even to drink, he pulled the bedclothes over his shoulder, burying his head in the pillow as if shutting out both time and space.

Later, David, hungry and alone, fended for himself, finding a silent, apprehensive Maria who fed him. Several whiskies later, growling with discontent, he strode to Faye's bedroom door. Knocking on it perfunctorily, he opened it, angry at such neglect, primed for confrontation.

But the room was empty.

Puzzled now as well as angry, he turned and opened Tommy's door. In the shadows, curled up in the chair beside Tommy's bed, was Faye, asleep.

27

Paediatric surgery. There was nothing quite like the tension of operating on an eight-month-old child with an intestinal obstruction to bring you down to earth after the frustration of a disastrous trip to America. At least David, dropping gratefully into a chair in the surgeons' sitting room, thought so. Children a few months old take a surgical battering with surprising resilience, provided all goes well. The rewards are great, with childhood, adolescence, maturity, old age all to come. But there is a flip side – one small mistake and perhaps eighty years of life are wiped out, with the parents' adoring gratitude converted in an instant to predatory hostility.

But this one had been a piece of cake, a sitter, a breeze. David stretched his legs and arms, holding his breath while tensing his muscles until they bordered on cramp. He was relaxing, his breath emerging like air out of a tyre, as Drew and Beavan walked in. They sat opposite him, seemingly in no hurry to get away.

'That went well,' Beavan smiled.

'One of the easier ones,' David said modestly.

'You should never say that, David,' Beavan told him. 'It's the sign of the master, making something very difficult look very easy.'

'I'm glad it went well,' David said. 'It's some time since I last did an intussusception.'

The silence that followed was not entirely comfortable. David raised one eyebrow in Beavan's direction.

'Is that why you came to watch?' he asked. 'To check I could do one?'

'No, of course not.'

Beavan laughed, but it was obvious there was still something left unsaid.

'I thought Brian usually did them for you, Roddy?'
'He did.'
'So – why not this one?'
'No particular reason.'
David raised the eyebrow once more, disbelief written all over his face.
'No, not really,' Beavan said. 'His results have always been very good, and they tell me he's operating better than ever now, less flamboyant, more cautious. It's just . . .' He shrugged.
'Just what?'
Drew looked interested too.
'Difficulty in communication, mainly. You must have noticed it since he came back. I can hardly get a word out of him. When you meet in him the corridor he creeps along the opposite wall. He looks absolutely pathetic at times.'
'The bastard could always creep.' Judging by the expression on David's face, Pullman also smelled.
'David!'
There was that sound again. Drew was really becoming a sanctimonious bastard. What did he know about life? Tucked away in his smug little suburban house with his smug little suburban wife, never *going* anywhere, *doing* anything. Always maundering on about how happy John was at Clavely Court. And what had John done? What had *he* achieved? Built a wall around the kitchen garden with money *Mal* had provided. Nothing more than that. And look what Tommy had done.
David became aware of their stares.
'Is he on drugs?' he asked disparagingly. 'Or the booze?'
'No, he's not,' Drew answered sharply.
'Because he'd better be fit if one of these comes in next week. Harry'll be on leave and I'm off to Newcastle for most of the week.'
'College again?'
Beavan was developing that tone of voice too.
'Yes, College,' David growled back.

There was a hum. People were impressed. A deaf man could
354

have sensed it. Row on row of heads nodded approval as, with effortless modesty, David answered a string of question arising from his paper. Everyone agreed – a surgeon's surgeon, bright but with his feet on the ground. Good pair of hands too, by all accounts. Seemed to have got over that awful business of his wife and his daughter. Make a good President. Understands the problems of the DGH.

The young man in the white coat, standing to one side of the seated ranks of blue and grey, shifted from one foot to the other. David had noticed him out of the corner of his eye, apparently trying to attract his attention without making it too obvious. As David, not without some reluctance, gave way to the next speaker, stepping down to a flood of genuine applause, the man aproached him.

'Sorry to bother you, Mr Royall. A phone call for you.'

'Take a message, would you?'

The flood of applause had not completely ebbed.

'Sounded rather urgent, I'm afraid, Mr Royall.'

'Who is it?' David snapped.

An elderly surgeon on the end of the row had another question he would like to ask.

'She didn't say. She seemed rather upset,' the young man added as if in justification of his impertinent persistence.

'She?'

Mundane matters began to register in a soaring mind.

'Oh, very well.'

The young man led him out and pointed to a phone. David picked it up, barking into it just the one word: 'Royall.'

'David, it's Dariella.'

'Dariella?' he sounded vague. It took a moment to change worlds. 'Oh, Dariella. Good morning.'

'David – it's Tommy.'

David's face clouded with irritation.

'What's wrong with him now?' he demanded.

'I'm worried about him, David. He's come out in a rash. It wasn't there last night.'

'So he's got a rash. Did you have to get me out of an important meeting to tell me that?'

'I don't think it's that sort of rash. I'm worried. He doesn't look at all well.'

'Where's Mal?'

'On his way home. He told me to ring you.'

Why couldn't people solve their own problems now and again?

'Dariella – I have to get back now. I'll be home later tonight. If it's not too late, I'll call in. Otherwise I'll see him in the morning. I must go.'

He pressed the phone back on its stand with the palm of his hand, crushing Dariella's voice into extinction, before hurrying back to the lecture hall.

The light on the telephone answering machine flashed its 'welcome home'. Someone had called. Closing his front door behind him, David crossed the tiny hallway in two strides. At the press of a button, he was informed that his car had been serviced and was back in his garage and that Dr Spicer was very worried about a lump his wife had just shown him. Then . . .

'David – it's Roddy Beavan.'

No ums and ers – just brutal urgency.

'We've been trying everywhere to get you. Ring me at the Merton as soon as you get in.'

Not 'in the morning' – 'as soon as you get in'. Not 'at home' – 'at the Merton'.

David bent to pick up his car keys from where they lay after being 'posted' through his letter box. Ten minutes later, he was hurrying along the Merton's deserted corridors. The door to Beavan's room was wide open. A weary consultant paediatrician looked up.

'Hullo, David. Sit down.'

David spoke one word as he slid into a chair: 'Tommy?'

'Yes, Tommy.' Beavan's eyes might have been those of a tired man, but they still managed to convey censure.

'I thought it might be. What's happened?' David asked.

'He ruptured his spleen.'

'He *what*?' David jerked upright in his chair.

'He ruptured his spleen.'

'But . . . Dariella just said he had a rash. She rang me in Newcastle.'

'A petechial rash. He had also had a nosebleed.'

'She said nothing about a nosebleed.'

'It seems she didn't have the chance.' There was no doubting the censure now.

'So – where is he?'

'On West 7.'

'West 7?' David's voice soared. 'That's Pullman's ward.'

'He did the splenectomy.' Beavan took his time, adding quietly, 'There was no one else around.'

'How did he come to rupture his spleen?'

'Seems he might have tripped coming downstairs to the ambulance.' Beavan smiled affectionately. 'You know the size of his feet.'

'You'd have thought . . .'

'Now, David – they don't need much in the way of trauma, as you well know. They can be almost spontaneous in these people.'

There was a moment's silence as everything slotted into place.

'Leukaemias, you mean?' Whisper the word.

'Yes.' Firm, unemotional, final.

'A lot of things are beginning to fit now,' David murmured, head down. There was something in his smile as he looked up that asked for forgiveness. 'How is he?'

'Not bad. We're doing our best to get some platelets back into him and he doesn't seem to be bleeding for the moment. So far, so good.'

'Can I see him?' Asked with all the anxious humility of the man in the street.

Pullman was emerging from Tommy's room as they approached. David hurried towards him, his hand outstretched.

'Brian. Thanks for . . .'

But Pullman's head sank lower, his shoulders pulled closer, as he hunched his way along the far wall.

David turned to call after him. 'Brian . . .'

Beavan took him by the elbow. 'Plenty of time for that later.'

Inside the side ward, centre stage, lay Tommy, asleep amongst a forest of plastic tubing. One cheek was pressed into a pillow, but the brilliant strip lighting showed up the other, grey-brown and sweaty, fluttering gently as he snored. In one corner, aglow with hatred, sat Dariella. At the bedside, his knees tucked under its frame, sat Mal, holding as if it were made of Dresden china a broad Simian hand into which a vital drip ran.

"Ullo, David. Glad ew could make it, boyo. I feel 'appier with ew around.'

Royall blinked at the generosity of spirit of one of nature's gentlemen.

'Mal – I'm sorry . . .'

'Wo' for?'

David could only shrug his shoulders.

'How is he?' he asked.

'Better. Better'n a few hours ago.' Tears welled in eyes Mal turned unashamedly on David. 'I honestly thought we'd lost 'im one time, coupla hours ago.'

'I'm sorry I couldn't . . .' David said, feeling trapped as he was forced to grind out the words, 'but he was in good hands.'

"Oo? Pullman?'

'Yes.'

"E's been magic.'

There was silence as they gazed down on Tommy.

"Elluva snore on 'im, i'n' 'ere?' Mal said proudly. 'Ever since 'e were a kid.'

'I know,' David said.

'David – I'm sorry to have kept you waiting.' Roderick Beavan threw an untidy bundle of folders on the floor before slumping into his seat. 'I thought outpatients would never end.'

David laughed to himself. How often had *he* said that? How often had he sat there, in total control, an expert in his field, putting out early feelers in the task of interviewing some anxious relative? Now *he* was the other side of the table, the recessive half of the duo on a stage where the steel looked colder, the furniture harder, the pathology forms more frightening. He tried not to look at the calendar as if that might be tempting Providence. He found he did not know what to do with his hands.

'That's all right, Roddy.' He waited for Beavan to settle. 'Is everything back?'

'Pretty well. Still one or two things to come, but we've had the result of the marrow now.' Beavan smiled. 'You've been very patient, David. I'm grateful.'

'I'm sorry, Roddy, for my part in all this. I should have realised earlier. After all, it was always on the cards with a Down's, wasn't it? Looking back, Tommy was ill out in the States and I didn't see it. Perhaps you can imagine how I feel.'

'What d'you expect from a surgeon?' Beavan pitched it just right.

'Hmmmmmmm.' The preliminaries over, David looked across at Beavan. 'So – what's he got, Roddy?'

'He's got an acute leukaemia, David, rather as we expected. That was pretty obvious from the peripheral blood – there were blast cells everywhere. But the marrow was classical. He's got an acute myeloid leukaemia.' He paused as if trying to find something optimistic to leaven the gloom. 'The platelets are better today. He's still going to need daily transfusions for a while, but I think the immediate danger of a major bleed is over.'

'Right.' David took a deep breath. He had long since discounted the chance of a miracle. 'Now – what about treatment?'

'I've had word with the boys at Queen's. They're coming to set that up for us tomorrow.'

'Chemotherapy?'

'Yes – chemotherapy.'

'Which?'

Beavan picked up a pencil, examined it closely and threw it down again. When he looked up, his stare was unwavering.

'What I'm going to say now, David, is as a friend. I've got to say it even if it offends. If I brought my daughter to you and you said she needed an operation, I would not expect to be taken into the decision-making as to what operation you should do. I might argue about whether she needed an operation at all – you might have to convince me of that – but once decided, I would happily leave the rest to you. I wouldn't dream of coming into theatre and looking over your shoulder. You would have my complete trust. David – leave Tommy's management to the experts. Be honest: you don't know your arse from your elbow in the treatment of leukaemia – leave it to those who do.'

He watched carefully for David's reaction, trying to soften the impact of his words.

'I know, with your level of knowledge, it's not totally possible – but try to be like Tommy's father. Tommy, after all, is the nearest to a son you will ever have.'

'I haven't been able to speak to Mal.' David's head began to drop. 'I feel somehow he might hold me responsible.'

'Nonsense. I get the impression he's far too big a man to do that even if it could possibly be true. It breaks my heart, I must say, to see him, just sitting there, not saying a word, holding Tommy's hands, looking as if he'd give every penny he's got if only he was fit again.' Beavan shook his head. 'And that's something else I'm grateful for – people with that sort of money, as you well know, usually pester for second opinions.'

'You'll have no trouble from Mal,' David smiled. 'To come back to the treatment. What about a marrow transplant? Am I allowed to talk about that?'

'Just so long as you don't get *too* technical,' Beavan grinned back before becoming serious once more. 'Yes. Obviously that's bound to come up for discussion if Tommy goes into remission. But that doesn't look too hopeful – the transplant I mean, not a remission.'

'Why not?'

'Tommy has no siblings. That's correct, isn't it?'

'Right.'

'So that only leaves his father. It's asking a lot for someone's only blood relation to be compatible.'

'I'm sure Mal would want to try.'

'He's already volunteered.'

'Good God.' David shook his head slowly.

'What's the matter, surprised?' Beavan raised an eyebrow. 'You obviously underestimate that man's intelligence, David.'

'There's an aunt – but she's out in Los Angeles. D'you want me to get in touch with her?'

'No desperate hurry at the moment. Let's wait and see.'

'So, Roddy.' David took a deep breath. 'What are the chances?'

'Of what?' Beavan asked cautiously.

David clucked irritably. 'Chances of a cure.'

Beavan's face screwed up as if he was ready to argue. 'You mustn't talk in terms of a cure on this one, David.'

'You mean there's *no* hope of a cure?'

'I didn't say that either. What I said is, you mustn't use the *word* "cure". "Remission", that's the term to use. A long-term remission is perhaps the best we can pray for. Permanent remission is a *possibility*, no more. It has been known, on very rare occasions, for acute myeloid leukaemias to go into spontaneous, permanent remission *without* treatment. But that would really be too much to hope for. As I say – from now on, you must learn to think in terms of possibilities, not probabilities.'

He looked at David's face and smiled. 'Cheer up – all is not lost. Tommy's lucky in that he's a big strong lad with no heart lesion; he should stand the chemotherapy quite well. At least we should get him into remission. But, as I said, after that who knows what the future will hold for him? His chances would be improved if we could find a suitable donor, that goes without saying, but even without a transplant, he could still die from natural causes. He's already older than his years, you realise that, don't you, David? The ageing process in a Down's is far faster than in normal people. They rarely make their three score years and ten. He might still die of old age before you do.'

Beavan's secretary put her head around the door. She smiled at David.

'Your ward sister just rang, Mr Royall. Could you call in when you've finished here?'

Faye Grainger was standing much as she had done after Mal's accident.

It had come full circle.

28

Something had changed. Nothing had changed.

It was an atmosphere.

David sat back, sinking into the cushions, wondering how one felt an atmosphere. Was this the sixth sense everyone talked about? What was telling him that he could relax, stop competing? The decor was no less elegant, the jade no less chilling, the bronzes no less menacing. Everything was as he remembered it, even down to the litter of papers strewn over the Chinese carpet. So what had changed?

'Have you eaten?' Faye Grainger asked.

He nodded.

'Which means you want a drink?'

He nodded again. There was a new peace about the place.

'What have you eaten?' she asked over her shoulder as she poured his drink. She didn't see him shrug his shoulders. 'Well?' she said as she handed him his glass.

'I can't remember.'

'You can't remember?'

'A cottage pie – I think,' he added. 'After two years, they all look and taste the same to me now.'

'Why don't you have someone in to cook for you? God knows you can afford it.'

'Just can't be bothered – and I can always scrounge a decent meal out of Mal if I'm desperate.'

She stood, strangely hesitant. At first he imagined her searching for some scathing remark about his forever scrounging off Mal, and it took a while for him to realise she was trying to decide where to sit. It gave him the chance to look up at her and release the smile that had been straining at his features.

She sat opposite him, annoyance obvious on her face as they took up their usual adversarial positions.

David prodded at some of the papers with his toe. 'How *is* the world of publishing?' Jackie's face flashed subliminally. 'Still bringing work home, I see.'

'I've sold out.'

'You've *what*?' He brushed at his trousers where he had spilt his drink. 'Everything? *Soigné*?'

'Including *Soigné* – though that was a bit different from the rest. I sold the rest for what I could get for them, but the *Soigné* management bought me out. I made them an offer they couldn't refuse, except, this time, I was selling.'

'So you're finished in Los Angeles?' His voice still rose in disbelief.

'Not entirely.' She spoke as if admitting to a small sin. 'I'd decided to stay on until they were on their feet again – *Soigné* took quite a knock after the Logan affair – but in the end they agreed to buy me out on the understanding that I kept my office and stayed on in some sort of non-executive job. I don't understand.' Furrows appeared around her eyes as she seemed to stare at some point midway between herself and David. 'They seem quite fond of me.'

'That's not so difficult to understand,' he said quietly. 'And Jo Logan?'

'Nothing. Not a word.'

David looked across at a dejected face. He smiled. 'You look the way I felt that day you came to see me at Digger Drew's.'

'In that dreadful old garage?'

'It's impossible to feel any lower than I felt in those days. Every concrete block I lifted was a penance.'

'Don't tell me I've got to go mixing cement somewhere.'

'No,' he laughed. 'We'll spare you that. There *are* other ways of being shriven.'

His intonation had Faye sitting straighter, her eyes narrowing. 'What d'you mean?' she asked.

'Obviously Mal hasn't said anything to you?'

'About what?'

'They might be looking for a bone marrow donor for Tommy.'

'Oh . . .'

Her sigh was long-drawn-out. She closed her eyes as she

leaned her head back, squeezing her lids tight as if holding back tears. But no tears came.

'Why can't I cry, David?' She opened dry, wide eyes. 'I haven't cried since I was eight years old.'

He put his drink down carefully.

'Am I going to come over there to you?' he asked softly. 'Or are you coming over here to me?'

'If I remember correctly' – she managed a small smile – 'it's my turn to come to you.'

Seated side by side, they turned on their shoulders towards each other.

'What are the chances?' she asked breathlessly.

'Of you being suitable?'

She nodded.

'Slim.'

Once again she closed her eyes, this time in disappointment.

'It's unfortunate Tommy has no siblings.'

She opened her eyes, enquiring. 'Siblings?'

'Brothers or sisters.'

'Ah.'

Another word locked away?

'Is Tommy going to die?' she asked.

'He might.'

'And with a transplant – is that the right word?'

'It would still be day to day, then week to week, month to month, year to year. At the moment, it's week to week.'

'It would be so beautiful,' Faye murmured.

He had never seen such blue eyes so close.

'It would, Faye.'

'Something money couldn't buy.'

'Yes.'

'I want the chance. I must have the chance.' He felt the vibration through his hands. 'But I'd need your help, David.'

'In what way?'

'I'd need you to keep telling me I was doing it for Tommy. I'm so afraid that, once again, I'd only be doing it for myself.' She gave a small shudder. 'But it would be so wonderful, *giving* instead of . . .'

David found himself kissing her with the touch of someone defusing a bomb. Not knowing what to expect, he drew his head back, just far enough to bring her face into focus.

'Please stay, Davy boy. Don't leave me. I'm so lonely.'

'If you're sure.'

'Oh, yes, I'm sure. It's just . . .' She hesitated. 'I can't promise . . .'

David smiled gently. 'And I won't expect.'

Slowly, Faye Grainger uncoiled, stood up and held out her hand, looking as serious as once she had in a school yard.

'We've wasted a lot of time,' she said, 'you and I. We've a lot to make up.' She led him amongst the trappings of wealth into a bedroom of soft, almost virginal simplicity that revealed the other Faye.

And there was warmth and softness, and tenderness in abundance, and patience and giving, and the fury of loving that drove out an eight-year-old's humping, heaving hell in cries and tears that left David Royall, Master of Surgery, feeling like a god.

Joe the Pug gave him the usual friendly if deadpan nod, but David walked past him as if sleepwalking. His 'Good evening, sir,' growled at David's back while waiting for the lift, was equally unrewarding.

The fact that, for weeks, David had been in and out of the apartment every day – and many nights – probably accounting for the radiant happiness in Miss Grainger's face – still did not permit him to ignore Joe.

'Good evening, sir,' he said ominously as David turned inside the lift to face the open doors.

'Oh.' Startled, David gave a brief smile. 'Evening, Joe. I'm sorry. I was miles away.'

As the lift doors closed, Joe, filled with wonder at the effect of love on grown men, settled back with his tabloid. Powerful thing, love. Had to be – anything that would make an intelligent guy like Mr Royall go walking the streets at night in the pouring rain. Without a raincoat. And no hat.

Joe gave his newspaper a shake.

First thing Miss Grainger would have to do was get him out of that soaking wet jacket. And those shoes. Those shoes weren't made for walking. And his hair was sopping wet.

Joe chuckled.

Best thing, strip 'im off and put 'im in a bath.

But the threat of pneumonia was far from David's mind as he hesitated in front of the door to the apartment. He made a last futile attempt to do something hours of tramping the streets had failed to achieve – marshal his thoughts.

Faye Grainger opened the door, turned and walked away from him. As he closed the door behind him, Faye crossed a room designed to have no focal point, a room in which to feel comfortable wherever you were. She turned to face him, her back to a wall.

She stood her full height, her hands behind her back, her face expressionless. Defendants in the dock, awaiting sentence in some TV court scene, stood like that. David picked his way between the furniture to stand in front of her. He leaned towards her, pulling her arms towards him, taking her hands in his.

It was not as he had planned it, but then, what had he planned?

'It's marvellous news, Faye, isn't it?' he said softly. 'I'm so happy for you and for Tommy.'

He searched her face for some sort of reaction but saw none.

'But why didn't you say?' he whispered.

They waited in a silence that became intolerable.

'Say it, damn you,' she whispered back. 'Say it.'

'Why didn't you tell me Tommy was your son?'

Beavan, as usual, had been the soul of compassionate understanding. He had rung to make sure David had been in his office.

'Are you all right?' he had asked.

'Yes, I'm all right,' David had replied, woodenly.

'I'm coming over to see you.'

David had not answered.

Beavan had found him slouched at his desk, staring into space. If there had been any expression on David's face, it had been that of someone tussling with a cryptic clue to some crossword. Beaven had sat opposite him, leaning to look into his face.

'You shouldn't have gone, sticking your nose into other people's business,' he had said, kindly. 'What did you do that for?'

A smile had crossed David's face so quickly as to appear a spasm of pain.

'I couldn't wait to find out.'

'So you go bullying some poor little lab technician into explaining results to you you shouldn't even have seen in the first place. And now, one of those rare birds, a thinking surgeon, is sitting there, adding two and two and coming up with the answer – five?'

David had nodded. There had been one flash of rebellion. 'Why the hell did you *have* to do their DNAs? Was it *absolutely* essential?'

'I don't know,' Beavan had confessed. 'Clinical acumen? Sixth sense? Sheer bloody curiosity?' Beavan had waited a moment to be forgiven. 'But I've decided,' he had gone on, 'that I must do that sum for you. I had no intention of telling you anything. I had decided that would be quite unethical and I had no desire to have Miss Grainger suing me for lack of confidentiality. But I knew, with Tommy and Miss Grainger being such a perfect match, sooner or later you'd begin to suspect.'

Beavan had paused, peering even more closely into David's face.

'But it's the other bit of information you've stumbled on you can't accept, isn't it?' he had said. 'Even though you've lived quite happily with the idea before.'

David had looked at him blankly.

'And you *must* accept it,' Beavan had banged the desk gently, 'if you are going to find any happiness in this. There is no doubting the fact that Faye is Tommy's mother just as there is no doubting Mal is his father.'

Then had come the dead time as Beavan's features had faded and Royall had wandered through the haze of his shock. He had taken to the street as he had once before, oblivious of the rain. But this time there had been a difference. Subconsciously he had known where he had been going even though his path had taken as many turns as a child tracing his way through a puzzle-book maze.

Faye's face was to become the first he would see again plainly.

'So what d'you think of me now, Davy boy?'

Faye's monotone conveyed neither defiance nor supplication while it was borne home to him what a waste of time hours of soul searching in drenching rain had been. He made sure Faye was looking at him.

'I love you, Faye.'

It took a moment, a fleeting, once lived moment, for both to absorb the significance of such a simple statement of fact. Seconds later, David braced himself as he felt the weight of Faye's body against him. He heard the racking sobs start deep within her as, too tall to bury her head in his chest, she pressed her face deep between his shoulder and neck. The sobs surfaced as a child's unfettered howls and he felt cold tears on his skin.

He could do nothing but hold her.

As the storm abated, dying away to become spasms of snuffling, jerking whimpers, David drew her down slowly and gently, to sit beside him. Now she was able to put her head on his chest and they remained like that until at last Faye spoke, hesitantly.

'What *do* you think of me, David?'

'I've told you. I love you.'

'In spite of?'

'In spite of what?'

'Oh, don't be ridiculous, David.' The first spark of a new life flared. 'You know exactly what I mean.'

'All right. If you must hear me say it – in spite of. Happy now?'

'You can still . . . touch me?'

He made a great play of rearranging his arms around her, enfolding her more closely.

'There are worse sins,' he murmured, speaking to himself as much as to her.

There was silence.

'It didn't last long,' Faye said quietly. 'And it . . .'

'You don't have to,' he said. He pressed her head against his chest as if to stifle the words. 'There's no need.'

'And it wasn't Mal's fault. It was all my doing. I . . . I was so lonely. And we were always so close. And . . . and . . . it was only just the once. And . . .' – the first small laugh of a new life – '. . . you know Mal. He can never say no to anybody.'

What of Mal's wife? And her suicide? David vowed not to think about that. 'What did Mal think of it all?' he asked.

Faye laughed for a second time.

'He said it was probably only half a sin as he reckoned it was highly unlikely we had the same father.'

'Any road, 'ighly unlikely ew an' I 'ad the same father, innit?' David could hear him saying it.

'And when Tommy turned out to be a Down's, Mal said he'd look after him and I went off to the States.'

David said nothing, piecing together a picture of the past.

'And then you came along.' Faye burrowed her head a little deeper, her voice now steadier. 'Damn you,' she said lovingly.

David laughed, a little smugly.

'Upset the applecart, did I?'

'You did – you and your life-saving act, sewing up people's livers.'

'I should have let him bleed to death,' he said, feeling the omnipotence of the life-saver.

'I kept hearing from Mal how well you and Tommy were getting on, how you were spending so much time together. I got jealous. That's why I came down to Port Grimaud.'

'You mean . . . ?' David frowned. 'You mean it was *Tommy* you came to see?'

'Well . . .' Faye hesitated. 'Yes.' It was a time for honesty. She lifted her head a little as if to soften the blow. 'I suppose I was jealous of you both really.'

David put his head back and roared.

'And I thought . . .'

'And, of course, that Logan woman had just kicked me in the teeth.' Faye thought for a moment. 'I tried to come over and watch Tommy win the Amateur, but I just couldn't get away.'

'And all the time, I thought it was my fatal attraction.'

He roared at the ceiling once more.

Faye raised her head, propping it now on arms folded across his chest.

'I've always loved you, Davy boy, ever since I can remember. If you didn't know before, and I suspect you did, the last few weeks must surely have convinced you. It was just that . . . there were so many secrets.'

'I know,' he murmured.

'So . . .' For a moment, some of the old Faye reappeared around her eyes and mouth as she prepared herself to endure pain once more. 'What happens now?'

'What d'you mean?'

'To us.'

David thought for a moment, a teasing smile twitching at his lips.

'Fancy a walk up the Maindy?' he asked.

Seeing tears begin to well once more, he spoke again, starting slowly.

'I think we go to my place so that I can change.' They both looked at the wet patches on his jacket. 'Then we start thinking about somebody else for a change, someone very important, and we go and give Tommy the good news.'

'In *my* car,' Faye said, sitting up. 'Not that old banger of yours.'

'It will have to be,' David laughed, looking down vaguely at his feet. 'I rather think I must have walked here.'

'What – from the hospital?' Her voice rose. 'All that way?'

'I can't remember coming any other way.'

Faye stood in Mal's hallway, waiting as David closed the door behind them. There was a gentle barging of shoulders as he handed back her key, and she leaned against him as they climbed the wide, creaking stairs. He somehow managed to keep his arm around her as they entered Tommy's bedroom.

Mal looked up, saw it, and grinned.

"'Ullo, ew pair o' sinners. We've been waitin' fur ew to turn up.'

Dariella got up from where she was sitting. She walked towards them and the door. David put out his arm.

'Please, Dariella?' he pleaded.

She stared silently at him for a moment and, if not transmitting forgiveness, her face signalled perhaps a truce and she returned to her chair.

Tommy, as bald as a coot, his ears at right angles to his pink scalp like twin range-finders, bounced his joy at his loved ones.

David and Faye glanced enquiringly at Mal, who shook his head.

'No, I 'aven't told 'im.'

He stood up and moved to the foot of the bed as if to allow them centre stage.

David and Faye released each other only to sit, one each side of Tommy's bed. They buried their elbows in the bedclothes as they huddled closer to Tommy. They looked at each other until Faye, choked with tears, nodded.

'There's something we both want to tell you, Tommy,' David said.

Slowly, drawing out the moment of happiness, he described to Tommy how his Aunty Faye was going to give him her blood and that it would make him strong again. But Tommy looked more worried than before.

'But . . .' David and Faye waited patiently, snatching glances as they did so. 'But what's Aunty Faye going to do if I've got her blood?'

Tommy's mouth screwed up as they burst into happy laughter once more. David leaned over to kiss him.

'Your Aunty Faye will be all right, I promise you. We'll feed her on raw meat and red wine and she'll soon put her own blood back.'

'But . . .' The anxiety was slowly fading from Tommy's face as he looked from one to the other but the reassurance needed some solid basis. He searched for some criterion by which to measure it. 'But Aunty Faye can't pull the sails up. If I have her blood, will I still be strong enough to pull the sails up?'

'Of course you will,' David said. 'I'm depending on you.'
'Down in Port Grimaud?'
'Down in Port Grimaud.'
'And can I come with you?' Faye asked. 'Please?'
Tommy began his bouncing once more.
'But that won't be until next summer,' Faye said. 'There's the long, long winter first. Tommy, as soon as you're better, will you come and stay with me in Los Angeles in the sunshine? And bring David with you? We can go sailing there.'
She looked as if she might now make a habit of crying.
'Can we?' Tommy asked David.
'I don't see why not.'
'And will I have to play snooker?'
'Only if you want to.'
Tommy tried, and failed, to put his arms around both David's and Faye's necks at the same time. They ended in tousled disarray in the middle of the bed.
'So . . .' Faye said, recovering breathlessly. 'I think that's about as much excitement as I can take for one day. The final decision to be made can, I think, be left until tomorrow.'
'What's that?'
David asked the question, but they all looked at Faye.
'Which place here in London gets sold. It's going to be ridiculous now, keeping two places. One has got to go. I say yours.'
'Why mine? Why should *I* move for *you*?'
'Because you love me. You've admitted it. And if you don't, you've been putting on one hell of an act over the last few weeks.'
That stopped him for a moment as he glanced anxiously at Tommy. He need not have worried, for Tommy looked back at him like some auctioneer inviting another bid.
'But my place is nearer the hospital.'
Tommy's head swung for the counter-bid.
'Mine is more central.'
'That poncy place? I couldn't live with all that marble and those horrible carvings.'
'They're negotiable. But that horror of yours is the sort of place any self-respecting, newly-wed, first-time buyer would turn

his nose up at. No – if you are going to be Sir David Royall, President of the Royal College of Surgeons of England, then the sooner you start living like him the better. So that's settled, Davy boy. It's my place. Yours has got to go.'

And Tommy laughed, and laughed, and laughed and . . .